RELENTLESS
MELT

ALSO BY
JEREMY P. BUSHNELL

The Weirdness
The Insides

RELENTLESS MELT

JEREMY P. BUSHNELL

A NOVEL

MELVILLE HOUSE
Brooklyn, NY / London

RELENTLESS MELT

First published in 2023 by Melville House
Copyright © Jeremy Bushnell, 2022
All rights reserved
First Melville House Printing: April 2023

Melville House Publishing
46 John Street
Brooklyn, NY 11201
and
Melville House UK
Suite 2000
16/18 Woodford Road
London E7 0HA

mhpbooks.com
@melvillehouse

ISBN: 978-1-68589-032-2
ISBN: 978-1-68589-033-9 (eBook)

Library of Congress Control Number 2022952078

Designed by Beste M. Dogan

Printed in the United States of America

1 3 5 7 9 10 8 6 4 2

A catalog record for this book is available from the Library of Congress

To the questioning, and the nonconforming

"She wanted to hear someone say this very thing, that the cruelty existed in time, that they were all unprotected in the drive of time."
    —DON DELILLO, "THE IVORY ACROBAT"

❡

"Precisely by slicing out this moment and freezing it all photographs testify to time's relentless melt."
    —SUSAN SONTAG, ON PHOTOGRAPHY

❡

"The past, he reminded us, and all at once we felt it slithering through our ears and throats like a bolt of silk . . ."
    —KATHRYN DAVIS, THE SILK ROAD

PART ONE

OCTOBER

1909

THE EVENING
INSTITUTE FOR
YOUNG MEN

1

Artie Quick restlessly paces the second floor of the YMCA building, passing the door to the classroom and then turning back, approaching it again, trying to build up the will to enter. It is 7:57 p.m., according to the wooden clock. Class begins in three minutes.

Three minutes to eight, Artie thinks, that's perfect. Three minutes to eight is the perfect time to arrive on the first night of class if you want to make absolutely no impression. It's safely on time by any measure—the class laggards will surely show up later than you—but it's also not too early. It reduces down to a mere shaving the period during which you have to sit there, waiting for class to start, looking at people while they look at you. It's the perfect time, Artie thinks, beginning to sweat, even though it's a cool October evening outside.

Go in now, Artie thinks. If it gets any later you'll lose your nerve. Any later and you'll have to admit that you weren't brave enough after all.

Go in now. But not quite yet. One last glance at the wooden clock that hangs on the wall between classrooms. Now it's 7:58. One last moment to squint at the tiny pentagonal window behind which the pendulum swings, to examine the face reflected in the dark glass. The willful jut of the jaw; the tiny notch of a frown line between the eyebrows. It isn't the face of a person who's not brave.

Slowly, Artie smooths an errant cowlick back to the scalp, then turns, walks to the door, grasps the handle, and goes in, ready, seemingly ready, to begin the first session of a thirteen-week course of instruction on the topic of Criminal Investigation.

Luckily, there's an open desk close to the door, and Artie takes a seat there. At the front of the room a big man, a bear in suit and spectacles, writes his name on the chalkboard. Professor Winchell. Some other students are already seated at their desks; Artie can count the backs of eleven heads. A moth flutters about the room, looping erratically in the room's unsteady electric light. The clock in the hall groans and begins to strike eight. Artie is still hopeful that a latecomer will hurry in—there are still a few open desks—but no one does. So much for three minutes to eight being the perfect time if you didn't want to be the laggard.

As the clock completes its chiming, Professor Winchell takes a watch out of his coat pocket and makes a tiny adjustment to it. Then, as the room falls back into silence, he looks over the assembled students and says, in an orotund voice: "Welcome to Criminal Investigation."

Standing beside his desk, he takes roll from a list, calling each student's name in turn. Each of the assembled students mumbles "here" or "present" in response. Everyone, Winchell excepted, seems a bit nervous, a bit uncertain that they're really supposed to be in this classroom: this is a bit reassuring. Even so, when

Winchell nears the bottom of the list and calls out "Master Quick?"
Artie elects to respond with "here," rather than with "present": it's
shorter by a syllable.

Two more names and Winchell puts the list down, taking a
moment to square it, so that its edges align precisely with the
edges of his desk. "A pleasure to make your acquaintance," he says
once the task is completed. "In advance of this session," he continues, "you should have acquired the course text; I see many of you
have it out already; that is good. Please open the text to page one."

Artie already has the book out and open, as well as a small
notebook. Winchell hefts his own copy of the book—his hand
trembles, and he takes a moment to steady it before he begins to
amble between the rows of seated students.

"Page one of our text," Winchell says, "concerns the character
traits every superior criminal investigator should possess. Vigor,
health, courage, tact—covered here on page one. Important, indeed, although my own youthful vigor is perhaps not entirely
what it once was."

A polite chuckle from the students, though Artie doubts
Winchell is much over forty.

"However. It is also crucial that the criminal investigator be
knowledgeable. The criminal investigator, our text tells us—allow me to quote—has to solve problems relating to every con-
ceivable branch of human knowledge; he ought to be acquainted
with languages; he should know what the medical man can tell
him and what he should ask the medical man; he must be as con-
versant with the dodges of the poacher as with the wiles of the
stock jobber, as well acquainted with the method of fabricating

a will as with the cause of a railway accident; he must know the tricks of card sharpers, why boilers explode, how a horse coper can turn an old screw into a young hunter. He should be able to understand slang, to read ciphers, to pick his way through account books, et cetera.

"Now," Winchell says—he looks up from the book—"if you do not see yourself reflected in this description, do not despair. It is critical that we not despair. You are young men, this fact ensconced in both the name of the Institute that you attend and the fine Christian Association that has founded it. The youngest among you, our Master Kuykendall, yes, hello, is but fifteen years of age. How much knowledge he has amassed in his fifteen years I cannot be sure. I suspect it is likely to fall short of what Doctor Gross, the author of our text, cites here as necessity. But Master Kuykendall should not lose hope, for he has his youth, as do you all. Thus, you have time. A precious commodity, time. With the expenditure of it, knowledge may be bought. Of this, you may feel confident."

Artie is listening. Winchell strolls back to the front of the room.

"However," Winchell says upon coming to rest again. "The expenditure of time will mean nothing without a correspond-ing expenditure of your powers of effort. And this effort cannot be falsified. The willingness, no, beyond willingness, the desire, to put in the effort to learn is more important than knowledge, more important than youth, vigor, all the rest. The desire to learn, which, at its root, is nothing more than a desire to observe—that is the trait, above all, which is central to all superlative criminal investigators. I return here to Doctor Gross, who writes that an Investigating Officer must be always picking up something in touch with his work. Thus the zealous Investigating Officer will note on his walks the footprints found in the dust of the highway; he will observe the tracks of animals, of the wheels of carriages, the marks of pressure on the grass where someone has sat or lain down. He will examine little pieces of paper that have been thrown away, marks or injuries on trees, displaced stones, broken glass or pottery, doors and windows open or shut in an unusual manner. Everything will afford an opportunity for drawing conclusions and explaining what must previously have taken place.

"Nor," Winchell continues, "ought the budding Investigating Officer to neglect any opportunity for learning to know men. For every man with whom we come in contact may be taken as an object of study, and whoever takes the trouble can always learn something from the biggest fool."

Winchell claps his copy of the book shut and places it upon the desk, next to the roll list.

"With that," says Winchell, "let us embark upon a short mutual endeavor that I believe will prove illuminating. Please close your eyes."

The students stir perceptibly at this request, which seems, frankly, a bit strange.

"Do not be afraid, children," Winchell says, not unkindly. "The world may be a dangerous place but I guarantee you that nothing will bite you in the darkness, at least not here, in the space of this classroom."

OK, then: eyes shut.

"Tonight, for our first session of this class—close your eyes, please, Master, Hardesty is it? Thank you—tonight, for our first session of this class, we gathered here, in this room. Ten minutes elapsed between the arrival of the first of you, Master Owens, and the last of you, Master Quick."

Artie flinches at being singled out, but manages to resist cracking an eye open to sneak a look at Winchell's expression.

"It took me perhaps three minutes to proceed through the roll call and to briefly summarize the first page or two of our text. In total, then, thirteen minutes elapsed between the arrival of Master Owens and the point, moments ago, at which I asked you to close your eyes. Each of you had some portion of that thirteen-minute interval to make some preliminary observations. Those of you who are cut from the cloth of the criminal investigator should have used that time to make a quick study of the men here in this class. And—as the biggest fool in the room, perhaps, certainly the oldest—I flatter myself by imagining that I might have sufficed to form the central focus of that study. And so I ask you: From your positions, there, in the darkness where you patiently sit, without recourse to refreshment of your initial perceptions: What did you observe about me? What information did you obtain? Owens, you had the advantage, the full thirteen minutes—why don't you begin? Keep your eyes closed, please."

"Ah," says Owens, an evident note of nervousness in his voice. "You're, um, male; you're white, approximately, um, fifty years of age—"

"Fifty! Good gravy, man. Anyone else?"

Someone else: "Approximately forty-five, sir."

"Still too high—but a reasonable approximation. I take a portion of the blame: I may be bearing my years poorly."

Owens: "Apologies, sir."

"I take no offense, Owens, and I do appreciate your participation; you've gotten us off to a good start. Anyone else? Hands up, hands up if you have details to share. Yes, McAllister?"

"You're wearing a suit."

"Yes, as is the custom. What can you tell me about the suit?"

"It's, um, black, sir."

"Correct, although that doesn't get us much further. What else about my suit. Anyone. Is it an expensive one? Cheap?"

It's somewhere in the middle, Artie thinks. It didn't show evident signs of wear or mending, like a cheaper suit, pressed into regular duty, might have. Yet at the same time, Winchell is a big man, not quite fat, but with a broad expanse of stomach, easily around 275 pounds. Despite that, his suit jacket is baggy, implying that he bought a factory-made garment off a downtown rack, whatever was large enough to fit into comfortably, rather than having a suit made and customized by a tailor. Artie waits for someone to supply these observations, but no one does.

"You wear glasses," someone says instead.

"Very good."

Someone else: "You have a beard."

"True. Recently trimmed? Beard in order? Or wild, like an anarchist's beard?"

"Neatly trimmed, sir, not anarchic."

"I have been known to throw my weight in support of the single tax," Winchell says, "but I suspect my anarchic tendencies are otherwise held in check, and you are correct, Wilkins, that whatever they may be, they do not manifest in my beard, which was, indeed, trimmed back into order just this morning. Well noted."

Artie suspects that the use of the phrase "throwing weight" is a way to coax someone into offering an observation about Winchell's size and shape, but, if it's bait, no one seems interested in taking it. A silence ensues. Artie frowns.

His wedding band, Artie thinks. He's wearing a wedding band. Surely someone will mention that.

"What else?" Winchell says. "Is there anything else?"

What else. Besides the wedding band, which no one is remarking on. Anything else. One thing: the tremor Artie had noticed in the man's hand. At nearly one thousand pages, *Criminal Investigation* is a heavy book, but not so heavy an apparently hale middle-aged man like Winchell could not comfortably lift it, hold it before him. The shakiness could have been just a moment's unsteadiness, but it could have been a sign of something more: a symptom of ill health, poorly masked—an indicator of . . . neuralgic pains? Or something else? The need for a drink? No one remarks on that, either, and the moment passes.

"Very well," Winchell says. "I see we have some ground yet to cover. You may open your eyes."

Artie does.

"Please turn in your text to page twenty-nine," Winchell continues, "where we will begin to read from Section Six, 'Knowledge of Men.'"

The class meets for ninety minutes, and it goes quickly: Winchell limbers up as they get deeper into the text; he sallies frequently to and from the chalkboard, and, once there, he moves swiftly across it, despite his bearish size. And he may have an unsteady hand—if Artie didn't just imagine it—but the notes he fills the board with are produced in a neat, tiny script, set in rows that are eerily, unerringly straight. He erases the board two times during the session and each time he fills it up again. Artie works hurriedly with a single dull pencil, struggling to sloppily copy down as much of the material as possible.

Finally, Winchell puts the finishing touch on a diagram— indicating how to discern a man's center of gravity from his gait—and then he steps back, checks his watch, and claps his hands together solidly. He turns to face the class.

"It is 9:30 p.m.," Winchell says. "We shall return here in one week's time to resume your course of instruction. Please read Chapter Three in your handbook, 'Inspection of Localities,' in its entirety; it is brief. And as you pass through the localities this week that are familiar to you, home and church and neighborhood, do not neglect the opportunity to assail them with your best investigative eye, and you shall find that the most familiar environments contain a host of detail from which we have become estranged, and only through the process of careful observation can we, with them, once again become reconciled."

Become reconciled, writes Artie hurriedly in the copybook before slamming it shut, turning an eye to the door, hoping to rise swiftly and be the first to leave.

But then: Winchell speaks. "Master Quick. May I speak to you briefly, here at the front of the room?"

"Yes, sir," Artie responds in a low voice all but drowned out by the beat of hot blood, the rush of shame into the face and ears.

The other students file out. Artie, eyes low, plans dashed, approaches the front of the room, stands before Winchell, clutching book and copybook, submitting to dreaded scrutiny.

"I would like to believe," Winchell says, breaking the silence that has formed between them, "that during the hour and a half we have just spent together, I have adequately conveyed, if nothing else, that there is some value to the process of careful observation. Am I correct in this assumption?"

Artie can't meet Winchell's eye. "You are, sir."

"To demonstrate this point, we embarked on an exercise at the outset of our period of instruction, during which I made it clear that I expected you, as a class, to have made at least a minimal set of preliminary observations about me, and to have committed some portion of those observations to memory; is that correct as well?"

"It is."

"I want to stress here, Quick, that I am not a hypocrite. In other words, I do not seek to instill values in you that I do not also practice myself. Thus, it follows that I would undertake the enterprise of making my own set of observations about you— the collective you, please understand, the body of students in my classroom."

A curt nod from Artie to signal understanding.

"So," Winchell says, "That is what I did, this hour and a half, and especially during that exercise. And during that exercise I noticed something interesting about you—the specific you, this time, Quick, distinct from the collective."

Silence.

"Do you know what that was?" Winchell asks.

"I believe so, sir," Artie says.

"What was it?" Winchell asks.

Artie doesn't say anything.

"I noticed," Winchell says gently, "that you knew more than you said. Of course, you didn't say anything, so any observation you'd made, privately, would have been more than you said—but I could see that you'd made observations that other members of your class hadn't made. It was written on your face, your—I think it's fair to say—frustration with other members of the class. Their inability to notice things that you had noticed, or to remember things that you had remembered. And yet you did not volunteer your observations, even when it became clear that no other member of the class was prepared to. I observed this, and I thought to myself, there must be a reason for this, and so, as investigators do, I produced a hypothesis. There is a reason, isn't there, Artie Quick, why you didn't speak in class today?"

"Yes, sir," Artie says.

"What is that reason?"

Artie doesn't answer.

Winchell sighs, removes his spectacles, polishes them with a rag produced from his pocket, while Artie waits for the blow.

And then it comes. "There are women's colleges," he says, finally, keeping his eyes trained down on the glasses in his hand.

"The Bradford Academy, the Wheaton Seminary—for a young woman as bright as yourself, even Radcliffe—"

Artie has spent the whole evening afraid. Afraid to raise her hand, afraid to speak, afraid to call attention to herself in any way, all because she knew that if she were noticed, if anyone were to see through her ruse, it would mean—at best—that she'd be kicked out of the class, that her plans would be ruined. But now—now that the worst is happening—the fear gives way, yields to a flare of defiance. She thrusts her chin forward, balls her fists. "It can't be those schools, sir," Artie says.

"And why is that?" Winchell asks. He snaps his gaze back to her face; she locks eyes with him, allows herself to meet the full blast of his acute, perceiving intelligence. "Why is it so critical that it be this school, which, as you know, is intended to give a practical education to young men? Critical enough that you would implement—not poorly, I might add—this disguise?" He gestures, to indicate Artie's short black hair, kept close to her scalp with pomade she'd lifted from the men's counter at Filene's, her suit jacket, her carefully knotted tie.

"I work, sir," she says. "I don't have the free hours to commit to a full course of instruction. The Evening Institute—"

Winchell cuts her off with a brusque motion. "If that's the only reason—" he begins.

"No, sir," Artie says. "It's not. Not the only reason."

"What is the other reason?"

"I want this class," she says. "I want Criminal Investigation. Those other schools don't offer that as a class."

Winchell nods with satisfaction, as though this confirms

another hypothesis he'd made. He seems to be suppressing a grin. But then his look grows sober. "Most of the young men taking this class are taking it with a vocational intention," he says. "They intend to seek future employment as policemen."

"I know, sir," Artie admits.

"You understand, I trust—you must understand—that the Boston Police Department does not hire young women, and has no apparent plans to?"

"Yes, sir. I—I have a job. My wish to take the class, it's—it's not about my future employment."

"What is it about?"

Artie thinks of Zeb. Bits of their complicated history emerge in her mind: strands of webbing in darkness, glinting as this beam of probing light chances upon them. But she keeps her face studiously neutral; she doesn't want to offer up any clue for Winchell to seize upon. Not about this.

"Miss Quick?"

"I'd prefer not to say at this time, sir."

"Ah!" Winchell breaks into a true smile, his first during this conversation. "You gift me, Miss Quick, with a mystery. I already have my share of mysteries to solve, of course—I have my share. Which is not to say that an additional one is not a source of some minor delight."

He takes a long look at her, as if giving the quality of the disguise another assessment, then he fishes out his watch and checks it again.

"Well," he says. "I believe I've kept you here long enough."

"So," Artie says, "what happens?"

"What happens? The same thing that always happens, young lady: time advances."

Artie's face breaks into a frown.

"If you want a better answer," Winchell says, "you must ask better questions." He sighs. "To be fair, however, that is material we shall cover later in the course— 'Examination of Witnesses and Accused,' it's in your book—but given that we have not covered it yet, perhaps it is incumbent upon me to provide some assistance. I believe that you are attempting to ask something akin to what happens now that I have discerned the truth of the matter, namely: that you are enrolled in the Christian Association and its Evening Institute under false pretenses. Are you asking whether I will see to it that you are expelled from the class?"

"Yes," Artie says.

"I will not," Winchell says.

Some tension Artie had been holding in her body half unlocks at this; her frame nearly buckles from relief. But she retains a certain level of wariness: Winchell's concession here seems to have been offered easily, too easily, and she knows that it could just as easily be rescinded.

Winchell continues: "Based on what I have observed of you thus far, I think you have a keen investigative mind and the potential to hone it. Certainly you possess, in abundance, the willingness to learn. I do encourage you, however, to speak up when I engage the class in questioning."

"But, sir," Artie says, a tightness returning to her body, beginning in the shoulders, twisting there like a screw. "My voice. If the other students hear—"

"Mm," Winchell says. "I can see that you have an interest in maintaining your disguise. I will, however, point out that not every young man in this class has a deep voice. Master Kuykendall, please recall, is only fifteen years old: I assure you that his voice sounds no deeper than your own."

Artie isn't so sure of this, but she nods, hoping this conveys confidence. Winchell looks at her, though, and seems to see through the front. He lets out a small sigh. "I can appreciate your concern," he says. "You have made your classmates the subject of a deception, and I cannot entirely predict how they would react were they to learn this fact. Does silence protect you from these consequences? Perhaps. At the same time, I believe that your silence will hinder your ability to learn in this classroom. The calculus that you have set before yourself, of these various advantages and disadvantages, is a complicated one; I ask only that you consider the question of how to weigh them against one another, how to attempt to keep them in a satisfactory balance. You appear to have a resourceful mind; I trust that you will give the question some serious thought."

"Yes, sir. I certainly will."

Winchell studies her face as if to make sure that her answer carries a requisite amount of conviction, and he seems to come away satisfied. "Very well. In that case you may be off. Remember to read Chapter Three."

"'Inspection of Localities.'"

"Yes, in its entirety. And I will see you back here in a week."

"Yes, sir. And, um, thank you."

"Do not mention it, Quick," Winchell remarks. He replaces his spectacles and turns to erase the blackboard one final time.

Artie takes the advice and hurries out, emerging from the YMCA building into the night. It was dark when she entered the building, just before eight, but now Huntington Avenue is awash in light thrown from a lamp standing where the street meets Gainsborough. This catches her off guard, though it really shouldn't: they've been putting in electric lamps all over the city this year, and they've been in the Ladder District since summer. Artie still hasn't quite adjusted to them, and, moreover, she's not really sure that she likes them: sometimes you want a nice shadow to disappear into.

Sounds like something Zeb would say, she thinks: the thought elicits a frown. So instead she thinks of Winchell, wonders whether these lights would get his nod of approval. They probably would: she can imagine him saying they're a boon to any young investigator, in that they leave the world open to deeper inspection—something like that.

Or, if not that, then this: time advances. Isn't that what he said: it's the same thing that always happens? She muses on this as she crosses the street, heading west, toward the Fenway. If it's true, and surely it is, then maybe she'd best try, at least try, to embrace whatever changes may be coming.

She strolls north, along the edge of the Fens, heading home. Clarinet notes drift down from an open window of the conservatory. A student, practicing a run of scales, late.

2

It's Friday morning, almost 9:30. The morning bell is about to ring, and when it does, the doors will open, letting the waves of shoppers in. Artie straightens the overcoats hanging on the nearest rack, even though she's straightened them just a minute ago, and even though they'll be in complete disarray fifteen minutes from now. She sighs, steels herself, runs her hands over the front of her plain wool dress, smoothing out the wrinkles.

Artie started this job in the winter of 1908, when Edward Filene opened an overflow shop—the Tunnel Bargain Basement— to offer surplus merchandise from his department store and needed to hire basically every young girl he could find to help staff it. The overflow shop was only supposed to be temporary, and Artie had expected only to be taken on as seasonal help, but it's almost a year later and the popularity of the store hasn't waned. The doors have stayed open, and Artie has held on to the job.

In a lot of ways, it's a good job. She only works a ten-hour day, and only five days a week—her father, a carpenter, works twelve hours a day, six days a week. It pays well, and she's been able to save a little money, under her own name, since she's now enrolled in something called a credit union, a kind of cooperative bank that the store runs. Maybe even more than a little money, at this point—she's always a bit surprised when she checks in on it and sees exactly how much she's accrued in her account. Mostly she tries not to think about it, or talk about it.

Her parents don't know that she has that money saved there.

In other ways, though, the job is pretty grueling. She'd been first drawn to Filene's by the shop windows, which depicted spacious, well-lit areas in which gowns seemed to float, suspended as though in a dream. She could envision herself in such a space, drifting among the garments, gesturing at them. She knew, right from the outset, that this vision was a fantasia—she knew, when she applied, that she was applying for a job, and that she'd have to work hard, not just drift blissfully in a cloud of electric light—but the shop windows had unshakably invested Filene's with an aura of Parisian glamour. So when Artie imagined herself working there, she imagined working on the upper floors, which, Artie knew from her few curious forays into the store, were passably close to her fantasies— they were clean and airy and attended by attractive people.

She's been asked to work on the upper floors four or five times— two days in a row, once, when they were especially short-staffed— but mostly she's been in the Basement. And the Basement is crowded, it's noisy, there's no decor, the lighting is harsh—it's hardly the stuff of dreams. The garments are still beautiful—Artie is looking, right now, at a black muskrat misses' coat (its glossy, almost oily shine draws the eye like a magnet)—but they lose a bit of their glamour once they're here in the Basement, and they lose a little bit more each time they spend a day getting banged around by the hands of a thousand half-interested bargain seekers and urban idlers.

But still. She can't really blame people for wanting a bargain. (She herself has been known to keep an eye on a few items, watching the prices dropping—just like every other employee here in the Basement—calculating schemes to get them home once they drop below a certain threshold.) She can, and does, blame people, though, for treating her like a store fixture—an automaton that can change money and wrap parcels but that isn't quite human. People look right through her, they pass without offering a greeting, they snap orders at her, they step on her toes. By the end of the day, typically, she feels about ready to return the favor—to stop thinking of the people roaming the aisles as people, to think of them instead as a single faceless mass.

The bell rings. The door opens. They begin to pour in: the Customers.

Artie watches them as they approach.

Artie watches them, and she thinks about Wednesday night's class. She remembers Winchell walking them through Section Six of *Criminal Investigation*, "Knowledge of Men." She'd made a project, yesterday, of taking Winchell's teachings to heart: she'd made a point of being extra alert, extra observant of her surroundings. She'd tried, as much as she could, to stop thinking of the Customers as an undifferentiated crowd, tried to train herself to see them once again as individual human beings, with traits that you could identify, commit to memory, recall later in the service of unraveling some mystery. She tried to figure out who had secrets that they were subtly revealing through their actions. (Her conclusion: everyone.) It had been fun, it had made her shift go faster, and, more importantly, she could feel herself getting better at it, noticing details she would never have noticed before: a rakish angle to a man's hat, the bitten nails of a woman in elegant dress.

The first customer to make it this far down her aisle pushes past her: Artie eyes his walrus mustache and sniffs inquisitively at his cologne, concludes that he must be in league with some sinister syndicate.

The day gets busy. A person needs something wrapped, then another one, and then there's a line, and before she knows it Artie has spent an hour with her head down, folding brown paper and cutting twine. Not much in the way of good investigative opportunity there.

With the morning rush having passed, she has the opportunity to walk the aisles for a minute, tidying disarrayed piles of scarves, rearranging hats. And then, in her ear, someone is saying her name—"Artie!"—in a voice that seems hushed and urgent.

Artie jumps—but it's only Theodore.

"Holy smoke, Theodore," she says, clapping her hand to her chest. "Don't sneak up on people like that!"

Theodore, grimacing apologetically, takes two swift steps backward. At six foot five, with a wild sprig of unruly hair that makes him seem even taller, he's never been accused of being a graceful man, and Artie watches helplessly as shoppers dodge his elbows. Plus there's the folding tripod protruding from his rucksack, like an awkward extra limb pointing out stiffly behind him—Artie winces as it grazes the ostrich feather in an old lady's hat. One more step back and his tripod would have caught her right in the jaw. But the danger has been harmlessly averted, and Artie lets out her held breath.

"What do you want?" she says, a bit more curtly than she really intends. She's annoyed at having been startled, doubly so because she'd been priding herself on her resolution to be extra alert, extra observant of her surroundings. If a steep, ungainly man like Theodore could manage to get right next to her without her noticing, it seems like she has to keep practicing, and the reminder feels like a rebuke. But she's also glad to see him, standing there with his tentative, crooked smile—an olive branch offered from a safe distance.

"I wanted to see how it went," he says.

"How what went?"

"The class," Theodore says. "At the men's college! In disguise," he adds as a conspiratorial aside.

He utters the word "disguise" quietly, but it still feels foolhardy to Artie that he even says it out loud in public. She looks from side to side, trying to see if anyone around has heard. She's less afraid that the president of the Evening Institute himself is down here rummaging about for a bargain overcoat—ready to expel her upon learning of her ruse—and more afraid that he'll be overheard by a coworker, that this will be the provocation for some weird rumors about her to start spreading. Artie, with her cropped hair and squarish jaw, is already considered a bit odd by the other shopgirls, and Theodore is a bit of an odd sight too. That's part of what brought them together, she thinks, despite the fact that he's from a wealthy family and she's from the laboring class: they're two strange people, and each of them realized that together they could navigate the world better than either of them could alone.

Nonetheless, her friendship with him is unusual. She has a standing invitation to drop in at his townhouse, and she's been taking advantage of it, especially lately—the townhouse is warm, and Boston is getting cold—but she knows that most people wouldn't approve of a young, unmarried girl making an unsupervised call to the home of a young, unmarried man. Nothing untoward has ever occurred—mostly he just excitedly shows her items from his collections of eccentric stuff: photographic studies of animal locomotion by this guy Muybridge, phenakistoscope discs that produce a moving image when spun and viewed in a mirror, tiny reproductions of gloomy paintings produced by the French Symbolists. But she keeps it quiet anyway. Her parents don't know that she's been going there; her coworkers don't either. She worries that his even showing up just to chat with her while she's working could be enough to provoke gossip, and that's before you take into account any loose remark about taking classes at a men's college.

But no one seems to have heard. If Theodore's clumsy arrival and incautious comments gave anyone pause, they've since gone back to their shopping. This is a thing Artie has noticed: there are a lot of strange men in the city, and when one makes his appearance and nothing all that bad happens, people tend to just look the other way—especially if the man gives off the impression of having come from money. At most, an observer will give a sniff of distaste. It's not the same for strange women, though. For a moment, she feels a certain pang at the unfairness of the situation: that Theodore, as a young man with wealthy parents, is able to get away with certain eccentricities that she, as a young woman from the laboring class, would be chastised for. Theodore gets to blunder awkwardly through the world and no one really pays it any mind, but she gets criticized by strangers because she wears her hair short. He gets to be weird and she doesn't. That's just the way it is. But sometimes she wishes it were different.

But his strangeness really is part of the reason she's committed to the friendship. Yes, she enjoys having access, for the first time in her life, to some of the pleasures of the well-heeled life. True, she can go to a restaurant with him, even the down-and-tumble ones that he enjoys, and he'll pay for her meal—the novelty of that hasn't worn off. But she's more drawn to the fact that he'll stop in the street on the way, fish a scrap of paper from a small pocket of his blazer, and read a bit of some odd poem. She's more drawn to the fact that he does some unusual experiments with that little Brownie camera, making ghostly images by exposing the film twice without advancing it. (He did a photographic portrait of her face a few months back, in summer, superimposed over a photo of rippling water: she has it hanging now, in a cheap frame, in her bedroom at home.)

Sometimes he gets a glassy, faraway look in his eye and afterward claims to have had a vision—it's a little spooky, she doesn't totally like it, but it's a rather remarkable thing to see. Most recently, he has begun learning magic at the Boston School of Magic—her coworkers would definitely gossip if they knew that—though he hasn't gotten very far in his studies, as near as she can tell.

"The class," she says, remembering that there's a question on the table. "It went—well, it was a little complicated. But I think I'm learning a lot."

"About crime," Theodore says.

"Yes, but"—another hasty look around the aisle—"that's supposed to be a secret, remember?"

"Yes, of course," Theodore says, although he looks vaguely distracted, and she isn't entirely sure that he's actually remembered. "I did have something for you today, though. Something that came to my attention, and that might also be of interest to you. That might, in fact, give you an opportunity to practice some of what you're learning in—in that area."

"In Criminal Investigation?" Artie says, though she hates, a little bit, that now he's gotten her to say the supposedly secret part out loud.

"Yes."

"Well, what is it? The—thing."

"It's an unsolved crime," Theodore says.

"Oh," Artie says. Her heart leaps. This does interest her. "I want to hear more," she says quickly. "But"—some impatient shopper edges his way between them—"this probably isn't the right time, or the right place. Can I meet you somewhere this evening? When my shift is over?"

"Absolutely," he says. "Meet me at the Frog Pond."

*

There are no frogs at the Frog Pond, and it isn't really a pond, or at least it hasn't been for a long time. What it is now is a built feature of the park, a kidney-shaped pool at the north end of Boston Common, shallow enough that children can splash in it, although at this time of year it's too cold. At 8:00 p.m. it's also too dark, even though some illumination is provided by the new electric streetlights, which have been installed here and there along the paths. A few years ago you'd never have seen a woman alone in the park after the sun went down: the lights have made it feel a bit safer, though, so now it's not unheard-of. Even so, she wishes that Theodore had asked to have this conversation at a restaurant: someplace safe and warm and dry, where she could have filled her stomach with a bowl of onion soup, instead of just eating her normal post-shift meal, the single apple and greasy parcel of crackers that she brings with her to work. But she suspects there's a reason that he wanted to meet here.

She finds him easily. He's standing in a thrown ring of light at the eastern end of the pond. He has his camera set up on its tripod, its lens pointing at the trees above. He has his watch in his hand, and, as she approaches, she can see him shift his gaze from the timepiece to the branches of the trees and then back again.

"Hey," she says when she's closed the distance between them. He turns to her, lit from above, beaming with unconcealed happiness. For a moment he looks handsome to her, but this thought is confusing, so she dispels it with a sharp shake of her head, and opts instead to get straight to business.

"So," she says. "You were saying something back at the shop, about an unsolved crime."

"Yes," Theodore says. He reaches down and depresses a button on the camera; Artie hears the shutter click. "Unsolved to the best of my knowledge. I believe it may even have gone uninvestigated. Nonetheless, it has come to my attention." He bends over the tripod, begins to unscrew the camera from its mount.

"OK," Artie says. "What kind of crime? A robbery? An assault?"

"Unknown," Theodore says. "The knowledge I have been provided with is simply that a scream was heard here late last night, after midnight."

"Here at the Frog Pond?"

"Here on the Common."

"A scream by itself doesn't necessarily mean a crime, Theodore."

Theodore shrugs. "A mystery, certainly."

"OK," Artie says, trying to get into the spirit, help him out a bit. "Was someone screaming for help? 'I'm being robbed'? That type of thing?"

"Ah. No, not to my knowledge."

"Male scream? Female?"

"Unknown."

"Could it have been revelers? Extra exuberant, on their way out of a saloon?"

"Unlikely," Theodore says. "The report I heard was that the scream was one of distress."

"A wordless scream of distress."

"A sustained, distressed, wordless scream."

"Sustained," Artie repeats.

"So I was told," Theodore says.

"Who'd you hear about it from?" Artie says. "You said the crime wasn't reported—"

"I was told about it this morning, from my acquaintance Flann—one of the men who maintains the Public Garden. Something of a visionary, if you ask me. He makes it a point to have a sense of all that goes on in the Garden and here on the Common—he sees them as areas under his stewardship. Any crime that occurs here must be troubling to such a man, troubling twice over when the details about that crime have not yet come to light, so that the crime itself serves as a reminder of fundamental ignorance, of the ultimate unknowability of all things."

Artie's only half listening to this. Instead, she's drifted back to the sustained, wordless scream of distress. She tries out some screams in her imagination, tries to think of how long one would have to be before someone would describe it as sustained. She's no expert, but most screams, she thinks, are pretty short. If you're badly startled, you might scream for a second, maybe two. It's hard for her to imagine describing a two-second scream as sustained, though. So how long was it? Five seconds? Six? Ten? She tries to imagine screaming for ten seconds straight; she isn't sure she could do it. It's humanly possible, she supposes, if you took a long breath beforehand—

"So!" Theodore says: she snaps back to attention. "Given that you are embarking upon a course of study in criminal investigation, I thought you might be interested in this as an opportunity to practice your skills? A sort of field test, as it were? I thought it might—I thought it might provide a quality diversion for us both, if we were to do it together, that is. If you were interested." He averts his gaze from her, shyly looking down at his camera instead, which he's removed from the tripod and is now clutching in his fidgeting hands.

Artie smiles, charmed by the notion. She remains interested, although she's not at all certain about the plan. She's only just begun her studies, and she's not sure she has skills to practice beyond just wandering around, trying to perceive in some all-encompassing Professor Winchell–type way. On the other hand, Theodore's nervous enthusiasm is touching, and a little infectious—why shouldn't she attempt to get some practice in the field first? What could be the harm?

It could be dangerous, she thinks.

But surely that's silly. How much risk could there be, poking at the cold clues of a scream that occurred twenty-four hours ago? If the scream was provoked by a crime, the criminal is surely long gone, and the likelihood that the two of them could somehow blunder their way into danger seems slim.

And yet. Artie looks around at the grounds and the walkways, reviewing the possible directions into which she and Theodore could embark, and this conviction begins to waver. She's been warned, of course, not to walk in the Common after dark, and it isn't hard to believe that a crime has been committed here just last night. In this mindset, the new electric lights don't actually seem to be providing that much illumination after all, and the safety they purport to offer seems nothing more than a flimsy illusion. Every object and every shadow in the park begins to take on a menacing charge. The walkways might be lit, but there are wide swaths of darkness between them, spaces where anything could happen.

But—she sets her jaw. It's important not to lose her nerve. The work she ultimately wants to do—the thing she ultimately wants to do—it's not like that won't be dangerous. She might as well start getting used to it.

"Lead the way," she says.

They walk the paths of the Common, senses heightened. She tries to perceive things with clear and objective eyes, the way Winchell would want her to. But after a minute or two she begins to feel foolish: she starts to suspect that there's maybe not that much to see. What kind of evidence gets left behind by a scream? In practice, it feels like they're bumbling around in the dark, looking at nothing. Maybe she should have brought her notebook to record her observations—but what would she note, anyway? Is it important to note the broken branch overhead? What about this page from a newspaper, trampled into the mud? Should she observe details of the footprint?

It occurs to her then that maybe the problem is not that there are too few things to observe, but rather too many, that anything could be a clue. She feels frustrated by her own inability to evaluate the details meaningfully, to say with authority that this one is more important than that one; but then the frustration gives way to a sense that the whole thing is just plain dumb.

She shakes her head to clear it. Start again. What would Winchell want her to do? The details that are probably the most important for her to gather, right now, are details about the scream itself. They've been looking around the Common—that's in line with the chapter in the book she read last night, "Inspection of Localities"—but she remembers Winchell telling her about a future section in the book, "Examination of Witnesses." She hasn't gotten to that section yet, but from the title she can guess what she'd need to do.

Theodore couldn't provide much in the way of useful details about the scream because he didn't hear it himself: he wasn't a witness. But someone was.

"Hey," she says, reaching out to touch Theodore's sleeve. "This guy Flann. The gardener. Let's go talk to him."

"That's an excellent idea," Theodore says. "I'd love to introduce the two of you; I think you'd find him fascinating; absolutely fascinating. He wouldn't be on the grounds at this hour, however."

"Oh," Artie says.

"Perhaps we could speak with him tomorrow," Theodore says.

"Sure," Artie says, but she's a bit dejected to have to postpone pursuing what feels like a lead. She kicks a rock up the path; she falls deep into thought.

"Well, wait a second," she says finally. "If he's not here late at night, how did he hear the scream?"

"I don't believe he did," Theodore says.

"Well, OK," Artie says, "but who did then? I mean, are we sure there even was a scream, or are we just chasing phantoms?"

"Ah!" Theodore says. "Flann—he's a bit of an eccentric, you understand—he always tries to maintains close contact with the transients who reside here in the park. The tramps? The hoboes? They help him to keep up his sense of what transpires on the grounds."

Together they look up toward the northern corner of the park, the triangle near the golden dome of the State House and the tall, white steeple of the Park Street Church. Vagrants congregate there at night, sleeping on the benches. So far her perambulations around the park with Theodore have kept away from that corner, perhaps out of a shared, unspoken sense that that area would be dangerous.

"I believe," Theodore continues, "that he pays them a small sum for any useful tidbits of information they provide to him. So one of them must have been the source."

"Or several of them," Artie says.

"Plausibly," Theodore says.

She's nervous, but she also knows that churchwomen have worked with vagrants, part of their charitable mission. If they can do it, so can she.

So, together, they make their way up the incline that leads to the wrought-iron gates at the front of the State House, until they reach a group of four men sitting on a stone bench in front of a bronze relief depicting Civil War soldiers on a march. Artie and Theodore hang back, right at the edge of the group, exchanging glances. They don't really have a plan.

It's Theodore who makes the first move. He takes a big step toward the men and throws his arms wide. "Gentlemen!" he says. "Good evening!" The men bristle, look up at him balefully.

Artie catches Theodore by the coat, tugs him backward. She might not know how to interrogate witnesses, but in the moment she finds it hard to believe that it could go worse than the approach that Theodore is trying here would.

"Listen," she says, to the man closest to her. In an attempt to draw upon some inner reserve of charitable fellow feeling, she crouches down near him, so that they can better see eye to eye. He has a grizzled gray beard, and part of his nose seems to have eroded, a result of either accident or disease, Artie isn't sure. She wills herself to hold her position, to carry on, even though she finds it a little difficult to maintain a sense of fellow feeling with someone who's missing part of his nose. "I'm sorry to bother you," she continues. "Just—my friend here and I are looking into something that happened here last night. A possible crime. We heard that someone might have been screaming—in distress?" The man stares back, seemingly uncomprehending. "Sustained distress?" Artie tries.

"What is she saying?" bellows the second man on the bench.

"Shut up," the first man bellows back.

The second man: "But what is she saying."

"I was saying—" begins Artie.

"She was saying that someone was screaming last night."

"Screaming?"

"Screaming."

"Last night?"

"Here, last night; she wants to know if we know anything about it."

"Well, I wasn't here last night; I was at Old North."

"I was with you, you damn idiot."

"Well, tell her that."

"I will."

"I see," Artie says. "I'm sorry to have bothered you—"

"Were either of you here last night?" the second man hollers down to the other two men on the bench. The third man sits there inert, his chin to his chest; even from a few feet away Artie can smell the odor of alcohol wafting off of him. He hasn't stirred during the entire conversation and he doesn't respond now. But the fourth man, wearing ragged overalls and a broad-brimmed fisherman's hat, who up until this point had been similarly inert, suddenly leaps to his feet and takes a lurching step toward her.

Artie, startled, rises from her crouching position and tries to back away, but the man reaches out and grabs the cuff of her jacket.

Artie looks down and, through her panic, notes the tattoo on the back of the man's hand: a crude anchor, just above the knuckle. A former sailor?

"Hey, now," Theodore says, stepping in: he interposes a long arm protectively between her and the man, although the man doesn't release his grip.

"Theodore, wait," Artie says. She doesn't want this to tumble into violence if it doesn't have to, and she isn't sure Theodore's presence is helping. She keeps her eyes on the old man's face, inspects the crinkled network of lines around his eyes, and he looks back at her, and then he begins to say something. Artie can't understand him, though: to her ears, it sounds like gibberish.

"What is he saying?" Artie says, to the two loud men still sitting on the bench, who have, for the moment, ceased bellowing in favor of watching this unfolding drama.

"He's Portuguese," says the first man. "Do you speak it?"

"No," Artie says.

"I don't speak it either," says Theodore.

"We're all outta luck then," says the first man.

Artie tries anyway. "Were you here last night?" she says, returning her attention to the man in the fisherman's hat in front of her. "Did you hear the scream? Did you see the crime?"

The Portuguese man releases his grip on her sleeve, says something else, pauses, as though trying to figure out how to say something in English. Theodore, detecting that he maybe doesn't mean Artie any harm, draws his arm away, although Artie can tell that he's still energized, ready to get into a scuffle if the circumstances warrant it, perhaps a bit too ready. The Portuguese man seems to give up on whatever he was trying to say, and instead he turns his attention to fishing something out of the pocket of his overalls with his free hand.

He pulls something out, presses it firmly into Artie's palm, and then releases her sleeve.

She looks down at it.

It's a human tooth.

She recoils a bit, but doesn't drop it.

"Is this—where did you get this?"

The Portuguese man reaches up into his overgrown mustache and hooks his mouth with his forefinger. He pulls it way open so that she can see the gap, all the way at the back of his row of teeth.

"This is yours?"

The man, listening, lets go of his mouth, nods.

"Did someone strike you?" Artie tries. She makes fists with her hands, mimes a punch to her own jaw.

The man shakes his head no.

"Did it just—fall out?" she says.

The man listens. Artie isn't sure he understands. He nods yes.

Artie holds the tooth up, mimes it falling from her head. The man nods yes.

"Did you hear someone scream?" she asks.

The man stares at her. She puts her hand on her throat, opens her mouth, does her best imitation of someone in distress. The man nods yes.

"Was it you? Were you the one screaming?"

The man nods no.

"Did you see who it was?"

The man nods no.

This is the closest thing to a witness as she's going to find, she suspects. But she's not sure what to ask next, especially given that she's not even really sure he's understanding her questions. She makes a mental note to read that chapter in the book, so that next time she'll better know what to do.

She offers the tooth back to the old man, but he wraps his hand around hers, closes it back inside her grasp. His hand is wrinkled and knobby, very much an old man's hand, but it is warm and dry.

"Thank you for your time," she says, and then she leaves, Theodore behind her, the man's tooth still in her hand.

❦

Once she and Theodore have put some distance between themselves and the group of men, Artie stops walking. She stands under a streetlight and inspects the tooth to see if it has signs of decay or damage, something to indicate that it might have been bashed out or yanked out with a coarse tool. But she sees nothing like that. It's just a tooth, normal, inasmuch as it can be normal when you have a stranger's tooth in your hand. She sighs.

She wants to get better at solving crimes. But she feels like she's getting nowhere with this one—if there even is one; she still doesn't really know. Loose teeth from strange men. A sustained, wordless scream of distress. She tries to make them fit together, but comes up blank.

Feeling frustrated, she looks over to Theodore. "What now?" she says, a look of dismay crossing her face.

Theodore mirrors back her look of dismay, and then, unexpectedly, he brightens.

"I propose," he says, "that we go and have a drink."

Artie considers this. After these adventures in the park and her shift at work, she's pretty tired, and the idea of going home holds some appeal. But the lack of progress at what she's begun to think of as her case has left her feeling thwarted, and going for a drink would be a way to erase that feeling—to blow off some steam, get a second wind, close the night out with a jot of disreputable fun.

"The Pickle?" she asks.

"I'd go," says Theodore.

"Let's, then."

3

At the Pickle, they order nickel beers—Theodore pays—and they carry them carefully up to the second floor, pausing at the bend in the staircase to suck up some of the foam wobbling at the top of their stubby glasses. Theodore looks ridiculous pushing his lips out like that: Artie knows she must look ridiculous too: she laughs, and the force of the laugh sends beer foam over the rim of the glass in a plume. Theodore giggles at this, and Artie finds herself suddenly, indelibly endeared to the fact that this high, girlish sound could emerge from a man of his size. She wants to hug him and spin. But he's already turned away, hurried the rest of the way up to the second floor, two stairs at a time, so all she can do is hasten along behind him.

They emerge into the upstairs room, which is dominated by a sagging dance floor: they spot a lone free table at the floor's edge and they angle through the room to seize it. The room is hot, having accumulated the warmth thrown off by the exertion of the dancing crowd. Nobody's dancing right now; the band isn't playing—this isn't a surprise, really, the intermissions between dances always seem to be three times as long as the dances themselves. More time for sitting and drinking. They quaff half their beers in a single gulp, slam their glasses back to the tabletop. The table wobbles crazily, one leg outlandishly shorter than the others. Artie rotates the table a few degrees, hoping to correct the imbalance by matching its short leg with some compensatory rise in the buckled floor. Theodore tests the new position: it wobbles just as badly as it did before. He rotates it back with a grin; Artie gives him a scowl.

Theodore responds by closing his eyes, losing himself in what seems to be a happy reverie. After a moment of this, Artie considers summoning him back with a playful prod, but he looks so peaceable that she can't quite bring herself to do it. Instead, she contents herself with leaning back in her chair, pressing the cold glass of beer to her neck, and watching the crowd for a minute.

There are men and women alike packed into this room—more men than women, as usual, although the balance is pretty close. Also as per usual: Artie finds her eye drawn to the women in the crowd. She likes looking at women, likes seeing them in this kind of rough environment, less guarded, more likely to laugh, to move with wildness. This time, though, with her class fresh in her mind, she tells herself that she's doing it not merely because she finds women beautiful—as though there's anything mere about that— but because she's trying to hone her powers of observation, trying to inspect this locality with an investigative eye. As she looks at the mixture of women, mostly she sees women like herself: women who look like other shopgirls, garment workers, laundry ladies, domestic help. There are also prostitutes, drawn here by the uneven ratio of men to women. They're hard to spot at a glance, but Artie's noticed them before, and as she watches the crowd tonight she tries to distinguish them from the other working women, and tries to figure out how she's making that distinction. She thinks it has something to do with the way they respond to men: they sit closer to them, laugh more readily at their jokes; they're more assertive about when they'll place a hand on a man's arm.

Artie also can't help but notice an upper-class woman, seated nearby, wearing a straw boater and a smart, citron-green jacket. Upper-class women do show up here occasionally, dressed in clothes that are too fine for the environment, drawn here to delight in the scandal of it all, to take pleasure in their own shock, whether it be feigned or sincere. When they show up, they usually leave early, before midnight—Artie can imagine them the next morning, telling tales about how they descended into the jaws of vice, how they witnessed, with their own eyes, this place where men and women mingled drunkenly, pressed their bodies together licentiously on the dance floor in unseemly displays of animal lust, et cetera. This woman stands out, though. She's young looking, and here alone: Artie concludes that she must be a little braver than the other women from her class, who generally show up in pairs. The woman is joined at the table by two sweaty men, loutish looking, who she clearly didn't arrive with; they seem to be competing to see which of them can talk to her the loudest. Artie feels a momentary pang of concern: the guys look a little rough, and Artie wonders whether the woman isn't in over her head. The woman seems to be trying to signal disinterest by looking away from the men, casting her eyes around the room: she makes eye contact with Artie for a moment, and rather boldly holds it. Although Artie has short hair, she's not really accustomed to getting this sort of attention from a woman here at the Pickle: her face flushes, and she breaks the shared glance, looks back at Theodore. Theodore, for his part, has emerged from his reverie: he's now looking thoughtful, chin in hand.

"What?" Artie says.

"I was just thinking," Theodore says, "About the man back at the park. At the statue. The gentleman with the tooth."

"What about him?"

"He could be our screamer."

Artie wrinkles her nose. "You think?"

"Possibly," Theodore says. "Let's review what we know about what happened last night. From Flann."

"We know that there was, what was it, a sustained, wordless scream of distress."

"Right," Theodore says. "So—hypothesis. This man, our man, he had a toothache. Dental pain. One of the worst pains, I've heard. He wanders the Common, crying out in agony, then chocks his own tooth out with a stone or something—problem solved."

"I don't know," Artie says. "Something about it seems off." She thinks about why she's saying that. "He seemed agitated," she finally concludes. "Don't you think? He seemed like there was something he really wanted to tell me. Something more than just 'Oh, that scream you're talking about? That was me.'"

"Honestly?" Theodore says. "I think you're exactly right."

Artie thinks about it for a moment, reviews what she knows. "You mentioned the groundskeeper," she says. "Flann, you said his name was?"

"That's correct."

"I'd still like to meet with him—if you're willing to make the acquaintance, that is."

"It would give me great pleasure."

"Maybe later this week?"

"Name the day," Theodore says, "I'll make it work."

"OK," Artie says. She's not sure there's more to say about it at the moment. "How are things at the School of Magic going?"

"Ugh," Theodore says. He grimaces, rolls his eyes.

"That well, eh?"

"Oh, you know," Theodore says. "It's not going poorly, not exactly. Gannett says—well, he's always saying I have promise, enormous promise."

"That's encouraging," Artie says, remembering similar praise that Winchell had given to her, after class the other night. She had—what was it?—a keen investigative mind, and the potential to hone it? She feels a tiny swell of pride in her breast.

"It is," Theodore says, but he looks glum. "It is encouraging. It is the type of statement offered to someone who needs encouragement, someone who, without the aid of such pretty words, might find themselves discouraged."

"Is that you, then?" she says. "Prone to discouragement?" She recognizes that Theodore is referencing himself, not her, but hearing Theodore speak dismissively about encouragement in this way causes a frown to flicker through her smile; her budding pride suffers a hit.

"Well, certainly," Theodore says. "I mean, I'm five weeks into my studies with him and I haven't yet accomplished anything. Isn't that what a teacher is pointing out when they say you have promise? Aren't they really saying you haven't accomplished anything yet, but one day you might?"

She reflects on these words, and her own inability to successfully investigate tonight's crime, and her face falls. She takes a quick sip of beer, hoping to mask her expression.

"Isn't that part of being a student, though?" she asks, after she's swallowed. "If you enter the class already knowing everything there is to know on the topic—having accomplished everything there is to accomplish—then you probably shouldn't be in the class, right? And so, early on, isn't it part of the role of a good instructor to recognize things like promise, or, or potential—?"

"Oh yes," Theodore says, "I'm sure that's true, I'm just—I'm used to learning things faster. I don't want to just be promising, I want to be excellent. I haven't even mastered the first spell. We've been working on the same one, over and over."

"What's the spell?" Artie asks.

"It enables the caster to move silently," Theodore says.

"I can see that being useful," Artie says, thinking of creeping up the stairs when she gets home tonight, hoping not to wake other people in the building; hoping not to wake her parents.

"It's an old bit of thieves' magic, I'm told."

"That's interesting," Artie says, and she means it. She's always heard the local magicians spoken of as figures who weren't quite to be trusted, people who might lure you into some misadventure or charm you into relinquishing your hard-earned money. Don't talk to a magician if you're carrying a pie; you'll end up giving it to him, thinking it was your own idea all along—those are the sort of warnings you hear. She supposes that these swindles and schemes are essentially minor forms of criminality, but it hadn't occurred to her that thieves might have their own entire branch of magic. She wonders if Winchell knows, whether he's going to discuss it as part of the course.

"So how does it work?" Artie asks.

"You cast it on your feet!" Theodore says. "It creates a sort of"—he churns his hands in the air like he's kneading a loaf of bread held out in front of him—"a globe, I guess? Sounds can happen inside it but they can't exit? You generate it with your hands, but then kind of push it down to your feet."

Artie considers this. "Makes sense."

"Well, kind of," Theodore says. "It's rather a challenging way to do it, though, in practice. Your feet are moving when you walk, and you have to move the globe along with them. To make matters worse, both your feet can't fit in the globe at the same time—it's not that big! So you have to move it when you take a step, and then push it again, move it from one foot to the other. You have to concentrate on it, but if you concentrate too much the whole thing dissipates—I think so far I've taken a total of one silent step."

Artie finishes her beer. "Learning something hard takes time," she says.

"It's been five weeks!" Theodore exclaims.

"Five weeks? That's nothing. You never learned anything that took you five weeks to learn before?"

"No," Theodore says.

"Then you're probably not working hard enough," Artie says.

"Have you? Learned anything that took you more than five weeks?"

"Yes," Artie says.

"What was it?" Theodore asks.

Artie thinks for a second. "Sewing," she says.

Theodore rocks his head from side to side, weighing this. He drains the last of his beer, blots his mouth with the back of his hand. "Gannett wants to meet you, by the way," he says.

"Me?" Artie says, surprised.

"I mentioned you to him," Theodore says.

"What did you say?" Artie asks.

"It was when we were talking about thieves. I said that I knew a young woman with an interest in crime—"

"Did you mention why?" Artie says, suddenly wary.

"He did ask. I answered simply that you had a wide range of unorthodox interests. Which is not, strictly speaking, a lie."

Artie smirks. "What did Gannett think of that?"

"Gannett said that you sounded like a marvelously bright young woman, and that he always enjoys the company of anyone, ah, how did he put it, engaged in the work of overturning orthodoxies. He encouraged me to bring you along some evening so that he could make your acquaintance, if you were interested."

"I see," Artie says.

"Are you?" Theodore asks. "Interested?"

"I don't know," Artie says. "Maybe." She turns the prospect over in her mind. Magicians are disreputable, yes, but Artie's certainly never shied from the disreputable corners of the world. And knowing that Gannett knows stuff about thieves sharpens her interest, takes a vague feeling of generalized fascination and refines it into something akin to a specific set of questions that she might relish an opportunity to ask.

Before she can say more, a black man in a shiny suit steps onto the cheap wooden platform at the front of the room, lifts his double bass, and begins to play. A second man, following closely behind, takes his position at a drum kit, and a third man takes a seat at an upright piano that abuts the stage. Both of them join in as the band's trombonist and clarinet player climb the platform, fiddling with their instruments. Couples begin to rise from the tables: Artie experiences a tiny flare of interest in seeing whether the woman she noted before will be dancing, and if so with whom, and how well. She looks around, but the woman seems to be gone: the flare of interest claps out. With it seems to go all of Artie's remaining energy: her day has been long, and the thought that she still has to trek all the way home feels exhausting.

"Would you like to dance?" Theodore shouts over the music, extending a hand across the table. They've danced before, though they don't do it every week. Theodore, for all his long-limbed awkwardness, is not a bad dancer.

"I don't think so," Artie says. "Not tonight. I'm too tired."

If Theodore is disappointed, he doesn't show it—or maybe only for a second. But his primary reaction is to smile, to be his ordinary, benign self. He pushes his empty glass across the table, next to hers.

"Of course," he says. "Let's go."

*

Outside, the temperature has dropped, and a heavy, cold mist whirls about in the night air. Artie calculates how wet she'll get, waiting for a street car at this time of night: wetter than she'd like is the answer she settles on. She frowns, uses the toe of her shoe to desultorily nudge at a loose cobblestone that the Pickle uses as a doorstop on warmer nights. Theodore steps out into the blowing damp, looks upward with an assessor's eye, mumbles something unhappily. Artie hangs back, hides out beneath the tiny canvas awning above the Pickle's door, tries to convince herself that she's somehow staying dry there. She looks up and down the street, trying to see if there's a better spot within range of the places she could dart to.

She sees a narrow, dark alleyway about twenty feet from her that might provide some shelter, but her entry to it is blocked by a rotten wooden handcart being fussed at by a large man. A heavy, wet cloak bunched about his head and shoulders, a knotted tangle of leather straps in his hands—the idea of sharing an alley with him strikes her as undesirable, so she passes it over and looks further. Just beyond the alley entrance, she sees the woman in the straw boater and the green jacket, struggling to open a parasol. At this, Artie has to suppress a smile—she doubts the parasol will help at all, even if the woman does ever manage to get it open.

There is a kick of wind. The awning pops and snaps. The woman's straw boater is blown from her head and it sails out into the street, toward Artie, gliding to a rest on the damp stone near the mouth of the alleyway. Artie steps forward, intending to retrieve the hat, with a half-formed hope that, maybe, upon returning it, she'll get the pleasure of getting to say a pleasant word or two to this woman, maybe she'll get to enjoy a short, courteous exchange of goodnight wishes.

Even as Artie is imagining this, though, the woman has crossed the mouth of the alleyway and has stooped to retrieve her hat. And in doing so, she has landed herself squarely within the range of the hooded man's grasp.

He moves quickly. Artie barely has time to register what's happening. A long, curved knife has appeared in his left hand, and he reaches over the woman's shoulder, places the blade at her throat. He clamps his other hand around the woman's mouth and yanks her upright by her head. Her hands fly up to clutch futilely at his arms; her parasol clatters to the ground.

"Hey," Artie shouts at the man. "Hey!" He's turned his back to her, though, busying himself with dragging the woman back toward his wet wooden cart, with getting the two of them largely out of the view of anyone passing on the street's main thoroughfare. But Artie's already seen them. She hauls the cobblestone she'd just been kicking at up into her hand and breaks into a run. Behind her, Theodore is saying something; it sounds like "Wait."

But Artie doesn't wait. She closes the distance quickly, at a sprint. "Hey," she shouts again, at the man's massive back. By this point the man has wrestled the woman down into the cart. Artie catches a glimpse of her for just a moment: it looks like there's a wire now looped around her throat like a rabbit snare. Artie feels her stomach drop at the sight.

The man turns to look at Artie.

"Run along," he says. He holds the knife out toward her. "Unless you want me to cut your face wide open."

Artie throws the cobblestone at him, using both hands to propel it as hard as she can. It catches him beneath his nose, right in his mouth. He hunches down, cups his free hand over the site of impact, lets a roar of pain spill out of him. Artie sees blood drip from between his fingers. But he doesn't drop the knife.

He stands erect. He takes his hand away from his mouth, spits a red wad into the street, looks at Artie with rage in his eyes.

Artie steps back into the street. She'd turn and run but she's afraid to take her eyes off of the man. He's coming at her with the knife; he slashes but only catches air.

She hears Theodore yell something but her pulse is pounding in her ears and she can't make out the words. Her assailant glares in Theodore's direction; she risks a quick glance and sees that he's fumbling with his camera, trying to get a picture that they can maybe use later, as evidence.

She turns her attention back to the man with the knife. She can see him, beneath his hood, looking from her to Theodore and back to her again. The presence of another man forces him to pause, to calculate the risk: the pause gives Artie the ability to back a little farther out of slashing range; it gives Theodore more time to get his camera into position; it gives the woman, back in the alley, time to slip the wire noose off from around her neck and begin to clamber out of the cart. Artie can see grim resignation in the man's face; he knows he can't fight on all three fronts at once.

He screws up his face and then spits one last time, at Artie's shoes: even with the added distance, he's still close enough to her that the thick rope of blood finds its target readily.

She looks back up from the disgusting splat only to find him bolting away from the scene, disappearing into the gloom, leaving the three of them standing there, badly rattled, whipped by the chilly wet winds of October.

4

So now, finally, she knows. This is what it's like to come face-to-face with a crime. Artie can't say that she loves it. She's shaken, and wet, and scared, and her palms are scuffed from heaving the cobblestone, and she didn't even get to talk to the woman in green, who bolted like a foal while Theodore was off finding a policeman.

The investigation part is interesting, at least, although it's also frustrating. Only one officer arrives, an Officer Long, a curly-haired, chubby young man with a mustache that he's struggling to grow in all the way. He doesn't seem entirely equipped to cope with the situation. He has a notebook and a stubby pencil, and he tries to write things down, but the pages of the notebook quickly get damp. He tries to dry them on the hem of his shirt, but as near as Artie can tell this doesn't solve anything. He paces once around the handcart, gives it an experimental heft, handles the leather straps and the wire loop with a deepening look of distaste on his face. Theodore takes a photo of the cart and the policeman glares at him.

As he questions Artie, she finds herself wondering whether he's hewing to the guidelines laid out in the chapter on examination of witnesses, from *Criminal Investigation*, and, if he is, how well.

She reminds herself to check his examination style against whatever style the book recommends, which she'll figure out, she hopes, once she gets up to that part in the book. She tries to come up with questions about his style that she could ask Professor Winchell, once she sees him again. Did he do Thing A right? Did he do Thing B wrong? How could the examination have been done differently?

The policeman looks a bit foolish trying to scratch out notes in his sodden book, but if she's being fair, though, she'd have to admit that, as far as she can tell, the policeman is doing a good job. He asks her good questions: He tries to get her and Theodore to reconstruct what happened; he asks them for details about the assailant's appearance. What was he wearing? What did his face look like? As far as she knows, these are the right questions. So her frustration with this phase of the investigation is not with the officer, but rather—if she's being fair—with herself. Because she doesn't have the answers. She'd been feeling good, in the classroom, about her capacity for scrupulous observation, about her promise, but now, in the real world, faced with a real crime, she finds that she has retained almost no clear memories of the event.

Could she describe the facial features of the assailant? She can't. She remembers instead a flapping, wet cloak. She remembers the anger flashing in his eyes, yes, but can she remember the color of those eyes? No.

What was the assailant's approximate age? He wasn't elderly, and he wasn't a child, but beyond that? She can't say if he was twenty, or thirty, or forty-five.

Did he have tattoos or other distinguishing marks? She can't say. He moved quickly. It happened fast.

"He spat on me," she says, pointing at the blood on her shoe. The policeman pushes the flesh at his chin around with his hand, licks his pencil point, but doesn't write that down. Instead, he turns to Theodore, asks about the same questions, and gets about the same answers.

The policeman emits a long exhale of disappointment, like gas hissing out of a balloon. He then turns to Artie, giving it what is clearly one last try.

"Miss," he says, "can you tell me your single strongest impression of the assailant?"

Artie thinks about it.

"The knife," she finally says. "He had a knife. It was long, and it had a curve in it." And it came at my face, she thinks, but she's already told that part of the story and she doesn't feel inclined to tell it again. But she thinks about it. She replays, in her mind, the arc of the man's slash. She thinks, again and again, of just how short the distance was, between the tip of the blade and the tip of her nose. And she thinks, once again, that she needs to go home, for real this time.

Theodore insists on walking her to the streetcar stop, "for safety," he says, although it's clear that he's as rattled as she is. She doesn't look at him and get a sense that he'd be able to fight off the assailant, were he to return. But she doesn't say no.

◆

The Quick family, minus one, lives in three rooms on the third floor of a narrow brick building on Ipswich Street. Behind the building is a stretch of train tracks. During the day, these tracks are busy with locomotives heading to Newton: they roar past the house several times every hour, carrying passengers and freight, blasting soot onto the rattling windows of Artie's bedroom. Not the easiest environment in which to keep one's head. But right now, well past midnight, everything is still; the tracks are silent, the rain has stopped. Artie unlocks the front door of the building and makes her way up the stairwell cautiously, taking care not to wake the families on the first or the second floor with the sound of her tread. She's been going up and down these stairs ever since she was a kid; her legs know the exact number of steps in each flight, so the dark shouldn't pose any hazard, and it doesn't until she gets right outside her own front door, where she stubs her entire foot on her father's heavy satchel, stuffed with carpentry tools, which he's carelessly left there. She winces at the impact, not so much from the pain or the surprise, more just from the sound: kicking a bag full of tools makes an enormous clank, muffled by leather, yes, but still tremendously loud in the near silence of the stairwell. She releases her cringe almost immediately once the noise subsides, and the embarrassment passes not long afterward, but worry settles upon her in its place: the fact that the bag is there, just dropped at the top of the stairs, where it doesn't belong, is an almost certain sign that her father is drunk.

She opens the door quietly: when her father is drunk she can never be sure what mood he'll be in. Sometimes it's a joyous one—he'll reach down and lift her up, and she'll lean into him as he spins in a circle. It's a routine they did when she was young. She loved it then, and, if she's to be totally honest, she still takes a childlike pleasure in it now, even though that pleasure is tempered by her knowledge that alcohol is the fuel for his joy, by her awareness that the family below them probably doesn't appreciate hearing her father's heavy, stamping footfalls, probably doesn't appreciate having plaster dust knocked free from their ceiling. Even so: she prefers his joyous moods over his angry moods, the ones where he's shouting not with the enthusiasm of a father trying to delight his daughter but with the sullen, hateful intensity of a child trying to drive another child away: out of the room, out of the apartment, out of the family entirely.

Worst of all, though, these days, isn't her father's anger, but rather his despair: a new variety of mood that emerged after Zeb left. There's no shouting, there's just her father sitting there, silent, in his broad-backed wooden chair. He used to lean back in that chair, sprawled happily in it at the end of a hard day of labor, but now he's always leaning forward, pressing his face into his hands as though trying to keep a demon from escaping his skull. He'll hold that position for hours, breaking from it only for an occasional pull on his bottle of malt whiskey. Between these pulls he doesn't speak, or respond to being spoken to: Artie feels like he wouldn't even respond to someone attempting to physically shake him out of his slump, not that she or her mother ever dares to try. He's like a piece of the furniture, Artie has thought, at times, although that's not right, of course, because she knows that a piece of furniture would be something you wouldn't need to worry about, something that you could stand in front of and speak or laugh or think with no concern as to whether you were doing harm to it just by existing in its presence. By not doing the right thing, ever, somehow.

But when she enters the central room of the home tonight, her father isn't in it: he must have gone off to bed already. The room isn't empty, though: her mother is there, sitting hunched at the table, her face cast into an expression of deep concentration, her hands busy, doing something to the household's enameled colander. Artie freezes in the doorway. A plausible excuse for why she's returning home so late assembles itself in her mind, even though she knows it won't be necessary: her mother is not regularly in a state, these days, to know or to care how late it is when Artie comes through the door. She doesn't even look up.

"Ma," Artie says, in a whisper. No reaction.

"Ma," Artie says, a bit louder this time, but not too loud—she doesn't want to risk waking her father. Her mother, seeming to hear Artie as though from a great distance, frowns distractedly, the weak glow of the oil lamp exaggerating the expression into a mask of distaste.

Artie steps closer, places a tentative hand on her mother's shoulder. Her mother shrugs it off with an irritated *tsch*. Artie stiffens. Fine, she thinks. To hell with you. She feels a sudden impulse to walk away, to turn her back on her mother, to stomp off to her room and fling herself facedown onto her bed. But she doesn't move. She's determined, for some reason, to stand here, damp and weary, and try to find a way to calm her mother's disquieted mind instead of tending to her own restlessness, retreating to her room, trying to sleep, if she can, trying to forget about the man, the knife, the horrible wire snare. She wonders, for a moment, what it would be like for the tables to be turned, to be in a position to receive comfort, for her mother to be in a position to offer it. She wonders what it would be like to be able to say I was attacked on the street tonight and have someone in the house care.

Instead: "What are you doing there, Ma?"

"It's this colander," her mother says. She clutches at one of its metal handles, which is held on now by only one screw, the other one lost to time. She rotates the handle back and forth.

"What about it, Ma?"

"It's broken."

"That's right," Artie says. She leans in, points out the tiny pock marking the rusted-out spot where the screw once was.

"It needs to be fixed."

"It's not—it's not gonna be fixed, Ma. It's broken."

"I can see that it's broken, girl; that's what I'm saying. It needs to be fixed."

"I don't think you're gonna be able to fix it; that's what I'm saying." She detects the irritation in her voice, forces herself to strive to make her tone pleasant again, inoffensive. "You can see the metal's gone, here?" She points to the same spot. "You could get someone to patch it there, maybe, but you can't mend it on your own. Not just with—not just by hand."

"But—" Her mother rotates the handle again, as though in search of a secret position that would allow it to perfectly snap into place.

"Just leave it be," Artie says. "How long have you been working on this?"

Her mother doesn't answer. She takes the colander in both hands, extends her arms until she's holding it out at a distance. She appraises it with a keen eye. When she was well, she always had this ability, to attend carefully to the quality in things; she lost it, slowly, through the years of her progressing mental decline. Artie hadn't quite realized how gone that trait was until this moment, when she feels her heart skip wonderfully at seeing it return. She knows it's likely that it'll only be there for a moment, so she tries to cherish the glimpse of it, to hold on to it for as long as she can. She doesn't say anything.

"It's pretty, don't you think?" her mother says, turning it this way and that. The lamplight jumps across it, lighting up the blue flowers painted in a chain across its white enamel.

"It is," Artie says, and she intends it sincerely.

"I used to have so many pretty things."

"I know, Ma," Artie says. Artie tries to put some conviction behind these words even though she's not really sure about this—their family has never had much in the way of pretty things. The colander is, in fact, one of the only things in the house that Artie feels certain was purchased partly for the value inherent in its beauty.

"It's ruined," her mother says.

"It's not ruined," Artie says. "It works. You just need to hold it by the rim, be a bit careful when you're—"

"I just want it to be fixed," her mother says, her voice rising. "I want it to be fixed and—" She uses both her hands to bring the colander down on the tabletop, hard. Artie winces, casts a quick look toward the doorway to her parents' bedroom, frightened at the thought of seeing her father's form loom up to fill the frame. But nothing happens. Her mother's face is fixed in a grimace of frustration.

"It's OK, Ma," Artie says. She touches her mother's shoulder again; this time her hand isn't shaken off. "It's OK. We'll—we'll fix it in the morning, all right?"

A long silence. Finally her mother says, "All right."

"All right," Artie repeats, letting loose a held breath. "Let's get you up."

Once her mother is off to bed, Artie heads off to her own room, the room she used to share with Zeb. The room is dark, and cold; Zeb's bed is empty. It's still made, as though one day he'll simply decide to return for good. Artie doesn't need to see it to know: it's been left that way for a long time now.

She puts on her nightclothes and crawls, finally, into her own bed. The bed is dry, and that, at least, provides some modicum of comfort. She closes her eyes, reviews the puzzle pieces the day has dumped upon her, turns them over in her mind. A woman in a green jacket. A man with a knife. A cart and a snare. Blood on her shoes. And then the earlier pieces, from the Common: the old man's tooth (which she dropped blindly into a ceramic dish on her dresser, not quite sure what else to do with it); the sustained, wordless scream of distress. Two separate sets of pieces, two separate puzzles, it would seem, although, in her exhaustion, she begins to jumble them together, to intuit a single picture into which they all could fit. And then she drops into sleep, and the picture is gone.

5

Artie awakens Saturday morning before dawn, right when the first locomotive goes by. She keeps her eyes closed, groans softly: she went to bed depleted, both physically and emotionally, from last night's misadventures, and the sleep she's managed to grab seems to have done nothing to refill her reserves. On top of that, Saturdays are always exhausting at the store: a lot of local workers enjoy a half day, plus on top of that there are the tourists. They may be drawn to town on a weekend visit to see any number of sights, but they know that if they've come to shop they have to do it Saturday, since on Sunday the stores will all be closed.

For a moment she entertains the notion of rolling over, pressing her face into her pillow, and going back to sleep, but she knows that there are two good reasons why she should get up now, early, get dressed, and get out. Reason one: she can go meet Theodore for breakfast, and they can try to sort out what they know about the week's events. And reason two, the reason she wakes and leaves early most days: she can be out of the house without needing to cross paths with her father.

She laid yesterday's dress, her best one, over a chair last night, in the hopes that it would have dried overnight. Out of bed now, she tests its fabric with her hand. It's still damp. She frowns: the prospect of putting on wet clothes first thing in the morning doesn't hold much appeal, so she'll have to shift to one of her other options. Probably that means she'll wear one of her two high-collared shirtwaist blouses, either of which she could pair with her long, heavy blue skirt. The result, as an outfit, would be fine, comfortable enough, easy to work in, relatively plain.

She moves to the closet, looks at the blouses on their hangers. And then she shifts her gaze to Zeb's old suit, the one he left behind when he fled the family. She pauses for a minute to handle the jacket; she lifts its sleeve, tests the texture of its twill with her thumb. She realizes, after a second, that she isn't breathing, and she forces an exhale.

It's this jacket that she wore when she went to the Evening Institute. It didn't fit perfectly; that must have been part of how Winchell detected her. It was too small: too short in the sleeves, and she couldn't button it across her chest. This felt like a surprise, even though it shouldn't have—she knows that she's caught up to Zeb, growth-wise. In fact, the last time they saw one another, probably a full year ago now, she noticed that she was taller than he was. He'd been putting on some adult muscle, growing wiry, but he had stopped getting taller. There was still something about him that hadn't outgrown the runtish aspect of his boyhood. She remembers watching him during that meeting, watching him eat furtively at the kitchen table before fleeing again, and she remembers wondering whether he'd always look that way to her from here on out, like someone who had lost his way, somehow, on the path toward becoming an adult.

Regardless, the suit was there when she needed a disguise. When she first tried it on—a test run, on Sunday, before wearing it out into the world properly on Wednesday—she was surprised to find that, after all this time, it still smelled like her brother. Some boyish mix of hair crème, sweat, sardines, and back-alley dirt. It hit her with a force that was literally flattening. She had to lie down on her bed and close her eyes, just to take a moment, to soak up some of his presence.

She wonders, this morning, whether the garment still holds some of that odor, or whether it's lost its potency, whether it smells like her now. She's tempted to try it on, just to see.

For a moment she extends this fantasy: she imagines what it would be like to go about in the world wearing men's clothes all the time. It was interesting to traverse the world in disguise. It was frightening, to some degree—she didn't really know what would happen if she was caught. She'd smuggled the suit out in a paper satchel, so that her mother wouldn't see what she was up to; she brought it over to Theodore's home and changed into it there. Putting it on in the privacy of a room with a closed door was one thing; walking out onto the street in it was something very different. She had a moment of panic in Theodore's vestibule before she stepped out into daylight: it was all too easy to imagine the very first passerby stopping, scrutinizing her, pointing a finger, shouting something, hollering for a policeman—after that her fears of persecution began to get a little fuzzy. She could be arrested, she supposed. Maybe she'd end up in the papers, paraded as a freak, bringing shame upon the family; she didn't really know.

But she summoned up the nerve and went out anyway. And it wasn't like she'd feared. People didn't come to a sudden halt as she crossed their paths: they went up and down the street as normal, engaged in the commerce of an ordinary day. Moving up the street, buoyed by the fact that her disguise was working, allowed the terror of the experience to slowly transmute into a sort of exhilaration. It felt good to wear pants! Before the walk was over, she'd imagined what a benefit they'd be in the workplace: She'd be able to move more comfortably through the aisles; she wouldn't have to look back over her shoulder all the time to make sure her dress wasn't dislodging some product from its position on a lower shelf. Just having a single pocket would be a huge help at times, and Zeb's pants—which had four—seemed almost an embarrassment of riches. It wasn't hard to understand this as one component of what makes men inhabit the world with the confidence that they do. Not to mention that the men working at Filene's get paid more than the women do: that's the regrettable fact of it. So now, as she's getting dressed in her blouse and skirt, she wishes, a bit idly, that she'd hit upon this disguise idea earlier, that she'd applied to work at Filene's in the guise of a man. She feels maybe like she could have pulled it off: her disguise didn't fool Winchell, true, but his eye is unusually discerning.

But she can't reinvent herself as a man now. And she can't just wear the pants to work, despite their obvious utility. All she can do is finish dressing, put these thoughts away, and head out into the cold dawn light, lured by the promise of Theodore buying her a hot breakfast.

She meets him at Durgin-Park, his usual morning haunt: he's sitting at the end of a long communal table, halfway through a plate of ham, eggs, corn bread, and baked beans. He brightens when he sees her, and greets her cheerfully, but Artie's mood, at first, is sour. She greets him monosyllabically and huddles down into herself a little, keeping her coat on while she orders to stave off the chill. Theodore offers up a few other conversational forays, but Artie offers little more than grumbles in return. This lasts only until the meal and her coffee arrive, whereupon Artie finds that, as always, a plate of hot fare on a chilly morning goes a long way toward lifting her spirits.

"OK," she says as her bones begin to warm up. Maybe it's the food, maybe it's just the comforting light of day, but now that she's feeling a bit better, last night's attack seems to have diminished somewhat in size: it's still a terrifying thing that happened, but it's also taken on the status of an object of fascination, something that can be held in the hand and worked over. A puzzle. And with a puzzle comes the promise of a solution. Maybe Artie and Theodore are just soaking up excitement from the noise and clamor of the crowded dining room, but as they eat and begin to compare notes over the scarred tabletop, this solution seems tantalizingly within reach: maybe just one more cup of coffee away.

"So not last night but the night before—" Theodore says.

"Thursday," Artie says.

"—we have the scream at the Common."

"Right."

"Then last night—"

"Friday," Artie says.

"—we witness the attack on the woman."

"Yes."

"So: hypothesis."

"Go ahead."

"The same man is the culprit in both cases," Theodore says, his eyes bright. "The scream from the Common was from a similar attack."

Artie takes a mouthful of coffee. She swallows, grimaces. "No," she says.

"No?" Theodore says.

"No," Artie says.

"Why not? They're no more than a mile apart; that suggests a pattern."

"Well, does it?" Artie says. "Think about it."

Theodore frowns.

Artie continues: "What's the one thing that didn't happen when the man grabbed that woman?"

Theodore's face goes blank as he thinks about it for a minute.

"She didn't scream," he says finally.

"She didn't scream," Artie says. She presses a finger into the tabletop to emphasize the point. "She couldn't scream. He got that snare around her throat quickly, and its whole purpose was to make sure she couldn't scream."

"Maybe he learned something. Thursday was a failed attempt; Friday he devises a solution so that he wouldn't fail again."

Artie considers it. "That doesn't seem right to me," she says finally. "He seemed pretty practiced with it—it didn't seem, to me, like he was using it for the first time."

"That's true," Theodore says. "But wait a second. If he'd used it before—then—are you saying that he's tried to snatch someone before?"

"Or—" Artie considers the worst. "That he's successfully snatched someone before."

"He's been doing this for a while," Theodore says, trying out the idea, a note of skepticism in his voice. "In this version of events."

"I don't know," Artie says. She uses a scrap of corn bread to sop up a puddle left behind by her vanished baked beans, pops it into her mouth, uses her tongue to wad it into a corner of her cheek so that she can continue speaking. "All I'm saying is that he seemed adept with that thing. It didn't seem like a thing he'd just invented overnight. He moved quickly and he moved deftly. Think back. You remember."

She watches Theodore's face as she chews, watches it turn grave for a moment. He remembers; she can see it. She, too, feels spooked at the knowledge that they might have been up against someone more formidable than he initially appeared: not just some random ruffian but someone who has actually trained himself to snatch people off the street, designed a tool for the job, and mastered its use. Scary, grim, sure, but the mood is leavened by her sudden hope that maybe her memory didn't betray her after all, maybe her powers of observation actually did grasp something useful, some piece that they can fit into the puzzle. A clue.

"OK," Theodore says. He taps the tines of his fork against the tabletop. "But. If we really are dealing with a serial abductor, that doesn't necessarily rule out my theory: that Thursday and Friday nights were the same assailant. We know from last night that he's not infallible. You're saying his snare technique wasn't invented overnight; let's say I agree." He lifts the fork, points it at her. "Let's say he tried to use the snare on Thursday, at the Common, but he moved just a bit too slowly. His target screams; he flees." Tap of fork on table again, as punctuation. He looks up at her to see what she thinks.

Artie considers it. Its tidiness has an appeal. And Theodore is right that their assailant was not infallible. But what triggered his failure was not him moving too slowly, but rather that he was up against too many people, on a city street. In the darkness of the Common, unobserved? Surely he would have gotten away with it—she thinks. And plus there are still pieces that don't fit: she thinks for a minute of the old man's tooth, in her dish back at home. So Theodore's version of the story is only tidy if you ignore the things it doesn't explain, and she's pretty sure that's bad detective work. She could always run it by Professor Winchell and see what he thinks, though.

"Could be," is her answer, finally—she doesn't want to hurt Theodore's feelings by coming down too hard on his theory. "We still don't really know enough about what happened on the Common to be sure."

"That's true," Theodore says.

"Last night," Artie says. "You said we might be able to talk to the groundskeeper, is that right? Flann?"

"Yes!" Theodore says. He snaps his fingers. "That's right. He's probably working on the grounds this morning; we could go find him right now."

Artie jolts with excitement, although it's tempered by knowing that the start of the workday is coming down fast: there may not be time. She cranes her head around, looking for a clock, but Theodore, perhaps anticipating this, is already glancing at his watch.

"You can make it," he says, "but we'll have to hurry." He signals the waitress with a hand gesture. "What do you think?"

Artie lifts her mug, glugs down the last of her cooling coffee. "I'm ready when you are."

◆

Artie feels absolutely no surprise at the idea that Theodore has made friends with the groundsman at the Common. That's sort of the way Theodore is: he's a collector of interesting people. He notices them, and he isn't afraid to engage them in conversation, to root after what they might know. This was, in fact, the originating motive behind their own friendship.

He had spotted her at Filene's one day as she was arranging a display of chamois gloves and ribbon on an oval table. It was a slow Wednesday morning in February: the Christmas rush, by then, was just a fading memory, and the slushy and wet conditions outside were deterring all but the most determined shoppers from their browsing. But along came Theodore, ambulating up the aisle. She'd looked up, noted him—tall man in a damp traveling coat—and then gone back to folding gloves.

"How do you do?" he'd asked her.

This was a bit unusual—typically, customers would open conversation to Artie with something closer to "Can you help me?"—but not, in and of itself, too surprising. "I'm fine, sir, and yourself?" she'd replied.

Theodore didn't respond to the question; he was busy scrutinizing her quizzically. "Your hair," he'd said. "You wear it short."

Artie, suddenly made self-conscious, flushed a bit, and her
hand reflexively went up to pat her hair, as though it had come
out of place somehow. It wasn't uncommon for women visiting
the store to criticize her for wearing her hair in this fashion—
it's mannish, they liked to say. She noticed that Theodore's tone
wasn't critical, though, that it had more of a bemused fascination
in it than anything else, but she'd already begun to utter her by
now somewhat canned response: "Yes, well, Filene's prides its
staff on being up-to-date on the latest fashions, including with
regard to hairstyle. The women in Paris are wearing their hair in
this style this year, we're told, and—"

Theodore had interrupted her here. "Fashion," he said. "I do
not understand it!"

Again, Artie was girded to interpret this as a criticism—it was
not entirely unheard-of for men to enter the store and grumble
noisily at what they perceived as the unseemly overabundance of
product—but, again, to Artie's ear Theodore's tone did not sound
like one of moralistic scolding: it sounded more akin to open
wonderment. It caused her to recall a line from the Shakespeare
she'd read in the final year of her public schooling: "How beaute-
ous mankind is!" Uttered by Miranda, at the moment she laid eyes
on strangers arriving on her island. Artie could imagine that line
delivered with Theodore's exact intonation.

"Are you—are you looking to purchase a gift, sir?" she'd tried,
although she was already beginning to feel like this was the wrong
approach, somehow.

"A gift?" Theodore had said. "No, no, I'm not here to shop. I just—I consider myself a worldly man."

Artie regarded this non sequitur with a touch of skepticism, given that Theodore appeared to be only a few years older than she—she couldn't imagine he was much older than twenty-one, and she wasn't completely certain that you could acquire all that much worldly experience in just two decades of life. But she let him continue.

"I appreciate the arts," Theodore said, the puzzled look on his face deepening. "Painting. Poetry. Photography. It seems evident to me that fashion has as much to recommend it as these other arts."

Artie raised an eyebrow at this. She'd certainly never heard a man say things like this before, although it did possibly explain how Theodore had found his way into the depths of a department store primarily devoted to ladies' wear without actually intending to shop. Drawn there by the lead of his curiosity? If true, this was a thing that made him a bit more interesting to her, cause to let her guard down, if only a little.

"But I fear I have no head for it," Theodore said. "I don't know where to begin." He gestured at the gloves that she'd spread out in an array. "I haven't the faintest idea, for instance, what makes the difference between a fashionable glove and an unfashionable one."

"Well," Artie said. "It is a bit complicated. Some of it is the quality. The material, the stitching." She lifted a glove, held the seam toward him. "It's unlikely that a glove made of cheap material, or one that is poorly stitched, will ever be truly fashionable."

"I see," Theodore said soberly.

"But that's not all of it, of course. A glove that is only well-made, without an eye for aesthetics, will only be utilitarian—not fashionable."

"So where is the aesthetics to be found, in a glove?" Theodore asked, staring at the glove she's holding as though it were an artifact from some long-ago civilization.

"Well, it's everywhere," Artie said. "It's in every choice that the designer made. The color of the material. The pattern of this embroidery." She traced a line of tiny pink flowers with the tip of her finger. "The cut of the glove. The effect it makes upon the wrist."

"Astonishing," Theodore said, so sincerely that Artie couldn't help but smile, imagining Miranda again.

They stood there for a moment, each of them lost in their own private reflections as they observed the glove.

"Theodore Reed," Theodore said, finally, offering Artie his hand.

"Artie Quick," Artie said.

"I'd like to continue this conversation at a later date."

"Oh?" Artie had replied, a bit surprised to realize that she, too, would like to keep the conversation going.

"I'll be dining tonight at Brooks' Dining Rooms, six p.m. You're welcome to join me, or, if you'd like to pay me a visit at a more convenient time, I offer you my card."

She'd met with him at the Dining Rooms, not quite realizing at the time that she was joining Theodore's rotating cast of interesting people: a wide network of informants and odd fellows through which Theodore worked, steadily, to make sense of a world that bewildered him.

It took some time for her to understand the true breadth of this network—that it had room for a shopgirl like herself but also contained newspapermen, aspiring politicians, gossipy bootblacks, landscape painters, magicians, perfumers.

And her understanding about Theodore's collection (as she calls it, not entirely kindly) continues to deepen as she gets to know him better. At first she thought he assembled it because he was interested in the world and wanted to learn—she still believes that, she knows it's true, but over time she's come to conclude that there's more to it. She wondered, for a while, if he assembled it as an enormous distraction, something to make just because he was bored. But that wasn't right: she's never known Theodore to be bored. Then, for a while, she thought he built it mostly just because he could afford to. It is true, after all, that his ability to maintain these connections is facilitated by his wealth, or, rather, his family's wealth: it's easy to wander around the city and have interesting conversations all day when you don't have to work a job because you're relying on your parents' money. But that wasn't fully satisfying either.

Her current theory is that he built it because he was lonely. As she's gotten to know him better, she's understood the extent to which he is alone. Theodore's father, a career diplomat, was named an ambassador to Belgium eighteen months ago, and he left for Europe along with Theodore's mother. Theodore—twenty-one at the time, in everyone's eyes an adult—was installed in a small townhouse and left to fend for himself. With no small assistance from one domestic helper, Artie is quick to remind herself. All the same. She—perhaps alone among his confidants—sees in Theodore someone who is drowning in his own solitude even as he fills his life with a cavalcade of people. She's reminded that Miranda's astonishment at the world, and the people in it, comes not just from some boundless capacity for wonder, but rather from the sheer, immutable fact of her isolation. Years spent on a remote island.

*

When they come upon Flann, in the Common, he's standing at the base of a tree, fists pressed into his hips, glowering at its barren canopy. His stance reminds her of Theodore's from last night, when she met him at the Frog Pond. She'd found him gazing up into the network of crisscrossed limbs, pointing his camera at it, trying to discern whatever pattern or beauty could be found there. Two men with their minds lost in the branches: she intuits immediately how Theodore might have selected Flann for his collection, even though Flann looks like he's probably thirty years Theodore's senior.

She wants more practice at recalling the details of the people she encounters, so as he turns and notes their approach she carefully observes the lines around his eyes, the discontinuity in his nose that reveals that it might once have been broken, the red complexion of his skin, the whiteness of his beard, cropped close to his chin, probably with scissors. His hair is gray, forced back from his face with pomade liberally applied and run through with what might have been a wide-toothed comb. He gives Theodore a curt nod, looks Artie over without a greeting, and then turns to his nearby cart. The cart, hitched to a tired-looking mule, is loaded with various tools: rakes, shovels, shears of varying sizes arrayed in a zinc bucket, a small wheelbarrow, even an unstrung ukulele, but Flann's attention is focused on a ladder held to the side by two hooks. He can't quite seem to get it free.

Theodore, hands in pockets, keeps his distance, silently watching Flann struggle to lift the ladder off of both hooks simultaneously, seemingly waiting for a good moment to attempt to make an introduction. But after Flann fails in his third attempt—uttering a low oath—Artie decides to intervene. She crosses the short distance between them and reaches out for the back end of the ladder.

"Good morning, sir, my name is Artie Quick," she says as he turns his eye to her. "I'm a friend of Theodore's. Can I offer you a hand with this?"

He weighs this for a moment. "Be careful," he says, gruffly but not unkindly.

"Oh, my father is a carpenter," Artie says as she grips hold. "I've been helping to move ladders around since I was a tot."

Flann's look changes slightly as he reassesses her in some way, and then the two of them lift at his command.

"Nice to make your acquaintance, Mister Flann," she says, once they've carried the ladder to the base of the tree and gotten it standing. She's not totally certain whether Flann is his first name or his last. She extends her hand; Flann takes it after making a bit of a show of using his green coveralls to wipe his own hands clean.

"A pleasure," says Flann. "And a pleasure to see you again as well, Master Reed." Theodore beams.

"It's a quick visit today," he says, striding forward to meet them. "Artie and I have only a few minutes, but we were hoping we could ask you a question about something that happened here the other night, Thursday night."

"Aye," Flann says.

"You and Theodore spoke previously about—a scream? A long, sustained scream of distress?"

"Oh, aye," Flann says.

"We're trying to learn whether a crime was committed here, and, if so, what the nature of that crime was."

"I've heard tell of this scream," Flann says. He shrugs. "Can't say I give it too much weight. There's more devilment than that about."

Theodore blinks. "There is?"

"Aye," Flann says.

"Um," Theodore says. "Like what?"

Flann loosens a trowel from his belt and levels it accusingly at the tree. Theodore looks at the trowel, then looks at the tree, then looks back at Flann.

"I don't know if I mentioned this," Theodore says, "but we're a bit short on time? Artie here has to be at work by a certain hour, and it's approaching rather rapidly—"

A pained look crosses Flann's face. "I'm trying to teach you something here, my young friend," he says. "It's the same lesson I try to teach you each time you visit. How long it takes for you to learn it—that's up to you, isn't it?"

Theodore sighs. "So, the lesson," he begins.

"The lesson," Flann interrupts, "is that groundskeeping, or indeed, any of the finer arts, is grounded in observation. You want me to explain what the damned thing is—I want you to look, and see what the damned thing is."

At the mention of the word observation, Artie's eyes widened: she might even have made a surprised noise. Flann turns his attention toward her, as if to say, You have something to add?

"It's just—it's just that—I'm taking this class, you see, and, ah, I'm reading a book for the class and it makes what very much seems to be the same point. About observation, I mean."

"What's the book?" Flann asks.

"Ah, *Criminal Investigation*," Artie replies.

Flann frowns, as if the topic is inappropriate subject matter for a young woman.

"The—class is also about Criminal Investigation," Artie offers, feeling like she might need to extend some additional explanation. She winces as soon as she says it, though—she doesn't really want Flann to know that she's been sneaking into an all-male classroom, and he seems like he might be clever enough to piece it together. He notes the wince impassively: it seems for a moment like he might remark on it, but then he lets it go.

"Not much of a reader," he says. "I don't know that a book is the best way to learn how to look at things—every moment I spend in a chair somewhere reading is a moment I can't be out here looking at the plants that are my charge."

"That makes sense," says Artie, hoping to mollify him. "And my instructor, Professor Winchell—he's a good man, I think the two of you would quite enjoy one another's company—but he really, ah, he emphasizes the importance of getting out in the field, and, um, observing, with our own eyes? There's a chapter in the book, 'Inspection of Localities,' and it, um, he, my professor, he urged us to visit actual, uh, places, and look around?" It sounded good when Professor Winchell had said it, but Artie can't find a way to get it out of her mouth without sounding dumb, and Flann maintains a skeptical look throughout.

"Well," says Flann, "why don't you see if the lesson took? Take a look around—both of you—and tell me what you see."

OK, Artie figures. You can do this. She looks at the tree; she looks up and down the row of them.

"What kind of tree are these?" she asks, partly to buy a minute of time.

"Red maples," says Flann.

"Red maples," Artie says, nodding with a sagacity that she doesn't really feel she's earned. She doesn't know anything about red maples, so it's hard for her to know if there's something specific that she should be noticing about them, something that would be obvious to someone with more horticultural knowledge. But she also believes that Flann's intent is to play fair here, that he wouldn't have given her and Theodore the task of finding something, through observation, that they wouldn't have a way of actually seeing.

Theodore's stepping closer, taking a deep look at the patterns in the tree's bark, so Artie decides to do the opposite: she steps back, trying to get a look at the whole row of trees at once. She remembers that Flann pointed out the one tree for special consideration, not the whole row, so maybe trying to spot what's different about that specific tree, in comparison to the others, might be helpful.

She thinks back to the chapter in the book. It was mostly about how to make observations of a crime scene, things like noting the precise position of a corpse, blood spatter on the walls, et cetera. Not exactly relevant. But there were instructions about noting the size, shape, height, and "peculiarities" of the items in a space, so she figures she can begin there. She looks at the trees, one after the next.

"Were all these trees planted at the same time?" she asks.

Flann instantly fixes her with his acute eye. "Yes," he says. "So you see it."

Artie frowns, a bit puzzled. "Well," she says. "I don't know. I see that most of these maples are—they're pretty young, I couldn't tell you how young, but they're mostly about, I'd say, ten feet tall. But this one—the one you pointed out—it's older, or it's taller, anyway; it's maybe twenty feet tall? That's the—I mean, I don't know if it's worth noting, really, but that's a peculiar thing about it."

"Peculiar indeed!" Flann says. "I planted each of these trees a score ago, all the same size then." He points both ways with his trowel to indicate the whole row. Artie looks up and down the path, following the line of trees Flann's indicating. "All the same size right up until last week."

Artie wrinkles up her face in confusion, looks over at Theodore, who is mirroring the expression back at her. "That can't be right," she says. "A tree can't double its size in a week."

"Aye," Flann says. "Devilment afoot."

"Are you sure you're observing this correctly?" Theodore says. Flann, looking sideward, fixes one keen blue eye on Theodore's skeptical face. "I mean, devilment notwithstanding, trees don't grow ten feet in a week, so in order for your observation to be correct, you'd need a theory that could explain it."

"Maybe someone replaced it?" Artie tries.

Theodore frowns. "So you'd need a person—a whole team of people, and probably a dray horse in addition—to come in here, hauling a twenty-foot tree, in the middle of the night, dig up the old tree, and replace it with a new one? And haul the old one off somewhere? That's the theory?"

Flann paws at the scruff at his jawline for a moment. "I don't theorize," he says finally. He spits in the grass. "I'm not one much for it. I observe."

Theodore pinches the bridge of his nose. "Yes," he says. "Observation is all. I understand the lesson; I promise you, I do. But we can use observation to rule out possible theories about what happened, can't we? There'd be more things to observe if a tree really were taken from here, wouldn't there? There'd be signs—things would be all dug up."

Artie, remembering Winchell's urgings that the superior Investigating Officer will note things like marks in the grass and displaced stones, has already had this same thought, and she has dropped down to her knees to inspect the base of the tree. It's late October; the city has already had some hard frosts; she'd expect the earth there to be packed and dense. But the soil around the roots is broken, loose; she's able to dig her fingers into it easily.

"Huh," she says.

"You could learn something," Flann says to Theodore, grinning, "from Miss Artie Quick here. She observes well." He returns to the cart, fishes a set of pruning shears out of the bucket, gives his mule a scratch behind her ears.

"I just think it's more likely that the tree grew faster over the span of several years," Theodore says, ignoring the broken ground that Artie's pushing her hand into. "That could be for any number of reasons. Better light, or soil conditions, or—something. It grew faster gradually, and you're only just noticing it now."

"You're a bright man, Theodore Reed," says Flann, as he returns to the ladder and begins to climb. "But you're also a young man, and for this reason I'll forgive you what you're saying this morning, as I don't think you recognize that it's an insult."

He raises his shears and begins to trim branches from the underside of the peculiar tree's crown.

"I do enjoy our visits," Flann says. "But I believe you and Miss Quick have someplace else to be?"

Artie wants to protest—she feels that with more time she could possibly gather more clues, look around to see if there's evidence that some team of horticultural mischief-makers might actually have hauled a tree out of the park under cover of darkness. But she knows when they've been dismissed.

She turns to Theodore to ask the time, but he already has his watch in hand, and from his grimace she can see that she's already late. She takes off at a sprint, the best sprint she can muster in her damnable dress.

6

It's Wednesday night, the night her Criminal Investigation class
meets, and Artie leaves work and begins to cross the Theater
District. It's chilly, and there's rain in the air. Not much, though,
just a mean, faint spitting, which actually qualifies as something of
a pleasant change. For five days now Boston has toiled beneath a
succession of oppressive downpours, each colder and steadier than
the last. They've flooded the gutters and drenched the shoppers
and made it almost impossible to pursue any meaningful detective work. The first storm arrived seemingly out of nowhere on
Saturday night, washing out her plan to lurk in the streets around
the Pickle with Theodore, in the hope of catching their mystery abductor preparing to make another attempt to snatch someone. And
then on Sunday, her day off, she stayed home, watching glumly
out the window, waiting for there to be enough of a break in the
rain for her to return to the Common, scout out the area around
Flann's mysterious tree, maybe lay eyes on a clue. Inspection of
localities—it was even her homework. But the break never came,
and after enough hours had passed she had to acknowledge that
any meaningful clue would undoubtedly have been washed away
by a long day of heavy weather. So she hasn't been back.

She's heading south, toward Theodore's. Class doesn't begin until 8:00 p.m., so she has a bit of time, and she intends to spend that time in Theodore's washroom, changing into her disguise, taking advantage of the washroom's privacy (and its mirror).

Theodore lives in a small two-story brick townhouse in Bay Village. She gives a quick rap on the door to signal her arrival, but she doesn't wait for him to answer; Theodore has always encouraged her to just let herself in, and she's done it enough times by now that she feels OK doing so. He doesn't lock his door, at least not when he's expecting her.

Just to the left of the entry hall is Theodore's parlor, a room he refers to as his salon. The room has an exotic feel: it has a heavy Oriental carpet laid on the floor, and the walls are covered in a wallpaper with an intricate vermillion-and-gold pattern. One wall is taken up with photographs and a large painting of a sunken-eyed woman in a diaphanous gown bearing a chalice; another wall is the home of a series of shelves that display a rotating collection of oddities: tonight Artie sees a chunk of coral, a stuffed owl, a small statuette of a sphinx, and a squat green urn.

In the center of the room is a blue backless settee, where Theodore sits, shuffling through a loose pile of photographs spread across his knees. He looks up when she enters the room, and he begins to rise to greet her, acting on reflex, not quite realizing until he's halfway up that the action, if completed, will spill the photos down to the floor. He slaps a palm down to hold them in place against his thighs, clumsily sits back down again, gives her a deprecating half-smile.

"Artie!" he says. "I have something that you need to see."

"OK," Artie says. She grabs a chair from the corner and drags it over to where he is.

"I was thinking over the conversation we had with Flann on Saturday," he says. "That business with the tree? You remember."

"Sure," Artie says. "I've been thinking a lot about that too."

"Then you probably remember that I made some remarks where I cast doubt upon Flann's observational acuity, where the trees are involved. I feel as though I may have offended the man," Theodore says. "Do you think so?"

"It's possible," Artie admits.

"Mm," Theodore says, frowning. "Well, I shall be certain to pay him an apology when next he and I cross paths," he adds. "Especially because—well, let me show you." He begins to rifle through the photos. "I've been taking photos of the park all year. So—I was thinking back on the conversation, and I realized that it was likely that I'd taken at least one photo of that particular tree. I confess that by looking for the photo, I was hoping to prove my-self right—that the photo, when examined, would show that the tree, earlier this year, looks identical to the tree now—taller than the others—thus disproving the idea that the tree was replaced."

"Flann didn't say that the tree was replaced," Artie says, with a bit of a grin. "Remember that he doesn't theorize."

Theodore visibly suppresses a sigh. "Regardless," he says. "I found this photo. I'd like you to examine it."

He hands her the top photo from his stack. It's a shot taken looking down the long path where they met with Flann on Saturday. The line of red maples can be seen, receding into the distance. It was taken during the day: light bounces off the leafy boughs.

Artie looks closer. "These were taken—when? Summertime? Spring?"

"Summer. July I think."

"This July?"

"Yes, that's right. And—forgive me, it's not that easy to tell in the photo, but—." He reaches out, indicating with a finger.

"No, no, I see it," Artie says.

The perspective plays its trick, making each one in the line appear shorter than its predecessor, but it's undeniable that the trees are, in fact, all about the same height.

"So the tree we saw on Saturday—" she says, putting it together.

"Is not the same tree in this photograph. Flann is right, and I was wrong. The tree didn't just grow gradually over the course of many years."

"How does that make sense?" Artie asks.

"You tell me," says Theodore.

Artie thinks it over. But she doesn't have a hypothesis. She thinks it over some more.

"I'll ask Professor Winchell," she says finally. "At the Criminal Investigation class tonight."

"Is it a crime?" Theodore says. "To replace a tree with another one?"

"If someone stole the original tree . . ." Artie says, trying it out. It still doesn't make much sense, but maybe Professor Winchell will have some insight into the matter that she currently lacks. If it's ever happened before, he'll know. Or at least that's what she tells herself.

She turns one eye to the carved wooden clock hanging high on the wall. "I'd better get ready," she says.

*

She heads upstairs, to Theodore's washroom, and she carefully unfolds the brown paper parcel she packed Zeb's suit into this morning. She gets out of her own clothes and swaps them for Zeb's, wrapping her own back into the paper once she's changed. Then she spends a sequence of long minutes at the mirror, straightening her suit jacket, knotting her tie, greasing down each loose curl with Theodore's pomade, hoping to convince herself that she looks like something more than a girl playing dress-up in her brother's clothes.

She can't quite seem to manage it. Last week she'd been nervous, but she'd been able to transform that jitteriness into a kind of energy that propelled her, perhaps sloppily, through this part of the process. This week, though, some of that energy has waned: her swell of first-week resolve has been undercut by her new awareness that she needs to now make a routine out of this. She needs to fool her classmates for eleven more weeks: twelve if you count tonight. That's not going to work unless she looks convincing. She finds herself scowling in the mirror at any feature that seems too feminine, no matter how minor: the length of her eyelashes, the thickness of her upper lip.

She tries a smile. She looks exactly like an obsequious shopgirl; terrible. She doubles down on the scowl, trying to play the role of a wiry street scrapper, but no matter how much she thrusts her jaw forward she can't quite make it look as pugnacious as she thinks the look demands.

She pulls a few more faces before growing too discouraged to continue. She decides it's time to change strategies. She gathers up her belongings and heads downstairs, back into Theodore's parlor. He's still sitting on the settee, and he looks up at her with his familiar smile. Artie frowns back.

"Theodore," she says, "answer me honestly. Do I look like a man?"

"Ah," Theodore says. His smile slips away, replaced by a look of calculated hesitation. Artie doesn't want to be seeing hesitation right now. Theodore must detect this, because he quickly rearranges his face, eventually settling into a pained expression that manages to be even worse than the hesitating look, an expression that could probably best be described as a wince. Artie's frown deepens, and she feels a fulsome oath brewing up inside her, demanding to be uttered. She bites it back, though.

"A—young man?" Theodore offers.

"Sure, yes," Artie says, irritated by the qualifier.

"I think—yes, I think you really quite resemble a very young man," Theodore says, cautiously. "It's just that—please understand—it's just that you don't have especially much around this area." He rubs at the stubble on his cheeks, to indicate.

"Well, that should be fine, Theodore, then, shouldn't it," Artie says. Her voice threatens to choke off; she compensates by doubling her volume. "The place is called the Evening Institute for Young Men, isn't it? So that's who they expect to be there—young men. So I should be fine. And maybe you should've just said that: yes, I think you'll be fine, Artie."

"Well," Theodore says, wincing, "yes. I think you'll be fine, Artie."

"Oh, what do you know, anyway," Artie says, and she walks out of the parlor, back into the entry hall.

"Artie," he calls, but he doesn't follow her. "I thought I was to take you to dinner tonight."

"I'm not hungry," she lies as she pushes blindly out through his front door, out into the city, hoping that impulse alone might compensate for her missing confidence.

The streets near Theodore's home are narrow and quiet, but before long she's made her way back to a street that's bustling with passersby. She braces herself for exposure, but it's the same as last week: no one on the street pays her much attention. That's a small but palpable relief. Most people are keeping their heads bowed, their chins close to their chests: it's chilly tonight. She hugs Zeb's jacket tighter around herself.

The closer she gets to school—and the more people she passes on the street—the better she feels, and she allows her mind to drift away from the way she looks and back to the list of questions she wants to ask Professor Winchell. This list has gotten long over the course of the week, questions atop questions, and she feels grateful that she'll be back in class tonight. She experiences the pure pleasure of anticipation. She's not quite sure how she's going to phrase all of her questions without sounding insane—she can't quite imagine opening her mouth and asking, hypothetically, could a criminal steal and replace a tree, undetected—but she allows herself to feel confident that she'll solve that problem, somehow, in just a few hours. She allows herself to believe that she'll be able to figure out the phrasing, and she even allows herself to believe in her ability to solve the more difficult problem, that of working up the nerve to speak. She allows herself to hope that, if she works up the will to ask, she'll get the answers she wants. She allows herself, in other words, to believe, just for tonight, that the world is fair.

✱

She reaches the Institute at three minutes to eight, same as she did last week. She sees one of the boys from the class sitting out on the building's stoop, smoking a cigarette—Kuykendall is his name, if she recalls correctly, fifteen years old. She slows as she passes him, trying to get a good look at how much stubble he has (gratifyingly, she doesn't see any). He looks back at her from under the brow of his newsboy's cap.

"Hey," he says.

She hurries on without responding. She knows that this probably appears odd, but she doesn't want him to hear her voice. She climbs to the second floor, pauses at the clock outside of the classroom. Two minutes to eight: the perfect time. Tonight she won't even call attention to herself as the last person to arrive: Kuykendall will have to play the role of laggard this time around.

But when she enters the classroom, it's completely empty.

"What?" she says, aloud, as her heart drops. For a moment she elects on a course of stunned denial: maybe she's just the first to arrive, she tells herself, and if she just has a seat everyone will trickle in soon? But before she takes more than a step into the room she realizes that this is absurd: last week at this exact time everyone was here, ready to begin.

Perhaps she got the night wrong? Only she's certain she didn't, and anyway, that wouldn't explain Kuykendall's presence outside.

Kuykendall. She hurries back out of the room, down the stairs, out to the stoop. Kuykendall is still there, inspecting the burnt-out dog end of his cigarette.

"Hey," she says. She tries to keep her voice low, hoping to maintain her illusion, but she's almost too upset to care. "What happened to class? Where is everybody?"

"Yeah, I was trying to tell you," he says. "Class is canceled."

"What?" Artie says. "Why?"

"The lady didn't say. She did say that they might be canceling the whole course, and that we could get our money refunded from the bursar if we needed."

So there it is. The world's not fair after all. She feels the oath from earlier rise up in her again, and this time she can't suppress it. She lets it out, because, fuck it, she just doesn't care. She doesn't care about the expression of surprise on Kuykendall's face as she blows her disguise; she doesn't care that she looks like exactly what she fears herself to be, a weird, swearing girl in a suit jacket, standing on a Boston street corner with a head full of questions and nobody at all whom she trusts to help her figure out the answers.

PART TWO

NOVEMBER

1909

THE BOSTON
SCHOOL OF MAGIC

7

The thing Artie really wants to know is just exactly how her family came to lose Zeb, and whether there wasn't some way, possibly, to have stopped it before it happened.

It's not all a mystery, of course. She knows the story, at least up to a point. Zeb was four years older than she, and that gap was significant enough that she was never quite able to think of the two of them as peers—she never was able to think of him just as her brother, always as her older brother—but still, they spent their childhoods under the same roof; she witnessed the unfolding details of his boyhood from her own vantage point, one step behind. They shared a bedroom for most of those years, and many of her memories of him are from that shared room: she can remember him crushing his ugly plug hat down onto his skull, trying to break it in; she can remember him paring his toenails with his penknife; she can remember him carrying in a snowball from outside one winter morning and hitting her with it, right in the back of her head.

Outside of that room, Zeb spent his youth with a group of boys, the Bleachery Gang. Artie knows about that too. She wasn't able to witness much of it firsthand, of course; the Bleachery boys indulged in the courting of boyish dangers: spending their days in some local sandpit, throwing stones at rival gangs. A young girl, tagging along? She wouldn't have been welcome. But Zeb was always able to tell a vivid story, and he seemed to relish having an audience: and so it became a common occurrence for him to return home at the cusp of evening, to show off his fresh scrapes and cuts, and to tell the tale of how he received each one.

Artie can recall the period when he first began to tell these stories, when she was perhaps eight, and Zeb twelve. He'd tell them in the common room, thrilling the entire Quick household with tales of the ongoing saga of the Bleachery Gang versus the Wharf Rats or the Eggmen. Artie and Zeb's mother, who was then well, might shake her head disapprovingly at some of the rougher aspects of the play, but their father would take it as an opportunity, not uncommonly, to reminisce aloud about participating in similar activities as a youth with a similar group. He took pride, in fact, in Zeb's involvement in some regular scrapping: when Zeb was younger their father had often openly worried that Zeb presented a promising target for other boys to plague, on account of his small size, and he would insist, over their mother's faint objections, that learning to fight was an important part of a boy's upbringing. He'd go so far, on occasion, as to playfully wrestle or grapple with Zeb after he'd had a drink or two, and he'd offer boisterous praise whenever Zeb could wriggle out of his clumsy holds or otherwise get the upper hand.

Artie can remember an instance where their father removed his own belt and offered it to Zeb as a means of defense. Zeb accepted it, doubled it up in his fist, and then their father roared and came at him with a woozy, off-balance ferocity unlike anything Artie could remember seeing in him before. Zeb, in desperation, gave their father a vicious lash across the eye; their father had bellowed like a stung bull and then dropped back, before nodding with a grim satisfaction. For a week afterward a bloody, broken thing floated in the white of his eye; Artie remembers being terror-stricken at the sight of it. Not just because it was gruesome to look at—though it surely was—but because it provided a reminder of the drunken, lurching hobgoblin that she now knew existed behind her father's face.

And so Zeb's stories of his afternoon sandlot battles had helped, somewhat, to put their father at ease, and the scuffles at home slowed down. And even her mother would often be won over by the tales of the Bleachery Gang's setbacks and victories, her mild tuts of disapproval giving way to a transfixed silence. But by the time Artie was ten, though, and Zeb fourteen, something had changed. The stories were no longer told in the common space. Instead, they were told in the privacy of their shared room, in excited whispers now, with Artie the only audience.

It was the stealing that had changed things.

Stealing was another commonplace activity for the gang: they'd wander around the markets, stealing apples or pears or doughnuts. Zeb, in his telling, excelled at it, on account of his nimble fingers, slight frame, and fleetness of foot. But the first time Zeb boasted about his thievery, their father glowered darkly across the table. "That's not how we make our way in this family," he muttered. Zeb shut his mouth, confusion and an early adolescent variety of resentment warring on his face. After a few repeat episodes of this sort, Zeb realized that he was no longer able to share any story featuring what he was coming to believe that he was the most good at, and so he became sullen and quiet when in the family's public eye, only really coming to life again when talking to Artie privately.

For her part, Artie wasn't bothered by Zeb's thievery, at least not when it began. She was only ten, after all, and his escapades often meant that he'd return home with a little extra something in his pocket for her: a bit of lemon candy, or a bit of ribbon. Once he brought her a tiny ceramic tiger, no larger than her thumb to her first knuckle; she placed it at one corner of her windowsill, and it still stands guard there even now, seven years later.

Over the course of the next few years, Zeb got better at thieving—and as his expertise in that area grew, the split between him and the other members of the family deepened. Zeb wasn't only stealing something sweet for him and the boys to eat for lunch anymore, nor trinkets for his sister; he had moved on to larger things. And the gains were returning home. He'd come home with a bolt of fine linen for their mother, lifted from a warehouse. He'd come home with a crate of lager beer for their father, lifted from a beer team's wagon. He'd come home in winter with a sack of coal. Every week it was something. It was obvious to everyone in the home that the items were ill-gotten, although only Artie would hear the full story of the exploits.

By this point in time, Artie understood a little bit better that her family was struggling, financially—the money her father brought in as a carpenter allowed them to keep their hold on their apartment, but her mother had begun to suffer episodes where she was unable to get out of bed or complete any but the smallest of mending jobs she could do, from home, as a seamstress. The items that Zeb brought home helped to make some of the difference between living in relative comfort and living in relative deprivation. Their father accepted the ill-gotten gifts without asking questions, but also without joy or signs of gratitude: he would accept them with his face set in a thin-lipped rictus of resolve. And Zeb allowed this to rankle him: he took it as hypocrisy. Artie would listen to him, at night, explaining that he wanted their father to either accept the offerings with a full acknowledgment that they came from thieving, and that the thieving, therefore, was valuable, a real way that Zeb was helping the family, and worthy of praise—or he wanted their father to refuse the gifts outright, to stand by his word that thieving wasn't a thing the family did. This middle ground—accepting in a silent, dour way—struck Zeb as a cowardly acquiescence, the worst of both worlds. It sickened him. He'd mutter bitterly about how their father was a weak man who didn't stand for anything, who lacked conviction.

Artie didn't delight in these tales the way she delighted in the adventures of the Bleachery Gang—it scared her to see this split in her family, opening before her eyes. She'd retreat into silence. But Zeb didn't seem to notice or care. She wasn't even sure whether he knew she was listening anymore, or whether he thought she was asleep, whether he thought he was just talking to himself in the dark.

By the time Artie turned fifteen, Zeb wasn't bringing home food or fuel or sundries anymore: he was just bringing money.

He'd figured out ways to convert the things that he stole into cash. This took some fairly simple forms at first—he'd steal rags from a ragman, run them up the street, and sell them to a different ragman. He'd share these stories with Artie, in the same way he'd shared his earlier exploits, expecting her, perhaps, to respond with that same familiar glee. But it didn't feel the same, to Artie, as a story of chasing another boy out of a sandpile. Maybe it was because she'd grown older? Maybe it was because she had some sense of how her own family was only barely staying out of poverty? It was hard for her to imagine how a robbed ragman could subsist in this world.

"We'll just rob from the other one next week," Zeb said when she pressed him on this point. "It's all a great cycle; no one man suffers in it more than any other." Artie didn't find this convincing, and she was old enough and brave enough to say as much. And Zeb offered no further point in his defense, but rather withdrew into his familiar sullen silence, and after that he didn't tell her stories of the Bleachery Gang much any more.

By that stage, it didn't actually seem like there were many stories left to tell. From the scraps of information Zeb would occasionally let slip, it sounded like the gang was breaking apart. They were all growing older; some of the eldest boys had gone off to work as longshoremen or grocers, others had entered into trade apprenticeships. Her father had been trying to pass on his own skills to Zeb—carpentry and woodcarving—but Zeb was good at managing to vanish on the days he was supposed to accompany his father on a job. Sometimes, to avoid his father's ire, he'd be gone for days at a time.

Gradually, the absences got longer, and the periods of time he'd be home got shorter, until finally, now, it seems like he's truly gone for good.

She remembers the last time Zeb returned from one of these long absences, last year around this time, in the fall. It was during the day, but she was at home: she'd completed her schooling in the spring, but she wouldn't be employed by Filene's until December, when they hired her as one of many new employees recruited to cope with the surge of Christmas shoppers. And she was alone: her mother had been between bad episodes, and she'd taken an interest in going out to do the shopping, a task that had fallen to Artie more and more. When Zeb entered the house, he registered her presence with surprise: it was clear that he had expected her to be at school, that he hadn't quite grasped exactly how the passage of time had changed things, here at home.

He looked like he'd been roughed up recently, a cut congealed nastily above his eye, his coat torn at the sleeve. She'd sworn to greet his return stone-facedly, in an attempt to profoundly convey her disapproval of these disappearances, but she immediately went back on this promise, and instead cooed and fussed over him stupidly, getting angry at herself even as she was doing it. In the process, she blurted out a question about how he was getting money, how he was keeping himself fed. She knew the answer must have had something to do with stealing, but she couldn't, then, quite understand how someone could live solely on the money they might be making as a thief.

He'd responded by talking to her—with more than a touch of his old, boyish boastfulness—about a fence whom he'd begun working with. She didn't know what a fence was, and she told him so. He began to explain, then broke off his explanation midway through, and it was only then that she began to understand: that crime was not just something that you did, not just an action among many possible actions, but was a force in the world, a system, a tentacled thing that could reach out and envelop you, that could take hold of your family and simply rip it apart.

She helped to clean his cut. She fed him some dried fish and what remained of the week's loaf of bread. She mended the sleeve of his coat while he ate. She didn't push for more answers, not then. And he didn't offer them. What he offered her was a tight, ferocious embrace before he slipped back out the door.

I'll ask more next time, she thought, as she watched him disappear back down the stairwell. I'll talk to him, and I'll ask the right questions, and learn what it means to be a criminal and why you might choose that over being with your family.

But there was no next time. She hasn't seen him since. A long year during which she hasn't known whether her brother is dead or alive. She chooses to believe that he's alive: he's always been canny, and she suspects that this canniness has enabled him to escape some of the worst pitfalls of the criminal life.

She still wants to grasp the system of crime, however. She still has questions and she still wants answers. Even more urgently now. In her brother's absence, however, she has needed to seek answers elsewhere. This was how she found her way to the Evening Institute, and why it felt so important to be in Professor Winchell's Criminal Investigation class, important enough to dress in Zeb's suit and to risk ridicule, scorn, or worse on the street. When she took the textbook off the shelf at the bookshop, held it in her hands for the first time, it felt like she'd taken grip of a sledge, a tool, something that, when swung correctly, could do damage to the structure of crime, could amplify her ability to do the work of breaking her brother free. Assuming he's even still alive. She does assume this: although she suspects that his canniness has enabled him to escape some of the worst fates that can befall criminals.

But a tool by itself won't get you very far. She's musing on that tonight, out for a walk up Charles Street with Theodore, whom she's forgiven. You need more than just a tool: you need training, an education in how to use and handle it. She's heard her father say these words many times while holding a carpenter's chisel up to the light, turning it this way and that—wisdom intended for Zeb, she supposes. So without the benefit of the class—? It's been two weeks now since the class has met, and she's kept on reading the book, diligently—she's almost all the way through now. But without classroom instruction, without guidance on how to use the book as the foundation for action, the lessons that it has to impart feel inert, advice intended for someone else, someone—more serious.

She and Theodore have paused in their walk at a construction site, at the corner of Charles and Phillips Streets. The intersection is consumed by a wide trench in the ground, crowded with wooden ballast and bracing: the early stage of a new tunnel leading beneath the city.

This trench, a good fifty feet long and twenty feet deep, is surrounded on all sides by a waist-high wooden fence, erected to keep curious passersby or blithe drunkards from falling in. It's a November evening, thankfully mild, and the workers appear to have gone home for the night, or something—there's one sleepy-looking watchman down at the mouth of the tunnel, looks like a Boston cop from his uniform, who is resting his elbows on a barrel, making sure no one hops the fence or makes their way down the wooden ramp that the workers use for entry, but other than that the site is abandoned. Artie distractedly picks at the fence until a long splinter peels off in her hand.

"So my class is over," she says.

"Over?" Theodore says. "It's only been a few weeks."

"It's canceled," Artie says. "The second class was canceled, then last night I went back for what would have been the third class, and some lady told us it was canceled for good." She drops the splinter over the edge of the fence and watches it flutter down into the gloom of the pit.

"Is the professor—Winchell, you said his name was? Has he fallen ill?"

"I'm not really sure." She sighs. "I'd just gotten started with something," she says, "something that felt really important, and already it's over." She stares down into the pit, frowning.

Theodore watches her sympathetically. After a respectful interval, he offers "Were you able to get your money back?"

Artie's frown deepens. "Yeah, that lady sent me over to the bursar's office; I got my money back. But—"

"That's good, at least," Theodore says. "At least you're not—"

"No, Theodore—the money's not the point. I spent the money in the first place because I wanted to take the course.

Getting the money back but not having the course just leaves me where I started."

Theodore nods solemnly. "Perhaps they'll offer it again in the spring. You could set the money aside—?"

"Yeah," Artie says. "Sure. That's true. It just—"

"I think I understand," Theodore says. "You want to do something now."

"I want to do something now," Artie says.

They muse on this together for a moment. Artie watches the night watchman's head grow heavy: It looks like he's falling asleep at his station. His head drops precipitously forward, and he catches himself at what seems like the last possible second, giving a great start and standing upright again.

"Maybe I should visit him," Artie says.

"Winchell?"

"Yeah," Artie says. "Pay him a social call."

Theodore frowns a bit at this.

"He's probably listed in the city directory," Artie says. "Don't you think?"

"It's likely," Theodore says. "But—"

"Do you have a city directory?"

"I believe so," Theodore says. "It's—there's a pile of books on my desk; I think it might be somewhere in there?"

"Could I use it?" Artie says.

"Yes?" Theodore says, a bit absently. "I'll look for it." He seems to be distracted from the promise while he's making it, as though his mouth is operating independently of his brain. Artie waits.

"What?" she says finally. "What's wrong?"

Theodore blinks. "It's only," he says, "it's only that, well, if you were to pay him a visit, what do you think you might say to the man?"

"I'd—I'd ask him why he canceled the class."

"Is there an answer he could give that you'd find satisfying?"

"I don't know," Artie says. Her frown deepens. "Maybe I'd ask him if he could give me—private lessons, or something."

Theodore considers this. "I offer this only as a gentle suggestion," he says, eventually. "But you may remember that Gannett, my instructor at the School of Magic, has expressed an interest in meeting you. If you really wanted to do something now, maybe you could—"

"But I don't want to learn magic, Theodore," Artie says. "I want to learn Criminal Investigation."

Theodore sighs. "I understand that," he says, after a moment. "I do. But Gannett knows things, and some of those things might be useful to you. He knows about thieves' magic, so it stands to reason that he must know something about thieves."

Artie had forgotten this detail.

"It could just be something to pass the time while you're waiting for your course to be offered again."

Artie purses her lips.

"It's not far from here," Theodore continues, growing enthusiastic. "And he keeps late hours." He fishes his watch out of his pocket and checks it. "We could go over there right now. Surely there's no harm in just facilitating an introduction."

"I don't know, Theodore," Artie says, remembering Flann and his mysterious tree. "The last guy you introduced me to was— pretty strange."

"Strange, yes," Theodore says. "But did he do harm? No. In fact he gave us an interesting mystery to chew over."

"True. We never got anywhere with that mystery, though," Artie says, wrinkling her nose, still frustrated by the loose end.

"That's the nature of the world, though, isn't it? More questions than answers. It's cause for wonder."

"Not very satisfying, though, is it?" Artie says.

Theodore shrugs blithely, as though he's never lost a moment of sleep over the world's lack of satisfying answers.

"You say it's not far from here?" Artie says.

"It is not," Theodore says.

"OK, then," Artie says. "I'll meet him."

8

A rtie looks up and reads the long sign mounted on the fa-çade: Boston School of Magic. 103 Court Street. Eastern Headquarters for Magicians. W. D. Gannett. Then she looks through the windows, into the shop. The store is dark inside—it seems closed—but she can make out a spread of its available wares: a few decks of cards, an array of dusty, multicolored balls in wooden cups, some sun-bleached trick boxes, a cheap-looking turban propped, slightly askew, on a crudely painted dummy head. Beyond that, just clutter and gloom. This place doesn't look, to Artie, much like a headquarters for occult activity: it looks more like an outlet for the sale of tawdry claptrap. This impression is reinforced by a series of signboards that hang across the front of the building, each pitching some fresh enticement: Master Dealer and Importer of Magical Apparatus. Conjuring Entertainments Furnished. Tricks for the Stage. Puzzles, Jokes, and Novelties For Sale.

"Don't pay all that too much attention," Theodore says, perhaps seeing the dejection playing out across her face. "The shop helps Gannett to pay the rent, you understand, but it's not the real work that's being done here."

"OK," says Artie, not quite convinced.

"Here," says Theodore. "Let me show you." And with that he leads her past the storefront door, instead directing her to a smaller door, painted with a black lacquer, set back from the street between a pair of heavy stone buttresses. Set into the door is a very small wooden carving of a sphinx in profile.

Theodore knocks gently on the door, then pauses, cocks an ear, and then knocks again, in a rapid pattern. A secret knock? There's something tricky about the pattern: even though Artie just watched him do it, before her eyes, she's not sure she could recreate it exactly. It seems, interestingly, to defy her ability to hold it in memory.

"How'd you do that?" she asks. But Theodore doesn't answer: he doesn't, in fact, even give any sign of having heard her. He has his head cocked again, listening for something. Artie gives a listen too.

There's a sound, deep within the door, of something falling into place. Theodore grins, a bit giddily.

"You ready?" he says.

Sure. She nods.

Theodore pulls the door open and ushers her inside. They're at the western end of a long corridor, wallpapered in burnt orange. Artie starts, just briefly, at the sight of a pair of stuffed owls, mounted near the ceiling. They're dramatically lit by the unsteady light of the hallway's gas lamp: talons out, beaks open, eyes agog.

Beyond the owls are a number of other mounted birds, smaller ones, black in color. Almost a glossy blue, really. Sharp beaks. Artie doesn't know what kind they are, although her mind turns to the word "shrikes." She feels, momentarily, a responsibility to learn the names of all the world's different kinds of birds: How can she observe things properly if she doesn't know the name of anything she's looking at, if all she can make of a flock is bird, bird, bird?

They walk the length of the corridor, toward another door at the eastern end. Artie determines that the corridor must run adjacent to the magic shop, but it seems longer than the magic shop seemed deep, so once they pass through the door they'll have reached some room behind the shop, deeper within the heart of the block . . .

They pause at the door for a moment, long enough for Artie to notice that this one has a wooden carving as well, a monkey, covering up its eyes . . .

And then—without a knock—they pass through the door. What's back there is a tiny theater, the walls painted black. Theodore and Artie have entered from the rear: about five rows of seats stand between them and the stage. And on the stage stands a lone figure, an older man, with wire-rimmed spectacles and a rather bushy mustache. He's not wearing any theatrical finery— no cape, no exotic robes—just a rumpled gray suit. But in his hands are three steel hoops, and he tosses these up in the air and they flash in the stage light and they clang and ring against one another, and Artie finds herself mesmerized. And he reaches up to catch them and then there only seems to be one ring, and he tosses it and then there are two, and then he catches them and tosses them and then there seem to be three again.

"Mister Gannett, sir!" Theodore calls, and Artie starts at the unexpected sound of his voice, and for a moment—just for a moment—Artie wishes that he hadn't opened his mouth. She wishes that she could have lurked there, in the darkness of the theater, for longer, that he hadn't broken the spell by speaking, that she could have just gone on watching the rings rising and falling and joining and separating. When she was watching them it seemed like time wasn't passing at all. She liked that: the way the act brought her to some still point, immersed her in an instant that didn't need to end, that might not have ended had Theodore not spoken . . .

Gannett catches all three rings, brings them down to his side, whereupon they all vanish, leaving just a man onstage in a rumpled gray suit, alone. Gannett shades his eyes against the light, peering into the darkness. "Theodore Reed," he says, "is that you?"

"Yes, sir, it is," says Theodore.

"I didn't hear you come in," Gannett says. "You must be practicing that spell, eh? The Cat's Approach?"

A puzzled look crosses Theodore's face. "No, sir," he says.

"No?" Gannett says, wryly smiling. "Must be my hearing going, then," he says. "A peril of old age. One of many." His smile seems to falter a bit.

"Perhaps, sir?" Theodore says. He doesn't quite seem to know whether Gannett is making a joke or not; Artie isn't sure either. Gannett nods once or twice, somewhat soberly, as though Theodore has said something wise; then he removes his glasses, polishes them briskly with a bit of cloth drawn from a pocket of his suit.

"Well, lad," he says, donning his glasses again, "don't just stand there in the dark, come on up and say hello. What brings you down here tonight?"

"I've brought a friend," Theodore says, beginning to make his way down the aisle. Artie follows along. "Miss Artie Quick? I mentioned her to you; you might recall?"

"Ah, yes," Gannett says, climbing down from the stage, meeting them just before the first row of seats. "Your unorthodox friend."

"Yes, sir, that's right."

"My hearing may be going," Gannett says, "but my memory has stayed sharp at least. It's the little things that one must be grateful for, don't you agree, Miss Quick?" The smile has returned to his face, and he extends his hand.

"Yes, sir," says Artie, though she hasn't really given it much thought. She puts her hand in his—for a moment, she thinks he's going to give it a genteel kiss, but instead he clasps it, placing his other hand over hers. It's difficult for Artie to see his eyes—there is glinting stage light captured in the lenses of his glasses—but she can tell that he's looking her in the face, and that there's a perceptive attentiveness in his gaze as it travels over it.

"How old are you, Miss Quick?"

"I'm—I'm seventeen."

"Seventeen," Gannett says. Something wistful settles into his tone of voice. "It's a wonderful age," he says. "So much yet ahead of you. An age of rich potential."

"Yes, sir," Artie says, a bit uncertainly.

"Well, then," he says, releasing her hand. "It's agreed." The wistful tone is gone, replaced by upbeat cheer. "So, Miss Quick, Theodore tells me you have an interest in—what was it—criminology?"

"Criminal Investigation, sir," Artie says. "And Theodore tells me that you have some knowledge of, uh, thieves' magic."

"Some," Gannett concurs. "And you thought this might be a useful adjunct to your studies?"

"Well, yes, sir—although"—she thinks of the birds in the entry hallway—"to be quite honest, sir, I think a good criminal investigator needs knowledge in a wide variety of disciplines, not merely in the ways and means of thieves. You say that seventeen is an age of, uh, rich potential, and I agree. So I think it's important, at this point in my life, to be broadening my area of study rather than narrowing it? Toward that end, sir, I'd be willing to learn just about anything that you'd be open to teaching."

Gannett, beneath his mustache, smiles, spreads his hands. "Ordinarily," he says, "I'd embrace this enthusiasm in a young student; it suggests, indeed, that you are well poised to embark upon a course of study with me. The traditional route is a bit tricky, though, given, ah, certain particulars."

"How do you mean, sir?" Artie says, although she suspects she might know what he's alluding to.

"Well," he says, "ordinarily, my course offerings have been available to men only."

"I see," says Artie. Something inside her crumples a bit. She wasn't even sure that she wanted to take instruction from Gannett—she's still not sure that learning magic is exactly how she wants to be spending her time—but she wanted to at least have the option to decline the opportunity. Having the opportunity taken away from her stirs up, once again, that grinding sense that the world isn't fair. She's angry, and, more than that, she's afraid—afraid that she'll always have to jump through a hoop to get any version of what she wants, to get even the most minor scrap of knowledge. Will she need to dress up in Zeb's clothes here as well? Will that make her a less conspicuous visitor? She considers, for a moment, explaining to Gannett that this is an option.

Before she has an opportunity to decide whether that's really wise, Gannett continues. "It's just that, well, a certain amount of risk is involved, when it comes to training young women in the magical arts. A churchgoing New England man might look upon my trade of instruction as disreputable, but if he sees it as doing no more than serving as a diversion for a few wayward bachelor males, he may be willing to shrug it off as largely harmless. If, on the other hand, he begins to understand me as offering a dangerous attraction for his virtuous daughters—"

"My father was never much of a churchgoing man," says Artie, trying to keep her tone light, to match Gannett's own tone. She tries to beam a smile at him—the same smile that she uses to win over resistant customers—but something in it goes sour, and a tight frown reasserts itself on her face. "With all due respect, sir," she tries, "I can certainly understand the issue from your perspective, and I don't intend to ask you to take on more risk than you can bear. But—Theodore told me that you were interested in meeting me, and, so, forgive me, sir, but I can't quite understand—why invite me to come here if only to turn me away upon my arrival?"

"Oh," Gannett says, "don't misunderstand me, Miss Quick. It's not my intention, here, to turn you away. I'm merely—musing on some of the curiosities of the circumstance. As you may know, the magical arts have long enjoyed a parallel evolution with the arts of the theater, and the true practitioner of magic must also be a masterful practitioner of performance." He turns, indicates the proscenium arch behind him with a gesture of his hand. "This is not to suggest that the work we do isn't real, whatever we currently mean by that term; it is merely to say that a magician is not truly considered adept unless they can perform their work on the stage, before the eyes of an audience. And as we have seen women taking to the stage in ever-greater numbers, the emergence of a generation of talented actresses, we have also seen the emergence of a parallel tradition in the arts of stage magic, that of a magician performing with a female assistant."

"Oh," says Artie. She's a little perplexed as to what, exactly, is happening in this conversation. Is Gannett asking her if she wants to be his—stage assistant? She isn't entirely sure how she feels about that. She's used to being looked at as part of her job—and her short hair definitely draws stares—but it's not her favorite part of the job by any means, and she's not sure she can see herself thriving beneath the heightened scrutiny of the theatrical audience. The idea makes her want to shrink away, to disappear, but she strives to keep a neutral expression on her face, evincing attentiveness, she hopes, but no more.

Gannett might detect some of her discomfort, though, for he continues: "I am merely remarking on the precarity of the contemporary magician's situation, his uncomfortable perch on the horns of these twin expectations. The theatergoer of Saturday night clamors for the appearance of a young enchantress on the stage; the churchgoer of Sunday morning demands that young women be kept safely cloistered away from those who would train them in the mystic arts. That the average Bostonian can be both of these men in this sequence, and see no contradiction—well, it is merely a sad irony of our contemporary moment. A thing to be worked around. I've found my workarounds in the past; I expect to be able to work around it again, in a—in a different time ahead."

He smiles at Artie again, from beneath his mustache, although the upbeat tone has drained from his voice and there's something off about the smile; it seems a bit thin, like there's pain in it. Artie sneaks a quick look at Theodore to see what kind of reaction he's having, but she can't quite read it before she has to snap her attention back to Gannett.

She feels as though some response is expected here, but she's not quite sure what to say. A prickling sensation plays over her, stirring a memory in her of last November, when she went in to Filene's to apply for a seasonal position; she remembers sitting in an office, being looked over expectantly by a department manager, hoping that she looked presentable, smoothing her skirts with a nervous hand. She has that same sense of uncertainty about her course of action, that same sense that her life would change if she were to accept a proffered position; that same acute awareness that, in fact, no such proffer had yet been put on the table, that the decision about whether it would be offered or withdrawn hadn't yet been made, and that, ultimately, that decision depended, uncomfortably, on what Artie would do or say next.

"Well," Gannett says. He removes his glasses again, gives them another quick polish. He spares a moment, during this process, to take a quick look at Artie: with no lenses serving as interference, glinting with caught stage light, Artie can get a good look at his eyes for the first time; she can see that they are deep, serious, and sad.

Gannett returns his glasses to his face, and he blinks at her as though he's just met her for the first time. He smiles welcomingly, benignly even, although this doesn't quite dispel the impression of his sorrowfulness that Artie picked up just a moment ago.

"Why don't you tell me something," Gannett says.

Artie's mind goes blank—she's a bit caught off guard by the open-endedness of this request. She looks to Theodore again, hoping he can offer some sort of guidance; he gives only a quick, quiet, perplexed shrug by way of response.

"Something—about myself, sir?" Artie says, again recalling her interview at Filene's, remembering that the department manager had asked her to tell him something about herself.

"Yes," Gannett says, "certainly. Something about yourself."

Artie struggles for a moment. She struggled similarly at Filene's, trying to make sense of what might be an appropriate biographical detail to offer, only—something is different here. Filene's had been badly in need of holiday help, and it only took a moment of observing the manager's harried, distracted demeanor before Artie was able to conclude that the manager hadn't really cared about her answer, that the question was little more than just a method of ensuring that she could hear, speak, and correctly string two sentences together. In this way she had been able to put herself at ease. But this situation is different. Gannett, calmly observing her, doesn't seem to be just hurriedly rattling through a formality: He seems interested in her answer; genuinely interested in whatever she might choose to say. He seems genuinely interested in her as a person. It reminds her of the way Theodore looks at her sometimes, and she suddenly gets a sense that Gannett might be the kind of man that Theodore could potentially grow into, given time. She understands why Theodore has been drawn to study with this person: he must see, in Gannett, some vision of his older self.

None of this, of course, is helping her to figure out what to say. "Anything in particular you'd like to hear about?" she says.

The phrase that leaps into her mind is "relevant experience"—one final memory of her Filene's interview. The manager had asked her, What do you have in the way of relevant experience? She didn't have any relevant experience then—she'd offered her faculty in calculating sums, but that was just something she'd acquired in her basic schooling—and she doesn't have any relevant experience for this situation either: she doesn't do magic, or understand anything about it; she doesn't know anything she's ever done that a magician might be interested in—

Except, maybe:

"I know a few things about herbs," she says. "My grandmother worked with them."

Her grandmother, on her father's side—Gweneth. Gweneth had emigrated to the United States from Wales, with her husband and Artie's father, then an infant. The name Quick, in fact, was an Anglicized version of the family's last name, Cynwric. Her grandfather had worked as a slate quarryman in New Hampshire, and it was family lore that her grandmother had maintained a small herb garden out behind their house. Artie never saw that garden—by the time she was born her grandfather had died in an accident at the quarry and the family had moved to Boston—but her grandmother still was able to grow herbs in a small plot on the grounds of the Presbyterian church where she was a parishioner, and Artie can remember her doling out mysterious ointments to cure various ailments and illnesses suffered by the family. Chickweed ointment, marigold ointment, a peppermint salve that her father would massage into his hands nightly to alleviate the aches and pains of his carpentry work.

"I never knew that!" says Theodore.

Gannett, for his part, only smiles: a smile that appears, to Artie's eye, to be genuine. "Is that so," he says finally.

"Yes, sir," Artie says.

"I hope you will permit me a follow-up question," he says.

"Of course," Artie replies, a bit of nervousness creeping into her voice even through her attempts to banish it.

Gannett, again, must detect her nervousness, for he provides a gentle clarification. "I will underscore here that my intention in asking this question is not to test you, or to make some other assessment of your knowledge. The herbal arts are not my field of expertise, and so my question here is sincere."

"OK," Artie says, still a bit tentatively.

"If you were to prepare an herbal sachet," he says, "something, say, that could be placed on a pillow, to create a relaxing effect, something that could stave off the terrors of the night, what herbs might you choose to include?"

The terrors of the night? Artie thinks. She finds the phrasing curious, though she supposes there's something in Gannett's slightly haunted demeanor that suggests he might not be getting enough sleep. He didn't say it was for himself, though, this hypothetical sachet. She doesn't pursue this line of thought further; instead, she's trying to remember her grandmother, and what she might have recommended for this purpose.

"Chamomile," Artie tries. "Chamomile is a soothing herb. I might also add, maybe rose petals? And—lavender?"

Gannett reflects on this for a moment, as though trying out the combination in a mental sensorium. "Yes," he says. "I can see that being an effective combination. Perhaps your advice shall occasion me to make a visit to an herbarium."

"I hope you do, sir," Artie says, with sincerity.

"Well," Gannett says. "It's been a pleasure to meet you, Miss Quick, but the hour grows late."

Apparently the interview, such as it is, has concluded. Artie waits for a moment, to see whether he plans to extend an offer to her, but he just looks at her silently.

"Uh," Artie says, when the pause has grown overlong. "Yes, sir, it does. And I have a bit of a journey to get home."

"I hope you will return for another visit in the future," Gannett says.

"Yes, sir," Artie says. She wants to ask whether there's a particular day or time that might be appropriate for her to return, but a hush seems to have fallen in the room, and she's hesitant to dispel it with a fresh question.

"Good night," she says.

"Good night, Artie Quick," Gannett says. "Good night, Master Theodore Reed."

"Good night, sir," Theodore says.

Gannett reascends the stage, stands in the spotlight. Artie spares him one backward look as she and Theodore head back out, the way they came in. They walk the length of the burnt-orange hallway, under the gaze of the shrikes, or whatever kind of bird they actually are. Neither of them speak until they're out of the building, and are in fact some distance away.

9

Artie stands in front of the door to Professor Winchell's home, a two-story Georgian bordered with a thick hedge. It's cold out, but she's sweating. She reaches out and grips the door's heavy brass knocker, but she doesn't lift it. She holds it, and then releases it, tries to work up the nerve to try again.

She still can't quite believe she's here. She's been operating on impulse for a few hours now, ever since she found the city directory at Filene's.

Since last night, when she'd first had the idea to look up Winchell's address and pay him a visit, she hadn't stopped thinking about where she might be able to find a city directory. Her family didn't have one, and she wasn't quite satisfied with Theodore's promise to hunt for his, which struck her as a little half-hearted. On her way home, she crossed in front of a hotel, and she paused for a minute in the glow of its gaslights, trying to guess whether there'd be a directory in there. It didn't matter anyway, because she probably couldn't enter a hotel unobtrusively: she knew that the staff would look askance at a woman entering alone, especially at that hour of the evening. If she'd been dressed in Zeb's clothes she could have tried to sneak in, dressed as a man, but she'd left the suit at Theodore's place, so that was out. She held it in her mind as a possible scheme, though, just in case Theodore didn't make good on his promise.

As it turned out, though, it wasn't necessary. She'd been working today at Filene's, getting new stock ready to go out to the floor, when her attention got snagged by a wooden nook in the back room, crammed with paper. She'd walked past this nook a hundred times and had never given more than a half glance to the mishmash of printed matter crammed into it: she knew that, basically, the managers used it as a storage area for ephemera that had piled up in the store, stuff that probably needed to be thrown out but might still be important: obsolete product catalogs, old inventory records, and, maybe—she dimly remembered seeing them there—outdated city directories.

She put down the box of emollients and cold creams that she'd been carrying, and stood in front of the nook, giving it the once-over with her best investigative eye. It only took a moment to affirm her memories: there they were, down on the bottom shelf, two well-thumbed city directories: 1906 and 1907.

She crouched, pulled 1907 into her hands, blew dust from the top of its pages. She wanted to see if Winchell was listed in it. She just wanted to check. Just to see if it was possible to reach him that way. She flipped to the Ws. She didn't know his first name, and there was more than one Winchell listed there, but all she had to do was look over the occupations listed next to the names. He wasn't Winchell, Charles, boots and shoes; he wasn't Winchell,

Frank, metal worker; he wasn't Winchell, J., confectioner—he was Winchell, Silas E., pol investigr. And there was his address, which she hastily committed to memory before returning the book to its slot and returning to stocking the shelves.

After work, she headed to Theodore's. She's taken, these past few weeks, to leaving Zeb's clothes there so she doesn't need to smuggle them in and out of her house anymore. Theodore was a bit surprised to see her at his home on a night other than a Wednesday—the one when her class formerly had been scheduled—but he let her in nevertheless.

"I'm going to Winchell's," Artie said, by way of explanation.

"Oh," Theodore said. "You know, I think I might have an idea as to where that directory is."

"I don't need that anymore," she said. "I used the one at work."

"Ah," Theodore said. "Then—do you require my company as you pay Winchell this visit?"

"No," Artie said, after thinking it over for a second. She's been enjoying her outings with Theodore lately, but what she really wants to talk to Winchell about is the Criminal Investigation class. Why he canceled it, what she should do to improve her skills now that the class has disintegrated, that sort of thing. And she couldn't really see what part Theodore might have to play in that conversation.

"Then," Theodore said, "forgive me for phrasing the question this way, but why are you here?"

Artie blinked. "I have to change?" She pointed at the ceiling, by way of indicating the upstairs bathroom. "Into Zeb's clothes?"

"Why?" Theodore said.

Artie blinked again.

"Perhaps I've misremembered," Theodore said. "It's just that, from your retelling of the events that occurred in your first week of class, it was my understanding that Winchell had already perceived that you were a young woman, disguised as a man."

"Well, that's true," Artie said, although she felt faintly wounded by this retelling of events, in a way that she couldn't quite put her finger on.

"And it was my recollection that you were continuing to dress as a man as a way of maintaining a subterfuge among your fellow male students. But the class is over; the students dispersed. So—"

"OK, sure," Artie said, seeing where Theodore was coming from. She frowned. She looked away. She tried, for a moment, to envision her rationale, to figure it out in the privacy of her own brain. Part of it was that dressing as a man felt appropriate to the occasion. This is the way she dressed when she began studying Criminal Investigation, and so if her plan was to show up to Winchell's house tonight, uninvited, to see if she could somehow continue those studies, then it stood to reason that she should show up dressed this way again, looking a way that Winchell would remember, a way that he might respect, so that he wouldn't have to wonder, even for a moment, Who is this stray girl, arrived upon my porch?

But that wasn't all of it, and Artie felt a bit vexed at not being quite able to puzzle through what she was feeling. She looked up again, locked eyes with Theodore. "I just want to," she said.

Theodore looked perplexed for a moment, and he opened his mouth as if he were going to ask a question, but he must have seen something in her eyes that conveyed the force of her conviction, because all he said was, "OK," and then he settled back into his chair and picked up a copy of a magazine, *The Sphinx*, which he'd clearly been in the middle of reading when she'd arrived. "Can I be of assistance?" he asked before he began to read again.

Really the use of his bathroom mirror was assistance enough, and she said as much before retiring upstairs and speedily changing. The two of them parted ways warmly. And now, after a quick hackney cab ride, she finds herself standing on Winchell's porch, sweating in Zeb's suit jacket. Her suit jacket. Now, faced with the prospect of having to lift the knocker and announce her presence, she finds herself experiencing her first true failure of nerve. She may be dressed in a way that's appropriate for the occasion, but she still can't quite shake the feeling that she is exactly what she was afraid she'd be: a stray girl, arrived upon Winchell's porch, a place where she has no reason whatsoever to be.

And yet. She can't have come all this way and not go through with it. She's not going to leave just because she can imagine Winchell glowering sternly at her, banishing her back into the darkness. If he ends up sending her away, then fine, but she refuses to be scared off just by the prospect that that might happen. And so she knocks.

Of course, when the door finally opens, after an uncomfortably long, sweaty interval, it's not Winchell standing there at all, but what must be his housemaid, a rather tall, aproned woman, with a few sprigs of curly brown hair escaping from her bonnet. Artie, caught off guard, curses herself for being so focused on what Winchell would do or say when he saw her that she didn't prepare for the possibility that he might not be the one to answer the door at all.

"Good evening," Artie says, attempting a quick recovery. She tries to keep her voice deep, but is not at all sure that it's working. She lowers her chin. "I'm here to speak with Professor Winchell?"

The woman looks at her with a touch of mild perplexity. "I'm sorry," she says, eventually. "Mister Winchell is not taking visitors at this time."

"I'm not—" A sudden frustration flares up in Artie. She doesn't want to have come all this way—to have spent a day's wages on the cab—only to be turned back by someone other than Winchell himself. Her voice gets louder (and, to her chagrin, it rises in pitch; it can't be helped). "I'm not here on a—on a social call. I just need to talk to Winchell; I have some things I need to ask him."

The housemaid's perplexed expression deepens. "Forgive me," she says, "but you don't appear to be connected with the investigation."

Artie grasps for this, a possible lifeline. "Ah! But I am! I am connected with the investigation."

The woman winces, as though Artie's falsehood has caused her physical pain. She opens her mouth, and Artie waits, expecting, and dreading, the arrival of whatever the next question might be, certain that she won't be able to answer.

But then, a male voice from beyond the entry hall: Winchell. "Gertrude? Who is that?"

"It's a—a young person," the housemaid replies.

"My name is Artie Quick," Artie offers.

"Artie Quick," Gertrude repeats, to Winchell.

"Yes," Winchell says, sloping into view from an inner doorway. "I thought I recognized his voice. You may see him in."

Gertrude stands aside, allows Artie to enter, and then disappears through a side door into what must be the kitchen. Artie is a bit surprised to have made it past the front porch, and she has to dry her sweaty palms quickly on her pants legs before she can accept Winchell's offered paw for a handshake.

"Good evening, Master Quick."

"Good evening, sir!" Artie says, gratitude beaming through her face. But her expression grows more solemn as she takes note of Winchell's demeanor. He looks more ragged than she remembers: his sideburns are growing out a bit unevenly; his beard, once neatly trimmed, has grown bushy, and there's a streak of white in it that she doesn't remember. His eyes look upon her kindly, but the kindness seems to rest uneasily upon a sadness, something broken, and she also notices a rheumy bleariness in them that she associates with drink. She realizes, with a jolt, that his eyes remind her of her father's eyes, and for the first time she wonders if Winchell is really an adult whom she can trust.

"Will you join me," Winchell says, "in the study?"

"Certainly, sir," Artie says, hoping that Winchell doesn't detect the slightest touch of a nervous quaver in her voice.

He leads the way down the hall, the floorboards groaning under his tread.

"You shouldn't have lied to Gertrude, you know," Winchell says. "It wasn't nice."

There's a touch of mirth in his voice, but Artie feels compelled to offer an apology nevertheless. "I'm sorry, sir," she says toward his back as they enter his study. "And I'm sorry to be bothering you at home, and to be arriving unannounced, and—"

Winchell dismisses these concerns with a wave. He doesn't turn around; he seems barely to have heard them.

"It's just," Artie continues, not quite able to stop herself, "it's just that so much has happened, since our class, and I just—there were just a lot of questions I wanted to ask you."

Winchell retrieves a glass from his desk, which is covered in heaped piles of paper. He tilts the glass this way and that, assessing how much liquor remains in it (about an inch, Artie notes).

"Yes," Winchell says, a bit absently. "Yes, a lot has happened." He retrieves a bottle from the sidebar and refills his glass, looks to her as if to offer her a glass as well, then seems to think better of this, replaces the stopper in the cut glass bottle. "Please," Winchell says, "have a seat."

He gestures at one of two enormous leather armchairs, a standing ashtray between them. Gertrude seems barred from the study, perhaps: the ashtray is brimming with what appear to be pipe knockings. Artie sits, and as the leather creaks beneath her, she realizes that this is the most comfortable chair she's ever been in.

Winchell takes the seat across from her, sips from his glass. "Artie Quick," he says, after swallowing. "It's a pleasure to see a promising student, even in an unorthodox context. So what did you wish to ask me?"

Artie has stored up so many questions over the past few weeks, and now, with Winchell finally at her disposal, they all threaten to jump to the forefront at once. Did the police officer questioning her after the attempted abduction outside the Pickle do a good job or not? Is it possible for a criminal to steal a tree and replace it with an even larger tree? If so, why would they do that?

She inhales sharply, clears her head, remembers what she really wants most to ask.

"Pardon me if I seem impertinent, sir," she says. "But what I'd really like to know is: Why did you stop teaching our class? I was enjoying it, and I guess—I guess I'm just sad that it's over."

Winchell nods. The gesture seems sorrowful; there's something defeated in it.

"I'm sorry, sir," Artie says. "You don't owe me an explanation, it's just that—"

"No," Winchell says. "I believe I do owe you an explanation. I know how important the class was to you. The reason, however, is a difficult one." He lapses into silence.

"Gertrude mentioned an investigation," Artie tries. "Is there—" She's not quite sure how to phrase this. "Are you involved in a case?"

He turns his glass in his hand. "I have a daughter," he says. "Lillian."

Lillian Winchell. Artie commits this to memory. She wishes she'd thought to bring her class notebook tonight. It'd normally be rude or odd to be taking notes on Winchell's daughter, she supposes, but there's a gravity in his voice as he utters her name that leads her to believe that he isn't just a prideful father steering the conversation to his child. It leads her to understand that the name is important, one she'll need to remember.

"She's twelve," Winchell says. "Her whole life ahead of her."

Artie listens.

Winchell heaves a sigh. "On the evening of October 29, I was not here. I was out for the evening, attending a fundraising dinner. A male assailant forced open the dining room window"—Winchell points his glass at the wall, indicating the direction of the dining room—"and proceeded to the kitchen, where he subdued Gertrude, leaving her tied to a leg of the stove. A length of rag stuffed in her mouth sufficed to muffle her cries for help. This assailant then proceeded to my daughter's room, upstairs"—Winchell gestures with the glass again, raising it to direct Artie's eyes ceilingward—"whereupon he seized Lillian, my only child, and made off with her. Where she is now I do not know."

"Oh, sir," Artie says. October 29 was just under two weeks ago, just a few days after their first class session. "That's—I'm so sorry to hear that."

"Thank you, Master Quick," Winchell says. "Your words are a kindness in a difficult time." He drains his glass. "I'm not in charge of the case, of course. I'd be too close to it, emotionally I mean, to be able to observe with the dispassionate eye required of a practiced investigator. In fact, they've moved me off of any case with the faintest scent of blood in it: instead, I'm supervising a team of young cadets working on insurance fraud cases. I don't think they trust me at the moment with anything that's not sublimely dull." He permits himself a thin smile. "All the same. All the same, it's been . . . difficult not to want to look over some of the documentation regarding my daughter's case." He indicates the heaped paper on his desk with a nod of his head. "To . . . review it, to make sure there are no inaccuracies, no dropped leads, no missed details. That's how I spend my evenings now: hunting. Hunting for that which has been overlooked. There must be something, you understand, there must be something that will lead me to her. Criminals always leave some clue, it's just a matter of finding it."

"I'm sure that's true, sir," Artie says, though her voice sounds very small.

"Under these, ah, circumstances," Winchell says, "it's been difficult to, to focus on other things. So, the class, I couldn't. Couldn't make the time. Not any longer. My time, you understand. It's been given over to this. To finding my daughter. To making sure she's safe."

"That's very understandable, sir."

"It's very unlikely," Winchell says, "you know. Very unlikely that she is safe. Unlikely that she'll ever be found, even. With these sorts of cases. It's—generally you find them, children, missing people—generally you find them very quickly or not at all."

Artie, uncertain of what to say, gnaws nervously at her knuckle.

"She's all I have left," Winchell says. "My wife, eight years ago, she had an illness. The doctors at the General Hospital thought they could—" Artie notices, here, that his hand has begun to shake, just like it did the first night of their class, only stronger, more violently. He shakily raises his glass to his lips as though to take a sip. His lips work at the rim of his glass as he tilts it back. Fruitless, really—the glass was empty before he even lifted it this time— but just the motion seems to calm his hand. "Since her passing," Winchell says, "it's just been us. Lillian and I. She's all I have."

Artie feels a wave of emotion begin to crest in her. Sorrow, of course, sympathy—horror, even: the horror of watching another human being, right there before you, suffering a pain you can hardly imagine. But she also feels an enormous sense of responsibility: an awareness that the moment is calling upon her to offer some form of comfort. She doesn't know how to comfort an adult, though, not really, especially not an adult like Winchell, whom she looks up to, whom she admires specifically because he is a person who knows what to do in any given situation, even in the face of a crime. And now, here he is, laid low, spinning helplessly in the wake of this massive tragedy, and here she is, the one who needs to know what to do, who needs to know what sort of assistance to give.

"I—" Artie says. She's grasping about for something she can offer by way of assistance. Anything. Winchell is trying, she reasons, to solve a crime. And what does someone want when they're trying to solve a crime? They want a clue.

"Forgive me, sir," Artie continues. "I do not know if this is going to be helpful. But—I witnessed an abduction, an attempted abduction, of a young woman, not all that long ago. It would have been—if I have this right, it would have been the night before—what happened to your daughter."

Winchell looks sharply at her. Not angrily, but keenly, with a revived ferocity in his eyes, an attentive ferocity that she remembered from the first night that she was his student. "You're saying Friday? October 28?" he says.

"Um," she says. "I think so, yes, sir. Two nights after our first class—I was downtown—"

"Did you report the incident to a policeman?" Winchell asks.

"Yes, sir," Artie says.

Winchell rises, makes his way to the desk, lifts a few stacks of paper, in search of something buried deeper in the stack. "Do you remember the name of the officer?"

"I believe it was an Officer Long, sir."

"Ah," he says. "I'm familiar with Officer Long's report from that night. Officer Long was, in fact, one of the police investigators under my command, until recently. I hadn't realized that you were the witness named in that report."

"Yes, one of them, sir." Remembering how few details she was able to provide to the officer, Artie feels a sudden sense of shame. "I tried to give a good description of the assailant, although I—I'm not sure that—it happened very quickly, and my ability to recollect was—it was inexpert, sir; I believe you would have been disappointed in me."

"Not at all, Master Quick, not at all. It's difficult to observe accurately even under the best of conditions. In a stressful circumstance—witnessing a crime in progress, for instance—well, I won't say it's impossible to observe accurately, but I will say that it gets easier with practice, and, of course, with the proper training, which I appear, this fall, to have denied you. So I am disappointed only in myself."

"Do you think—do you think the cases are related? Part of a pattern of similar attacks?"

Winchell squares the edges of the stack of paper. "A pattern," he says. "I will say—I will say—" He hesitates, clears his throat. "I will say that I was—we were—we are in the process of investigating the assailant you witnessed; we believe him to be a repeat offender. The case is no longer under my supervision, and I should say no more about it. The investigation is ongoing."

Artie's mind swims. A repeat offender! "So then—it could be related to—?"

"To Lillian?" Winchell says. Something rueful crosses his face. "Do you know what a modus operandi is, Master Quick?"

"Yes, sir," she says. Winchell raises his eyebrows. "It's in the textbook, sir. *Criminal Investigation*?"

"Ah," Winchell says. His rueful look develops, a bit cautiously, into a smile. "You read ahead."

"Yes, sir," Artie says. "I am interested in the topic."

"So—a modus operandi?"

"It's the manner in which the criminal has committed the crime," Artie says.

"Correct," Winchell says. "A characteristic style. And you may recall that *Criminal Investigation* says that a criminal rarely departs from his modus operandi, and is incapable of getting rid of it altogether."

"Yes, so—"

"So." Winchell raises his hands in a gesture of futility. "I appreciate your instinct here. But in reality, the case of the assailant you witnessed downtown and the individual or individuals who abducted my daughter are very different. The woman was older, not a child. The abduction was attempted on the street, not inside a house."

"I understand, sir," Artie says, though she really doesn't. It seems to her that if your primary intention was to snatch women or girls you could go about it any number of different ways. She lets her expression deepen into a frown.

"I see you're intending to help," Winchell offers, not unkindly. "And the information you've given me—regarding the most recent abduction attempt in the Ladder District? It is helpful. It may not be my case any longer, but I will give Officer Long's report a careful review, now that I know you were one of the witnesses present on the scene. I may need to ask you some follow-up questions, if that would be all right?"

"Certainly," Artie says. She's not sure she believes Winchell when he says that the information she gave him was very helpful—she thinks he may just be humoring her, because he's fond of her—but his words put her at ease nevertheless, or at least begin to relieve the enormous pressure to do something. She provides Winchell with her work schedule and her home address as he's seeing her to the door.

She still wishes there were more that she could do. As she steps off of Winchell's porch, she turns over what little she can remember of the crime, hoping that she'll be able to jog free some forgotten thing, but the most vivid images that swim up to her mind are the same ones that are already in the report: the assailant's blood, spat on her shoes; his knife, coming at her face.

❦

Back at Theodore's, she doesn't change back into her other clothes, not immediately. Instead, she enters Theodore's salon, flops herself across the settee, and tells Theodore what she knows.

"You're sure he said that?" Theodore says, when she gets to the part about how the attack they saw might be part of a pattern of repeated attacks.

"Of course I'm sure," Artie says. Her hands alight upon Theodore's discarded copy of *The Sphinx*, which she picks up and wrings restlessly. "I'm a good listener. He said—oh, what did he say, exactly—he said the assailant was being treated as a repeat offender, and that the attack we saw was the most recent one."

An expression of consternation crosses Theodore's face. "What?" Artie says.

"I just feel like I'd have heard about it," Theodore says. "I read the newspapers—I read them every day. If there is some ongoing wave of kidnapped girls here in Boston, I just feel like the papers would be reporting it. Don't you think so?"

"I don't know," Artie says. "The papers don't know everything that goes on. Or they don't report everything that goes on, or something. I mean—did you see an article in the paper when Professor Winchell's daughter was kidnapped?"

Theodore considers it. "No," he eventually concedes.

"So maybe the police keep these kinds of stories out of the papers for some reason. Maybe they're trying to minimize a panic or something. Or maybe the papers have decided not to print it for some reason or another. Who knows why they do what they do."

On this note, she unrolls the copy of the magazine in her hands, and for the first time she looks down at it. The cover features a photograph, printed within an ornamental cameo frame, of a man and a young woman, little more than a girl in age. Artie looks at it for a moment and frowns thoughtfully.

"That's Gannett," she says, pressing a finger into the cover. There's a caption, in fine print, under the picture: W. D. Gannett, Magician, with Dorothy Gannett, Assistant.

"Hm?" Theodore says.

Artie holds up the issue. "Gannett," she says. "He's on the cover of this magazine. With"—she looks at the cover again—"I guess his daughter?"

"Oh," Theodore says. "Yes? I think so."

Artie flips the magazine open, hunts around until she finds what looks like a short article on Gannett, set in dense rows of tiny type.

"Huh," she says.

In the back of her mind, she's still been turning over the visit to Gannett's, the odd note it closed on. She still can't quite figure out if he was inviting her to train as his stage assistant or not. And she still isn't sure whether that idea really holds much appeal. She tries to imagine herself onstage, in front of the scrutinizing eyes of an audience. She feels hot and embarrassed just thinking about it.

It occurs to her, for a moment, that she'd feel more comfortable if she could do it wearing her suit. If she could be seen as—not exactly a man, but maybe something other than a girl. Whatever that might mean. A set of ramifications seems to radiate out from this thought, but they disintegrate when she tries to hold them squarely in her consciousness.

She looks down at the magazine again. It seems like it might be about Gannett's stage act; maybe she could understand better what it would be like, working for him onstage, if she read the article? But something in her feels restless; she's not in the mood to read.

"Did you ever see his stage act?" she asks Theodore.

"His?" Theodore says.

"Gannett's."

"Oh," Theodore says. "No, I haven't."

"How come?" Artie asks. "I'd think you'd be interested."

"I am interested," Theodore says. "It's just that—I think he's been spending most of his nights at the School. It seems like he's been studying something, puzzling over some magical problem. It doesn't seem like he's had much interest in preparing a public performance."

"Hm," Artie says. "The way he was going on about it last night, he made it sound like a key part of his work."

"Maybe he's waiting until he has a new stage assistant," Theodore says, crooking a bit of a wry smile.

"It says here his daughter is his assistant," Artie says, frowning. "If she even is his daughter. You ever meet her? Dorothy Gannett?"

"I haven't," Theodore says.

"Hm," says Artie. She looks back at the article, but her attention slides away from the dense print. Thinking about Gannett's daughter causes her thoughts to return quickly to the tragedy of Winchell's missing daughter. She slaps the magazine back down on the settee.

"I just feel," Artie says, "that that guy—the guy who tried to grab the woman outside the Pickle—I'd just like to know who he was. Winchell doesn't think he was involved with the kidnapping, 'cause of this modus operandi thing, but I don't know. It just seems that if we're looking for a person who has kidnapped a little girl, and we don't have any place to start, we might start by trying to figure out more about a guy who has been trying to grab a bunch of women."

"I don't disagree," Theodore says. "I haven't stopped thinking about that man since that night. Regardless of whether he is involved with Winchell's daughter, he is undeniably a dangerous individual. Frankly, I don't like the idea of him roaming free. If we knew more about him, we might be able to aid the police in securing an apprehension." He sighs. "But we have no way of finding the man. We don't even know where to begin looking. I can't tell you how many times I've regretted my failure to get that photograph of him; it would have given us something to work from."

"I don't know if we need the photograph," Artie says, pondering it.

"Neither of us can even remember what the man looked like. He could walk by us on the street and we wouldn't even know it."

"I don't know about that," Artie says. She's still thinking. "I can't remember him well enough to describe him, but I feel certain I'd recognize him if I saw him again. And I think I have an idea of where to look."

"Tell me."

"Well," she says, "when I think back, the one thing that I do remember about that night was the man's knife. Do you remember that?"

"I remember he had a knife," Theodore says. "And that it was quite frightening."

"OK, but—beyond that?"

"Beyond that? Nothing."

"I remember it," Artie says. "The knife. It was long, it was thin, it was—curved?" She makes a shape in the air with the tips of two fingers.

"OK," Theodore says. "That's something."

"It is something. I know what kind of knife that is."

"Go on."

"It's a fisherman's knife. It's a fish filleting knife. I've seen them hanging in the fishmongers' shops."

"OK," Theodore says, taking this in. "So maybe our assailant works as a fishmonger?"

"Maybe a fishmonger," Artie says. "Maybe a fisherman. And if you wanted to look for a fisherman, where would you look?"

"The wharf," Theodore says.

"The wharf," Artie says.

10

Artie spends the night at Theodore's. Nothing untoward occurs—she sleeps, poorly, on the settee. Even so. Just spending the night, as an unmarried woman, would be untoward enough to ruffle the sensibilities of most people. She entered Theodore's house in her suit jacket, though, so any nosy Puritan observer in the neighborhood watching his place late at night would—hopefully!—have only seen the arrival of a man, nothing there to besmirch Theodore's reputation. What her own parents might think is another matter. That is, of course, if they even noticed that she didn't come home. Last night, when she was deciding to stay, she thought they probably wouldn't. Now, though, as she tosses and turns in the predawn darkness, she's not so sure. The thought that her mother and father might have waited up, in increasing stages of distress, for her return stirs up a feeling of remorse, which simmers hotly within her, making it all but impossible to find a comfortable position on the settee and go back to sleep.

She should have gone home, she tells herself. Staying was the wrong decision. She has taken real advantage of her parents' laxity when it comes to her spending evenings out with a strange man whom, when you come down to it, they probably wouldn't even very much like. What if they start taking a more strict approach, demanding that she come directly home after work, insisting that she use that time to tend to chores around the house instead of running around trying to solve crimes? (She has noted the dirt in the corners at home, the pile of undone mending: she knows it'll fall to someone to do it eventually, and she knows that she's the only real candidate.)

So, fine: it was stupid to stay; staying opened her and Theodore both to unnecessary risk. And yet last night it had seemed like the only option. She'd been exhausted. She'd been upset about Winchell's daughter. She'd spent the last of her money on the hackneys to and from Winchell's place, and the thought of getting home on foot seemed insurmountable. She admits to herself, this morning, that Theodore would have loaned her the money, or just given it to her outright, but it didn't occur to him to offer and she didn't want to ask.

Also? As long as she's being honest, she has to admit that mixed in amongst last night's weariness and distress was an indelible streak of pleasurable anticipation. There was an undeniable thrill to the idea of going to the wharf—a dangerous place—with the intention of trying to brush shoulders with the city's criminal element. She wanted to start the day at Theodore's—he lives closer to the waterfront—wake up early, and go out there to take as long a look around as possible before she has to turn around and go in to her shift at Filene's. She's not totally sure whether the criminal element is up and about this early—she suspects they may be more of a late-night crowd—but this does little to deter her excitement.

Theodore isn't up this early either, unfortunately. She was awake when the clock in the corner of the room chimed five, and now it's chiming six. The sun isn't up yet, but through the window, and beyond the bare branches and rooftops, she can see lightening bits of sky: surely by now there will be activity at the waterfront worth observing.

She considers going up to Theodore's bedroom and trying to rouse him, but the thought feels uncomfortable: better, she figures, to wait for at least a little while longer. But she's feeling too restless to fall back asleep. She sits up on the settee, stretches, runs a palm down the front of her shirt to try, with limited success, to smooth out the wrinkles. She drums her fingers on the legs of her pants (also quite wrinkled). Waits a few minutes: still no sound from upstairs.

With nothing else to do, she picks up that copy of *The Sphinx* that she was looking at last night. Cover story: Gannett, plus Dorothy Gannett. His daughter, presumably. By now there's enough light in the room to read by, so she flips the magazine open and digs in.

The article is just a two-page spread, reporting on—yes— the father-daughter magical team causing a sensation in Boston. Gannett's a figure who is probably already known to readers of *The Sphinx*, he's had an illustrious career, runs the School of Magic out of Boston, Eastern Headquarters for Magicians, helped launch the careers of a bunch of magicians Artie's never heard of, best known for his stage trick with the three hoops, show-stopping illusion where he throws the hoops into the air and they freeze there, suspended as if anchored by some internal force, et cetera. That's page one; so far, so good.

Page two: now his daughter, fifteen-year-old Dorothy, stepping into the spotlight, taking her place on the stage at his side, et cetera, clearly a prodigious talent in her own right.

Write-up of the show: Gannett wheels a grandfather clock onstage; Dorothy walks a circle around it and the pendulum stops. She walks the aisles of the theater and audience members present their personal timepieces to her: regardless of their make or model or quality, Dorothy is able to stop them with the gentlest touch of her dainty hand; they are stopped as surely as if she'd struck them with a hammer. Members of the audience, fearing that their watches have been permanently damaged, begin to grow agitated: just as they're about to cry foul, Dorothy returns to the stage, circles the grandfather clock backward, and all the timepieces, clock included, begin to work again. Most amazingly, they all seem to still have the correct time, regardless of when in the act they were stopped: even the grandfather clock, stopped for the longest, has the same time as a timepiece in the audience that Dorothy never touched. A magnificent debut, a powerful new voice in the field of chronomancy, Dorothy is one to watch, full of astonishing promise, given time she may one day eclipse the chronomancers of the Vienna School, whatever that is, the end.

Artie raises her eyebrows, flips to the next page to see if there's anything more, turns the magazine over, and inspects the back cover as though some additional detail might have been stranded there. The article was pretty interesting, and the act sounds impressive, but there's something about the whole thing that seems a bit odd to her.

She checks the date on the front of the magazine: 1908; Dorothy would be sixteen now. So where is Dorothy now? If she's his stage assistant, Artie thinks, why would he need to try to get me to be his assistant? Artie opens up the article again, reads it over for some mention that Dorothy might be leaving town, taking her watch routine on tour, going off to study in Vienna, joining a convent, anything. But there's nothing.

Theodore's voice from the doorway, unexpectedly: "Good morning!"

She starts; she hadn't heard his approach. "Theodore!" she says, irritated. "I thought I'd told you not to sneak up on me! I don't like it."

"I know," says Theodore, looking rueful. "But I thought you'd want to see."

"See what."

"Last night," he says. "After I retired upstairs and left you to, ah, your rest? I was practicing, and I really think I have it down now."

"Have what down?"

"My spell," he says. "The Cat's Approach. Watch!"

He points his finger at his left foot, and takes a step forward. He places his foot on a floorboard; Artie can see it sink a bit under his weight. But it doesn't creak. It doesn't make any sound at all.

"Oh, Theodore!" she says, legitimately delighted, her irritation melting away.

"Wait," Theodore says. He's frowning, and his eyes are tightly closed. "This is the tricky part. You have to move it—the area of effect, they call it—you have to move the area of effect to your other foot—"

He points backward to his right foot, and then steps forward with it, places it on a different floorboard. Again: no sound at all. He opens his eyes and begins to beam.

"You did it!" Artie exclaims.

Theodore, grinning hugely, raises both hands in a whaddayaknow! gesture. "I made it the whole way down the stairs like this," he says. "I've never done it more than a single step before. It must have taken me ten entire minutes to make it down here, but I was silent the whole way."

"I'm amazed," Artie says, "and I'm happy for you. But speaking of how long things take—"

"I know," Theodore says. The rueful look returns. "You probably want to go, and here I am holding you up."

"I'm glad the spell worked," Artie said, "and I'm excited to see where you go from here. But I do want to go. We only have a few hours—"

"Say no more," Theodore says. "Let's go."

*

It's a wet, blustery day at the wharf. Not quite raining, but the air is full of thick mist: a pervasive damp, half descended from the slate-colored clouds above and half kicked up from the ocean below as the breakers smash into the dock pilings. The pier itself is covered with a metal roof on thin pillars, but that does little to shield anyone from the whirling mixture. Artie and Theodore are jostled by men in huge coats, reeking of sodden wool, carrying heavy coils of cordage or baskets heaped with fish. Big gulls, perilously low in the sky, scream at the fish. The men scream back at the gulls.

Theodore has brought his camera, but he's been too shy to aim it at any of the bustling, swearing fishermen, and after nervously making his way to the edge of the pier and taking a few shots of the boats and their tangled rigging, tilted dramatically against the dead backdrop of the sky, he settles on occupying himself with just trying to keep the device dry and safe, holding it protectively close to his chest. He looks unhappy, and Artie begins to feel guilty about having dragged him out. She knows that coming to the wharf was an idea they came up with together, but somehow, now that they're here, aimlessly walking about, squinting into the cold and damp, she feels herself taking more than her share of ownership of the matter.

What even was the plan again—to just come here and see if they could miraculously catch a glimpse of their assailant? It seemed to have promise last night, but now, in the light of day, it looks more than a little stupid. She underestimated the sheer number of people who would be active on the pier, overestimated the ease with which she'd be able to get a really good, close, investigative look at any one person in the hubbub. If anyone in the fray stands out, it's actually they: even wearing her men's suit, it's still clear from her clothes that she doesn't work the ocean or the docks, and Theodore's fancy suit is equally out of place. They look like the interlopers that they are, and this earns them some unfriendly glares. And there are a few moments, here and there, where the skin on the back of Artie's neck prickles and she feels like she detects something more, something sustained: less the feeling of being the subject of an occasional glower, and more the feeling of being watched. But each time she turns around, looking for someone who might be following them, or observing them with true malicious intentions, she sees nothing more than the undifferentiated din of working men.

The edge of Long Wharf that isn't up against the Atlantic is lined with shipping businesses and fish markets, and they investigate those for a little while, weaving in and out of coughing motorcars and heavy, horse-drawn carts. As a strategy, this feels a bit smarter: they begin to have success at spotting things that indicate that they're on the right track. The fishmongers, busy at their stalls, do use curved filleting knives like the one that she remembers from that night outside the Pickle; there are carts, heaped here with slit and gutted fish, that do resemble the cart their assailant tried to snare that woman into. Artie wonders what time it is—there's no clock in sight—but she doesn't want to ask Theodore to check his watch: she knows she should be heading to work right now if she wants to be there on time, and that isn't even counting the time it'll take to get back to Theodore's to change back into her clothes. But she doesn't want to quit. Not now. Not when she finally feels like they might be getting somewhere. She half expects Theodore to chime in, to offer a warning about the hour, but he still appears to be a bit glazed by whatever happened to him back on the pier, and in no real state to be minding the time. Artie's not above taking advantage of his disorientation if it means it'll give her a little more time to investigate.

But more time spent looking doesn't equate to more clues. The first time she spotted a knife that resembled the one she was looking for, it was thrilling; the second time, it was intriguing; the third time, it was meaningless. The men she saw holding those knives didn't jog anything in her memory: they all looked about equally likely—or unlikely, really—to have been the man she encountered that night. The atmosphere of the wharf does have a faint whiff of the criminal—she experiences a momentary thrill at seeing some rough-looking men in tattered coats huddled together around a dice game in an open garage—but she doesn't know how to translate any of it into a lead, not really. Before long, she's grown frustrated. She's tired, she's cold, and she's hungry, and she says as much to Theodore.

"I think I see an oyster saloon, just over there," says Theodore, craning his head to peer above the crowd. "Interested?"

She is. She knows that she shouldn't spend the time sitting down for a meal, but at this point she's late enough for her shift at work that another hour or two hardly seems like it will matter, and she's feeling gloomy enough that she's not sure that she cares. Plus the lure of food is strong. They didn't have breakfast before they came down here, and even though she knows it shouldn't, the thought of a hot cup of coffee or a warm bowl of chowder is able, right now, to tempt her more powerfully than the thought of hurrying across town to spend a long, miserable shift at work.

They edge through the crowd and enter the saloon, take a seat at a table in the corner. Artie sits with her back to the wall: she still hasn't quite been able to shake the feeling that they're being followed, and she wants to eliminate the possibility, however fanciful, that someone might creep up behind her, ready to slip a snare around her neck.

Even with this precaution in place, she still misses his approach. She's not quite sure how he appears out of nowhere: maybe it's just because he's still small. All she knows for sure is that one moment she's scooping the last chowder out of her bowl with a sop of hard bread, and then, when she looks up, the next moment, he's there, standing at the edge of her table, examining her with a gently puzzled smirk on his face. Zeb.

"Nice coat, sis," he says, and he pulls up a chair.

11

The first thing Artie feels is a rush of shame, a desire to cover herself up, to rise, to run. She's not ready to be seen in these clothes, not in front of a member of her family. Out in public, where maybe no one will notice, is one thing. In front of Theodore, a trusted friend, ready to support her every scheme, is another thing. But this is another thing entirely.

"What are you," Zeb says, pulling up a chair, "in disguise or something?"

"Yes," she manages to say, grasping for whatever will help her appearance make some kind of sense. "In—disguise."

She expects him to ask the obvious question—why—and she tries to untangle the various threads of an answer she might give. But he doesn't ask why. Instead, he plops down on the chair, drops his elbows on their table, looks her over with a careful eye, as though she's asked him to assess some criminal skill, one professional to another. He nods with admiration, but there's something exaggerated about it, something off, something false, something cunning and mean behind it: he wants her to know that, yes, indeed, he is wondering why, all the why questions—why on earth are you here, in this strange dive, with this strange man, why is your hair cut too short, why are you wearing the wrong clothes—but he also wants to deny her the chance to answer any of them: having caught her doing something she obviously shouldn't be doing, he wants to let her twist for a moment, while he works the questions over on his own, a set of private puzzles. She can see him working them through, reserving a part of his brain for the purpose of observing her, and tumbling those observations over and over, even as another part of his brain keeps up a stream of steady patter, all the better to keep her off balance while he figures out whatever the angle here might be.

"Disguise, huh," he says. "Well, I gotta hand it to you—it's working. Ace stuff, absolutely ace stuff. In fact, you know what tipped me off? It wasn't that I recognized you, it was that I recognized the coat. Can you believe it? There I was, minding my own business, when I see somebody go by wearing this coat, and I think to myself, gee, I used to have a coat just like that, I wonder whatever happened to that coat, and then, as I'm ambling along behind the person, I think ohhh yeah, that coat, that coat is still at home, with Mom and Dad and, who else, oh yeah, little sis, little Artie, I wonder how she's doing anyway, and then I get a look at the person from another angle or two, maybe I'm a little suspicious by now, and what do you know, it *is* my coat, and would you look at that, it *is* little Artie, all grown up now, it looks like"—a glance here at Theodore—"so here we all are, looks like it all came together, although to what end, to serve what design, who can say. Who can say." The waitress approaches, and Zeb, detecting this somehow without ever taking his eyes off of Artie, waves her off with the back of his hand.

Artie's face has grown hot. She twisted uncomfortably, just as Zeb seems to have wanted. But she's also taken advantage of the moment: while he was observing her, trying to make his assessment, she was doing the same to him. It's been a year now, since she's seen him, and she's trying to detect what might have changed in that time, she's trying to read in his face whether his fortunes have risen or fallen, whether he's suffered, and, if so, how badly.

He looks older, but whatever experience he's been having out here, in what she thinks of as the grip of the criminal underworld, doesn't appear to have done an irrevocable damage to him: she doesn't see a brokenness or sorrow haunting his face, just the same canny intelligence that's always been alive there. Or—no—not the same, exactly, or perhaps the same but different: it's deepened somehow, the old boyish canniness in his eyes has changed into something more like an animal cunning. She wonders, for a moment, just how dangerous he is now, and whether he poses a danger to her.

Before she can pursue that thought to a conclusion, Artie recognizes, belatedly, that this is her opportunity to say something. Although Zeb was quick to dismiss the waitress, her arrival did cause him to break from his patter for a moment, leaving an opening. She hurriedly sifts through the various fragments of things she might say, attempting to assemble them into an actual remark. But before she gets a chance to, Theodore pipes up.

"I beg your pardon."

Zeb flicks his attention from Artie to Theodore. He doesn't say anything, but his expression changes: he looks as though he might spit.

"I don't know who you are," Theodore says—it's clear he didn't listen that closely to Zeb's opening monologue, "but—"

"And I don't know who you are," Zeb interrupts, giving Theodore a look of withering assessment. "So stow it."

"Please, sir," says Theodore, trying to stay polite but clearly evincing a growing agitation. "I'm going to ask that you leave us to allow our meal in peace."

Zeb regards Theodore calmly, reaches into his pocket, and withdraws a stiletto, presses its flat edge to his lips for a thoughtful moment. "And I'm going to ask, mister, that you shut your face."

"OK," Artie says. "Enough. Both of you. You're both being ridiculous, and I don't want to see anyone get hurt. Theodore, this is Zeb, my brother. Zeb, this is—this is Theodore. Also, put that knife away. I've had more than enough knives pointed at me recently."

"I wasn't pointing it at you," Zeb says, a bit sulkily. He lowers the knife's tip to the tabletop, proceeds to make a show of being momentarily engrossed in using it to dig some minuscule particle out of the wood grain.

"Zeb!" Artie says. "Put it away."

He does. A thoughtful look crosses his face. "What did you say?" he says.

"I said put it away."

"Before that."

"I said . . . I've had more than enough knives pointed at me recently."

"More than enough knives," Zeb says. He frowns. "How many is that, exactly? Not counting mine."

"One," Artie says.

Zeb purses his lips, seems to weigh whether this is a reasonable answer. "And who did you say pointed it at you?"

"I didn't say."

Zeb gives Theodore a baleful look. "It wasn't this guy, was it?"

"Excuse me?" Theodore says huffily.

"Both of you," Artie says, slapping her palms on the table. "Zeb, no, it wasn't Theodore. Use your head. Why would I be out to breakfast with someone who'd pointed a knife at me?"

Zeb contemplates this for a moment. "I've seen stranger things," he concludes.

Artie concedes the point. "Yes, OK, but—can you just stay calm for a second?"

Zeb shrugs. "Sure," he says. "It's just that—if someone is threatening my sister, I'd like to know who."

"I don't know who," Artie says.

"In fact," Theodore says, suddenly cheerful, "that's part of what we're here to find out."

"Theodore, quiet," Artie says, although she notes that for the first time Zeb casts a look at Theodore that is not entirely charged with contempt. But no one builds on it, and an ill humor settles about the table.

"Well, anyway," Artie says. "Hello."

Zeb grins. "Hi. How've you been?"

Artie's not entirely certain how to answer the question. "OK," she says. "I've been OK. How have you been?"

"Pretty good," Zeb says.

"You're keeping safe?"

Zeb chuckles a bit at this. "There's not much that I do that you'd call safe," he says. "Not that kind of trade. I've got all my fingers and both eyes, though; that puts me ahead of some."

He holds out his hands, taking a moment to inspect both the palms and the backs. Theodore seems to maybe blanch slightly. Artie doesn't say anything. She's not sure what else she really wants to say. No: what she really wants to say is, I wish you'd come home. But she doesn't say this. Something—something like fear—causes her to hesitate. She hesitates, and she goes on hesitating, and her coffee goes cold before her.

Zeb fishes out a watch and checks the time. It's a nice watch, Artie notes. Expensive. Maybe he's doing well for himself. But probably it's stolen.

"Look," Zeb says, returning the watch to its pocket. "We could go back and forth like this for a spell—I could ask, oh, how are Mom and Dad doing, and all that—but let's be honest, if I really wanted to know, I could just drop by and see for myself, which I haven't done and which I can say I am not going to do anytime soon. Now, the thing I am interested in, here, today, as we enjoy a breakfast together, is the part of the story where someone pulls a knife on my beloved sister, which leads her, if I am understanding correctly, to dress like a man and wander around on the wharf, so maybe we could just go back to that?"

At this, Artie's mood darkens. She frowns down at the tabletop.

"Artie," Theodore says gently.

"What," she says.

"This is why we're here," he says. "Isn't it?"

"What is?" she says.

"We're investigating a crime. And this—this man here—who claims to be your brother—"

"He *is* my brother, Theodore."

"Yes, well," Theodore says, and suddenly Artie becomes aware of how her brother must look through Theodore's eyes: nothing more than a disreputable little man with grubby fingers. And quick on the heels of that realization comes a second one: she realizes that seeing her brother this way must impact the way Theodore sees *her*—just for a moment, it must take her humble background, her family's lack of wealth, and transform it from something that appears to Theodore as maybe an adorable curiosity, or a distantly interesting detail, into what, she is now certain, will be the thing he will eventually come to permanently regard it as: a liability. A marker of an unsuitability within her. She feels a hot rush of shame, and then anger, a brief flare of brilliant anger.

Theodore is continuing: "In any case. We're investigating a crime, and this man seems like he knows more about the—criminal element in and around this place than either of us."

Zeb beams at this. "Very true," he says. "Your friend here, sis, is a bit of a drip, but that is actually very true. Not much happens around here that I don't get to hearing about."

Theodore ignores the insult. "We're here for information," he says, to Artie. "We should—you should—ask him if he has any."

Theodore is right; she knows he is right. And yet, all the same, she finds that she doesn't want to ask Zeb about the crime, about all the mysteries that she's dragging around with her. She has Zeb here, in front of her, for the first time in months: she wants him safe at home; if she must ask him something, she wants to ask him something important, something that will help her understand why he won't come home. She wants to ask him: What is it? What on earth is the thing that keeps you out here, in this place, among these people, doing these things, when you could just come home? But she hesitates again, feeling that fear again, and for a moment she thinks that what she's afraid of is simply the possibility that he won't answer, but then she understands it's not that; what she's actually afraid of is the possibility that, even if he deigned to answer the question, he might give an answer that she could not recognize.

"We're investigating a crime," Artie says slowly.

"Yeah," says Zeb. "I kinda pieced that together."

"We encountered a man," Artie says, "downtown. In the process of attempting to abduct a woman."

Zeb settles in, listening. He presses his pointer fingers together and rests them against his lips. His eyes watch her carefully. The look he gives her is attentive. It almost trips her up: She's not used to seeing this expression on his face. It's not a smirk or a boastful grin or a snarl. It's the face a concerned adult person might make.

She continues. "He had a knife—a fishing knife. And he had a kind of wooden cart with a wire snare in it. Based on the knife we thought we might be able to find him down here."

Zeb winces. "There are a lot of people who have that kind of knife," he says. "He could have been someone who worked for one of the downtown hotels, cutting up fish for the kitchen—"

"That's true," Artie says.

"Do you have anything else to go on?" Zeb says. "Did you get a good look at the man?"

"I didn't get a good look at him," Artie says, "no. But"—this suddenly occurs to her—"I do have something else to go on."

"Tell me," Zeb says.

"His nose," she says.

"What about it."

"I broke it," Artie says.

Something flickers in Zeb's face. He doesn't say anything, but the concern in his eyes changes character somehow; it seems to hone itself to a sharper point. Artie suspects that Zeb has crossed paths, somewhere, with someone who is in possession of a recently broken nose. She waits for a moment, hoping he'll offer up a detail. But he doesn't, so she continues.

"I talked to a police officer about it," she says, remembering her conversation, last night, at Professor Winchell's.

"Police don't know anything," Zeb says immediately, although the expression of sharpened concern doesn't leave his face; it isn't replaced with one of his more familiar expressions of contempt.

"This particular police investigator is smart," Artie says. "He's smart, and I think he's a good man, and—"

"Police don't know anything."

"Maybe you're right," Artie says, changing tack. "But what he told me is that the police consider this man—the man with the knife—to be a repeat offender. So there's a man out there who has been abducting or attempting to abduct women and girls, multiple women and girls. So maybe you're right, Zeb; maybe the police don't know anything. Maybe they know only a fraction of what there is to know. I mean, it seems like it would be hard to do something like that, again and again, and to keep it hidden from everyone. So sure, the police don't know. But somebody does." She watches Zeb's face very carefully. "You say there's not much crime that happens in this city that you don't know about. And you know what, Zeb? I believe you. So maybe you're the one who knows something about this guy. Maybe he works in a hotel kitchen, maybe he works here at the dock. But he's out there, the man who pointed a knife at your beloved sister." Artie smiles sweetly. "And I wanna know who he is."

"Why?" Zeb says, after a moment.

"Because I wanna talk to him."

"What if I told you he was too dangerous for you to talk to?" Zeb says.

"She did break his nose," Theodore says. Zeb pays no notice. He keeps watching Artie.

Artie thinks it over. "Are you scared of him?" she asks.

"No," Zeb says, instantly. "He's not—he wouldn't come up against me. It's hard to explain, exactly, without getting into the details of a whole bunch of stuff that I don't want to get into with you. But there's guys out here who are on top and there's guys out here who are underlings. And let's just say I know which one I am."

"On top," Artie says.

Zeb's familiar boastful grin returns.

"And this other guy is an underling, then."

"Basically," Zeb says.

"Whose underling?" Artie says.

The grin disappears. Zeb opens his mouth, then shuts it again.

"I wanna talk to him," Artie says.

"OK," Zeb says. "OK. So do I, actually."

He stands up.

"Wait here," he says. "Order some more coffee, on me." He throws a stained dollar bill, produced seemingly from nowhere, onto the table. "I'll be back in an hour."

12

It's clear that he didn't come in without a fight. His eye is swollen, and the bandage across his nose is disarrayed; a stripe of fresh blood hangs beneath his nostrils, damply coagulating. Artie wonders whether his nose has now been broken twice in a row: she winces to think it. An involuntary burst of empathy, perhaps misplaced. She tries her best to stuff the feeling back down, to put a different feeling in its place. She tries thinking this man is a monster; he deserves whatever he gets. The thought doesn't quite sit well within her, though; it doesn't feel good, like a desire for vengeance should, once satisfied.

It's definitely him, though, definitely the man they saw trying to stuff a woman into a cart, and the blood on his upper lip helps to confirm it, helps bring back the memories of that night. She remembers his injured face, remembers him spitting blood at her through the rain, remembers the glare he directed at her, the rage contorting his features.

When he looks at her now, though—looking at her, then at Theodore, then at her again—it isn't rage she sees; it's puzzlement, followed by a light surprise, followed by a look of weary contempt, almost a boredom.

"Oh," he says. "It's you two. For a second there I thought I was in trouble."

"Sit," says Zeb. He's standing close behind the man, his left hand holding the man's shoulder. Artie wonders for a moment at the odd, awkward stance the two of them seem forced into, as though they're unwilling partners bound together for a three-legged race, and she guesses that Zeb has his knife out, in his right hand, pressed up behind the man, at the ready to perforate the man's kidney if necessary. The man sits, and Artie catches a quick glimpse of steel as Zeb returns his stiletto to its hiding place.

"OK," Zeb says, taking a seat of his own. "This fellow here is one Mister Spivey, Horace Adolphus Spivey. Horace, these are—well, let's just say they are some friends of mine. You'll understand if I don't introduce them by name."

"A good day to you, Mister Spivey," Theodore says, his voice emotional, full of shaky bluster. "And let me tell you that you *are* in trouble, very much in trouble!"

"Oh, yeah?" says Spivey, his voice flat with disinterest. "And why's that? What exactly are you gonna do to me?"

"Why—I'm going to—I'm going to turn you over to the rightful authorities."

No one says anything. Theodore looks around, as though there might be a policeman standing by, ready to make an arrest. There isn't, of course; the only person nearby is the waitress, who has begun to approach the table.

"I told you no thank you, nothing for me," Zeb says, to the waitress, without looking at her. As far as Artie can remember

Zeb never said anything like that, but she figures now isn't the time to point that out.

"I'll have a cup of coffee," says Spivey.

"No he won't," says Zeb.

The waitress looks from one of them to the other, the pencil unmoving in her hand, and then she leaves. It's unclear whether any coffee will be coming.

"OK," Spivey says. "OK, Mister Fancy Pants. So you're gonna call in the cops on me. And what exactly are you going to tell them?"

"I'll tell them," Theodore says, "that, that on the night of the"—he tries to count backward for a moment—"that a few weeks ago I witnessed you attempt to abduct a young woman, downtown."

"Uh-huh," Spivey says.

"I have—I have a corroborating witness," he says, pointing at Artie.

"Uh-huh," Spivey says. "Your corroborating witness doesn't even know how to dress."

The hot flush rushes, stupidly, into Artie's face again.

"So, OK," Spivey says. "The two of you saw me try to grab some woman. What was the woman's name?"

Theodore frowns.

"Where is this woman now? Did anybody actually report her as missing? Did she ever file a report to the police? 'Cause the last I saw her she was running straight back to her safe little home, and I, for one, hope that she stays there. But without her you got no evidence that a crime was ever even attempted. Whereas I, I can say that I saw the two of you coming out of a saloon, where you shouldn't even have been, and that, drunk, you attacked me, you hit me in the face with a goddamn cobblestone"—he points at his nose—"and that you made up this cock-and-bull story to protect yourselves."

"The police found your cart," Theodore says.

"So you were trying to rob me," says Spivey. "Two fancy brats, out to knock over a merchant. It's been known to happen, ya know."

"They found the snare that you use—"

"A piece of twisted wire?" Spivey says. "You're gonna let your whole case rest on that? Hell, they coulda found the knockout drops that I use to keep them from screaming and I still could explain it away."

"Can you explain away the break-in and abduction at the Winchell residence?" Artie asks.

At this, Spivey blinks, not once, but several times. "Ah, heh," he says, sort of speaking a laugh as he tries to assemble an expression of casual jocularity. But that's different from the half-bored expression he was wearing before.

"Lillian Winchell," Artie says. "Age twelve. And somebody actually has reported her as missing. And if I recall correctly, the assailant in that particular incident encountered and assaulted a maid? Do you think she would recognize you, if she saw you again?"

"Maybe the person who abducted that kid was smart enough to wear a mask that night," Spivey says.

"Sure," Artie says. She's thinking back now to *Criminal Investigation*, to the things she's learned from reading deep into the book on her own. "But—it had been raining, you might remember—so are you sure your boot didn't leave an impression in the mud? If we hauled you in to the police right now, this morning, are you sure the boots you have on right now wouldn't match a print found outside the Winchell residence?"

"Look," Spivey says.

"Or, did you know—I just learned this recently, and I found it very interesting—did you know that the pattern of an individual's fingerprint remains the same throughout their entire lifetime? If you have the impression of someone's fingerprint, on a pane of glass, say, you could distinguish the print from the print taken from the hand of any other individual, did you know that?"

"Listen," Spivey says. "I see what you're trying to do here."

"And what would that be?" Artie says.

"You're trying to scare me," Spivey says. "You have some stuff on me I didn't know you had. You're a smart little bitch, I'll give you that."

Artie wrinkles her nose.

"But it's not going to work," he says. "You want to run me in to the cops this morning, try to pin the Winchell girl on me, go right ahead. You don't scare me."

"And why not?" Artie asks.

"Because," Spivey says, "the police are in on it."

Now it's Artie's turn to blink. This sounds improbable to her. For starters, just to begin with the most obvious thing, she can't imagine Winchell going along with the abduction of his own daughter. Although didn't he say that they'd moved him off the case? That they'd shunted him into doing something with—how did he put it—no hint of blood in it? Insurance fraud cases or something? An unsettled feeling stirs up in her, and it refuses to subside.

"I highly doubt," says Artie, trying to sound more certain than she really is, "that the police would have any investment in covering up the actions of a murderer. A murderer of women and children."

"Hey," says Spivey. He puts his hands up, and for a moment he actually does look afraid. "These people. I don't hurt them. I mean, they get a little banged up when I grab them, maybe, sure, but I knock them out with drops. They wear off, those drops. They don't kill you. I didn't kill anybody. I grab people for money. That's it. They want any young woman I can grab off the street? Sure. They want a specific girl, grabbed from some specific guy's house? This guy Winchell? Sure. That might cost a little more money, but I'll do it. But I don't kill anybody. And if any one of those women has turned up dead, you can't pin that on me. You don't have anything that connects that to me."

"Are you telling me that Lillian Winchell is alive?" Artie asks.

"She was alive," Spivey says, "when I dropped her off."

"Where?" Artie says. "Where did you drop her off?"

Spivey looks anxious now, as though the full amount of just how much he's given away is finally coming to light. A sheen of sweat emerges across his face. He looks away from Artie, over to Zeb. Zeb has, sometime during the course of this conversation, drawn his knife out again: he's back to digging something out of the table with it.

"I dunno, Horace," Zeb says, without looking up from this work. "I'd tell her, I were you."

"I dropped her off with—with a policeman."

"What policeman?" asks Artie.

"I don't know his name," Spivey says. "I didn't need to know his name. They just told me go to the drop-off point and drop her off with the policeman, same as I'd done with the other girls."

"At a police station?" Artie says.

"No," Spivey says.

"Where?" Artie says.

"Just—a drop-off point," Spivey says, wringing his hands together. "In Cambridge. Not much to see there really. Just at the corner of Charles and Phillips."

Charles and Phillips? She knows Charles Street runs along the river, of course, but Phillips she can't quite place. She looks over at Theodore, who knows some of the local urban geography a little bit better, due to his propensity for long walks. He's looking up and to the left, also trying to puzzle out the address. And then his face lights up.

"Artie," he says. "Artie, you know where that is. It's that spot where—"

At that moment, everyone's eyes are on Theodore, and Spivey, sensing his opportunity, leaps up and bolts for the exit.

"Hey!" shouts Zeb, "Hey!"

Spivey overturns a table behind him, sending cutlery clattering everywhere. Someone's cup of coffee bounces to the floor, then shatters. It takes Zeb only a moment to round the obstacle, but it buys Spivey enough time to disappear out the door. Zeb follows close behind.

This leaves Theodore and Artie to deal with the waitress, who regards them grimly after setting the thrown table back upright.

"Sorry," Artie says "It's just that—"

"Out," the waitress says.

13

The corner of Charles and Phillips. It's the intersection where the city is building the new subway tunnel, the one that'll link Boston and Cambridge. The long open trench: Artie remembers dropping splinters down into it when the two of them stood there, just two nights ago, taking a pause in their evening walk.

Theodore wants to go straight over, get to Phillips Street, investigate, see what they can find. Spivey said nothing much is there, but Theodore remembers the site, knows that this is a lie. Once they start sniffing around, they're sure to find clues. It's a big hole in the ground, and one thing you can do with a hole in the ground is hide stuff in it.

"Evidence, Artie, we could get our hands on real evidence!" Theodore says, throwing his arms wide. Artie frowns, looks away from him, looks up and down the street, checking again to see if there's any sign of Spivey or Zeb. Still nothing: both of them have disappeared into the crowds, and she has no way of finding either of them again, no hope that either of them might provide more information. She peers out, across the wharf, fixes a glare at the gray water.

"And time is really of the essence," Theodore insists, to the back of her head. "If there's evidence to be found over at Bay Street, Spivey is probably on his way over there right now, getting ready to move it, or destroy it. He has a head start on us, but if we hurry . . ."

"But hurrying," Artie says. "I think it's a mistake."

"A mistake," Theodore says, incredulous. "You've been the one, all along, who has wanted to pursue this case, even when it seemed all our leads had dried up. Now, finally, we have something real, an obvious next move, and you want to drag your feet? How could that be? Are you frightened?"

"I'm not frightened," Artie says, though it has occurred to her that rushing over there underprepared might land them in a dangerous situation. And it also occurs to her that Theodore seems to have forgotten that she's supposed to be at a shift, for work, in just over an hour. "And I don't want to drag my feet," Artie says. "I want to act. I just want to act in the smartest way possible."

"And what do you believe that to be?"

"We go to Winchell's," she says, pushing Filene's out of her awareness for the moment.

Theodore sighs.

But Artie feels determined. She has some important bits of information now, and her first and strongest impulse is to bring them to him, the way a cat with a mouse in its jaws instinctively brings it home and drops it proudly on the doorstep. She wouldn't admit this out loud, but she's gone so far as to privately assemble a fantasy of being invited into Winchell's study again, only this time getting to sit next to him at his grand desk, engaging in the work of comparing notes. Theodore isn't in the fantasy, and she wonders whether his obvious resistance to the idea comes from the fact that, on some level, he understands that going to Winchell's will require him to be shunted to the sidelines.

"After all," Artie tries, "if what Spivey said is true—if there's some kind of cover-up within the Boston Police Department—then surely it's of critical importance for Winchell to know that as soon as possible?"

Theodore looks unconvinced, but eventually he relents and finds them a cab. It's a long journey, and the cab heaves and sways at it makes its way through Boston's crooked streets. The relentless motion soon renders Artie queasy, and she spends half the ride attempting to get back to the pleasurable fantasy of working side by side with Professor Winchell. Reality intrudes, though: each time she's jostled up against Theodore, each time he mutters irritably about the cost of the cab, each time she grows irritated with him, in turn, because she knows he can afford it and doesn't understand why he's complaining so much, it gets harder and harder to imagine herself in Winchell's sumptuous study, spending the day arranging her clues and his together into some masterful joint solution.

"I still think this is a waste of time," Theodore says, and her fantasy collapses entirely. "We should be going to Phillips Street and investigating the site! Going to Winchell's, taking this detour—"

"For heaven's sake, Theodore," Artie snaps. "The man's daughter is missing. Put yourself in his shoes for a moment. If your own child were missing, and someone out there had information that might help you to figure out where she was, would you want that person to delay getting that information to you? Would you want them galloping all over town in search of more clues, or would you want them to come straight to you?"

Theodore screws up his face at this. She suspects it's less because he's trying to wrestle with the question she's presented him with and more because he's struggling to assemble a vision of himself with a child. She's never heard him say anything about being a father. She assumes, of course, that the idea must cross his mind sometimes—he's twenty-one years old; by now he must have felt some pressure from his parents to extend the family line—but today he's doing a pretty good job of convincing her that the entire notion that he could ever produce offspring is a completely alien one to him. She wonders if he really just manages to get through life without considering the possibility, whether this is part of what contributes to her sense that Theodore is weightless, somehow, a person unburdened by life's more serious matters.

This raises the question of whether she herself is going to have children. Or not so much whether, as when. Or not so much when, as with whom. Hard to think about Theodore as a father without also considering him as a father to the children she knows she is expected to one day produce. But contemplating the idea makes something in her stomach flop over. Or maybe it's just the cab's continued bouncing over cobblestones, or the odors of mildew and horse dung that have been assailing her over the course of the ride.

All the same, something in Theodore's demeanor has softened slightly: his irritation seems to have lost its edge. Perhaps he's undertaken the empathetic exercise she's asked of him. "You're right," he says, "of course. I wasn't thinking. I'm sorry."

"It's OK," Artie says, sighing as she tries to dash these thoughts of the future and return her mind to the here and now. "I know you're excited to get to Phillips Street and take a look around."

"I am," Theodore says.

"And we will go over there," Artie says. "As soon as we can. I promise."

Theodore brightens a bit at this.

Once they're at Winchell's residence, Artie leaps from the cab, lands clumsily, nearly twisting an ankle in the process, and she rushes up the walk, leaving Theodore to sort out paying the driver. It isn't Winchell who answers her breathless raps on the door, however: it's Gertrude again, the housemaid. Gertrude didn't seem especially impressed by Artie last night—she seemed convinced by neither Artie's disguise nor her hasty lie that she was somehow involved with the investigation into Lillian's disappearance—and the light of day in no way appears to have improved her estimation of Artie. Indeed, she fixes Artie with a bland gaze that communicates, very clearly, I am not going to help you, and Artie feels her fantasy slip out of her grasp once again, but with a finality to it this time, as though it has hit the brick of the walkway and shattered.

"Inspector Winchell is unavailable," Gertrude says.

"OK, but is he home, though?" Artie says, craning her head to get a look past Gertrude into the hall beyond. She can see the foot of a staircase—

"Inspector Winchell," Gertrude repeats, "is unavailable."

"I understand, but," Artie says, and then frowns. She considers the option of yelling Winchell's name up the stairs, then thinks better of it. She tries to compose herself, to get her thoughts in order. "I have information," she says, "urgent information about Lillian. It's critical that Professor Winchell get this information as soon as possible."

"I will ensure that he gets whatever message you leave with me," Gertrude says.

"It's just that—Lillian Winchell may still be alive," Artie says, dropping her voice to a conspiratorial whisper.

"I see," Gertrude says impassively.

Artie scowls: she'd really thought that might be enough to get her in the door. Theodore, having paid the cab driver, ambles up the walkway, smiles at Gertrude. "Hello," he says.

"Good day to you," Gertrude says to Theodore, taking in his presence without really ever taking her eyes off of Artie. "Is that the entirety of the message?" she says, dryly. Artie doesn't think Gertrude has blinked once since she opened the door.

"No," Artie says, frowning. She tries to think: If she can't see Winchell, what information is it actually most important to relay? "Tell him—tell him that I have information about who broke in here, that night. I know the name of the man who abducted Lillian, and who—assaulted you, who tied you up. His name is Spivey. Horace Adolphus Spivey."

"I'll pass that along," Gertrude says. Artie, knowing how easily things can be forgotten, wants to demand that Gertrude write down the name somewhere; she wants to grab her and shake her in a desperate attempt to use physical force to lodge the name into some deep fold of her brain. But she doesn't.

"Also—?" Artie says. She didn't necessarily want to reveal this, but a sense of desperation has crept in; she's willing to put all her cards on the table if she thinks it'll help convince Gertrude to pass the message along. "It's my understanding that Spivey isn't working alone. I have reason to believe he may be working with other police officers. If they know that Winchell is on their trail they might—well, I'm not sure what they might do, but it's probably better that they don't know."

Gertrude listens. Her face remains studiously neutral, but Artie can detect that something has shifted, however minutely, in the quality of Gertrude's attention; for the first time, Artie feels certain that Gertrude is actually listening: not only that, but that she has taken in every detail of this message, and will relay it to Winchell thoroughly and completely.

"There's more," Artie says. "Tell him I know more. If he wants to reach me he can call my, uh, associate here, Theodore Reed. Do you have a card with you, Theodore?"

"Oh, ah, of course," Theodore says. He pats down his pockets until he finds one, and he passes it on to Gertrude.

"I'll see that he gets this," Gertrude says. Her voice seems to have warmed, not much, maybe only by the smallest detectable increment. "Good day to you both." And she closes the door.

Theodore turns to Artie. "So, wait," he says, "we're not going in?"

◗

They've let the cab go instead of paying the driver to wait, and they end up spending the better part of an hour trudging through the streets of Winchell's neighborhood looking for another one. Over the course of that hour, Theodore's earlier irritation with

Artie returns in full force. Maybe his bad mood is further facilitated by the morning's coffee wearing off as the day crawls into
afternoon; Artie can't be sure. For her part, she spends the cab ride
worrying that maybe she revealed too much to Gertrude: If there's
a criminal conspiracy out there, organized against Winchell,
couldn't Gertrude be a part of it too? Couldn't they—whoever
they are—have . . . something—paid her to just go along with
Lillian's abduction? To allow herself to be bound in the kitchen?
Once you know there's a conspiracy out there, it's hard not to start
thinking that everyone is in on it.

They disembark at Phillips Street. The site itself looks about the
same as when they last saw it. The city is building a tunnel to meet
the new streetcar that'll come across the new Cambridge Bridge.
What it looks like, currently, is mostly just a long trench carved
into the earth. One day there will be tracks there, but right now
it's just mud and gravel crowded with a lot of wooden ballast and
bracing to keep it from collapsing in on itself. At the east end, the
trench descends to meet a pair of large masonry archways, newly
constructed. Twin openings to a tunnel. A big hole in the ground.
Artie isn't sure exactly how far underground the tunnel goes: you'd
need to stand there at the mouth of the tunnel and look in to be sure.
And someone's already down there. It's the sleepy-looking police
officer they saw the last time they were here. Spivey claimed to
have dropped Lillian off with a policeman: Is this the one?

They walk the fenced-off perimeter of the pit, trying to appear like casual strollers should the watchman look up and spot
them. They're still not really talking, but now that they're finally
at the site, Artie can see Theodore's enthusiasm for undertaking an

investigative endeavor begin to surge back: His clouded expression brightens, his eyes grow alert. He looks ready to find some clues.

There aren't really any clues to be found here at the rim of the trench, though. All they encounter is just the normal array of street trash. Half a loaf of rat-nibbled bread. A bent comb. Theodore prods the comb with the end of his shoe. Beyond that the only point in their circuit that's of real interest is the point where there's a break in the fence: the spot where workers, not that there are any right now, could climb into or out of the site via a wooden ramp wide enough to wheel a cart down.

They walk the perimeter again. Artie can feel an unspoken sense beginning to grow between them, a knowledge: the knowledge that if there's any clue at all to be found here, today, it's down there. Beyond the watchman. In the tunnel. This knowledge grows in their minds, becomes a certainty, and the certainty then swells into a quality like yearning. Both of them keep casting long, desirous glances at the twin archways of the tunnel mouth as they complete their second circuit of the pit. When they pass the ramp that leads down into the trench for the second time they exchange a meaningful look.

They've begun to feel a bit paranoiac, so even though the watchman still doesn't appear to have noticed them, they begin to worry that a third lap of the site might elicit some suspicion. They drop back some distance, to the shelter of the entryway of a vacant building—formerly a bookbindery, according to the weathering sign.

"What do you think?" Artie says quietly. "Should we go down and question him?"

"No," Theodore says. "I don't think so. If he's in on Lillian's abduction and the other abductions—if he's Spivey's contact person then—" He thinks it through. "Then any questions we'd ask—"

Artie finishes the thought: "They'd just serve the purpose of revealing that he was under suspicion. They'd tip him off."

"Maybe he'll leave," Theodore says, hopefully.

"If he left," Artie says. "If we had the chance—would you go down in there? In the tunnel?"

"Would you?" Theodore asks.

"It'd be dark," Artie says. "We'd need a lamp or something."

"It's a work site," Theodore says. "There are probably lanterns in the tunnel, for the workmen—?"

"It's a work site," Artie says, "but no one's working. When we were last here I thought everyone had just gone home for the evening, but now it's the middle of the afternoon and there's still no one here but that watchman."

"Hm," Theodore says. "That's true."

"Something's going on down there," Artie says. "We just have to figure out what."

∅

The problem, though, is that their ability to figure out what is limited to mostly just waiting and watching. They sit on the stoop of the abandoned bookbindery and keep their eyes on the top of the ramp, hoping to see the watchman emerge eventually. But it's cold out, and, after an hour or two, their joints have begun to hurt; periodically Artie gets up, flaps her limbs, hurries to the corner and back, in attempts to keep her circulation moving. But she doesn't ever want to stray too far from the pit.

Finally, though, they need to eat. As the sun begins to go down, Theodore disappears into the warren of streets and returns a few minutes later with some handheld meat pies: they're warm, and Artie devours hers rapaciously, licking each greasy flake of buttery crust from her fingertips afterward. Thus heartened, she advances on the wooden railing again, looks down onto the watchman again: she scrutinizes his stance for some sign that he's cold, or hungry, or even that he needs to use a toilet; but she finds nothing: his body just hangs there in its same bored slump, same as hours ago.

Theodore comes up behind her, and they drop a few steps back from the rim of the trench so they can speak without danger of being overheard by the watchman below. "Maybe I could sneak down there," Theodore says quietly. "I could try my spell? The Cat's Approach? I could try to advance silently, behind him . . ." It's an idea, but there's dejection in his manner.

"You're getting better at that spell," Artie says, matching the dejection in his voice with dejection in her own, "but you've never used it in a dangerous situation. And to come up behind him you'd need to be coming out of the tunnel, not heading toward it . . ."

Theodore frowns at the trench, as though there's a way to make the physical dimensions of it somehow different through the force of disapproval alone.

"What I wish we had was your camera," Artie says. "If we got a photograph of him, we could share it with Winchell—he might be able to identify the man; maybe we could get somewhere from that."

"I could run home and get it," Theodore says. "Leave you here on watch? It might take me an hour to get there, maybe an hour to get back—?"

"It'll be dark by then," Artie says, eyeing the sky. It's pretty dark already: the shadows of the buildings surrounding them have grown long, begun to merge into deep pools of gloom. "I doubt you'd be able to get a good photo, even now." She thinks for a moment. "I could maybe try to describe the man's distinguishing traits to Winchell: Do you think I could do it well enough so that he'd know who I meant?"

"Well," Theodore says. "Let me close my eyes, and you describe him to me, and I'll see if I can visualize him."

"OK," Artie says. Theodore closes his eyes dutifully. Artie, preparing her attempt, takes a step toward the fence, stares intently down into the pit, tries to get a good look at the watchman through the welter of wooden beams, tries to make out his features in the gathering dark. The angle isn't great. The first phrase that comes to her mind is "the top of a hat."

She edges her way along the fence: once she's moved a few feet down, she has a better angle; she can at least see his chin and his facial hair now. She's trying to commit the exact shape of his mustache to memory when a black carriage comes rattling along. She's seen a hundred carriages go by in the hours they've been stationed here, and about an equal number of motorcars, but the driver wheels this one around to the break in the fence—maybe twenty feet from where she's currently standing—and draws the horse to a halt there. That's new.

"Theodore!" Artie hisses.

Theodore is still standing there with his eyes closed. "Are you starting?"

"Theodore, no, look!"

He looks. They watch as a man gets out of the carriage. Identifying characteristics, Artie thinks. Get his identifying characteristics.

He's not a policeman, or at least he's not in police garb. He's dressed in a thick overcoat. It's not buttoned all the way, and Artie can see a triangle of dark suit underneath—she's too far away to see if the suit looks expensive, but the coat does, at least (looks warm, too, Artie notes with some jealousy). He's tall, and although the coat adds bulk to his form she can tell from his long neck that he's a wiry man. She observes gray in the sideburns that curl out from beneath his olive-colored homburg hat; she'd guess he's maybe fifty. His hands are large and knotty, and he twists something between them—a bolt of fabric, perhaps? She can't get a good enough look at it to tell more. They watch as he steps through the break in the fence to the top of the ramp, they watch as he pauses before descending: he looks that way, up one side of the fence, then this way, looking now right at where she and Theodore are standing—

His gaze meets Artie's, and he frowns at her. She immediately turns around, trying to adopt the demeanor of just an ordinary evening stroller, and she grabs Theodore's sleeve and gives it a tug so that he'll turn around and walk with her.

"Who is that?" Theodore says under his breath.

"I don't know," Artie says.

"What do you think he's doing?" Theodore says.

"I don't know," Artie says. Her mind is frantic with the arrival of new details: she wants to grab up as many as she can, but she doesn't want to turn around for another peek for fear that she'll be spotted by the wiry man again. Her brain is on fire with ferocious indecision. She walks determinedly away, all the while trying to will herself to look casual, trying to figure out whether the prickle she's feeling is the man staring daggers at her back or just her imagination. Finally she can't resist: she looks over her shoulder to see if he's still watching them.

He isn't. He's descended into the trench.

OK. She lets out a long breath. She's hungry for one more look at the man, so she braces herself, then sidles up to the fence again and looks over. The wiry man is down there, talking to the police officer, but he immediately senses her presence. He whips his head up to look at her. She mutters the strongest oath she knows and steps back so that she's out of sight.

"Did they see you?" Theodore whispers.

"Yes," Artie says.

They hurry away from the trench. By some unspoken agreement, they retreat back across the street to the bookbindery; they drop into the recessed doorway, hoping to disappear into the shadows.

It's only the shadows that are protecting them, though, for there's an unobstructed line of sight between them and the trench. They watch helplessly as the police watchman appears at the top of the ramp, near where the carriage is parked. He comes through the break in the fence, peers up and down the street. It's clear that he's been sent up here to look for them, to chase them away. Artie tries to remind herself, though, that the watchman has no reason to believe that they were anything other than two young men out for an evening stroll . . . They're not a threat, they're just two lads with perhaps a bit too much curiosity . . . No need to be too aggressive in chasing them off, surely . . .

And perhaps she's right. The watchman doesn't seem to be in any special rush. In fact, he pauses, takes a few moments to exchange a greeting with the driver of the cab, who has descended from his perch to brush his horse. Artie can read a certain level of familiarity between them. They're greeting one another, but not introducing themselves to each other. They know one another, she thinks. Whatever is happening here right now has happened before.

But the greetings don't last forever. The watchman gives the horse a pat on its flank and then steps off the curb, one more step toward them. He frowns into the gathering darkness, takes a moment to fiddle with something clipped to his belt, a metal tube of some sort. He lifts it up and thumbs a button on the side, and a thin beam of light issues from a lens at the end. He sweeps the beam from side to side along the street.

Oh no, Artie thinks, though a part of her marvels at the novelty of a handheld electrical lamp. She pulls Theodore deeper into the bookbinder's entryway with her. The two of them press their backs against the door. If they can stay out of the range of that weak beam for a minute longer, the watchman will surely assume that they've already wandered off.

So she tells herself.

Even so, her heart is hammering against her ribs.

The watchman takes another few steps toward them. He peers directly in their direction, squinting into the gloom of the doorway. The light in his hand falters; he looks down and twists the metal tube in his hands, knocks on its brass end with the heel of his hand.

Then there's the sound of a scream.

Badly startled, Artie nearly leaps out into the street. The scream only lasts a second, though, and she's able to keep herself pressed back against the door, even though her heart is banging in her chest twice as fast as it had been.

The sound of the scream appears to have caught the watchman's attention, thank goodness. He turns away, looks down into the trench, so for the moment she and Theodore can continue to go undetected. Artie notes, however, that there's no urgency in his manner. Whatever the situation unfolding down in the trench—in the tunnel?—might be, he doesn't seem to be especially interested in intervening in it.

A woman is in trouble—why isn't he helping? Artie thinks frantically. The police are in on it, she remembers, that's what Spivey said. It's one thing, however, to believe that this could be true—and another thing entirely to watch a police officer responding to a cry of distress with only the most mild interest.

Artie's instinct, in the face of the watchman's apathy, is to rush out herself, see if the woman needs aid—but she knows she can't, at least for the moment. The watchman might not be looking in her direction currently, but he's still right there, just two dozen feet beyond the doorway . . . Theodore, perhaps sensing her struggle, places his hand on her shoulder, only lightly, but clearly a suggestion that she should hold herself back, even if just for a few moments.

So in an attempt to occupy herself for those necessary moments, she hands the situation off to the investigative part of her mind. Because she understands now that the investigative part of her mind has a certain coldness to it, and that coldness is useful right now. Her investigative self, dispassionate, doesn't want to treat the scream as a sign that someone nearby might need help: Her investigative self only wants to treat the scream as a clue, to turn it around and see if it can't be made to fit with some other clue. Wasn't there another scream? it asks. Way back at the start of all this?

Yes. Artie remembers the report from the Common: a sustained, wordless scream of distress. And she knows that trying to match two separate screams in the city, weeks apart, is nothing more than a fool's errand, especially when she wasn't a direct witness to the first one, but her analytical mind, now activated, insists on completing the comparison. So no, she doesn't think the two are the same. The scream she just heard sounded like someone distressed, that much was for sure, but it wasn't sustained: it lasted for maybe a second, maybe two, before sort of descending into a raspy sob that lasted for a few seconds more before ceasing entirely or at least dropping completely out of earshot.

What else? This new scream is evidence in her investigation. She may find it necessary to recall it in detail at some future point, to facilitate some future comparison; she wants to commit each quality of this scream to memory. She replays it in her head, looks for the words that will lock it into place. It sounded: ragged. It sounded: hoarse. As though emerging from a throat that was dry from disuse. Or sickly. Or aged.

The investigative part of her brain, seeking more information, as ever, asks: the woman who screamed, is she old?

Artie doesn't know. The investigative part of her brain says: find out.

The watchman is at the break in the fence, busying himself at the top of the ramp. He's crouching, extending his hands. Then Artie sees it: he's giving aid to an old woman who is stumbling up to the top of the ramp.

The woman passes through the break in the fence, helped forward by the watchman. The wiry man pushes her along from behind. For a moment she stands in the street and raises her anguished face to the moon. Artie observes her shock of wild white hair, the crude shift that she's dressed in. No shoes.

The wiry man reenters the carriage, and the driver and the watchman hoist the woman up after him. The door to the carriage closes. Artie can hear the click of the latch.

"Theodore," she says as the driver climbs back to his seat. "We have to follow them. We have to figure out where they're taking her."

The driver snaps the reins, and the horse starts off. Artie and Theodore dart out of the doorway, looping the long way around the pit, trying to ensure that they won't be seen by the watchman, who is making his way back to the break in the fence. They complete the loop, blessedly undetected, keeping their eyes on the carriage as it heads north, up Grove Street. They follow it up Grove and around the corner onto Cambridge Street.

Cambridge Street is a wide boulevard, but it's hardly open road: although the carriage is able to pick up a little speed, it still has to contend with the presence of other carriages and motorcars, so Artie and Theodore don't have any real difficulty keeping behind it. They don't get too close—they don't want the wiry man to spot them inadvertently—but they're not too worried about being seen, as a number of other people are out on the street at this hour: bankers and shopkeeps heading home a little late; drinkers and revelers heading out a little early. It's not that hard for them to blend in; the briskness of their pace is maybe the only giveaway that they're in the midst of a mission.

The carriage follows Cambridge Street as it begins its wide curve through the center of town, and Artie and Theodore stay behind it. At the fork it turns left, onto Court Street. They pass Gannett's School of Magic, Eastern Headquarters for Magicians; Theodore crooks his thumb at it as they pass and casts a smile Artie's way. Artie suppresses the urge to roll her eyes: she's glad that Theodore is enjoying his studies, but in the heat of this chase, she feels less interest than ever in revisiting Gannett, to serve as his stage assistant or whatever it was he wanted in exchange for learning a trick or two. What she's up to now is more interesting.

The carriage turns to follow the street in its circuit around Court Square, and when it reaches the corner of the square the carriage comes to a halt. Artie and Theodore wait at the opposite corner. The carriage is parked across from the entrance to an alley.

The wiry man descends from the carriage; he helps the old woman down, and together they enter the alley. With his passengers discharged, the driver directs the carriage off, around the square, back toward Court Street, and although Artie is reluctant to let the carriage go—they might get more clues by following the driver—she knows that they need to stay here. The wiry man and the woman are more important right now.

Artie and Theodore creep up to the alley entrance and peek around the corner. They watch the wiry man come to a stop in a square of lamplight. He's facing a tall building, the woman hunched over by his side. The lamplight is falling from the upper-story windows, but the first floor is a windowless assemblage of rough-hewn granite blocks, marked only by a single door, barely visible from their vantage point.

The wiry man knocks on the door: a single, firm rap, audible even from this distance. After only a moment, the door opens, and someone—a nurse?—Artie only glimpses a pair of hands and a sliver of white sleeve—leads the old woman into the building.

The wiry man turns back toward the mouth of the alley, and they duck back around the corner to avoid being spotted. They drop back to the far corner of Court Square so that he won't see them when he exits the alley.

He emerges back onto the street, arranges his overcoat for a moment, and heads south, toward a brick walkway that leads to School Street, up the side of City Hall.

"Let's follow him," Artie says. "If we can figure out where he lives, we could figure out a way to get his name."

Theodore nods.

They keep after the wiry man, maintaining a careful distance. They don't have to follow him for long, though. He reaches School Street, turns right, and then turns immediately into the courtyard of City Hall. He crosses the slate flagstones, climbs the short flight of stairs, passes between the columns, enters the archway, opens the door, and disappears inside.

14

So this is where the string of clues has led: the plaza in front of City Hall. Theodore glances at Artie, and in that glance she can read an implicit dare: Go in. Follow the wiry man. See what he's doing in there. And she gives him a look back, with its own implicit dare: You first.

But they both hesitate. They stand there in the courtyard, at the foot of the edifice, hands thrust in their pockets, feeling thwarted and cold, hoping that their quarry will come back out so they can resume the chase, in the hopes that it will lead somewhere, anywhere, other than here. Looking for a criminal at the dodgy end of the Long Wharf is one thing; following a criminal directly in through the front door of City Hall is another thing entirely. The windows of the building are mostly dark—it's after hours, all legitimate city business should have concluded for the day. And yet the wiry man just walked straight in. Like he owned the place.

"I'll go," Theodore says finally. "I'll follow him." And instantly Artie regrets that she wasn't the one who offered first. You're not a person who isn't brave, says a voice inside her, a reminder.

"We'll go together," Artie says. "We've been investigating this together—"

"It's safer for just me to go," Theodore says. He looks at the door doubtfully. "I'm a—I'm a young gentleman; if I encounter anyone in there, even at this hour, they will simply see me as an ordinary citizen who perhaps wandered in mistakenly, disoriented but posing no threat—"

This gives Artie a moment of pause. On the one hand, the idea that you could just wander into a place where you weren't supposed to be, and that, if confronted, you could just feign that you didn't know any better, that you'd just gotten turned around—? It's a new idea to her, a strategy she wouldn't have attempted on her own: she can barely believe that it would work, regardless of whether you were a young gentleman or not. At the same time— assuming it would work at all—Artie takes a certain amount of umbrage at Theodore's not-so-subtle insinuation that he's the only one of them who could come across as an upstanding member of the public who has lost their way. So she scoffs. "Come on," she says. "Your family may be wealthy, mine isn't, but we're not destitute either. I don't look like some dangerous street urchin."

Theodore gives her an assessing look. She's used to him looking at her with open affection, and when it pivots to this other type of look, which it does on occasion, she always finds it discomfiting. She's not really sure she wants to know what lies on the far end of his assessment; if she looks like an urchin in his eyes, she'd rather never find out. Or at least she'd rather not find out right now—there are more important things going on right now.

"Look," Artie says. "We don't know who that guy is. We just know that an encounter with him could be dangerous. Remember the first time we ran into Spivey. He came at us with a knife. We only got away from him safely because there were two of us, dividing his attention."

"That's true," Theodore says thoughtfully. But Artie isn't waiting for him to weigh the decision any further. She's making her way to the door, leaving it for him to follow.

❧

It's dark inside City Hall. The building has been outfitted with electrical lights, but they're all turned out at this hour. One neglected lantern, burning low, hangs on a peg near a grand central stair: the thin rind of sputtering blue light enables them to perceive the basic geography of the entry hall, but its range is feeble: the ceiling overhead is lost in gloom.

Artie suspects that there's a switch somewhere that she could flip, that she could fill this space with cold illumination, but feeling her way along the wall turns up nothing, and she's not sure that she'd flip it if she even found it—she's fully aware of how much attention that would draw. Doing it would probably be in line with Theodore's strategy—flipping a light on might make it easier to nonchalantly feign that you are just undertaking normal business in a place; creeping around in the dark certainly doesn't— but she also notices that Theodore, behind her, doesn't seem to be searching for a light switch either.

Instead, the two of them listen. It's been a few moments since the wiry man came into the building; maybe they'll hear footsteps, if he's moving around. He might even be close by. Artie's skin crawls at the thought. But they hear nothing.

They cross the entry hall, peer down the hallways that flank the central staircase. Nothing much to note: no sound, no light.

"Upstairs?" Theodore says. He's whispering, but his voice sounds loud in the silence. Artie replies with a curt nod only.

They climb the stairs, find themselves deposited in a wide second-floor hallway lined with doors. Each door is inset with a panel of frosted glass. Most are dark, but three doors down, on the right, one of the panels glows, lit from behind. An electric light is on, in someone's office.

Could the wiry man be there, behind that door? They creep up. Artie peers at the glass, her heart pounding in her chest. Nothing can be seen through the frosting, but painted on this side of the door, in stately letters, there is a name, and a title: Jameson A. Briggs, Commissioner of Police.

Artie shoots a glance at Theodore, nods at the text. Theodore, looking nervous, nods back.

On its own, though, it means nothing. It's just a light on, in a building, at an hour when a light maybe shouldn't be on. Neither of them knows whether this is where the wiry man went, or whether there's even anyone behind this door. And Artie has to know.

She reaches out, takes the doorknob in her hand, and turns it, as slowly and quietly as she can. The door isn't locked. She opens it a crack, looks through.

There's someone in there. It's him. Standing in the center of the room. It's the wiry man. She doesn't have time to notice anything else, for he looks up immediately, looks right through the narrow opening. His eyes fix on her, a predatory alertness in them. Artie lurches backward, away from the door.

"Hello?" she can hear the man call.

"Run," Artie blurts.

"Hey!" shouts the man.

She runs. Theodore runs. They hit the stairs at top speed, urgently praying that their footing is true. She can hear the man in the hallway behind them, shouting again: "Hey!"

They don't stumble. They make it down the stairs and they sprint across the entry hall; they slam through the door and spill out into the plaza. They turn a corner, and another, trying to create an untraceable path through Boston's convoluted streets. They finally stop to catch their breath when they're at the populated downtown corner where Artie normally catches her streetcar home; not far from the Pickle. They look up and down the street, trying to be sure they haven't been followed.

"So," Artie says, wiping sweat from her brow, her heart still beating fast in her chest. "So that's it, then."

"That's something," Theodore says, bent over, panting.

"Spivey is right," Artie says. "They're all in on it."

"They," Theodore says. He pauses, sucks a whooping intake of breath, gathers himself, stands upright. "Fill me in. Who is they again?"

"The police," Artie says, quietly, so she won't be overheard by passersby. "Spivey said he would grab women and drop them off with a policeman."

"For money," Theodore says.

"And we went to the place he said and we saw a policeman there."

"Yes," Theodore says. "And a woman. Though—an old woman. Not who we're looking for."

"We don't know that Spivey isn't also grabbing old ladies," Artie says. But she frowns. Now that she has a moment, she has the opportunity to reflect on the inelegance of the information she has. Old ladies, little girls—the lack of pattern doesn't quite sit right with Artie; it makes her feel like there's some piece that she's missing. She remembers what her textbook said about modus operandi, and she has to admit that there's no modus operandi here that makes sense, not that she's figured out, anyway. But she also remembers that Winchell, on the grounds of modus operandi, decided that Spivey wasn't involved in both kidnappings—and that was wrong.

"In any case," Theodore says, "you're right. Enough of Spivey's story adds up that it looks like he's telling the truth. Whatever is happening, the police are in on it—and we know now that they really are."

"But Winchell," Artie says, puzzling it over. "He's a police investigator. And he isn't in on it. He's a victim of it."

"And what even *is* it?" Theodore says, after a minute.

"What do you mean?" Artie says.

"We keep talking about it," Theodore says. "This guy Briggs is in on it, Winchell isn't in on it—but what is it? I mean, what we have doesn't really make sense, does it? We went to this site because we knew it was a point of interest in a kidnapping—but we didn't see a kidnapping."

"That's true," Artie says.

"We saw—we saw the opposite of a kidnapping. We saw someone being taken from a hideout and being—returned to someone. How does that make sense?"

"Well," Artie says, thinking it through, "maybe what we saw is the back end of a kidnapping. Like, a ransom scenario? Crooked police kidnap someone, then they return them once a ransom is paid."

"You think that's what we saw?"

"Maybe," Artie says. "Except—"

"Except what?"

"Except nobody ever came to Winchell with a ransom demand."

"That we know of," Theodore says. "He might just—not have told you."

Artie winces at this, because she realizes it has a high potential of being absolutely correct. Ultimately, she knows that she probably must appear, to Winchell, as just some bright young thing, a student with promise. She's not his confidant or his investigative partner, much as Artie might wish otherwise—there would be no reason, really, for him to remark on private details about the investigation surrounding the disappearance of his daughter.

And yet. Theodore wasn't there. He hadn't seen that Winchell had spoken to her frankly, unguardedly. And—more importantly—by the point when Artie had seen him, Lillian had been missing for two and a half weeks. If a kidnapper had presented Winchell with a ransom demand in that time period, Artie doesn't doubt that he would have paid it, and that Lillian would have long ago been returned to safety. She remembers Winchell's words about missing children: you find them very quickly or not at all.

"Tomorrow," she says darkly, after thinking on this for

a moment. "I'll go see Winchell again tomorrow, and I'll ask. Besides—we have another name now. What was it—Briggs. Something Briggs."

"Jameson," Theodore supplies.

"Jameson Briggs. Winchell should be told that he's involved."

"Of course," Theodore says absently, "the man we saw? We're not even sure that that was Briggs."

"How do you mean?" Artie says. "We saw the name on his door—"

"That's true," Theodore says, "but all we can say for sure is that we saw someone nefarious inside Briggs's office."

"A criminal," Artie says.

"Yes," Theodore says. "We know this man is a criminal, and so we shouldn't assume that his presence in Briggs's office is legitimate. He could have broken in, in the pursuit of further criminal acts; he could have been pilfering evidence, planting false records, doing any number of things."

"That should be easy enough to figure out, though," Artie says. "We could go back, during the day. See if we can find him in the building during regular hours."

"Would you feel safe enough letting him get another look at you? In better light? We know he's a dangerous man. There's a case to be made that the less he knows about us, the better."

Artie has to acknowledge that Theodore has a point. "Well," she says, "I could just describe him when I go to Winchell's again. He's a distinctive-looking man; I think I could relay his identifying characteristics. If he really is the commissioner of police, Winchell will know him."

"That's a good idea," Theodore says, though maybe not quite as encouragingly as Artie might like. He's a bit distracted, eyeing a streetcar that's coming up the avenue. And Artie's faith in the idea crumbles a little bit: she realizes that when she goes—if she goes— she probably won't even get to talk to Winchell; she'll probably just get to his door and be turned away by Gertrude again.

"You should get on board," Theodore says as the streetcar comes to its whining halt before them. "Get home. I still don't feel like we're safe. That man could still be out here, looking for us."

Artie's still trying to figure out a next course of action, and she bristles a little at the idea of separating from Theodore before they have a plan, but ultimately he's right—they might not be safe. So she gets on board, lost in her head—neglecting even to say goodbye—and she lets the car carry her off, homeward, into the night.

❦

She sleeps late, and even so, when she wakes she's still tired after the previous night's events. Nevertheless, she's enormously grateful that it's Sunday, and that she won't have to work. If she even still has a job after skipping yesterday's shift. The idea that she might have been fired makes her feel queasy, although she knows the holiday season is approaching, and Filene's is once again in need of workers to handle the rush, so maybe they'll show some lenience.

She stays in bed for a while, repeating the important name in her mind: Jameson Briggs. She could get up, go over to Winchell's, get past Gertrude somehow, tell him that Jameson Briggs is involved. It sounds important. It is important.

But is it true? Theodore was right: they saw a person in a place, but that alone doesn't prove the man's identity. She wonders how flimsy what they have really looks. If she's going to make the trip all the way over to Winchell's, she wants to bring him something more, something valuable, one more clue. She doesn't want to show up on his doorstep looking stupid.

So she heads back over to City Hall first. The offices are likely to be closed today, but she wonders if there might be something that she could spot, something she overlooked. She even reasons that someone with a round-the-clock job like the commissioner of police might make an appearance there even on a Sunday; maybe she could lay eyes on him again, could get confirmation that the wiry man really is Briggs and wasn't just an intruder. For this reason, she wears her shopgirl clothes instead of her suit—the wiry man saw her in the suit, and maybe the risk of him spotting her again might be mitigated this way, maybe he wouldn't recognize her. She wraps her suit in a parcel of brown paper, carries it with her—if she goes to Winchell's afterward, she'll want it. She's not quite sure where she'll change, but she'll figure it out.

It's almost winter, but the day isn't that cold. She arrives at the plaza and walks a careful circuit. Pedestrians cross through the space, and she squints intently at one after the next, hoping she'll spot her culprit, but she has no luck.

After her third time around the plaza, boredom begins to set in: there's no obvious clue just sitting here, and she can't just squint at people all day. This is pointless, she thinks.

Her gait slows; she stops. She thinks to herself—what else could she find out? There must be something.

She thinks about last night, replaying the chain of events that led her here, to be standing in front of the gray edifice. She retraces her steps, heading up the brick walkway that flanks the east side of City Hall, the walkway the wiry man had taken to get there. It leads her back to the mouth of the alley where she and Theodore had hidden, the vantage point from which they had watched the old woman getting handed off. Into some building.

She remembers Chapter Three from *Criminal Investigation*: "Inspection of Localities."

Artie enters the alley. The space is narrow, compared to the wider boulevards that surround it, and it's gloomy, almost dark. She passes what seems like the back of a newspaper printing office: bits of broken, discarded metal type can be discerned amongst the other assorted rubbish. A suspendered newspaperman, enjoying a cigarette by the back door, watches her pick her cautious way along. She takes a quick glance at him, notes the expression of mild curiosity playing across his face. He doesn't seem threatening, but she passes him briskly nevertheless, just to be safe.

She stops in front of the door she watched the wiry man knock upon. Black lacquer, largely unmarred: it's not fresh, exactly, but it looks like it's been applied sometime within the last year, maybe. Other than that, the door gives away little: it bears no signage or nameplate to indicate the building's inhabitants or function, which may itself be notable, Artie realizes. An unmarked building.

There are no windows on the ground floor to peer into for a look inside, and Artie finds herself wondering how she could get more information. She looks back over her shoulder at the newspaperman, who continues to watch her with interest. She could go talk to him, ask him some questions: it seems possible that he might know something about his neighbor across the way. At the same time, she feels hesitant to approach him. she isn't sure that to do so would be safe.

So what, then? She's already drawn attention to herself just by virtue of being alone in this alley: she can't very well just lurk here for hours waiting for the door to open. Even if the newspaperman weren't staring at her—even if he were to go inside in another minute or two—she's not sure she'd be up for another session of standing and patiently watching for long hours. She had more than enough of that yesterday, at the edge of the trench.

Maybe the best thing, since she's already standing here on the stoop, looking suspicious, would be just to knock on the door. If anyone answers, she could probably just pass herself off as a girl here on a charity mission, sent by the church to collect alms for the poor. Or something like that. If someone answers, she could at least get the opportunity to take a quick look inside.

Before she can talk herself out of it, she reaches up and knocks. Knocks hard, as she remembers seeing the wiry man do.

She shifts from foot to foot, waiting.

She's almost ready to leave, to head home after all, when she hears some activity on the other side of the door. She smooths the front of her blouse, affixes a polite, entreating smile to her face, and looks up as the door opens.

She finds herself looking into the face of William Gannett.

15

Gannett? What on earth is he doing here?

He peers down at her; recognition passes over his face. "Artie Quick?" he says.

"Hello, sir," she says.

Her face feels hot. She's been caught off guard. She was only half expecting anyone to answer the door in the first place, and she certainly wasn't expecting it to be answered by anyone she knew. She finds herself immediately certain that Gannett won't believe her story about collecting alms—he doesn't know much about her, but he might know enough about her to know that she isn't the best example of a faithful, God-fearing New England girl. Maybe? She does vaguely remember, on the occasion of their first meeting, saying to him that her father wasn't much of a churchgoing man.

She remembers Theodore's strategy: the one they didn't get to deploy the night before, in City Hall.

"I think I'm lost," she says.

"I'm sorry?" Gannett replies, as though he hasn't quite heard correctly.

"Yes," Artie says, absently. "I turned into this alley, it must have been accidentally, and I think I must just have gotten turned around a bit. I thought I'd knock, to see if someone couldn't help me with directions."

It's a transparent lie, and she winces inwardly at not having thought quickly enough to come up with anything different. But it keeps Gannett off-balance for a moment. She sees the opening, and she maneuvers into it. Literally, as well as figuratively: she angles a shoulder into the doorway.

"May I come in?" Artie says.

"Ah," Gannett says, plainly hesitating. He looks out past Artie, looks up and down the street. Artie, undeterred, steps forward, putting Gannett in a position where he'll either need to step aside or he'll need to physically block her. He chooses the former, and Artie gains entrance to a narrow entry room.

She takes a look around. There's a small station at one side of the room, really not much more than a chair and a small desk, where a white-gloved nurse is sitting: this must be the woman whom Artie saw answer the door last night. The nurse looks up, her attention stirred by Artie's arrival.

"I'm sorry," Gannett says. "You said you needed directions?" Artie turns to look back at him. His hand is still on the door handle; his face bears a look of open unease. He looks prepared to usher her out as soon as he can find a way to do it with a modicum of grace.

Artie ignores his entreaty. "Is this where you live?" Artie asks, though it plainly isn't. She just wants to get him talking.

"Ah, no," Gannett says.

"So—what is it, then? This place," Artie says, hoping this doesn't sound too pointed.

"It's, ah," he says, then he breaks off. He blinks his eyes behind his spectacles, takes a long moment to compose himself, then tries again. "It's—something the city is trying. A bit of an experiment. It's a charitable home for the elderly. There's a bit of a problem, you see—" He hesitates here, as if struggling with which approach to take to his description of the problem.

"Generally," he begins, "when someone nears the end of their life, they have their family to take care of them. They—play out their last days at home."

Artie nods. This matches her experience: she remembers a week or so when she was age ten, when she and Zeb, as part of the family, were tasked with keeping an uneasy vigil by the deathbed of Gweneth, their grandmother.

"But sometimes," Gannett continues, "through some misfortune or another, people reach the end of their life without—without a family to care for them. Should these people lose the capacity to support themselves financially, the city traditionally has had no choice other than to place them in poorhouses, in amongst drunks, debtors, the mentally infirm. It leaves them vulnerable to abuse. It's a monstrous system—or, rather, one that provides a unique opportunity for reform; let's put it that way."

Artie listens.

"And so the city has attempted something new here," Gannett says. He's hitting a sort of stride; the explanation is coming more freely. "A facility devoted to the humanitarian care of what effectively amounts to the orphaned elderly. They're kept here in the best comfort we can manage, and tended to with care by a small staff of nurses, tended to until—well, until the inevitable."

"We?" Artie says.

"Yes," says Gannett. "I worked closely with the city on founding this facility. It's financed, in part, with a portion of my family fortune. It's a new experiment—we only set it up earlier this year—but the mayor already has intentions to expand it. We believe that it is doing some good. And of course, I don't just contribute money to the facility—I visit when I can. Every evening, or nearly so, offering my skills wherever they may come in handy."

"I see," Artie says.

Gannett says nothing. He looks down at her, the expression of discomfort gradually creeping its way back onto his face.

"Well," Artie says, after a moment, "it seems like a noble experiment. I think I'd better get home now."

"Yes," Gannett says distantly. "Do you still—need directions?"

"No, sir," Artie says. "I'd just grown disoriented for a moment. I have it now."

"Good day to you then, Artie Quick."

"Good day, sir," Artie says.

She turns to leave, without looking back. Gannett closes the door behind her. She can hear it lock.

*

She hurries to Theodore's place, bangs on the door.

"Hello there," Theodore says.

"I have information," she says, coming in. "I learned something."

"Go on," Theodore says.

Artie shakes her head, as though hoping to get her thoughts in order by rattling them into position. She's learned something, yes, but the rush through the streets to get here didn't quite help her to draw a larger conclusion from what she's learned.

"My suit," she says, gesturing at the parcel in her hands. "I have to think. I need my suit."

"Of course," Theodore says. She takes the stairs two at a time, struggles into the suit as quickly as she can, leaves her dress balled up at the foot of Theodore's bed.

When she returns downstairs, she finds him in the dining room, where he's enjoying an early supper. He blots his lips with a napkin when she enters.

"It's Gannett," she blurts. She pulls a chair up next to him.

"What's Gannett?" he says.

"Gannett's in on it," she says. "Whatever it is. Whatever is going on. He knows about it."

"William Gannett?"

"Yes, Theodore."

"Well, that can't be right," Theodore says, and he cuts off another piece of roast and forks it into his mouth.

Artie frowns. She feels rather incensed at seeing Theodore dismiss her hypothesis so offhandedly, without hearing the new evidence that she has in its defense.

So start with the evidence, she tells herself. What you can say for sure. What you actually observed. And so she does. "The building in the alley," she says, while Theodore chews placidly. "Where we saw that man drop off the old woman."

Theodore swallows. "Yes?"

"I went back there today. To see if I could learn anything more about it. I knocked on the door."

Some interest makes its way back onto Theodore's face; he raises his eyebrows. "Yes?"

"And Gannett opened the door," Artie says.

Theodore flinches. He casts his eyes about, as though he's looking for some distraction, something that might allow him to delay having to consider the ramifications that might stem from this piece of knowledge.

"You're sure it was him?" he asks.

"Am I sure it was—? Theodore, he answered my knock! He was standing right there before me, as close as I am to you right now. He recognized me, by name; we spoke—"

"OK," Theodore says. A troubled expression has settled in on his face; he pushes his plate away, his roast unfinished. "What did you speak about? Not the case, surely!"

"No, not the case. But I did ask about the building, what it was." She relays Gannett's explanation, as best she can recall it: that the building is a home for the orphaned elderly.

"I see," Theodore says. "And—then what?"

"Then I came here," Artie says.

"So—what leads you to believe that he's a part of this conspiracy?"

"I know it's not what you want to hear, Theodore," Artie says, trying to set aside her feelings of annoyance and to approach the matter with some diplomacy, for Theodore's sake. She knows he doesn't want to hear anything bad about his teacher. "But we have to look at the facts that we have before us. The man in the carriage knew where he was taking that woman. And the people there knew to expect her. There wasn't any negotiation there at the door. It was just—a quick drop-off. It was prearranged. So that means—"

"We didn't see Gannett there," Theodore says, interrupting. "Whatever arrangement these people have devised—we don't know that Gannett is himself involved. It could be something that's happening under his nose."

"OK," Artie says, a bit reluctantly. Gannett didn't strike her as the type of person whom it would be easy to sneak something past.

"We'd discussed the possibility that maybe what we've been uncovering is a ring where women are kidnapped and held for ransom," Theodore says, after a thoughtful moment.

"Yes," Artie says cautiously, though she's still not quite on board with this theory: there are still a few pieces that don't quite fit.

"So maybe a woman had been kidnapped from this home, and we were witnessing her return."

"OK," Artie says. "Except the whole point of Gannett's enterprise, as he explained it to me, is that these are old people with nobody to care for them. The—orphaned elderly, he said. They'd otherwise be in a poorhouse, he said. Who would have paid the ransom, then?"

Theodore snaps his fingers. "That's just it—Gannett must have paid the ransom!" Theodore brightens at this prospect, and she understands why: it would mean that Gannett, like Winchell, had been a victim of the crime; it would place him beyond suspicion.

"Do you think he'd do that?" Artie asks, unconvinced. "Pay a ransom for one of the women he was attending to?"

"Why wouldn't he?" Theodore says. "He's taken these women into his care, has he not? Why wouldn't that extend to ensuring their safe return in the event of their abduction? I think he would be rather affronted to hear that you think so little of him as to foreclose on this as even a possibility."

"For heaven's sake, Theodore. Forgive me for pointing out that you sound more than a bit affronted on the man's behalf."

"Yes, well, I suppose I am."

"And I suppose that I'm a bit affronted that—"

She doesn't get to finish: there's a knock at the door. Theodore and Artie exchange a glance: no one is expected.

"Could you have been followed here?" Theodore asks in a hushed voice, and it's then that Artie understands that he's maybe given more credence to her theories than he's let on.

"I—I don't know," Artie says. "I mean—yes. I could have been."

Theodore rises cautiously from his seat at the table, crosses into the entry hall. Artie follows, pauses in the doorway.

He opens the door, and there, on the stoop, wrapped in a massive greatcoat, stands Winchell. Artie breathes a sigh of relief to find Winchell there rather than Gannett, and immediately thereafter she realizes several things in quick succession—their message got through after all; the case isn't cold; their involvement is still seen as valuable—and these things, taken together, provide a surge of pleasure, indelible, undeniable.

"Theodore Reed?" Winchell says, by way of confirmation—it takes Artie a moment to remember that the two of them have never met before.

"Yes," Theodore answers, a bit cautiously. "And you are?"

"Police Inspector Silas Winchell. May I come in?"

"Ah!" Theodore says. "Of course. A pleasure to make your acquaintance."

Professor Winchell comes in, stamps his feet on the mat, and only then sees Artie. Winchell looks worse than he did the last time she saw him. His beard is wild, unkempt. His eyes are blood-shot, and there are deep circles beneath them. Artie's earlier pleasure gives way to a precipitous sense of concern—although then a genuine smile opens up Winchell's face, dispelling the haunted look for a moment, and Artie can't help but smile back.

"Master Artie Quick," he says. "A pleasure, as ever, to renew our acquaintance."

"Thank you, sir," she says. She rises, crosses the room to join in the round of handshakes.

"You two have been rather helpful," he says, shrugging him-self out of his coat.

"Is that so, sir?" Artie replies.

"Indeed it is. Of particular help was some information you pro-vided me about one Horace Spivey. It was not especially difficult to locate Mister Spivey, once I had the name. I have him, presently, in my custody. I've questioned the man. A very interesting character, Horace Spivey: a bad man. A very bad man. He's done some very unsavory things." A great involuntary tremor seizes Winchell's face for a moment; when it passes, his breathing has grown labored. He takes a moment to recover. "It is worth noting, perhaps, that Mister Spivey spoke to me about the two of you." He permits him-self a brief smile. "He is not especially fond of you, but he made a particular assessment of your character which is worthy of note: he suggested that the two of you were, how shall I put this, two young people who were unlikely to rest for very long in your amateur investigation. Mister Spivey indicated that he had provided you with certain facts—an address, among them—and he seemed to believe that you were likely to act on the facts he had provided you with. Would you agree with Mister Spivey's assessment here?"

"I would, sir," Artie says.

"I did as well," Winchell says. He settles into one of Theodore's armchairs. "Mister Spivey did not seem to feel that character trait was especially commendable in a pair of young people—a matter, as on many others, on which he and I must disagree. In any case, it became clear to me that your investigation may have had something of a head start on the official police investigation, which may help to explain my arrival here tonight."

"You want to know," Theodore says, "what we found out."

"Indeed I do," Winchell says.

And so they invite him into Theodore's study, and they tell him. They tell him of the pit, and the policeman down there. They tell him of the old woman, and the wiry man. They relay the man's identifying characteristics. And they tell him that they followed the man and the woman in the carriage, and that the wiry man went to City Hall, and that they watched him disappear within.

"We suspect the man may be Jameson Briggs," Artie says cautiously. "Commissioner of police." She half expects Winchell to show some shock or surprise at this revelation, but he gives no evident reaction beyond his standard-issue alert listening.

"And the old woman?" Winchell says, after a pause. "Did you note what became of her?"

"We did, sir," Artie says, with a sidelong glance at Theodore.

Theodore, sensing her prompt, supplies the basic facts: "Just before the wiry man disembarked at City Hall, he discharged the old woman at a local institution of sorts."

Here Winchell raises his eyebrows with interest.

"It's a social project of some kind," Theodore continues. "A home designed for care of the elderly."

"I see," says Winchell. "What else do you know about this institution?"

Theodore's expression turns pained, and he looks back at Artie. "We know the proprietor, sir," says Artie.

Winchell maintains the interested expression but doesn't ask anything.

Artie continues: "The proprietor is a Mister William Gannett, sir, a local magician. He runs the Boston School of Magic, over on Court Street. Theodore is his pupil."

"Ah," Winchell says. "William Gannett. I am familiar with the man."

"Oh?" says Theodore.

"Oh yes," Winchell says. "The police and the community of local magicians have had some uneasy relations throughout the years. Any police investigator worthy of the name should maintain a working knowledge of powerful magicians operating in the area, as, indeed, it is a tool of indispensable value. Magicians are often people of interest in an investigation—I'm not saying suspects, mind you, not necessarily, but questioning them can often supply an investigator with useful leads or other insights into a local case. And it's not uncommon for a magician, hoping to maintain a convivial relationship with the local police, to drop by the department, to give the police some advance notice of any especially unusual arcane feat they may be attempting. I believe I've seen William Gannett in the department a few times this year, though I've not spoken with him myself."

"We believe he may be involved with the kidnappings in some way," Artie says.

Theodore quickly clarifies: "We believe he may have been a victim of the kidnappings—that he may have been forced to pay a ransom. We think that maybe what we saw was one of the kidnapped women being returned to Winchell's safekeeping."

Winchell looks from Theodore to Artie for confirmation that this is, indeed, the theory that they're working with. Artie still doesn't have much faith in that theory, but she keeps her face neutral: she doesn't want to deepen her rift with Theodore over this issue. Winchell watches her for a moment, then blinks and looks away.

"Perhaps," he says. "Perhaps. In any case, I think it may be useful for William Gannett and me to sit down and have a conversation."

"That may prove difficult, sir," Theodore says.

"How do you mean?"

"Well—it's just that—Gannett, as I understand the man's habits, spends most of his evenings at the School these days."

"Yes, well, perhaps I shall visit him there."

"But you see, sir, the School—it's protected by a ward."

"A ward?"

"Yes, sir, a—protective magical field. The doors can't be forced, the locks can't be picked. The doors to the building can only be opened by Gannett himself, or by a very particular secret knock."

"I'm not intending to force Gannett's door, lad; it hasn't come to that. My intention is simply to approach in the spirit of openness, friendliness"—though Artie notices not a trace of friendliness in his grim expression here—"to knock on the door—an ordinary knock, mind you, with my own ordinary knuckles. Perhaps I shall call out 'Greetings, Mister William Gannett, it is your local police investigator, Silas Winchell, won't you kindly let me in so we can undertake a brief chat?' Surely you see no difficulty there, Master Reed?"

Theodore looks unconvinced. "It's certainly worth a try, sir," he says. "But I must warn you that when Gannett is deep in his studies he doesn't always respond to a rap on the door. He doesn't wish to be bothered by peddlers or solicitors, you see—"

Winchell frowns. "Well, for heaven's sake, lad—you're the man's pupil. When it's time for you to arrive for your studies, how do you get in the godforsworn building?"

"Me?" Theodore says, blinking in mild confusion. "It's easy for me, sir—I know the secret knock."

There's a moment then where the other two just stare at him.

16

The secret knock can't really be taught, Theodore explains apologetically, or, rather, it can only be taught by someone showing you. And not just anyone. It has to be Gannett himself who shows you; it's one more layer of protection, one more part of the ward. Winchell listens to about a minute of Theodore trying to explain ward mechanics before he pinches the bridge of his nose and emits an enormous sigh. It occurs to Artie that she's maybe not sure she's ever seen him impatient before. Theodore falls into an abashed silence, waiting for the sigh to conclude.

"I have an idea," Winchell says finally. "I am authorized to deputize both of you in order to obtain your aid in a police investigation. The procedure would only take a few moments, and then we could proceed to Gannett's together."

This doesn't actually sound entirely legal to Artie, but her face lights up anyway: the prospect of being a police deputy, even a fake one, is too enticing to pass up. She looks quickly over at Theodore to assess his feelings. She's expecting to see evidence of some reservations. If she were in his position—asked to lead an expeditionary force on her own teacher—she suspects she'd be experiencing some profound reluctance. But Theodore's face—raised eyebrows, slightly open mouth—really only reveals interest, anticipation. She forgets, sometimes, that he's like her in a certain sense: that he can derive joy just from being included in something, just from being asked to come along.

Winchell produces a slim, battered-looking edition of the police code from his vest pocket and reads a passage of dense legalese out of it in a rapid mumble. Artie tries to follow along, but she gets lost in the first tortured loop of syntax and after that she can't quite ever catch up enough to make sense out of what she's hearing.

"That's it," he says upon completion. He claps the book shut and returns it to his pocket. He can't quite seem to resist glancing at Artie's expression, as if checking to see whether she bought the ruse.

"That's it?" Artie says, skeptical.

"Well," Winchell says, a guilty flinch crossing his face, "there will also be some paperwork, you understand, to make the matter official. I think it best, however, that I complete that at a later time, so that we can make haste tonight."

"Well," Artie says, "OK."

They're standing in the evening darkness outside of Gannett's place, the Boston School of Magic, the Eastern Headquarters for Magicians, and Theodore, perhaps more nervous than he initially appeared, keeps fumbling the knock: once, twice, a third time. Artie hopes that secrecy isn't part of their stratagem: assuming Gannett is inside the building, there's no way this fusillade of rapping at his door could have failed to catch his attention. Artie looks up at Winchell to see if he's evincing any concern at the clumsiness of this approach. He doesn't look concerned, exactly, but he doesn't look well, either, not by any means: his shoulders are hunched, his face is twisted into a kind of pained grimace, he's breathing heavily, and he seems to be sweating even though the night is cold. An odor pours off of him, a sour, alcoholic sweat that reminds her of her father, coupled with a sweet stink like something decaying, as though some organ within Winchell has died, but he can't stop carrying it around with him . . .

She turns away. She can't look, not at Winchell nor at Theodore; observing either of them closely feels distressing in this moment. Instead, she looks through the window at the magical props there. The decks of cards. The multicolored balls. The dummy head with its turban. They haven't moved since the last time she's been here; they haven't changed at all except maybe to bleach a little more beneath the rays of the feeble autumn sun, except maybe to gather another layer of dust. For a moment she feels a strange, queasy sensation that the objects exist outside of time somehow, that they've always been here, just waiting for the city to catch up to them, and that they will still be here far into the future, that the city could burn again, like it did in 1872, before she was born, and the objects would somehow persist, in this specific arrangement, untouched in the center of the inferno.

The tissue of time seems suddenly, perilously thin, as though it might tear. She has no idea what might lie beyond it, and contemplating the notion makes her feel lightheaded, dizzy. She tries to blink the feeling away. She wants to reach out and touch the wall to counteract the yawning sense of vertigo opening up within her, but she has a sudden fear that maybe the wall isn't real, that her hand might pass through it, that she might tumble, and fall, and keep on falling, through a hole ripped in time . . .

The door unlocks with a click, and the world immediately refocuses itself, solidifying around the small, precise sound. All three of them seem to breathe a sigh of relief.

Theodore opens the door, revealing the orange hallway beyond. It isn't dark, like they might have expected—it's lit by a pair of gas lamps in wall brackets. From this, Artie deduces that Gannett is indeed here, present in the building. For a moment, she lets herself go further, lets her deductive mind indulge a fantastic possibility—that the corridor has in fact been left lit for them, that Gannett knew that they were coming all along, before they even started knocking, and has prepared the way accordingly. She shakes her head—surely that's not possible. Or is it? She doesn't have any idea, really, of what a powerful magician like Gannett is capable of, no idea of what they're walking into here. She's not sure any of them do, but they walk into it nevertheless, advancing down the hallway beneath the gaze of the owls and the other birds, beneath the shadows acting out a fearsome drama on the ceiling.

They enter the blackened auditorium. Gannett is onstage, practicing with the metal hoops, as he was the last time Artie entered this room. Artie counts three of them in the air, and then Gannett catches them—they chime against one another as he brings them down to his side—and when he releases them again there are only two. He catches again, releases again: this time, only one rises to shine in the beam of the spotlight. When he turns to face them, no rings remain at all, and he is able to prop both hands against his brow, shielding his eyes against the light.

"Master Theodore Reed," he says. "I see you have brought me some visitors. I recognize the young Artie Quick from your last visit, and—ah. Police Investigator Silas Winchell." He emits a sigh. "I should begin, Investigator Winchell, by saying that I am sorry for your loss."

Artie can feel Winchell's body stiffen in the darkness next to her.

"You know who I am?" Winchell says. His voice comes out nearly as a bellow, even though he needn't really have raised it at all: the theater is quiet, and she can hear the relatively soft-spoken Gannett just fine.

"Oh yes," Gannett says. "Your reputation precedes you. Silas Winchell, the only honest policeman in Boston! That's what I've been told, anyway, although by people who do appear to know of what they speak."

"And what do you know of my loss?" Winchell is lumbering down the aisle now; Artie and Theodore exchange a concerned glance and hurry to follow.

"More than I'd wish," says Gannett. The thin sigh again. "And please believe me when I say I understand your pain."

At the edge of the stage are three short stairs. Winchell climbs these and crosses into the spotlight, approaching Gannett. He pauses about ten feet away, and, as Artie watches with alarm, he draws a revolver from a side holster hidden within his jacket, trains it at Gannett's chest. At this distance he'd be unlikely to miss, were he to fire. Professor, no! Artie thinks, freezing in the aisle.

"Where is my daughter?" Winchell says grimly.

Gannett gives the revolver a look for only a brief moment. "There's no need for the weapon, my good man," says Gannett. He then pats down his vest, delves his slender fingers into his breast pocket, and withdraws something microscopic, held in a pinch: something invisible from the aisle where Artie stands. Gannett rubs his fingers together, examining whatever he holds there with an air of light distraction. "I'll answer your questions," he says then, returning his attention to Winchell. "Were you to discharge your firearm and injure me, I don't think you'd find that my answers would become any clearer or more informative, or that they would be produced with greater haste. Please, let's discuss the matter like gentlemen."

"My daughter has been missing for nearly one month," Winchell says. "I am no longer interested in discussing things like a gentleman." He takes two large strides forward, looping his left arm out in a wide arc as though intending to capture Gannett in a headlock, to press the gun in his right hand up against Gannett's skull. Gannett, in response, releases whatever he's holding in his fingers, dashes it directly into Winchell's face—it's some kind of dust or sand; it glitters in the spotlight's beam. Winchell blinks, stumbles, tries to raise the gun, but his arm reels loosely off to one side.

"I think," Gannett says, "that you may need to rest for a moment." And Winchell drops, his body landing heavily in an armchair that Artie is pretty sure wasn't there a moment before. His chest rises and falls with the rhythm of heavy sleep. After a moment, the revolver slips from Winchell's slack hand—Artie braces for an accidental discharge, but it just drops to the floor with a clunk. Gannett approaches it and slides it away with the edge of his foot.

"A shame, you know," Gannett says, removing his spectacles and busying himself for a moment with the act of polishing them.

"What is?" Artie says. Her voice sounds small, here in the aisle, with Theodore behind her.

"From what I've heard of Winchell," Gannett says, "he sounds like a good man. There were a number of people who wanted to ensure that Winchell was kept on the outside. He must be kept outside at all costs, they said. I always said that it was a mistake, to automatically consider that he would be opposed to our endeavor."

Artie takes a cautious step further down the aisle. "What endeavor?" she asks.

"The endeavor of protecting this city," Gannett replies, donning his spectacles again.

A hand on her shoulder. It's Theodore; she turns, catches a glimpse of the look of betrayal on his face as he pushes past her and advances down the aisle toward the stage. "I don't understand," Theodore says. "Do you know something about all this? The kidnappings? The disappearance of Winchell's daughter?"

"Lillian," Artie says quietly.

"Are you working with Spivey?" Theodore says. "And the—the man, the wiry man?" Theodore climbs the stairs onto the stage: if he fears that Gannett will send him into a mystic sleep, he gives no sign. "Please, sir," he says, approaching with open hands, "I intend no disrespect. But as your student—I always believed that I could ask you any question and that you would answer truthfully."

Gannett smiles politely. "It is permissible, don't you think, for a teacher to withhold information from a student? To present information only when the student is ready? Only when it arises in the due course of study?"

Artie follows Theodore up the stairs. "I'm not your student," Artie says, jutting her jaw forward. "And my due course of study, as a student of Criminal Investigation, as a, as a deputy of Silas Winchell, has led me here. Whatever you're doing here—you can't keep it a secret any longer. Whatever conspiracy you're trying to hide—it's been cracked open."

Gannett regards her and lets out a sigh. "I never wanted a conspiracy," he says. "I hope you can understand that. I believed that we could have made the case for—for our endeavor—to a wider audience. Maybe not the public, no, not the whole public, but—others believed that no one would understand, but I never endorsed that approach. I never endorsed that way of thinking about it."

"Then tell us," Artie says. She takes a cautious step past the sleeping Winchell, sparing only a quick glance for his gun on the floor before returning her attention to Gannett, now only a few steps away. If he's going to put her to sleep with some magic dust he could certainly do so from this range. "You say your endeavor here is in the service of protecting this city—that it's noble? Tell us. Let us be the judge."

A look of agony suddenly escapes through Gannett's face, catching Artie off guard. "It's," he begins, "it's a story that's difficult to tell. Please forgive me. Please forgive my reluctance. It's— this story is one in which I suffer. If you are to judge me, I want you to understand that at the outset. I want you to know that I haven't escaped suffering."

"You said you understood Winchell's pain," Artie says.

"Intimately," Gannett says.

"Tell us," Artie says.

Gannett takes a moment, in which he seems to be attempting to pack the agony back into his face, to contain it within his customary calm expression. And then he begins.

"Earlier this year," he says, "the city began construction of a new tunnel, designed to join a tunnel being constructed across the Charles River, to Cambridge. This is a large, complicated job, although one certainly not beyond the reach of the city's engineers. However, in the course of their excavations, they uncovered something. An anomaly."

"An anomaly," Artie says. She curses herself for not bringing her notebook, but she can at least be sure that she commits the facts of the story to memory.

"A structure," Gannett says. "A piece of architecture. Buried under the city."

"Indian?" Theodore asks. "Wampanoag?"

"No," Gannett says. "Wampanoag structures are primarily made from wood, reeds, rushes—materials that wouldn't survive a long burial. This structure was made from metal. A city metallurgist identified it as lead, worked with a fine level of craftsmanship. Once the workers had cleared the surrounding material, the structure was revealed to be cubical in shape, approximately twenty feet to a side. It had some decorative elements as well. Although badly damaged by virtue of having spent some sustained time underground, these decorative elements were still able to be interpreted—they were believed to be funerary in nature."

"A mausoleum?" Theodore asks.

"A tomb," Gannett says.

Artie frowns at this, but she doesn't interrupt the story.

"One side of this tomb had a door. The door supplied no apparatus by which it could readily be opened, and although the city's engineers could likely have cut it open or melted it, they elected, instead, to pause. Partly, I believe, because they wished to minimize further damage to the structure—they recognized it as a unique and possibly valuable artifact—but also because they were able to make out a set of engravings on the door that they interpreted as being magical in nature. The city has been known to reach out to local magicians for their assistance with matters of a mystical nature, when they arise—and here one was. Boston Elevated Railway came to believe that the door was protected by a mystical ward, and I am the local magician with expertise in mystical wards. And thus our connection was made.

"I wasn't able to read the engravings—they were in a language unknown to me, and they had suffered too much deterioration to undergo translation—but from their arrangement and some patterns of repetition I was able to conclude that the door was, indeed, protected by a ward. At first glance, it appeared simple—I dispelled it easily. Or at least I thought I had. But the door still would not open.

"This ward, you see, was unique. It required some study before I realized that it was deploying chronomancy—time-based magic. The ward existed in more than one point in time simultaneously. Suprasimultaneously, to be precise. I could work on the ward here—in the present—easily enough, but there were also versions of the ward that existed in the past, and other versions existing in the future, all operating to keep the door before me, in that moment, in the now, sealed tight.

"Those other wards were beyond my reach; I have no expertise in chronomancy. But as it happens, I did know the most talented chronomancer in all of New England."

Gannett pauses, and the agonized look returns.

"Your daughter," Artie says. "Dorothy Gannett."

Gannett looks at her, a fragment of surprise surfacing within the sorrow.

"I read about her in an issue of *The Sphinx*," Artie clarifies. "Her act with the grandfather clock, and the audience's watches. She was—in that act, she was playing with stopping time and starting it back up again."

"That's correct," Gannett says. He calms his face again. "Boston Elevated Railway had sought my help. I endeavored to be helpful. Dorothy was in Vienna at that time, studying with the master chronomancers there—and, by all reports, surpassing them. I arranged quickly for her return passage. I thought together we could solve the problem—she could locate the wards in time and shuffle them into the present, and I could dispel them, one by one."

"Did it work?" says Theodore.

"Yes," says Gannett.

"Astounding," says Theodore. "Except—how did it work? I'm just still having some difficulty getting my mind around the concept of chronomancy, exactly. Is it more like an enchantment, like when you're enchanting an object, only the object is time itself? Or is it more like a sorcery, where you're trying to manifest something, only in this case the thing you're trying to manifest is a—a—another frame of temporal activity? The implications are—the implications could be profound—"

Gannett permits Theodore a polite smile. "I see you maintain your zeal for knowledge, Master Reed—a thing we have in common. As Dorothy and I worked through the final wards, I, like you, found myself enticed by the prospect that here, before me, was a thing to learn. Dorothy's talents were prodigious, easily the match of the unknown chronomancer who had established these wards; she was performing feats far beyond my capacity to replicate or even to grasp, and all I could think was, What a joy. What a joy, I thought, to be outpaced by my own child, to be able, once the work is done, to reverse roles, even if just for a moment, to be able to be the pupil again, and her the teacher—to sit, to listen, to receive an edification.

"But this was not to be."

"Why not?" Artie asks.

"My daughter is—Dorothy is—"

"Is she alive?" Artie asks after Gannett falters for a moment.

"Yes," Gannett says. "But she's not the same. She's in no position now to explain anything any longer."

"What happened?" Artie asks, as gently as she can muster.

"The wards fell," Gannett says. "The door opened. And then—instantly—we realized our mistake. We realized that these complicated, powerful wards, strung intricately through time—they were never intended to keep us out. They were intended to keep something in. There was a thing in the tomb, but it wasn't dead. It was alive, and we knew because, the moment the door opened, the thing began to scream."

17

"This was no ordinary scream," Gannett says. "It was a scream of unimaginable, endless pain, a bottomless pain. The scream of an entity that couldn't die, that had been alive for an eternity, but for whom the experience of being alive was a ceaseless agony. It was as though I were overhearing an entity that was suffering in hell."

A sustained, wordless scream of distress, Artie thinks. She blinks.

"What did you do?" Artie asks, after a moment has passed.

"My first instinct, upon encountering any being in pain, is naturally to extend compassion," Gannett says. "But again this case was different. Within the pain there was also something else—a malevolence. In the manner found in some wounded animals. We do not reach out to a wounded lion hunched in the corner of its cave; we read the hatred in its glare and we know to keep our distance. In that moment I felt that hatred—that animal hatred. Only the entity in this crypt was no animal. The malevolence in that scream came at me with a force a hundred times greater than any beast could produce. It was as though we had uncovered a wounded god."

"A god?" Artie says.

"This is no mere metaphor. I've been doing the research—I have come to believe that what we are dealing with is best understood as a manifested aspect of the god Saturn, exiled or imprisoned in our plane of existence, mutilated somehow, insane . . ."

He exhales, a long, ragged sound.

"So what did you do," Artie says again. It's not really a question this time.

"What did I do, child?" Gannett replies. "Confronted with this mad fragment of a god?

"I ran.

"It pains me to admit it, but yes: I abandoned my own daughter in my terror. Oh, certainly, I clutched at her, before I ran, I reached out and clawed for her, catching only air. When I failed to secure her in my grasp, I allowed myself to believe that she was right behind me; I allowed myself to imagine that I could hear her footfalls. In reality, of course, it was only my brain playing a trick on me, giving me the permission I needed to run—there was no sound of footfalls; there was nothing but the scream. And I ran, blind with panic, through the rough-hewn tunnel, until that scream was behind me and I emerged into daylight, blinking uncomprehendingly at the sky. Within a moment I had gathered my wits, and I looked behind me for my daughter and found, of course, no one there—nothing but the mouth of the tunnel.

"I couldn't leave her in there. I quickly secured the assistance of a police officer near the site. Pointless, really—even then, I felt certain that a gun would be useless in the face of whatever was down there. But I had to go back, and I felt too cowardly to go alone. So together we went.

"As we entered the tunnel, I was struck by one thing: the silence. The scream had abated. I allowed myself, for a moment, to hope that the being might be gone, fled somewhere, although I didn't think about what it would mean for the being to have left its crypt and emerged into the city. We would have to contend with that problem later, although I did not know that then. All I knew then, as we reached the open tomb, was—"

The agonized expression that Gannett has shown her a few times reappears, only this time it cracks fully open, becomes a grimace, revealing the full abyss of grief that Gannett carries within him.

"All I knew then was pain," he says, his voice choking with it. "For there was Dorothy. Crumpled—in a heap—but even then I thought she might still be all right. I rushed to her aid but—as I began to turn her over—the moment I took her shoulders in my hands, I knew something was wrong. Her body felt wrong. It felt too light. She felt frail. And as I turned her over, I saw—the face of an old woman. Staring back at me, uncomprehendingly. My mind rebelled at the notion that this woman could be my Dorothy, but the eyes—her eyes—they were her eyes. There could be no mistake. The being—the god—whatever it was—it had fed on her."

"It bit her?" Theodore blurts.

"No," Gannett says. "It did not appear to have made physical contact with her. But somehow it drained her. It consumed her. It had devoured her youth, leaving me with only a broken old woman, feeble, insane—"

"Insane?" Theodore repeats, aghast.

"She'd gone mad, of course," Gannett continues. "The human mind cannot survive the strain of aging seventy years in a matter of minutes. She could neither speak nor walk. The officer and I slung her between us and carried her back here; in my grief I tried wildly to reverse what had happened to her. I used every scrap of chronomantic magic I had at my disposal. But no magician has yet learned a way to make an old person young again. Many have tried throughout the centuries. None have succeeded.

"I wanted, at that point, only to be left alone—I wanted to mourn, and beyond that I wanted only to work, to research— maybe there was still a way to restore my daughter to some semblance of her former self. But the threat had not gone away. There was still a malevolent being beneath the streets of this city. The officer I'd taken down there, once he had left my company, brought the matter directly to the commissioner of police; the commissioner of police brought it to the mayor. I was summoned to an emergency council, an attempt to make a plan to deal with the matter.

"During this council, we began to refer to the being as the Shrieker.

"We concocted a series of plans. Our first thought was simply to close the tunnel, that we could rebury the tomb, trap the Shrieker down there—but when we sent a crew of engineers to the mouth of the tunnel, the Shrieker detected them, advanced to meet them, began its scream. The engineers began to age, before one another's eyes—and so they dropped their tools and fled. We sent a pair of demolition experts who assured us they could close the tunnel quickly with explosive charges—they lasted on site for fewer than five minutes. The team of National Guardsmen that we sent down there with rifles, attempting to kill it, fared no better—"

"So now you're feeding it," Artie says.

"We're controlling it," Gannett says, a bit sharply.

"You're bringing girls to it," Artie says. "As an offering. That was the thing that placated it, when you first uncovered it. It fed on your daughter and—it stopped screaming."

"For a time," Gannett says.

"And now, each time it starts up again, you bring it someone new. You pay that man Spivey to snatch a girl and you bring it to that thing as—an offering. As a sacrificial offering."

"You have to understand," Gannett says, "what happens if we don't—"

"I know exactly what happens if you don't," Artie says. "It gets out. It gets out and wanders the streets of the city, and feeds on whatever it comes upon."

"A policeman guards the entryway," Gannett says in a low tone. "He keeps people from entering the tunnel. But he cannot keep the Shrieker in, when it decides to emerge. He is instructed to fall back, a matter of self-preservation. He falls back, sounds an alarm—"

Artie turns to Theodore. "That's what happened," she said, "that night at the Common. That sustained scream? This thing was there. They hadn't brought anyone to the Shrieker in a while—we saw Spivey trying to grab a woman the very next night, remember? And so the Shrieker went—and you remember that man," Artie says. "The sailor? He was trying to tell us something—"

"The man with the tooth," Theodore says. "The tooth that had fallen out."

"That's what he was trying to tell us," Artie said. "We were asking about the scream, about whether anything unusual had happened—and here was a man who was trying to tell us that something had aged him."

"Good god," Theodore says.

"It must have happened near the base of that tree, Flann's tree. The tree aged too. We had it wrong, Theodore, it wasn't that that tree was larger than the others, it's that that tree was older than the others. It aged forty or fifty years in just a few moments. Just like that sailor. He was aged until his teeth came loose from his head."

"And so you see," Gannett says.

"No," Artie says, wheeling to stare Gannett in the face. "No, I don't see."

"My dear child," Gannett says. "This evening at the Common you're describing—it appears to have affected no one but a tree, a transient out late. But that was merely good fortune. Imagine were it to enter a business district at the height of midday. Imagine if it were to enter a shopping district. Imagine dozens of people, possibly hundreds, damaged irreparably by this mad being. Beyond that. Imagine the panic that would result. Imagine the risk posed merely by people stampeding to get away. Imagine what would become of the city once the existence of the Shrieker were impossible to conceal. Imagine it becoming common knowledge that Boston was under assault by a supernatural force. What do you imagine would happen?"

"But—you just give it girls? That's your solution?"

"It's not our solution," Gannett says. "We have no solution. It is a mechanism to buy time, to prevent worse things from happening. It is a bad option chosen from an array of bad options."

"But how could you?" Artie says. She's trembling. "You know how it feels to lose a daughter to this thing—how could you want to subject other people—other parents—to that same pain?"

"We've tried to minimize that," Gannett says. "There are girls in this city whom no one wants. Who won't be missed. Urchins. Wastrels. You needn't look far—Spivey has instructions to—to find those girls. They're suffering anyway, living on the streets—"

"You don't get to make that choice," Artie says. "You don't get to make the choice of whether they're suffering enough to be sacrificed." Her voice catches in her throat. She wonders if, to these men, she'd look like a girl who wouldn't be missed.

Theodore speaks in the gap left while she tries to regain her composure. "I'm not so sure Spivey has been following your instructions," he says. "We saw him try to grab someone outside of the Pickle—she was no urchin, just someone Spivey thought might be easy to grab."

"And—Winchell's daughter? Lillian? You knew she would be missed. You knew you were doing something that would—that would shatter her father."

"That wasn't my decision," Gannett says.

"Whose decision was it?" Artie asks.

"I can tell you whose decision it was," says Winchell. "Jameson Briggs, commissioner of police." He's awake, in the chair. His revolver is back in his hand—he must have quietly hooked it with his heel and dragged it back without any of them noticing. Gannett's hand moves reflexively up to his pocket—

"I wouldn't," Winchell says. "You caught me unawares with that trick the first time, commendably. But you're unlikely to catch me that way a second time. So unless you have a pinch of sand that can stop a bullet, I'd think very carefully about your next move."

Gannett lowers his hand again, regards Winchell with a cautious eye.

"I'm correct, aren't I?" Winchell says, slowly hauling his body up out of the chair with a grunt. "Commissioner Briggs is part of your emergency council, I heard you say as much. He knew I was working on investigating the kidnappings—he knew I was getting too close to uncovering what you had concealed. This grotesque bargain. He knew I would not brook it. In this regard I posed a problem. He knew that he could deal me a blow; he already had Spivey as the implement. Once I'd been damaged by this horrendous loss, he knew he would have a justification for moving me off the cases that pertained to the missing girls, he'd have the ability to shunt me aside, into insurance cases, something suitably distant—"

"Yes," Gannett says. "That's right. Please understand, I—"

"I want to see my daughter," Winchell says.

"I'm not—I don't think that's a good idea," Gannett says.

"She's alive, though, isn't she?" Winchell says. "The being that you've described—this Shrieker—it doesn't kill the people it feeds on, does it? It doesn't drain them to the point of death."

"No," Gannett acknowledges. "It doesn't appear to want to do that. It wants to keep them alive."

"And you've been bringing the survivors to your convalescent home?" Winchell says. "That's why you set it up."

"Yes," Gannett says. "It seemed like something of—a kindness. A way to ensure that the girls—the women—"

"Do not speak to me of kindness," Winchell says. "I do not want to hear the word in your mouth."

"Very well," says Gannett, still keeping an eye on Winchell's revolver.

"Horace Spivey is dead," Winchell says.

Artie gasps.

"He was, shall we say, reluctant to provide me with the information that I required," Winchell says. "I thought perhaps a bullet to his knee might persuade him to cooperate. He did, in fact, become more cooperative after that, I believe in part because he believed that he could avoid receiving a second bullet, this one to the head. An erroneous belief, as it turns out, but his misunderstanding of the situation did serve me, for a time. And so I would like to ask you, Mister William Gannett, a question. I do not intend to ask it a second time. Are you cooperative?"

Gannett hesitates before answering, but only for a beat.

"I am," he says.

"Then show me," Winchell says, "what I need to see."

18

They're met at the door by a nurse, who eyes them immediately with suspicion. Artie half expects that this will
be the end of their investigation for the night: it would be easy
enough, in this moment, for the nurse to detect that something is
wrong, perhaps attempt to bar their entry.

They can try to pass off their arrival on the doorstep as police
business, Artie imagines, but they must surely look more disreputable than official. She tries, for a moment, to imagine how they
must look, through the nurse's eyes. The appearance of Gannett
is probably no surprise, Artie figures, since he basically owns the
place, but tonight he's been marched over here at gunpoint, so
he looks distressed, disheveled: he's sweating, even though it's a
cold night. He's hatless. And behind him is Winchell, grim-faced,
who hasn't even bothered to conceal the tiny pistol that he has
pressed up against Gannett's back. Gannett's body serves the purpose of blocking the pistol from the nurse's view, but the way that
Winchell looms directly behind Gannett must surely look odd,
undoubtedly menacing, even to someone who doesn't know a gun
is involved. And the picture is completed by Theodore and Artie,
who always look a bit weird even under the best of circumstances,

and Artie imagines that that impression is multiplied a hundred-fold under the current circumstances: quietly participating in the infiltration of a home for the elderly that's, in reality, part of a government cover-up of a supernatural incursion.

"Good evening, sir," the nurse manages after she's finished taking them all in.

"Good evening, Lucy," Gannett replies. "How are things going this evening?"

"Everything is in order tonight, sir," says the nurse. "Nothing out of the ordinary." Artie can almost hear the unspoken ". . . until now."

"The gentleman here with me is Police Inspector Silas Winchell," Gannett says. "He's come to examine the facilities—to, ah, ensure that all the women are being properly cared for."

"Evening," Winchell says gruffly.

"I see," says Lucy. Lucy gives Winchell a curt nod, and then turns her attention to Artie and Theodore, still openly perplexed as to their presence. After an uncomfortable moment—Artie has to bite back the temptation to introduce herself—she looks back at Gannett, an open expression of expectation of her face, but he doesn't offer any explanation.

Instead: "I think you can head home, Lucy. Thank you for your hard work this evening, as ever."

Lucy starts a bit at this. "But, sir. The night shift replacement nurse won't be here until—"

"It's all right, Lucy," Gannett says. "This may take some time. I have matters fully in hand until they arrive."

"Well," Lucy says. "All right, sir. If you're sure."

"Very much so," Gannett says.

While Lucy busies herself, gathering her coat from the coatrack, Artie takes a look around the narrow entry hall. There's a small station at one side of the room, where Lucy must have been sitting before she answered Gannett's knock at the door. Artie looks over the assortment of paper and small cards arranged neatly on its surface. Artie lights upon an idea that they might hold value as evidence—might they contain documentation about the disappeared girls? their names?—but she checks this impression against Winchell, who is paying the paraphernalia no mind.

She's still trying to do something with the knowledge that Winchell has murdered Spivey, to make it the basis for some important decision about how she feels about him, about what she's doing, tagging along here, though her mind rejects her attempts to focus on it.

The other side of the room is taken up with a staircase that leads to the second floor. The first few steps are lit by a low-burning gaslight mounted to the wall, but the light doesn't extend far: the first landing is half shrouded in gloom. Then the stairs turn a corner, and whatever lies beyond, on the floor above, Artie can scarcely imagine.

Lucy, now bundled in her heavy coat, pushes out through the door, disappears into the night. Gannett pulls the door shut behind her.

"Clasp your hands behind your back," Winchell says, attempting to forestall any potential magic use. Gannett complies.

"Now," Winchell says, "let's go upstairs."

Gannett leads the way—a bit slowly, since he can't use the banister with his hands behind his back. They make it as far as the landing before Gannett pauses, and turns to offer an entreaty.

"Inspector Winchell. I understand that you feel compelled to pursue this course of action. But I—I've seen what you are about to see. I've seen it with my own eyes. My own daughter—transformed in this way—gone mad—it's—it's a thing no man should ever see. I can tell you firsthand—it will provide you with no solace."

"I'll be the judge of that," says Winchell.

"Please, Inspector," Gannett says. "You and I—we're both men who seek knowledge. I understand the urge to try to understand the unimaginable. Yet—"

"You and I are not alike," Winchell says, "and this is not a matter for debate. I am going to ask you to stop speaking now. I will not ask you a second time."

Gannett stops speaking. Everyone has stopped speaking. Artie wonders whether Gannett doesn't have a point, though, and she considers breaking the silence to offer this observation, but she quickly loses her nerve.

Together they continue to make their way up through the building. Once they've turned through the dark corner of the landing, they reach the lower depths of a pool of light, filtering down from the gaslights on the second floor, and they climb the stairs and ascend into it.

Artie blinks as she enters the ward and gets a full sense of the size of the space. The entry hall was narrow, but the second floor is wide: it must span a good quarter of the block. She hadn't realized how many of the windows she'd seen from the outside looked into this room. But her attention isn't on the windows right now. It's on the beds.

The long ward has a dozen beds on each side; twenty-four in total. Each has a small table by its side, each table supports a vase with a single cut flower. A lamp hangs at the head of each bed, a ceramic pot sits at the foot. A few freestanding screens stand here and there in the room, printed with a vaguely Chinese decorative motif; these could be rearranged, presumably, to create private areas as needed. The room smells of talc and laundry soap and the sharp scent of human waste.

And about half the beds are occupied by women. Old women. Girls, Artie tries. They're just girls. A dozen girls, destroyed and left here. Broken things, arranged in two neat rows, six on each side, an aisle of available space between them. Artie tries to grasp the magnitude of what she sees before them; her mind can't quite seem to take it in, though.

"My god," Winchell says, standing behind Gannett at the head of the aisle. "You really did it, didn't you? I wanted to disbelieve it until the last."

Gannett continues to observe the injunction not to speak. He remains bound by it even as Winchell steps out from behind him, finally, takes a preliminary step deeper into the ward, down the aisle. Artie, still in the rear with Theodore, watches as Winchell's hand—the small pistol still clenched in it—drops down to his side for a moment. She watches Gannett's back for a moment, wonders whether he'll take this opportunity to cast a spell, to put Winchell back to sleep, to do something, to snap his fingers and send them all back home, or, better, to make this all go away, make this room go away, undo the things that happened. She wants that. She doesn't want to have solved this mystery: she wants there to have been no mystery in the first place; she wants none of this to have ever even happened.

Gannett doesn't snap his fingers, though. Gannett doesn't do anything. He just stands there, his head faintly declined, as though hung in shame.

She turns to look at Theodore. He's a step behind her, still at the top of the stairwell, one hand still frozen on the banister. His face is white with what might be a variety of rage.

Uncertain of what else to do, she steps quietly around Gannett, falls in beside Winchell. Maybe Winchell is right: if no one is going to make this horror disappear, maybe there is something to be gained from bearing witness to it. She looks up at him, wanting to signal her presence at his side. He looks down at her for a moment, his face lost in the depths of an unimaginable, cavernous grief: he seems to be expending an enormous effort to remember even who she is, or why she is here. But together they walk down the aisle. Theodore and Gannett follow.

Artie watches Winchell turn his head from side to side, looking at each bed in turn as he passes them, fixing each madwoman with a steady gaze. Artie realizes that she's avoided doing this so far—she's looked at the lamps, and the flowers, but she hasn't looked at the women's faces. She wills herself to follow Winchell's lead, to observe. It's a crime, she tells herself; what has happened to make this room exist is a crime, and, like any crime, it warrants investigation, close inspection.

And so: She looks at their sunken eyes, their lolling mouths. Shadows from the flickering lamps make their faces masklike, but Artie tries to peer past this, to perceive the humanity beneath, damaged and shattered though it may be. Artie thinks, for a moment, of her own mother.

A few of the women are awake, staring emptily at nothing, and Artie tries to make meaningful eye contact with each of these women in turn, hoping to extend compassion in a form they can feel, but not a single one of them seems aware of the presence of visitors. She continues her observations, attempting a dispassionate recounting of details, even though her throat is tight and her shoulders are shaking. She makes herself perceive the knotty tendons in the women's frail hands, examine the skulls beneath their loose skin. She listens to their ragged breathing, the low moans they issue.

She wonders whether Winchell will be able to identify Lillian. She can't imagine looking down into one of these women's faces and being able to identify the girl that she once was, sane and whole. But she's only just concluded this thought when Winchell freezes at the foot of one bed. He emits a noise that sounds a bit like he's just been punched, once, in the gut.

"Oh, my dear," Winchell says, his voice choked with grief. "My darling girl."

Gannett and Theodore join them, and they stand there for a moment, at the foot of the bed, looking down into the face of an old woman, a spill of unkempt white hair framing the small and tender oval of her face. She's asleep, and Artie wonders whether this is some small mercy: at least Winchell is spared the experience of seeing his daughter look at her own father and fail to recognize him.

Artie hears Winchell make another noise, a kind of groan, and she turns away from Lillian, looks up at him. His body is shaking. Artie feels an impulse to take his arm and steer him back out of the room, now that he's seen what he's come to see. But she does not act.

"Gannett," Winchell manages to say.

"Yes," Gannett replies.

"Do they suffer," Winchell says. It isn't really a question. "These women. Are they—are they in pain?"

"I—" Gannett says softly. "I'm not sure that's for me to say."

"I asked you, sir, did I not?" Winchell growls. "You would do well to answer."

"They—they are infirm, sir," Gannett attempts. "Physically speaking, do they suffer? They suffer the—the ordinary ailments of the infirm."

"Physically speaking."

"Yes."

"And mentally?"

"I—" Gannett says. There is a long pause. "Yes. It is my belief that, mentally, they suffer."

"I see," says Winchell. He sounds more composed now, as though he has resolved himself to committing to a decision.

Gannett doesn't say anything.

"What can be done?" Winchell asks, after an interval.

"Sir?"

"I believe you heard the question. What can be done for these women?"

"What can be done—" Gannett tries. "I mean, with all due respect, sir, we are doing what can be done."

Winchell looks down, into the face of his daughter.

"We are—" Gannett continues. "We have given them a place where they are comfortable, as comfortable as possible, where they are fed, where their needs are met—"

"Allow me to speak plainly," Winchell says.

"Of—of course."

"The misfortune that has befallen these women—it is supernatural, is it not?"

"It is."

"And you—" Winchell says. "You are a man endowed with a significant prowess, with regard to the supernatural, correct? You purport to teach it, as a subject."

"I—that's correct."

"So, what I am asking, then, is perhaps not so much what can be done, but, rather, what can you do? This supernatural misfortune—certainly there is a way, there must be a way, for a man such as yourself to undo it, reverse it?"

"No, sir," Gannett says. "I cannot."

"Given enough time?" Winchell prompts. "Given enough resources?"

"No, sir," Gannett says. "The magics involved—they are—they are far beyond my ken. The condition of these girls—these women—is quite irreversible. The best we can do is attempt to alleviate their sufferings, in whatever small ways that we can muster."

Winchell nods. "I see," he says solemnly. "I see."

He lifts his hand, the pistol in it.

"Sir—" Artie has time to say.

"Lillian," Winchell says, training the pistol on the sleeping form in the bed. "I'm sorry."

He pulls the trigger.

The report seems enormous in the room: it echoes back from the eaves. Lillian's body jerks once in the bed. Artie screams, jumps back, colliding with Gannett, who is looking at Winchell in horror. A woman somewhere in the room begins to wail.

"My good man!" Gannett blurts before Winchell raises the pistol a second time and takes aim, over Artie's head—

Gannett begins to raise his hands—Artie can't tell whether he's trying to cast some protective spell or just protect his face from the bullet—it doesn't really matter which: there's no time for it to make any difference either way. Winchell squeezes the trigger, and another colossal bang rends the air. A hole opens between Gannett's eyes, and he staggers back a step. He stands there, teetering on his left foot, while his right foot drifts back and forth in the air, as though he were hesitating for a moment before stepping into a puddle at a curbside, angling for the shallowest spot, hoping merely not to ruin his shoe. And then he crumples backward, falling into Theodore's arms for a moment. But Theodore can't hold him, and the man's body slides down to the floor in a heap.

"No," Theodore says, falling to his knees. "No!" His voice cracks.

Winchell pays him no mind; he's busy fussing with the pistol in his hand. Two spent casings clink as they fall to the floor: Artie realizes, a moment too late, that he's reloading.

"Please, sir—" she manages. Her face is wet with tears, although she can't place in time any specific moment when she began to cry.

Winchell looks at her, his face grim, impassive. Then he looks across at Theodore, and then back at her again. His face contorts itself, struggles to contain a torrent of emotional energy. His lips move for a moment, but no words emerge.

"Oh, children—" he finally says, his face settling into an expression of unfathomable sadness. He looks, for a moment, as though he is preparing to extend a long, heartfelt apology. And then he places the gun in his mouth and pulls the trigger.

"No," Artie says as the sound of the shot resounds. "Oh, please, no." But her protestations go unheeded: no god elects to take this moment to intervene. Winchell drops, his eyes blank, his mouth slack: the tiny pistol drops from his hand and clatters to the floor, he slumps to one side, and all is still. The wailing woman's cry diminishes, down to a low whimper, the sound of a child recognizing that it won't be consoled.

Artie can't take any more. She covers her face with her hands and whirls toward Theodore, who has just climbed back to his feet moments ago: she presses into his chest; he's the nearest solid thing she can slam herself into. His arms come up and clutch her. She takes whatever animal comfort she can get from being in his grip and tries to return it: she clutches him back, holds his trembling, jerking frame. Surely, she thinks wildly, surely in a moment we will collect ourselves, one of us will collect ourselves and figure out what to do next, where to go from here. And then everything will be all right. Surely, then, everything will be all right.

Any moment now, she thinks. Any moment now, she thinks again as she sobs.

Outside, in the streets of Boston, the first snow of the season begins to fall. You can see it through the long row of windows: flakes whirling in the air. But neither Artie nor Theodore will notice this, not immediately. Not for some time.

PART THREE

JANUARY

1910

THE EXCAVATED
PRISON

19

Artie hadn't wanted to leave.

She hadn't felt that it was possible to leave. The only thing that seemed possible was to stay there, crouched down by Winchell's side, crying uncontrollably.

She'd stayed like that for a long time, until finally Theodore touched her gently on the shoulder. She'd looked up, into his tear-streaked face.

"I think—" was all he managed to get out, but Artie knew what he was getting at. She'd gotten up, wiped her eyes and her nose, straightened her suit.

"Yes," she'd said. "Let's go."

And they'd gone, leaving behind three dead bodies and a roomful of suffering women: they left them behind for whoever might arrive first, whether that be an investigator drawn by the sound of the gunfire or the night shift nurse who would be arriving to relieve Lucy. They just left, both of them steeling themselves to not look back. On their way out, Artie had grabbed the paperwork from the desk at the nurses' station: she hadn't been thinking clearly, really, and she still believed that there might be a mystery that she could fruitfully solve, something toward which the paperwork might count as a clue.

Three dead bodies. A triple shooting. And yet they both know that they shouldn't contact a police officer. To report the shooting would at best be pointless; at worst it might put them at risk. They both know what Briggs does to people who might learn about the thing in the pit, to people who start figuring out how they've been keeping it down there. He broke Winchell. He directed a man to abduct Lillian, Winchell's daughter, just because he knew it was the way to break him. So neither of them doubt whether Briggs would come after them if he knew who they were—if their names were locatable in a police record. Spivey might be dead, but, in the absence of any other plan, what choice does Briggs have other than to carry on, to keep feeding the thing, the damaged god, whatever it is? He's probably already enlisted someone else to do the snatching, Artie presumes, and there's no reason why he wouldn't target her to be the next person to be dragged down to the mouth of its violated tomb . . .

But Commissioner Jameson Briggs doesn't know who she is, or who Theodore is. That's what Artie told herself as she broke away from Theodore and hurried home in the night. Some attempt at reassurance. He doesn't know who they are, and he doesn't know that they've figured out the details of the conspiracy that he's assembled.

Everyone who knows that Artie and Theodore know those details is now dead.

Two days after the shootings, she met with Theodore for breakfast, and the two of them sifted through the materials she'd grabbed. The mood was solemn. They spoke as little as possible. Mixed in among the nightly log reports were some intake cards, and these felt promising: but they were able to access none of the joy that they once felt when first confronted with new mysteries, when presented with fresh clues. The clues no longer felt tantalizing and the work of unpacking those clues—sitting there, at the table, drinking coffee, sorting cards into chronological order—no longer felt like a pleasure.

What it felt like, instead, was a duty. She felt a duty to bring justice to those girls, left to die in that horrible room. Maybe there was something in this pile of paperwork, she told herself grimly, that would help her to singlehandedly ensure that Jameson Briggs would be thrown into his own prison.

But there wasn't. It only took her a few minutes to get the cards in order, and it didn't take much longer to discern the pattern in them. The earliest cards—two, both dated April 1909—document the intake of two girls: Dorothy Gannett, listed as such, followed by someone just listed as Alice. No last name. There's no follow-up card for a month, and then there's one dated May 1, listed as Bea. There are nine other cards, each about three weeks apart, but none include a last name, and the names that are there are clearly decoys. They proceed in a baldly artificial alphabetical order: Cora, then Doris, then Emily. Because she knows the timeline, she can determine that Lillian Winchell—intake late October—must be the woman listed here as Kate. There's a final woman listed, Laura, intake mid-November: the date matches the night that they saw Briggs at the pit, the night they followed him to Gannett's ward.

These are bits of knowledge: scraps that help, in minor ways, to clear up the picture. But the rest of the names offer up no such additional knowledge. They are utterly unyielding. They can barely even be counted as names: it is probably more fair to say that they're just words, scratched onto lines. Impenetrable. They may as well be blots of ink. It occured to her that the true names of these girls might, in fact, never have been known by any of the men involved in their capture and destruction—not Spivey, not Gannett, not Jameson Briggs. And certainly not by the thing in the pit.

This is a dead end, she thought. There's nothing in there to implicate Briggs. And there's nothing else in there to help her fulfill any other sort of duty, either: she'll never know who these girls are, she'll never figure out who their parents are, she'll never learn whether there wasn't someone—a mother, a father, a brother—she'll never be able to find those people, she'll never be able to tell them: I know what happened to her, the girl you've lost.

The realization crushed something inside her. She fought back a sudden urge to vomit. She got up from the table, her breakfast half finished, and left. Theodore, behind her, called her name, tried hastily to gather up the spread paperwork, but she didn't look back.

*

In December she didn't see Theodore. During that time she tried not to think about the destroyed girls, or the thing in the pit. The approach of the holidays helped, a little: she hadn't lost her job, and the store was thronged with shoppers, and it was possible, although not easy, to lock herself into the activity of helping them, one after the other. Stay smiling, remain pleasant, keep cheer in her voice.

She half expected, during this time, for Theodore to show up at her work, but he must have sensed that she needed some distance from the whole affair. She bought him a Christmas gift—a handkerchief, navy blue, dotted with stars—but they didn't see one another at Christmas, and she ended up leaving the kerchief on her bureau, in a wad, next to the dish holding the man's tooth, the tooth that fell out in October, the night the Shrieker was on the Common, four weeks after Jane, a few days before Kate.

She'd left her suit at Theodore's, and she misses it—she wants it—but she can't bring herself to visit him.

❦

It's only once they're in the New Year that she begins to feel ready to talk about it. She knows where Theodore usually has breakfast on Saturday, and on the first Saturday in January 1910, she wakes surprisingly early—she feels fully rested for the first time in weeks—and she has an extra hour before work that she wasn't expecting. The sun is coming up and the skies are clear. So she goes.

❦

She arrives at his table, takes a seat uninvited, startling him—he's concentrating on carefully navigating a forkful of drippy egg up to his mouth—but his look of surprise instantly gives way to his familiar smile.

"Artie!" he exclaims, dropping his fork back to the plate, the triangle of egg forgotten. "Happy New Year!"

"Happy New Year, Theodore," she replies, a bit wearily. But she smiles, too, not without reluctance. If she's to be totally honest, she'd have to admit that this is part of the reason she held back from visiting him earlier: she knew he'd be happy to see her, and she knew that she'd, in turn, feel happy to be seen. But on some level she wasn't ready to feel happy. To be happy, she knew, would mean that her grief would have to cede its position at center stage, and it has taken her some time to feel ready to let it do that, even for a moment, without feeling like she was betraying Professor Winchell, Lillian, the other destroyed girls. But maybe now, in a new year, in the clamor and warmth of this restaurant, with the smell of hot grease in the air and wintry light falling on the street outside, maybe she can permit happiness to have this moment. So she smiles.

"Do you still have my suit?" she asks as she takes a seat.

Theodore fastidiously blots his mouth with a napkin, nods. "Of course," he says, "of course! It's just been waiting for you to come by and retrieve it. I would have brought it to you, but—"

"Can I get it tonight? After work?"

"Certainly." He checks his watch, looks from it back to her, hopefully. "Do you have a bit of time? Before you need to run? Can I order you some breakfast?"

"Maybe just a cup of coffee."

"With pleasure," Theodore says.

It only takes a minute for the coffee to arrive. She spends most of that minute silent, looking out the window, considering that feeling of happiness as it flits away, considering that which rushes in to replace it. She catches Theodore looking at her a few times, an anticipatory eagerness in his eyes, but it doesn't take long for him to seemingly figure out that she'll talk again when she's ready: he returns to quietly working through his plate of eggs and beans.

"I got you a Christmas gift," she says finally.

"Oh?"

"A little something from Filene's," she says, fishing the hand kerchief out of her clutch. It's still rather crumpled and wrinkled, and she tries abashedly to shake it out, make it presentable.

"Oh, Artie," he says, taking it from her. "I love it." After holding it in his hands for a long time, admiring the pattern and the quality of the fabric, he smiles, tucks it into a pocket, and turns his attention to his rucksack. "Actually," he says, digging into one of its side pockets, "I got you a Christmas gift as well."

"Theodore," Artie says. "You needn't have."

He clucks his tongue at this rather feeble protestation, and emerges from his sack with a small box, cradled in his hand. Printed in tidy type on the lid are the words W. F. Woodman Co., Jewelers. For a moment Artie believes it might be a ring, or a necklace—an uneasy feeling, for some reason, accompanies this— but then she opens it and reveals a shining pocket watch, impossibly handsome and smart. She gives a small, sharp gasp of pleasure.

"I hope it's OK," Theodore says.

"Goodness, Theodore, it's perfect," she says, fishing it out of the box to get a feel for its weight in her hand.

"It is?"

"What could possibly be wrong with it?"

"They had it available in a chatelaine style also—something you could have worn at the waist? Which is, ah, more traditional. But I thought this style might work better with your—your suit. Which I was assuming you'd come to claim, when you were ready."

"Yes," Artie says, clasping the watch to her chest. "Oh, I love it."

Her coffee arrives. She returns the watch to the box for safe-keeping, and places the box in her clutch. Then she wraps her hands around the warmth of the mug, blows gently across the surface, sends steam across the table, waits for it to cool enough to drink.

"So," Theodore says.

"So," Artie says.

"How are you?"

Artie gives her coffee an exploratory sip; it's still too hot. "I'm . . . I'm OK," she says. "It's hard, though."

Theodore nods.

"I think the worst thing," she says, groping for a way to articulate something that she's spent some time trying to keep cloistered at the back of her mind, "is knowing that it's still going on. That they're going to take more girls and—and give them to that thing."

"We can't know that for sure," Theodore tries gently. "Spivey is dead—"

"Spivey is dead," Artie says, "sure. But Briggs isn't dead. You think he can't find some other two-bit lowlife willing to grab girls off the street in exchange for whatever favors Briggs might have to offer?"

"No," Theodore says. "No, I don't think that."

They're both quiet for a minute. Artie tries her coffee again, manages to get a full swallow of it this time.

"If they're still doing it," Theodore says, "they've done it again. Since we were there. It's been five weeks. I don't know of any indication that the Shrieker has emerged, so—"

"I was thinking about that too," Artie says. "It's hard to bear. Knowing that it's just—still happening. And there's nothing we can do about it."

"I've been investigating some options," Theodore says. "Some time ago I made the acquaintance of a man at the *Globe*, a one Mister Julius Roop. I've been thinking about calling upon him again. I wanted to discuss it with you first, so I haven't really made progress on it, but—if we could go to Roop with the facts that we have, with the paperwork that we have—if we could convince him that the story was true, then perhaps the *Globe* could help us to expose Briggs's malfeasance—put a stop to, to what's happening?"

Artie purses her lips thoughtfully. "The last time we met," she says, "when we went through the paperwork?"

"Yes," Theodore says.

"That was two days after—what happened in Gannett's ward. After the shootings."

"Yes."

"And you'd been looking in the paper," Artie says. "To see what the *Globe* was going to say about the shootings."

"Yes."

"But they hadn't printed anything."

"No."

"And—since then? Did they ever print anything?"

"No," Theodore says. "Not to my knowledge."

"Triple shooting," Artie says. "Death of beloved police investigator. By any measure that's a big story, isn't it?"

"Yes."

"So that raises the question: Is the *Globe* covering it up? Can the *Globe* be trusted?"

"I don't know," Theodore says. "Maybe they are covering it up. Or maybe it never got to them. Maybe Briggs just made sure no whisper of it ever escaped. It could have been done; the police aren't especially keen on talking to journalists to begin with. And I trust Roop; I believe he's a good man."

Artie takes a sip of coffee, holds the sip in her mouth for a moment before swallowing. There's hope in what Theodore says, a moment of hope; she allows herself to feel it. But the shine goes off the idea before the coffee in her mouth has even cooled. Briggs is a criminal, yes, a destroyer of lives; Artie wants to see him brought to justice, yes. But—something she's been thinking about, for the last month—handling Briggs doesn't really solve the real problem, the problem of the thing in the tunnel.

She swallows. Disconsolately: "Here's the thing, Theodore. What if they were right?"

Theodore frowns. "What do you mean?"

"What Gannett said. He said that what they were doing was— how did he put it? He said it wasn't a solution, it was—"

"A mechanism. To prevent worse things from happening."

"A bad option from an array of bad options," Artie says. "And so—what if they were right? What if what they were doing— what they are doing—is actually the best of all possible solutions?"

Theodore's face is very still. "You mustn't ask that," he says.

Artie looks down at the surface of the table, the whorled knots in the wood.

"Those girls—" Theodore tries.

Her eyes flick back up to him. "Yes, Theodore, I know. Don't think that a night has gone by this past month where I haven't thought about them, where I haven't thought about that horrible room. Don't think that a night has gone by when I haven't thought about whatever girl was next; the one we knew about but couldn't save. Every single night I'm thinking about them. Can you say the same?"

"Yes," he says, meeting her gaze. "I can."

She softens toward him, slightly, at that; she releases a ragged-edged sigh. "I'm just saying. We've inherited Gannett's problem. There's a thing down there that threatens us all. A god, a monster, whatever it is, we don't know. All we know is it's a thing that demands to be fed. We can get the help of your Mister Roop to tell the world about what this city has done to feed it, and, who knows, maybe we should. Maybe it'll help get Briggs brought to justice. But that doesn't make the thing down there go away. That doesn't get it back in its prison. As far as I know, the only thing that could possibly get it back in its prison is a chronomancer. And we don't know where to find one of those."

She drains the last of her coffee. She has to get to work. She and Theodore cast somewhat despairing, apologetic looks at one another before they part ways. She does her shift at the store, a blessed reprieve from having to think about this problem, and after work she retrieves her suit from Theodore. She doesn't stay to visit for long; it doesn't feel like there's much to say.

When she gets home she closes herself in her room and puts on the suit. She wants to be back in it; it's been too long. She puts on the suit, and she puts the beautiful new watch in its pocket. And then she sits there on the edge of her bed, the watch ticking next to her heart, and she thinks about the problem, and she replays the conversation she had with Theodore, and it's only then that she realizes that she does, in fact, know exactly where they can find a chronomancer.

20

"But Artie," Theodore says. "She can't help us. She's gone mad."

Artie is pacing Theodore's living room. She's wearing her suit so that she can think. She turns on her heel, points her finger at him.

"We were told that she'd gone mad, sure," Artie says. "By Gannett! But Gannett—he was a liar!"

Theodore raises his head to look uncertainly at her, from the settee where he is reclined. "I'm not sure he actually ever lied to us," he says.

"Are you kidding me? He sought to—to deceive the entire city!"

"Didn't he say that he wanted for there not to be a conspiracy? That he'd hoped to get the truth to a wider audience?"

Artie clucks her tongue at him by way of reproach.

Theodore lowers his head again, looks up at the ceiling. "Besides," he says, "Gannett is our primary source of information about this whole thing. Why would he tell us the truth about everything else but lie about that detail?"

"To—" Artie tries. "To protect her."

"Try again," Theodore says.

Artie turns a corner in her circuit of the room. "I feel like I'm onto something here," she says.

"With the idea that Dorothy Gannett might not be mad?" Theodore says. "Artie, my dear, it is unfortunate, but we are in a position where we have to trust what Gannett told us. If we decide we can't trust Gannett, then we're back to knowing nothing. If we disregard this one piece of information—"

"OK," says Artie. "OK. So we don't disregard the piece of information. Instead, we look at it a bit more closely. Dorothy Gannett is mad. But what does that mean, exactly?"

Theodore waits a moment. "What does it mean?" he asks finally.

"Well, that's just it," Artie says. "We don't really know, do we? Does it mean she's catatonic? Does it mean she can't form a sentence? Or does it just mean her faculties are clouded? I mean, take my own mother, for example."

Silence from Theodore. Her back is toward him so she can't see whatever his face might be doing. She stops for a moment in her pacing.

"Could you describe my mother as mad?" Artie says. "Yes, you could." She winces at this, caught off guard by the fact that it hurts to say this out loud. "And yet, some days—some days are better than others. Some days she's—almost well."

"Would you trust her," Theodore says, very softly, "to help you solve a problem?"

"I might," Artie snaps, "if we didn't have any other option." She begins to walk again.

"Well," Theodore says, "OK. Here's what we know. We know that Dorothy Gannett is mad enough that she's been put in her father's home for the mad, and mad enough that she hasn't left on her own volition."

"We assume she hasn't left," Artie says.

"You think she's left?"

"I'm just saying that we don't know. She could have gotten better."

"You've been in that place," Theodore says. "Did it strike you as the kind of place that one gets better in?"

Artie thinks back to the room, remembers its sounds, its smells. No, she thinks. But she doesn't say this. Instead, she turns a corner.

"I'm not really sure," Theodore says, "that what happened to Dorothy is the kind of thing that one's mind ever heals from. The shock . . . of aging so much, so fast . . ."

"But that's just it," Artie says.

"What is?"

"You're not sure."

She looks at Theodore, watches him weigh this.

"It's just," Artie says. "it's just that—we were in a room with the person who knows the most about this thing, the Shrieker, whatever they're calling it. We were in a room with the only person masterful enough to work the lock on the door that held this thing in place, and we didn't try to talk to her. We were in the room with her, and it didn't even occur to us to try to lay eyes on her. I think that was an oversight on our part. Would you agree?"

Theodore thinks it over. "I would agree," he says finally.

"And I think—I think that if we want to try to solve this problem—if we want to try to make that thing in the pit go away—then we have to get back in that room."

"OK," says Theodore. He sits up, swings his feet to the floor, blinks his eyes twice, claps his hands on his knees. "But how do we do that?"

"Whoever is at the nurses' station will try to stop us," Artie says. "At least one of the nurses has laid eyes on us before, the night that Winchell—the night of the shootings. And even if we were to encounter a different nurse, who didn't recognize us, I'm sure they wouldn't just let us casually waltz in."

"So we sneak in?" Theodore says. "We use the Cat's Approach?"

Almost in spite of herself, Artie smiles—it's been a while since she's thought of Theodore practicing magic. The thought leads, though, inexorably to her memories of Gannett's death, and her smile wanes.

"How is that going," she says as gently as she can muster. "After what happened to Gannett—I mean—it must have disrupted your studies."

"Well," Theodore says. "Yes and no." He gets a funny sort of look on his face: half smile, half embarrassed grimace.

"Yes and no?" Artie says. "What does that mean, exactly?"

"Well," Theodore says, "I have this." He cranes over to dig into a pile of books on an end table and emerges with a heavy tome, bound in cracked leather, which he drops into his lap.

"What," Artie asks, "is that?"

"It's a grimoire," Theodore says. "A—compendium. Of thieves' magic."

"Huh," Artie says. "Where did you get it?"

"Ah," Theodore says, looking a bit abashed. "Well. You remember how the School of Magic is protected by a ward?"

"I guess?" Artie says.

"You remember that I could get in by doing a secret knock," Theodore says.

"Yes."

"Well," Theodore says. "That's because Gannett sealed the building with a ward. The secret knock allows passage through that ward. Now, the ward—it's a strong one. It's still on the building. It didn't dispel upon Gannett's death. But what that means is—"

Artie's figured it out. "The secret knock still works."

"I thought I would try to see whether it did," Theodore says.

"And it does."

"Yes, it does."

"So you stole this book?" Artie says, delight creeping openly into her voice. Theodore's embarrassed smile widens.

"I just—I do still want to learn magic," he says. "If I can't learn it from the man, I'll learn it from his library."

"OK!" Artie says, unable to repress a grin. Then she turns thoughtful for a moment. "You should let me in there at some point," she says. "There are probably all sorts of clues lying about in there."

Theodore shrugs. "There's a lot of interesting stuff in there."

"Sure," Artie says, "but I want clues."

"OK," Theodore says. "But for now—back to the matter at hand. We were trying to decide whether or not to sneak in?"

"Oh, right," Artie says. She thinks it over for a minute.

"Well—I don't know. The Cat's Approach would be great if we could get upstairs and wanted to move around up there quietly, but it doesn't really help us in getting past whoever is at the nurses' station. Do you think there's a back way in? A service door?"

"I'm not sure," Theodore says. "There are second-story windows looking in to the ward . . ."

"Sure," Artie says, "but how would we get up to a second-story window?" They both muse unhappily on the question for a moment. Visions of getting up to the roof (somehow) and having Theodore lower her down on a rope (or something) flit through her mind: these visions have an appealing heroic flair about them, which recommends them, but that flair disintegrates the second she tries to imagine going through the actual actions, to imagine letting herself be dangled above the street.

She sighs, drops down into the armchair that faces Theodore's settee. She looks over at him, her eyes eventually coming to rest on the book that he has cradled in his lap. "Is there anything in there that would help?" she asks, indicating the book with a nod. "Some spell? That would enable you to scale walls?"

"You know," Theodore says, "I think there is? But that—that's beyond my level. It would take me months to get to a place where I could even begin to learn it, and without instruction—" He shakes his head.

It doesn't make much sense, anyway. Even if they made it to the window—either by lowering themselves down or by magically creeping their way up—what if it were locked? Would she be expected to just batter at the glass, smash her way in? There's no possible amount of catlike sneaking that would keep that disguised.

"So it's back to going in through the front," she says.

A conflicted look passes over Theodore's face. "I'm not the strongest person," he says. "But I could probably overpower a nurse—"

"No," Artie says, sharply. "I don't want to hurt anybody. There has been enough suffering—there have been enough suffering women—involved in this mess already. I don't want to do more harm."

"Even if it were part of taking steps to stop this problem? You could argue that there's a greater good to be considered—"

"No," Artie says. "That's the kind of logic that Gannett used, that Briggs used—that some people's lives were OK to destroy."

"To protect the city, though."

"That doesn't matter," Artie says. "I mean, yes, I understand why they did it, but nobody—no man—should put themselves in the position of being able to choose who gets to be protected and who has to be sacrificed. Who has to suffer. That's wrong. If you grant yourself the moral authority to start grabbing nurses and—doing what? Wrestling them down to the ground? Then you're just a thug, no better than Spivey."

Theodore nods at this, a bit glumly.

"What we need—" Artie says, rubbing her temples. "What we need is some way to just take the nurse out of the picture, painlessly."

"Like a distraction?" Theodore says. "Something that could get her to leave her station?"

"Yes, a distraction," Artie says, "or—you know what I wish we had?"

"What's that?"

"You remember when Winchell barged up to Gannett? On the stage, at the School of Magic?"

"Yes?"

"Gannett had some pinch of, like, fairy dust. Magic powder or something. He blew a bit of it into Winchell's face and Winchell just—"

"Fell asleep."

"It didn't hurt him," Artie says. "It didn't cause him to suffer. He just—fell asleep. You can get us into the School of Magic, right?"

"Well," Theodore says. He hesitates.

"We could just go in and take a look around," Artie says.

"I already did that," Theodore says.

"Yeah, but we could go in and see if there's a leftover supply of that magic dust. That way we could—"

"Artie," Theodore says. The guilty smile again. "I already did that."

"What?"

Theodore gestures helplessly. "I knew that some of the spells in the grimoire require ingredients for their proper preparation. A lot of those ingredients are hard to find, and I knew that one place I could find them was Gannett's study. So I—I gathered a few necessities and a few other things that—looked interesting."

"Theodore!" Artie jumps back to her feet, out of the armchair. "You have the dust?"

"I do," Theodore says. "A small amount, just a few pinches, in an envelope. But I must caution you—"

"That's it," Artie says. "That's our way in."

"I must caution you," Theodore says in a slightly sterner tone of voice, "that we're playing here with magic that I don't really understand."

"OK," says Artie. She turns in a circle suddenly, a bit giddy at having found what she thinks of as a solution.

"So don't get too excited, in other words," Theodore says.

Artie frowns. "Why not?" she says.

"The powder might not even work in the hands of someone who can't wield it correctly," Theodore says. "We don't know if it worked because Gannett enchanted it in advance, or if it worked because of something particular about the way he flung it, or the way he drew it out of his pocket—it could be anything. If he enchanted it in advance, we don't know how often it might need to be re-enchanted, or if the enchantment still works after his death—we don't know anything."

"Well," Artie says, "the ward on his building still works after his death, right?"

Theodore considers this. "That's true."

"So we know that when Gannett died, his enchantments didn't all die with him."

"I suppose not," Theodore says. "But we don't know if an enchantment on a building works the same as an enchantment on a dose of powder—"

"OK," Artie says. "Get up."

Theodore blinks.

"Get up," she says. "Get your envelope. We'll give it a test."

Theodore puts the grimoire back on the end table, struggles to his feet. "Well," he says, making his way to his crowded desk in the corner of the room, "I'm not so sure that this is—"

"You want to learn magic, don't you?" Artie says as he bends over the desk, rummaging.

"Yes," he says.

"'If I can't learn it from the man, I'll learn it from the man's stuff,'" she says. "That's what you said, isn't it?"

"Essentially," Theodore says, a note of weariness in his voice. He rises to his full height again, a small glassine envelope in his hand. He holds it up to the gaslight uncertainly.

"Then this is your chance," she says. "Think of this as practice."

"What would you have me do, exactly?" Theodore asks as he crosses back over to where she stands.

"I would have you put me to sleep," she says. "Knock me out. Just to test it."

She positions herself at the end of the settee, tries to maneuver herself into the right spot for falling backward onto it, then she looks back up at Theodore. His face is pained, uncertain. "I'm really not sure this is safe," he says.

"You said yourself that probably nothing was going to happen," Artie says.

"That's—not what I said," Theodore says. But his fingers delve into the envelope, and they emerge with a pinch of the stuff.

"Just—toss it right at me," she says, attempting to sound more brave than she really feels. "Oh, and—keep an eye on your watch. Time this. If we know how long I'm asleep for, we'll have at least a rough idea of how long we might have to try talking to Dorothy."

Theodore looks at the bit of powder between his fingers, regards it suspiciously. He looks up at her: the suspicious expression doesn't change. "Are you sure about this?" he asks.

Is she sure about this? How could she be? Among other concerns, it suddenly occurs to her that Winchell was a big man, with a hundred pounds or more on her. The dust knocked him out for just a few minutes: she expects—hopes, actually—that it'll knock her out for longer—they'll need the time—but not too much longer. She doesn't want to be in a coma. She's heard the story of Rip van Winkle: she doesn't want to wake up to find twenty years have passed.

But if it isn't safe—if it causes her to suffer—she doesn't want to use it on a nurse either. That's part of what she wants to test here. And to do that, she has to be brave.

You're not a person who isn't brave, she tells herself.

She sets her jaw, smooths the front of her suit jacket with the edges of her hands. It's now or never.

"I'm sure," she says. "Do it."

21

She comes to. She's on her back, on the settee, looking up into Theodore's face; he's looking down, into hers, with concern.

"Did it work?" she asks.

"I think so?" Theodore says. "I'd say so? How are you feeling?"

How is she feeling? She tries to assess. She pushes herself up into a half-seated position, wipes a bit of drool from the corner of her mouth with the back of her hand. "I'm OK," she says. "I think." She blinks experimentally. "How long was I out?"

"Fifteen minutes, give or take," Theodore says, taking a glance at the clock on the wall.

So they could knock out a nurse—assuming she was around Artie's size—for fifteen minutes. That's a bit longer than Winchell was out, when he was hit with the dust, so that's good. It's still not a lot of time. It's enough time, though, to get upstairs, to find Dorothy Gannett's bed, and to figure out whether she can speak, can hear, can understand.

But—then what? Artie wants to figure out what Dorothy knows about the Shrieker, to figure out whether it can be stopped, and, if so, how. But she can't imagine opening the conversation with that question. She can't imagine, really, how the conversation will go at all.

You don't have to imagine it, she tells herself. You just need to do it.

Easy enough as a thing to say. But it doesn't quite dispel the question. She and Theodore agree to wait forty-eight hours before attempting to enter Gannett's secret facility—mostly to see if any side effects emerge from Artie having inhaled the knockout dust; they still really want to be certain that they don't do anything that might inadvertently cause lasting harm to the nurse. So Artie has two days to wait, and although she's able to go through the motions of those days, working her shifts at the store as normal, her mind restlessly turns over the question of what she will say, picks at the edges of the question as though it were a scab on her knee.

What do you say to a person who is crazy and broken? It's not as though Artie hasn't had experience with trying to do this: She knows what it's like to try to get through a conversation with her own mother; she knows how hard it is to get anywhere when her mother is in the grip of an episode. And Artie has gotten no better at this, recently, even though she now has more opportunities to try, what with winter having settled over the city. In the summer or the fall she could spend some of her evenings just taking walks or loitering around on the streets, which might earn her some suspicious looks after a certain hour but at least allowed her to delay going home. Now the cold forces her, more nights than not, to go home while her parents are still awake.

It's not all bad: her mother is still well enough to cook, so there's at least the pleasure of a warm meal to be had, unifying the family around the common table. Minus Zeb of course. Wrapping her hands around a hot bowl of stew on a cold night still brings her the same feelings of comfort as it brought her when she was a child. But there's nothing happening around that table that could really be called a conversation. Neither her mother nor her father ask her how work was, or where she's been on the nights that she's been over at Theodore's, and she's reluctant to offer that information unprompted. Her father asks no questions of her mother, her mother asks no questions of her father, and Artie asks no questions of either of them. It ends up feeling like three strangers dining at the same table. So if she can't start up a conversation with these people—her own family— she can't begin to think of how she'll start up a conversation with a stranger, a shattered girl, slowly dying in a bed in a secret ward.

She thinks of this over dinner the night before she and Theodore plan to meet, spooning stew into her mouth, chewing chunks of turnip, looking sidelong at her mother and her father, contemplating.

Maybe it's easier, she tells herself, to talk to strangers: when she's at Durgin-Park, having breakfast, somebody wants to strike up a conversation half the time, even if it's just about the weather. The flow of talk travels easily across the communal table. And the other half of the time, the days when no one wants to talk? At least she doesn't have to look at the collection of silent people, lost in their own thoughts, and think, This is what my family has become. There's not that sense of dejection. Anyone could start talking at any time, and you wouldn't have to shift the accumulated weight of weeks and months of things gone unsaid. Maybe she'll try talking to Dorothy and it will be easy.

But talking to Dorothy—even if she's well enough to understand—isn't going to be like talking about the weather. She needs to talk to Dorothy about the safety of the city, about matters of life and death. She needs to talk to Dorothy about chronomancy, which—she barely even understands what that is. Even if Dorothy is lucid, even if she'd spent weeks on her back in that ward coming up with a plan for how to contain the Shrieker again, Artie doesn't even know how to start asking about what that plan might be. She knows it's not that easy to do even a basic spell—Theodore's been working for months to learn his—so even if Dorothy knew some spell that could work, and was willing to explain it to Artie step by step—even then!—she can't imagine—

You're getting ahead of yourself, Artie thinks, setting her jaw. She sops the last of her stew up with a hunk of bread. You don't have to imagine it, she tells herself once again. You just need to show up and do it.

✶

And so, the next night, she shows up. She arrives at Theodore's place after her work shift, changes into her suit. She looks at herself in the mirror and is surprised, for a moment, to note that she looks how she wants herself to look. That she matches, somehow, her mental image of herself. And aside from her nervous energy, which hasn't dissipated over the last forty-eight hours, she feels good. She heads downstairs, feeling invigorated, alert. Inhaling Gannett's dust doesn't seem to have caused any lingering effects—in fact, if you looked at the two of them, there in the foyer, making their final preparations before embarking, you might think that Theodore had been the one knocked out: he's looking unusually pale, weary, the lines in his face drawn long.

"Are you sure you want to do this?" she asks as he's struggling into his overcoat. He pauses, one arm in the coat and one arm out, and he purses his lips for a moment, looking deliberative, but then he gives a single grim nod of assent. This rattles Artie's sense of determination: she'd expected him to be his normal, unfailingly enthusiastic self tonight, and she wonders if that expectation helped undergird her resolve.

There's nothing to be done for it except continue on. They leave Theodore's home, make their way through the steel-gray night, heading toward Gannett's building. They could hire a cab—it's cold out—but it's not that long of a walk, and they can use the time to go over the plan one more time. Keeping their heads down against the wind, they quietly rehash the details. Theodore holds the dust: he's going to be the one to approach the door while Artie stays back, out of sight. He'll knock, the nurse will answer, Theodore will use the dust and she'll go under, opening up their fifteen-minute window. Artie will enter, head upstairs, while Theodore waits with the nurse, both to keep an eye on her safety and also to warn Artie should she begin to wake up unexpectedly, before they're both safely out of there.

"I don't think it'll take fifteen minutes," Artie says, her doubt having crept back in. "I'm going to go up there, try to say something to her, and she won't respond, and then we can get back out. It'll take two minutes. That's all."

Theodore nods again. "Yes," he says. "You're probably right. Still, you'll have more time if you need it."

"Probably," Artie says.

"Probably," Theodore says.

And with that, they seem to be out of things to say. It's not long before they reach the alley, and they turn in and approach the door leading to Gannett's ward. Artie scouts ahead, looking for a good place where she can watch what happens while still staying out of view. She settles finally on a shallow niche of shadow across the street, near the newspaper building's back entrance but not so close that she might be errantly stumbled upon by a journalist stepping out to leave for the night.

When she returns to Theodore, she finds him with the tiny envelope of dust in his hands, turning it this way and that. He prods the ground uneasily with the toe of his shoe.

"You know," he says, "what we're doing here is a crime."

"I know," Artie says.

"At the very minimum the police would consider it assault," he continues, his voice low. "And given that we're using a magical substance? Use of a magical substance to facilitate a crime—that carries with it some very stiff penalties—"

"It's worse than that, Theodore," Artie says.

He stares at her blankly.

"I mean, think of what happened to Winchell. Think of what happened to Winchell's daughter. Remember that she was sacrificed just because Winchell got too close to figuring out what Briggs and Gannett were doing. We know that Briggs is willing to silence people. If they catch us in there, they're not just going to send us to jail. In jail we could threaten to talk, to tell the story." She pauses, reflecting on this unhappily. "I don't know what they'd do to you, exactly—your parents are rich enough that they might raise some trouble if you disappeared—but me? My dad is a laborer, and my mom is losing her mind. They don't have the capacity to raise that kind of trouble, the kind that might stick. They might not even try. They don't talk to me. My brother has disappeared and I think they half expect that I'm going to disappear any day now. You remember what Gannett said: they're looking for girls no one would miss. So that's what would happen to me. I'd be next in line to get fed to that thing. There'd be nothing left of me but a made-up name on an intake card."

"You don't know that," Theodore says.

"Maybe you don't know that," Artie says, a bit more sharply than she perhaps intends.

Theodore falls into a silence.

"Look," Artie says, after a moment. "You don't have to do this with me, if you don't want to. I think our plan makes sense—having both of us—but you can give me the dust and I can do it myself. It'll probably be OK. I'll probably just be in there for two minutes."

"Probably," Theodore says.

"Probably," Artie says. "It's just—I'm doing this. I'll take the risk. I just need to know. If there's anything that she knows that could help us solve this problem. If there's any chance at all that she knows something. I just want to be able to say that I followed every lead. It's what—it's what Winchell would have done. I want to be able to say that I investigated it as far as I could."

"I get it," Theodore says.

"If I go in there by myself," Artie says, "and I get caught—there are—there are still things you could do. You could talk to that re-porter—what was his name? Roop? You could tell him what you know and you could make sure that my—that I was investigated."

"No," Theodore says. "I get it. I'm with you. We're doing this together."

"OK," Artie says.

"Are you ready?" Theodore says.

"Yes," Artie says, "I am."

*

For all her bold talk—all her claims of I'm doing this, I'm going in—she still suspects that the plan won't work, that something will happen to thwart them. As she watches Theodore cross the street, she realizes that she's braced, fully braced, for him to lose his nerve. But he doesn't.

As he reaches the door, a pinch of dust held between his fingers—as he raises his hand to knock—she realizes that she's braced for his knock to go unanswered. But it doesn't. A nurse answers the door—Artie can't see her face, but she can infer puz-zlement from the nurse's stance—and Theodore flicks his pinch toward her. She slumps toward the doorframe: Theodore reaches out to catch her, lowers her gently to the floor—and Artie doesn't move. She's stuck; stupefied, caught off guard by the success of this first stage.

Theodore, in the doorway, turns to look at her; tries to beckon her by yanking his head in the direction she's supposed to go. Inward.

Go, she tells herself, go. You have fifteen minutes.

OK. She blinks. She closes her mouth, which has been hanging open in something like shock. She reaches backward: her fingertips find the cold stone of the wall behind her. She gives herself a push.

She's crossing the street. Gathering speed. She's in the intake room, Theodore hastily closing the door behind her. The room is narrow, and the nurse has been lain diagonally in the available space: some impulse in Artie threatens to balk at the unseemly act of stepping over the prone woman. But she's willful now, finally: she does it without breaking stride.

"If she starts to wake up—" Artie says over her shoulder.

"Yes," Theodore says. "I'll call you."

"Right away."

"Yes."

OK, then. Artie climbs the stairs. She reaches the landing, makes the turn, climbs the next flight. And then she's in the room, the ward.

She knows which bed is Dorothy's: Dorothy's intake card, among the documents she pilfered last time she was here, had a bed number listed on it, and she'd compared it against a diagram of the room layout; she knows how many beds she needs to count on her left before she will find Dorothy, in a bed on her right.

She keeps her eyes focused ahead. She doesn't look at the bed where Winchell's daughter died. She doesn't look at the floor, doesn't try to see if she can discern where Gannett and Winchell's bodies fell, whether there's some stain left there for her to perceive—some accusatory mark that might not be there if she'd acted faster, been better—

She stays focused. She doesn't look. She passes four beds.

She turns, and looks down into the face of Dorothy Gannett, the greatest chronomancer the world has ever seen.

Dorothy's eyes, sunken deep in her skull, are closed. Her eyelids delicate, like crepe.

"Dorothy," Artie says, her voice nearly a whisper. She tries again, a little bit louder: "Dorothy Gannett." She watches Dorothy's delicate eyelids, trying to see if they issue up any sign, just a twitch, any sign that she can hear.

Artie wants to ask: Can you hear me?

Artie wants to ask: Can you help us?

But Artie closes her eyes, and she says something else entirely, something that comes unbidden.

She says "I'm sorry."

She turns her face to the ceiling, and the words come in a rush. She says "I know what happened to you, and I just wanted to say I am sorry. I don't know if anyone has said that to you before, but—someone should have. I'm sorry for what happened to you, and I'm sorry that no one has been able to stop it from happening to other people, from happening to these other women. That's what I'm trying to do—I'm trying to stop the thing down there. Not to hide it, not to appease it, but to stop it. But I don't know how. And—it's not my fault, but I'm sorry anyway, I'm sorry that I haven't stopped it, that no one has stopped it, and that because of that—because of that you've lost your father, too, you've lost your father and I've lost my teacher and it's just, it's just going to go on. No one knows how to stop it, and no one knows how to help, and I just wanted you to hear someone say that it's wrong, that someone should have figured it out by now, and someone should apologize for the fact that we haven't figured it out, the stupid human idiocy of it, and that's me, I guess I'm the person, offering that apology, to you, because you deserve to hear it."

She looks down. Dorothy's eyes are open, fixed on Artie.

Artie starts, takes a step backward. She's alive, Artie thinks, in a state of alarm, Dorothy Gannett is alive, but this isn't really what she means; she always knew Dorothy was alive, no surprise there, so she must instead mean Dorothy Gannett is awake, that must be the thing that startled her. Except that isn't really it either, she realizes. What she really is reacting to is the fact that Dorothy Gannett is alert. Those eyes: They didn't look cloudy or unfocused. They looked alert. Artie steels herself, cautiously steps back up to the bedside, returns the gaze. Dorothy peers at her with a keenness, a probing intelligence. There's nothing in those eyes that looks insane.

And then, as if exhausted from the effort, Dorothy's eyes sag shut again. A pang goes off within Artie: maybe she only had this one moment, and maybe it's now over: maybe she's lost Dorothy forever. But no. Dorothy's lips are moving: she's struggling to speak. Artie remains very quiet.

"You're here," Dorothy says, and then the rasp of her voice descends into coughing. It takes what feels like a long time for the coughing to subside, and Artie feels the push and pull of warring impulses urging her to do something, to help this struggling old woman in some way. But she just waits, and eventually Dorothy is able to try again. "You're here because you want to stop that thing," she says. "The thing in the tunnel."

"The Shrieker," Artie says. "Yes."

Dorothy gives her head one curt shake. "It can't be stopped," she says.

"Oh," Artie says. "Then—" What she wants to say is, Then we've lost, but she can't. She's felt precariously poised over a pit of despair for some time now, for weeks; saying those words would tear away whatever platform keeps her suspended there, in the air, and she would drop. How far down she would fall she does not know.

"The thing in the tunnel," Dorothy says again. "It's"—she frowns, her brow knits, her face contorts, revealing something like disgusted effort—"it's a product of time itself. To stop it— to properly stop it—to kill it—you'd need to slay time—that isn't possible."

"I don't understand," Artie says. She feels as though she may burst into tears.

The effort on Dorothy's face intensifies. "The thing is a-a-an—an aspect of time made manifest. Personified. Except it's not a person. A god. A manifestation of a god of time."

"Saturn," Artie says, remembering.

Dorothy's eyes snap open. "Yes," she says sharply.

I heard this from your father, Artie wants to say, but she hesitates. Gannett was shot in this very room, and Artie doesn't want to stir this up if she doesn't have to.

"Saturn," Dorothy says. She seems to grow tired again: her eyes droop, but don't fully close. "The devourer of children."

"But why—" Artie struggles to formulate the question. "What's happening right now isn't time operating as normal. It's like—time has gone wrong. The Shrieker—it's in agony? It's consuming time—aging people—it aged you—but that's not right, that's not how time is supposed to work."

"No." Dorothy shakes her head. "No. It's—deranged. A mad fragment of time. That's why—that's why the prison. They made the prison to contain it. They couldn't stop it but they could contain it—put it in a box and move it—"

"Who did?" Artie asks. "Who made the prison?"

Dorothy shakes her head. "Don't know," she says. "People. People in a different time. They put it in a box, moved it here."

"Could we—is there a way to move it back? Even if that wouldn't properly stop it—"

"Not back," Dorothy says. "Not properly back. Don't know enough about where it came from. But away."

"Away to where?"

"Forward. Forward in time." Dorothy frowns, her eyes close, it looks as though she is trying to recall a fleeting dream. "Underwater."

"We could move it underwater?"

"In the future. The city. Underwater."

The city will be underwater in the future? Artie doesn't know what this means, but before she can ask, Dorothy continues: "That wouldn't stop it," she says, "still wouldn't stop it. But people couldn't find it, there."

Artie has questions—but she's also starting to feel like they're running out of time. She doesn't know how much of her fifteen minutes she's used up. Put the thing underwater, where it can't get to people: that sounds good enough to her. What they need is a plan.

"How?" Artie asks.

"Magic," Dorothy says. Her eyes open again. "Chronomancy."

"I don't—" Artie says. "I have a friend who can do magic—he studied with—" Artie bites back the words "your father," shakes her head to dislodge the thought. "He's been studying. But he can only do one spell—he can't do chronomancy."

"I can prepare the spell," says Dorothy. "I'll need—downstairs, there's paper, pencils?"

"I have those things," Artie says, holding up her investigator's notebook.

Dorothy nods. "Put them under the mattress for now," she says. "So the nurses won't see."

Artie does.

"I can prepare an incantation," Dorothy says. "For your friend to read. I'll also need something—an object—a timepiece?"

Artie pats the pockets of her suit. The pocket watch is there; she fishes it out. "Will this work?" she asks, lowering it into Dorothy's weathered hand.

Dorothy examines it with the sharp eye of an appraiser. She flips it over as though expecting to find an engraving on the back. "Yes," she says. "This will work." Artie secretes it away under the mattress, with the investigator's pad.

"I don't have much time left," Artie says. "How will—"

"Come to the street tomorrow night," Dorothy says. "I can stand. I can walk a short distance. I've been practicing; the nurses don't know that. I can't yet manage the stairs"—she smiles bitterly—"but I can get to the window. If you're waiting there, I will drop the notebook and the charm—your timepiece—down to you."

"OK," Artie says.

"It is imperative that you and your friend work quickly," Dorothy says. "Once the charmed timepiece leaves my possession, it will immediately begin to lose potency. Your odds of success will improve if you go to the tunnel right away."

"Oh," Artie said. She hadn't quite realized that doing the spell would need to be done in the tunnel, down where the Shrieker is. She'd maybe hoped that it could be done from the safety of Theodore's apartment. "It's—that's dangerous," she says, almost without really intending to.

"Yes," Dorothy says without hesitation. "The Shrieker—it won't want to go. It will try to stop you. Or—your friend. When he starts to do the spell, though, I'll know. I can try to aid from afar. Send some of my power through him."

"OK," Artie says. "And—that'll work?"

For the first time, Dorothy grins, and Artie can see, emerging from deep within the shell of the lined and withered face, the irrepressible expression of a sixteen-year-old girl who has found herself on the wrong end of an impossible situation, but who still, despite everything, remains spirited.

"I have absolutely no idea," Dorothy says.

22

"L et's go," Artie says, hurrying down the stairs.

Theodore, crouched down by the nurse's side, looks up at her, looks at his watch, looks up at her again.

"Ten minutes," he says. "Were you able to talk to her? Was she responsive?"

"Yes," Artie says, "and yes. I think she can help us. But—come on. It's important that we get out of here." She indicates the prone nurse with a curt nod of her head. "We don't want to be here when the nurse wakes up, remember? The plan was for us to get out the door and into a cab, get out of the area so that we're not still wandering about on the street when she decides to go looking for the police—"

"Yes," Theodore says, blinking back to the reality of the situation. "Yes, of course." He struggles back to his feet.

"You're distinctive looking, you know," Artie says. "That nurse will be able to identify you if we're still—"

"Yes," Theodore says. "I'm ready."

Artie pushes the heavy door open, and the two of them emerge into the night. Artie feels flushed, riddled with adrenaline: she can barely feel the cold air. They stumble down the two stairs and turn right, walking briskly until they're out of the alley and back on the main avenue. There are a few other people out at this hour, but not enough: their bodies, even taken together, do not form a crowd that they can blend into. Artie cranes her head this way and that, scanning the street for the familiar form of an available cab.

She sees nothing, save for a few coughing motorcars. They keep their heads down and they keep walking.

"She wants us back here," Artie says. "Tomorrow night."

She can hear Theodore's surprise, somehow, though he doesn't say anything.

"She says—she says we can stop it. The thing that's in the tunnel."

"How?" Theodore says. "Gannett told us that the city sent men down there with guns, trying to kill it—"

"It's not—" Artie says. "It's not that we would kill it. She said we couldn't kill it. That it would be—" She tries to remember exactly what it was that Dorothy said. "That it would be like trying to slay time itself."

"What?"

Artie frowns to herself. It does sound a little incoherent, in her retelling—maybe she misjudged when she decided that Dorothy Gannett was sane. But no. Dorothy's voice had been raspy, feeble, and her sentences didn't always begin and end where they should, but Artie remembers the alertness, the clarity in her eyes. All the same, Artie begins to worry—if she can't recount the conversation in a way that sounds sensible, she runs the risk of shaking Theodore's faith, and if Theodore backs out, then there is no way forward.

She continues: "She said we can't kill it. But we can stop it. We can move it. Move it through time."

A pause. "I have some questions about that," Theodore says.

"I do too," Artie says. "But I only had a few minutes. We had to use the time we had to make a plan."

"And did you? Make a plan?"

"Yes."

"OK," Theodore says. "So—what is it?"

They turn a corner. The wind bites harshly at their faces for a moment. Artie, squinting, looks for carriages, wondering whether the nurse is awake yet, wondering how much time they have.

"Dorothy is preparing a spell," Artie says, "for you to cast. We come back here tomorrow night, at ten. She will get to a window and drop some materials down to us, including an incantation that you'll be reading. From there, we go over to the pit, and we go down into the tunnel. You do the spell, and it'll send the Shrieker away."

"We'll go in the tunnel?" Theodore asks.

Artie thinks of some way that she could sugarcoat this, but can't, in the end, come up with anything. "Yes," she says.

Theodore is silent for a moment.

"Artie," he says finally.

"I know."

"Gannett said that when they sent men down there, with guns, that the Shrieker knew they were coming and—"

"I know," Artie says again. "I just—I don't have a better idea. This is the best shot we have."

"OK," Theodore says, after a pause. And then they're both silent for a bit.

Finally, Artie sees the shape of a carriage beneath a streetlight, though it's still some ways ahead. She reaches out, tugs Theodore's sleeve, which seems to stir him from his reverie. They pick up the pace of their stride while still trying to look as inconspicuous as possible to other people on the street.

"OK," Theodore says. "And what about at the pit? Last time we were there we were spotted by that policeman. He had a service revolver. If the entrance is guarded again, and I see no reason to believe that it won't be, we'll have to get around that problem. We're almost out of the dust, and even if I could get more I don't think I could get close enough to knock him out."

"Well," Artie says. "I thought about that. I think I might have a solution."

They've reached the carriage at last. Artie looks up at the driver.

"Good evening, sir," Artie says, deepening her voice, hoping she'll be taken as a man. "Would you kindly take us to Long Wharf?"

The carriage driver looks down at her. "It's a bit rough there, this time of night." She can't tell if he's saying this because he assumes she's a woman, or if he'd say that to just anyone.

"Yes, sir," Artie says, regardless. "It is."

*

They disembark onto a cold, wet curb facing the bay. It's too dark to see the water, but they can hear it crashing against the wharf's pilings.

A bit rough here, at this time of night: Artie replays the phrase in her mind. The driver's words; her assumption: if true, it shouldn't take long to spot people engaged in some sort of disreputable activity. And indeed it doesn't. All they need to do is look one way, then the other, and Artie spots a narrow alley between two buildings, a weather-beaten saloon and a brick warehouse. Long shadows dance on the brick, thrown by the bodies of men huddled in some activity around a fire. Artie thinks: crime.

It's not lost on her, as she approaches the men, how much has changed since the start of all this. At the start of all this, three months ago, she wanted to understand crime—understand it as a system. That's why she went to the Evening Institute for Young Men in the first place. She wouldn't say that she understands it completely—in fact, she feels certain now that you could study it for a lifetime and still not understand it completely—but she understands it much better than she did three months ago, enough to spot it in the streetscape.

At the mouth of the alley now. The fire is burning in a small zinc pail, the men gathered around a dice game, some crouched, some sitting on orange crates. A small pile of crumpled money, held in place against the wind by a broken half of a brick. A bottle of alcohol, changing hands.

It's frightening, and her fear grows with each additional step she takes. It's not hard for her to imagine that the men could hurt her, and she can't allow herself to believe that Theodore offers anything in the way of protection. There's a rotting wooden cart at the far end of the alley and it summons the sickening memory of Spivey grabbing that woman in the green parasol, choking her with a wire snare, wrestling her down into the cart's dank interior. It's not hard to imagine that these men could do the same to her. Take her away, make her disappear, God knows what would happen to her. Or they could just hurt her, right now, right here in the space of the alley. She remembers the fish knife in Spivey's hand, slashing at her face. There's not a man in this crowd who looks like he might not be ready to slide a blade out of some greasy pocket.

She's not just afraid. She's also weary. Weary of feeling afraid, of feeling disposable; weary of the threat of men, in their groups, whether they be huddled around a fire at Long Wharf, gambling for a few bucks, or gathered in a room at City Hall, deciding who to sacrifice to the god under the streets. She feels almost too weary to move. And yet. Within the heavy ashes of that weariness, something burns, unsmothered. A filament. Bright, twisting. An anger. She remembers not just Spivey's knife slashing at her face, but the cobblestone that she hefted into his. How it felt to see him crumple.

She remembers this same filament burning in her when she interrogated Spivey in the oyster saloon, not far from here, the way she was able to frighten him, shake him, break him down, just by looking him in the face and asking the right questions, saying the right words. The filament burns within her and it makes her feel wild. They're not strong, these men, the wild part of her says. They're a house of cards. Push them even a little, and they'll just fall down.

"Hey," she says.

The men in the alley turn their heads to look at her. One man, wearing a shapeless hat, gathers the dice swiftly into his cupped hands, sneers, then spits suddenly into the flames in the pail.

"What do you want," he says. She can somehow feel Theodore, behind her, tensing up. She hopes he doesn't speak.

"I'm looking for Zeb Quick," she says, before the silence can go on for too long. A flicker in the man's eyes. "I won't insult you by asking whether you know who he is. I want to speak with him tonight."

"Who knows where he is, at this hour," says the man.

"One of you does, I'd wager," says Artie.

"Find him yourself," says the man. He begins to shake the dice in his hand, turning away from her.

"I will, if I have to," says Artie. The man doesn't look at her; she raises her voice a little. "But I can guarantee you he's going to want to speak with me as well. For the next hour, my associate and I will be in the saloon, right here, waiting. That's a piece of news that will be of considerable interest to Zeb Quick, and I expect he'll look favorably upon whoever is the first to get it to him—if they get it to him in time."

Another young man, little more than a boy, really, at the edge of the ring, climbs to his feet. "I'll do it," he says, his voice high, his face uncertain.

The man in the hat glowers in the boy's direction. "Angus," says the man, low: a growled caution. An apologetic look crosses the boy's—Angus's—face, but the offer doesn't appear to be withdrawn. He keeps on standing, and the man in the hat keeps on glowering. Artie wonders whether the moment will tip into violence, but the uncomfortable peace seems to hold.

"What's your name?" Angus asks.

"Artie. Tell him Artie is looking for him. He'll know who I am."

Angus shoots an apologetic look at the man in the hat, and then disappears silently into the darkness.

"You happy now?" says the man.

She isn't, not really. What would make her happy is having a cobblestone to heave into this man's face. To see the whole unseemly crew scatter before her. But she's gotten someone looking for Zeb, someone who might know where he is, and that's enough to conclude the exchange. She turns to go. She doesn't answer the man's question, not out loud. She does not say goodbye.

*

In the saloon, they sit in the dankest, most shadowy corner they can find. Far from the stove, and an unhappy chill pours through the wall, but at least it keeps the inquisitive, vaguely hostile looks from the clientele off of them—as much as possible, anyway. They each drink a glass of beer quickly, to steady their nerves, and then they each order another one. They keep their eyes on the door, for Zeb's arrival, but long minutes pass and no one goes in or out.

"Let's go over this again," Theodore says finally. Artie blinks.

"Go over what?" she says, tearing her attention away from the door.

"Dorothy says we can't kill the Shrieker."

"No," Artie says. "She says we can move it."

"Move it through time."

"That's right."

"What exactly did she say about that?"

Artie sighs, rubs at her face.

"I just want to be sure I understand," Theodore says more gently, some of the skepticism draining out of his voice.

Artie takes another sip of her drink. "I'm not sure I understand," she says. "She wasn't making a whole lot of sense. But she said—she said she thinks that the Shrieker was sent here from another time. That it's not where it should be, or where it originated, in the timestream."

"OK," Theodore says. He takes a drink too. "So she wants to have us, what, send it back?"

"No," Artie says. "Maybe? I don't know. She said we could move it to the future. She was insistent on that point."

"Hm," Theodore says. "Will that really solve the problem, though? If it works, I mean. Won't we just be giving the Shrieker to another group of people?"

"I don't know," Artie says, frowning.

Theodore frowns too. "I suppose," he says, after another swallow of beer, "that people in the future might be better equipped to handle the thing? Perhaps they'll have devised some powerful weapon, or—perhaps the study of chronomancy will have advanced by then, and they could—do something—"

"Maybe," Artie says. "Dorothy also mentioned something else."

"What was it," Theodore says, after an interval.

"She mentioned that in the future some of the city might be underwater," Artie says. Theodore raises his eyebrows. "That the Shrieker could possibly be trapped underwater. That wouldn't kill it, but it might hold it in place—"

The door opens. They turn to look. It's Zeb.

He scans the room, spots them, and then approaches, pausing only to lean over and hook a chair from a table he passes on the way.

He straightens this chair once he's dragged it over; settles in. "Artie," he says. He does not acknowledge Theodore with anything other than a dismissive look.

"Zeb."

"I heard you were looking for me," he says.

"Yeah," Artie says. "I need you to do me a favor."

"Anything for the family," he says with an expression that's either an affectionate teasing grin or a contemptuous sneer. She can't quite make it resolve into one or the other. Maybe it's a little bit of both. "What's the favor?"

"Tomorrow night," she says. "I need you to make a policeman disappear."

23

"**W**ell," Zeb says. "Sounds like you've gotten yourself up to something."

"Yeah," Artie says, "you could say that."

"Some manner of criminal enterprise?" Zeb says. "I have to admit, I didn't think either of you"—a quick, appraising glance at Theodore here—"really showed the telltale signs of the, ah, criminal temperament."

"It's not a criminal enterprise," Artie says. Zeb raises his eyebrows, a touch skeptically. "Not exactly," she qualifies.

Theodore bangs his hand on the table, seemingly affronted. "It's not a criminal enterprise at all," he blurts. "Far from it. We're actually involved in trying to break up a criminal enterprise." He looks at Artie, perhaps expecting support, but finding only a glare in response, he shuts his mouth.

"See," Zeb says, spreading his hands, "that may pose a problem for me. If there's a criminal enterprise worthy of note in this town, you can be assured that I have noted it. Many of them—not all, mind you, but many—yield something for me in the way of profit. A portion of their proceeds tend to flow my way, directly or indirectly. So when you enlist my help in breaking up some enterprise—as much as I'd like to help you, I also need to be assured, you understand, that in doing so I wouldn't be working against my own self-interest. So I'm going to need some information about exactly what you two are busy getting yourself involved in."

Artie and Theodore exchange a glance: Theodore still looks a bit embarrassed about having revealed too much moments ago, and he doesn't seem willing to risk compounding that mistake. "It's complicated," Artie says finally, more to buy time than anything else.

"I'm sure," Zeb says.

"It's—OK," Artie tries. "We think there's something that the city is covering up. Including the police. Something bad. It doesn't . . . make profit. It just hurts people."

Zeb contemplates this for a moment.

"Spivey," he says.

"What?" Artie says.

"Horace Spivey," Zeb says. "Abductor of girls? You had me chasing him down the street last time I saw you?"

"I remember," Artie says.

"This 'enterprise' you're talking about. This has to do with that. Yes?"

"Yes," Artie says.

"And you think he was working with the police. Or that the police are covering up what he was doing."

"Yes," Artie says.

"Man came to a bad end, I heard. Shot twice in a downtown garage. You know anything about that?"

Artie doesn't answer: she looks down at the tabletop, feeling abashed.

"Some say a cop did it," Zeb says softly.

"That cop came to a bad end too," Artie says.

"I'd heard that," Zeb says. "Ate a bullet from his own gun?"

Artie doesn't say anything.

"Not the first cop to go that way," Zeb says. "Occupational hazard, they call it. Forgive me if I don't shed a tear."

"Didn't ask you to," Artie says.

"No," Zeb says, "you didn't. You just asked me to—how did you put it?—make some cop disappear."

"We don't want anyone getting hurt," Artie says. "We just need a distraction."

Zeb purses his lips thoughtfully for a moment.

"Sure," he says.

"Sure?"

"Listen," he says. "Cops are basically dumb. If you're here because you need me to distract some cop, I can do it." He emits the smallest sigh. "I can lure him wherever, point him in whatever direction you need him pointed, and I don't need to harm so much as a hair on his head to do it. I'll need the time and the place and all that. But—"

"But what?" Artie asks after a moment.

Zeb opens his mouth to speak, then closes it again. He turns to Theodore. "Hey, buddy," he says. "You think you could see your way to buying a drink for a fellow member of the Commonwealth? Especially one who you're asking for a favor?"

Theodore doesn't answer; instead, he turns to look at Artie.

Artie gives him a nod. Theodore stands, straightens his shirt fussily, and then heads off to the bar. Zeb watches him go, a faint expression of satisfaction playing around his lips.

"Do you have something to say?" Artie asks.

"I do," Zeb says. "Let me think of how I want to put this." He taps his lips twice with his pointer finger, then continues. "There used to be a time, see, and it wasn't even that long ago, but there used to be a time where I'd drop in, down at the house, the old homestead, and you'd take an interest in how I was doing, heck, I don't think I'd be wrong in saying you'd fuss over me a little bit. But nowadays?" He clucks his tongue. "I hear that you've come all this way, late at night, that you are looking for me, maybe I allowed myself, foolish, I know, but maybe I allowed myself to think that you might be here to check in on me, make sure everything was all right with old Zeb. But no, instead it's all business, you don't even ask, How are you? Instead it's straight to, I need you to do me a favor. Last time, too, straight to asking me about some piece of information you're in need of."

Artie blinks. "I asked you how you were doing last time," she says.

"I asked you first," Zeb says.

"That's not true," Artie says.

"Isn't it?" Zeb says with a shrug.

A moment goes by. Artie forces a tight smile.

"OK, Zeb," she says. "How are you?"

"I'm good," Zeb says, a plainly false smile surfacing on his face. "Things are good. And how are you?"

"I'm good," Artie says, matching Zeb's strained brightness with her own. "I've got a lot on my mind right now, though. There's kind of a lot going on."

"Sounds like it," Zeb says.

Theodore returns, bearing a tiny glass of beer. He hands it off to Zeb, who accepts it without thanks.

"You needn't sit back down," he says as Theodore pulls out his chair. "I can see that you're both busy. I won't keep you. Why don't you just let me know when you need me to be where you need me to be, and we can wrap this up."

"Tomorrow night," Artie says.

"Short notice," Zeb says.

"Is that a problem?"

"For you, I can make it work," Zeb says.

"OK," Artie says. She weighs for a moment whether she'd rather have Zeb meet them at the pit directly or at the home where Dorothy is kept. She's reluctant to bring him in too early—she doesn't think all three of them really work well together, as a team—but she also thinks it might be useful to have someone at the home other than just Theodore and herself. In the event that the staff at the home might somehow be on higher alert, it might be good to have a backup person around, someone who could receive the goods from Dorothy without risking recognition from a watchful nurse.

She decides. They'll meet together at the home. They fix the details, say their farewells, and leave Zeb to drink alone at the table.

Heading back to Theodore's place. A cab, rambling through the cold streets. Artie, in her seat, begins to worry, begins to wonder whether it was right to bring Zeb in on this. Maybe she should have asked him something about what he was thinking of doing, pinned him down on exactly how he was going to distract the watchman without hurting him. It would have given her an opportunity to test his plan, to double-check that it met her muster. Zeb hadn't really conveyed that he shared her concern about no one coming to harm, and even if he had, she's not sure that she could trust his word to be worth much. He's a criminal, after all, and criminals lie—

Everyone lies, though, she reminds herself wearily. Criminals lie, police commissioners lie, teachers lie. Even Winchell, she thinks, remembering how quick he was to perform his flimsy "deputization" of her and Theodore when it suited him. The night he shot his daughter. The night he died.

She sighs, pushes away the memories of that night, tries to find her way back to her previous line of thought: worrying about Zeb. But some of the animating force seems to have gone out of that particular fear now. Yes, she might have been wrong to introduce Zeb as a wild card, but suddenly it seems just as likely that she wasn't wrong; it feels now like maybe he's no more of a wild card than anyone else. They really have bigger things to worry about anyway. They're going up against some angry god with a plan lacking any guarantee of success, and if they fail they'll die, or, rather, they'll be aged beyond recognition and their minds will shatter. Maybe they'll be found the next time Jameson Briggs goes down into the tunnel, be brought to the ward, maybe over time their sanity will slowly knit itself back together so they can reflect on their failure for what remains of their days. Her frown deepens.

She glances up to face Theodore, across the cab from her, but he's looking down at his long hands, crossed in his lap, lost, seemingly, in his own thoughts of what has passed and what is yet to come. She opens her mouth but eventually decides not to interrupt.

*

She wakes in the morning on Theodore's settee. He's already up and in the room with her, she notices, seated at his desk in the corner. He's cleared some of the clutter, by moving a stack of it to the floor, and he's busy writing something. She blinks, wipes her eyes.

Theodore notices her as she struggles her way up into a sitting position. He turns, a gently apologetic grimace on his face. "Sorry if I woke you," he says. "I couldn't sleep."

"What are you writing?" she asks.

"I'm writing a letter to my contact at the *Globe*," Theodore says. "Julius Roop."

"Oh?" Artie says, wiping her eyes.

"Yes, well," Theodore says, "I got to thinking last night, as I was trying to sleep. I got to thinking and—well—forgive me for putting too fine of a point on it, but it occurred to me that Dorothy's plan—our plan—might not work."

Artie doesn't say anything, but she offers a sharp nod in response.

"So if," Theodore says, "if we—if it doesn't work, I just think it's important that somebody else knows about what happened.

We learned so much. About those girls, about Gannett, and Briggs, and—all of it. I don't want that information to be lost if we fail. I want someone to know. What do you think?"

Artie considers it. She remembers the conversation she had with Theodore over breakfast, four days ago, when they first talked about Roop. In that conversation, she'd raised the question of whether Briggs and his cohort were right to keep it all hidden, to make the decisions they made behind closed doors, in an attempt to keep the city from panicking. You mustn't ask that, Theodore had said, and she thinks that's wrong: it was important, she thinks, to consider the problem, to ask the question. She's glad she did it. But she thinks now that she has an answer.

"I think you're right," she says. "I want someone to know too."

So they write it out together, Artie suggesting turns of phrase and offering forgotten details. It takes an hour or so to get it all down. They package it up with the materials that Artie had grabbed from the nurses' station—the intake cards with their cryptic designations, the diagrams of the ward itself. Theodore binds the pile of documents with a piece of red string and seals it inside a large envelope made of creamy paper; he addresses it neatly.

"Well," he says, "there it is."

❦

As the appointed hour nears, they head to the street outside Gannett's home for the aged to meet with Dorothy. They arrive early, but even so, Zeb's there ahead of them, leaning up against the wall, bearing a greasy-looking cardboard valise.

"This is the place, huh?" he says once they're within earshot.

Artie, hoping to keep a low profile, only indicates confirmation with a nod. She uses a quick crook of her thumb, as surreptitious as she can make it, to point out the window they're to watch. Zeb nods, shifts the valise from one hand to the other, adjusts his position against the wall.

And then there's nothing to do but wait.

Artie had been worried about a nurse spotting them—she's been here a few times now, she'd surely be recognized—but this fear seems to have been unfounded. The front of the home is mercifully quiet and still: no one is peering out at them. It doesn't quite dispel her nervousness, though. There are only a handful of pedestrians out at this hour—another mercy—but every time one appears, Artie feels a jolt of anxiety, even if they're just crossing the mouth of the alley, even if they don't cast a single look in Artie's direction. This anxiety is compounded the few times someone turns into the alley and begins approaching: Artie wills herself, each time, to maintain the appearance of nonchalance, as though just lurking here in the dark and the cold is the most normal thing in the world, but each time she catches herself casting at least one worried glance at the approaching figure, half expecting it to be Jameson Briggs, caught up to them at last. There's one time when she looks up and is absolutely convinced, for an entire second, that the man she sees coming down the alley is none other than Horace Spivey, the boning knife glinting at his side.

Stuck in this state of apprehension—not to mention the deeper apprehension about what they'll need to do next, after they receive the handoff from Dorothy—makes time pass very slowly. They'd arrived half an hour before the appointed time: when Artie first nudges Theodore and asks for a look at his watch, it's a blow to learn that only five minutes have elapsed.

Twenty-five minutes left, then seventeen, then twelve: the more acutely uncomfortable she feels, standing out here in plain view, the slower time seems to pass. She wonders if the others feel equally anxious. Theodore looks typically benign, not counting the flash of irritation he gave her the last time she wanted a look at his watch. And Zeb just looks bored. She doesn't know whether this is a carefully maintained illusion or whether he really is just bored.

She's still trying to make this assessment when he pushes himself off of the wall and begins to saunter away from them.

"Zeb!" Artie hisses.

Zeb, still walking, looks over his shoulder. "What?" he says. "I want to see something."

Artie gives him her firmest look.

"You don't need all three of us watching a window," he says. "You really don't. If something happens, yell."

And then he slips around the corner and is gone. Artie catches Theodore looking at her, his expression not quite readable, although she detects some questioning of her judgment in it. She turns the firm look on him, and he blithely goes back to looking at Dorothy's window.

It seems to take forever for Zeb to return, although Artie knows that it's probably only been a few minutes. He strolls back up to them, the valise swinging at his side.

"What did you want to see?" Artie asks in a whisper.

"It's just something," Zeb says in a normal speaking voice.

"What is?"

"I mean, right around the corner: that's City Hall."

"Yeah," Artie says.

"You said this thing—this criminal enterprise, or whatever it is—you said the city was covering it up?"

"Yeah."

"So—you mean, like, the mayor?"

"The mayor, yeah," Artie says. "And the commissioner of police, this guy Jameson Briggs."

Theodore gives them both a cautionary look, as though by mentioning Briggs's name she may inadvertently summon him.

"And these missing girls," Zeb says, undeterred. "Do you know how many there were? How many Spivey grabbed?"

"Twelve," Artie says. "Twelve before Spivey was—before what happened to Spivey. There's probably been a thirteenth by now."

Zeb turns his head, spits.

"That's worse," he says.

"What's worse?" Artie says. "Worse than what?"

"I'm just saying," he says. "What they get up to here, right downtown, right in City Hall? That's worse than anything I ever did, down on the wharf."

Artie nods grimly, feeling certain he's right, although this certainty is compromised by an accompanying note of doubt struck within her: it occurs to her that she isn't equipped to agree, not really. She doesn't have the necessary information. She doesn't, in fact, know the worst thing Zeb's done. She frowns at this awareness, which swells and grows in her. She's working up the nerve to ask when Theodore stirs, points.

"Both of you," he says in a hushed tone. "Look."

Movement up above, at the window. A smear through the glass, a face.

"That's her?" Theodore asks, but Artie is already in action, moving quickly, preparing to be in position. She tries to make eye contact with Dorothy as she crosses the street, but the face disappears as suddenly as it appeared, and once she's at the base of the building she's of course at the wrong angle to see anything through a second-floor window at all.

Artie scarcely has time to worry about this: only a moment passes before she hears something from above: the window rattling in its frame. Dorothy struggling with the latch?

For a moment nothing happens.

Please, Artie has time to think.

Then another short burst of rattling; then it subsides again. The window doesn't open. Please don't let us be thwarted by this, Artie thinks. By a single windowpane.

Before she reaches the end of the plea, though, there is a soft crash. Artie steps back, hand up to shield her face, as a few shards of glass spin down and smash to glittering dust on the paving stones at her feet.

"Dorothy," Artie calls, just loudly enough that she can hope she'll be heard. "I'm here."

A glimpse of something. Dorothy's hand, holding a sack of some kind. A pillowcase, containing objects.

"I'm here," Artie says, just a tiny bit louder. "Let go. I'll catch it."

The case dangles there, above Artie's head for a moment, twisting this way and that, in eccentric orbit, and Artie wonders whether she'll really need to yell to be heard. But then it drops. Artie is in the perfect position. It drops directly into her outstretched hands. OK. That's something.

She looks into the pillowcase: sees her watch and her notebook, just as expected.

OK.

She backs away from the building until she can see up into the window. Sees Dorothy's face, framed there in the darkness, looking down at her. She stands there, in the middle of the street, looking back, wondering what to say, or what to do. Wave?

"Go," Dorothy says, her voice surprisingly clear and strong. "You don't have much time. With each minute that passes we grow weaker. Remember that I will be with you."

So now she knows what to do. There's only one thing to do. She has to go. She turns, she goes, she doesn't look back.

*

It doesn't take long for the three of them to find a cab and pile in. Once they're seated, Artie hands the contents of the pillowcase off to Theodore so that he can study the incantation that Dorothy has transcribed into the notebook's pages, at least for the few minutes it'll take them to wend their way to the pit. It's not much of an opportunity, but it's the opportunity they have.

"Goodness," Theodore says, peering at Dorothy's tight, crabbed handwriting.

She figures she'd better let him concentrate, so she turns her attention instead to Zeb, who is seated across from her, his knees knocking against hers each time the cab jostles. The greasy valise is in his lap; he traces an idle pattern on its surface with a fingertip. She detects an ódor coming from it that she can't quite place, something like paraffin.

"What's in the case?" she asks.

"You wanted a distraction," Zeb says. He keeps his eyes trained on his hands. "I brought a distraction."

"You remember I said I didn't want anyone to get hurt, right?"

"You remember I said I could do that, right?"

These answers aren't entirely satisfying, and she begins readying herself to say so, but then she realizes there's another question she wants answered more; the question she asked herself back when they were waiting outside Dorothy's window.

"Zeb," she says. "What's the worst thing you've ever done?"

This gets his attention. He stares flatly at her face.

She continues: "I guess what I really want to know is this," she says. "Did you ever kill anybody?"

Theodore looks up at this, eyebrows raised. He looks at Artie, then at Zeb, then at Artie again, and then goes back to studying the notebook.

Zeb offers up a small, thin smile, something wistful in it. "I've owned guns," he says. "I've used them, sometimes, when I've had to. I don't always think it's been a bad thing. But I'll tell you this. It was back, oh, seven or eight months ago. There was a boy. Thirteen years old. About the same age as I was when I started thieving. Wily little bastard, agile too, he could wriggle through a fence like a snake. I took a liking to him. Always looking for more people I can bring up, you know? So I start giving him some little tasks. Stand at the corner and holler if you see a policeman coming, that's maybe where you start with someone like that. You know, low-level. Nothing big. That went OK, so I moved him up a little. Here's a warehouse full of items that I shouldn't technically have. I'm going to go get the buyer for these items, back in an hour, you just wait here and make sure nobody comes around trying to stick their nose in, OK? OK. Only something feels off, so instead of being gone for an hour I stop in at the bar at the end of the street, have a drink, quick one, then circle back, and sure enough, there's the kid, handing off a box of my goods to some other lowlife. The lowlife goes running—I'm not too worried about that, I know where to find him later. But the kid just stands there, the box still in his hands; he's caught, and he knows it, and he's, like, paralyzed, waiting to see what's going to happen. Now, as I said, I'd had a drink, and I had a gun, and a gun maybe leaps into your hand a little too quickly after a drink. So it's in my hand. Now, the kid, all he'd really done is made an error in judgment. I actually still like the kid; I still want him on my side, but I need to make sure he doesn't make a similar error in judgment next time. I need to make sure, in other words, that he learns—that actions have consequences, you know? So I raise the gun. And yeah, I pull the trigger. I'm a good shot. Even with some whiskey in me I'm a good shot. All I want to do is just graze the kid's shoulder. Just enough to give him a little reminder. Should be an easy target. He's just standing there, frozen, with a box in his hands. But I forgot how agile the kid is. I start to squeeze the trigger, and he drops the box. Damn kid can move like a whip. I have just enough time to figure out what's happening. I think he's gonna break left and I try to correct, instead he breaks right. The bullet, it catches him right—right here."

Zeb touches his throat with two fingers.

"So, yeah, that—there's no coming back from that. So that's it. That's the worst thing I've done. That sort of the kind of thing you're looking for?"

"Yeah," Artie says. "It is."

They ride in silence for a minute. Zeb goes back to tracing the pattern on the surface of the case.

Artie has one more thing to say. She's about to say it, and then she thinks better of it, and then she says it anyway.

"I'm not sure," she says, "that that's the kind of thing that can be forgiven."

"Yeah, well," Zeb says, "I didn't ask for that, now, did I?"

The cab judders to a halt.

24

The three of them huddle together, in the doorway of the defunct bookbindery. Zeb squints out at the fenced-off pit two dozen feet away.

"The watchman," he says, his hands twisting at the handle of his valise. "He's down there? In that trench?"

"Yes," says Artie. "Each time we've been here, anyway."

"OK," Zeb says. "Let me go take a look."

"Be careful," Artie says. "This watchman caught us peeking down at him last time, and let me tell you, he didn't really like it."

"If there's one thing a watchman can't stand, it's being watched," Zeb says.

"Yeah, well, he came up the ramp last time and shone a light around, looking for us, and he almost caught us, too, so just—be careful."

"I will," Zeb says. "Here," he says, pushing the valise into Theodore's hands. "Why don't you make yourself useful and hold this?"

Theodore wrinkles his nose at Zeb's rudeness, but he takes the case. "All right," he says.

"Don't drop it," Zeb says over his shoulder as he strides out of the doorway.

Together Artie and Theodore watch him approach the pit. He saunters up to the fence, leans on it, affecting the breeziness of a young man out for an evening stroll. The illusion doesn't completely work: the January wind is bracing enough that the sight of anyone casually lingering anywhere might attract attention, but Zeb doesn't overstay his time. He takes a quick look down into the pit, then steps away, fists in his pockets, whistling.

He returns to the doorway, takes the case from Theodore again, sets it flat on the ground.

"This is going to be easy," he says. "Or—getting him out of there will be, anyway. I can lead him on a merry chase for a bit but I can't promise that I can keep him away from his duties forever. At some point he's going to realize that he's left that tunnel unguarded and he may give up on me and return here."

"I think that's OK," Artie says.

"I mean," Zeb says, "if you needed more time, I could probably knock the guy out, leave him tied up somewhere—but you said you don't want the guy hurt. That still true?"

"It's still true," Artie says. "The important thing is that we get in. Once we're in—I don't know. If we survive, I don't think getting back out will be that much of a problem."

Zeb has dropped into a crouch, and he's placed his hands on the latches of the case, but the words "if we survive" appear to give him some pause. He looks up at her.

"Listen," he says. "I don't know exactly what you're expecting to find down there, and it seems like you don't want to tell me. That's fine—but, just—if you could use a little more manpower for what you're doing—somebody good in a scrap—"

"Well," Artie says, followed by a pause for equivocation.

Zeb, stepping into the gap: "I just feel like I might be of more use to you down there than running around the city creating a distraction—"

"The distraction is necessary, though," Artie says. "We can't get in the tunnel without it. As for what's going on down there— we won't need manpower. This isn't the kind of thing that can be won with manpower."

"Well," Zeb says, "what can it be won with?"

"Magic," Artie says. She looks over at Theodore; Zeb follows her gaze. Theodore gives a sheepish grin.

"A magician, eh?" Zeb says, looking back at her. "I've known a few. Some even had some technique, formidable technique. Not always the most reliable people, not by a far cry, but your boy here seems loyal enough." It looks like he tries to smile, but it comes out more resembling a scowl. Artie scowls back, without really intending to.

Zeb sighs. "Listen," he says. "I don't really like the idea of you going down there to do something dangerous, even if you do have some magic on your side." He watches Artie's expression change, holds up his hands defensively. "I'm not intending to stop you," he says. "But, just—at the end of the day, you're still my sister. I don't like the idea of not knowing whether you're alive or dead."

"I know the feeling," Artie says. "Believe it or not."

Zeb perceptibly winces at this. "Yeah," he says. "So just—let's check in, OK? Tomorrow night. I'll be at the saloon where you met me last night. I'll wait for you there. You can just come and— let me know how it all went. How does that sound?"

Artie thinks about it for a minute. "OK," she says finally. "It sounds OK."

"Maybe come by yourself this time," Zeb says, looking up at Theodore. Theodore offers a tight grin in response.

"So what's in the case?" Artie says.

Zeb pops the latches and removes from the case a ball of twine, an empty jam jar, a torn length of curtain, and a small, square tin tank of kerosene, leaky at its corners. Zeb waves away the fumes with his hand.

"What's all this, then?" Theodore asks.

"You meet some interesting people in my line of work," Zeb says, screwing the cap off the tank. He tips the tank into the jar: kerosene glugs from one container to another. "This is a little trick I learned from a big, ugly Finn. Wave of the future, I'm convinced."

He wraps the scrap of curtain around the mouth of the jar, ties it there with the twine, then turns the whole contraption upside down and sets it on the pavement. Artie watches apprehensively as kerosene slowly soaks through the fabric, a slow trickle of it seeping out onto the cold pavement.

Before too much can escape, Zeb rights the jar and rises, knees popping.

"That's about all there is to it," he says. "Nothing left but the fun part."

He fishes some matches out of his pocket and uses one to ignite a loose corner of the fabric that hangs down the edge of the jar. It goes up like a wick.

"Time to go," he says. "Best of luck to you and the boy wizard."

And he walks out of the doorway, the blazing jar in his hand, a beacon in the darkness.

He doesn't break stride; he walks directly to the edge of the pit.

"Hey, flatfoot," he calls, and he hurls the jar over the fence.

Artie can hear the jar smash, can hear the sudden whoosh of flame, but the loudest thing she hears is the watchman cry out in surprise.

Zeb rounds the perimeter of the trench, making his way over to the break in the fence, to the top of the wooden ramp, where he can easily be seen. He shakes both fists in the air, doing his best impression of a wild anarchist bomber.

Having made this suitable spectacle of himself, he drops back a few yards—not too far, though; he clearly wants to remain tantalizingly close, a target just out of reach, so the watchman will be lured in his direction, leaving Artie and Theodore unnoticed, invisible in the dark background.

The police officer comes charging up the ramp.

"You bastard," he says, laying eyes on Zeb.

Zeb drops back toward the mouth of a distant alley. For a moment the watchman doesn't engage in pursuit: instead, he stands there, at the rim of the pit, struggling to get his flashlight working. When it clicks on, Artie's breath catches in her throat: all he would need to do is swing around in their direction and he could spot them. And if he spotted them, and recognized them, the whole ruse could collapse.

Zeb intervenes. "I've got an even bigger bomb for your precinct!" he yells, and then he darts around a corner. This threat, invented on the spot as far as Artie knows, succeeds as a lure: the watchman jolts into action, racing off after Zeb into the maze of city streets.

If they're to have a window of opportunity, it's now.

"OK," Artie says. "Let's go."

They hurry out of the doorway, circling around the fence until they reach the opening. Artie raises her eyebrows as she catches sight of Zeb's handiwork: a two-foot-wide pool of flame licking at the gravel at the bottom of the trench. She spares a moment to wonder, absurdly, what Winchell would say about this new development in the world of improvised incendiary devices, this new milestone in criminal technology, were she able to relay news of it back to him. But then she shakes this off, and she sets foot on the ramp, and descends, Theodore right behind her.

They reach the bottom of the pit, begin to make their way across a walkway of planks through an expanse of loose timber and broken brick. They pass the flames from Zeb's bomb, and Artie gives over a moment to wonder whether she shouldn't look for a water barrel or a heavy work blanket, something she could use to extinguish the flames before they attract the attention of curious onlookers, or—worse—the local fire department. She doesn't want to have gotten rid of a single watchman only to have to deal with an entire scrum of firefighters. But the fire has already begun sputtering out: it's consumed its initial payload of kerosene and now it's safely ringed by nonflammable rubble and stone; it probably has only a few minutes of life left in it. So no need to do anything but advance.

Ahead of them, the tunnel. Two dark openings, side by side, a pair of arches framed by cold masonry, one intended to provide passage to an inbound train and the other intended for an outbound train, back before work on the site was abandoned.

Artie indicates the left entrance with a nod of her head. That seems to be the one that Briggs and the watchman have been escorting their victims into, Artie reasons, basing her deduction on a few glass lamps that hang there from a battered peg. Together she and Theodore approach, and they each take a lamp in hand. It takes Theodore a moment or two to get them both lit: he has to hold Artie's notebook awkwardly between his knees before he can complete the task.

"So this is it," he says once he's passed Artie her lamp, returned his lighter to his pocket, and taken the notebook back in hand.

"Do you feel ready?" Artie says.

"No," Theodore says. "But Dorothy says she'll be helping us? From afar?"

"That's what she said."

"I don't feel anything yet," Theodore says. He looks about in the night air, as though Dorothy might be hovering above them in the form of a spectral aurora borealis.

"She said she'd be able to assist once you started the incantation," Artie says.

Theodore nods, looking glum.

"She also said—not to rush us, but—she said that with each minute that passed, her ability to help us—"

"Grows weaker," Theodore says. "I remember. And for that matter the watchman may be returning soon. So we should go. I just want to say—I just want to say, if I don't get a chance to say it later, that it's been a marvel to work by your side through all this. An absolute marvel. And if this is—if this is where our time together ends, I hope it won't be, obviously, but if this is where it ends, I will want you to know that I won't have regretted a moment of this work."

"Thank you, Theodore," Artie says. "I feel the same way about you."

"Also," Theodore says, "you look very handsome in your suit."

Artie's cheeks flush at this.

"Thank you, Theodore," she says again. "You look very handsome as well." And he does.

This seems to dispel his glumness: his face breaks into a smile. "All right, then," he says. "Let's go."

Together they enter the tunnel. Artie raises her lamp to examine the arched ceiling above her head: it's lined with a string of electric bulbs, though these are dormant, dead. Nevertheless, she and Theodore continue on: their lamps throw light adequate enough to advance by, even though the ominous look of their dancing shadows on the walls stirs some uneasy primal feeling deep within her. Aside from their apprehension, progress into the tunnel is easy, at least at first: The work on the first thirty yards seems largely complete. The walls are smooth, and the ground beneath their feet is even.

But then the tunnel begins to curve, and the grade begins to descend. At this point, timber bracings begin to appear at regular intervals, and the walls take on a rough, unfinished look. The paved floor gives way to a slapdash configuration of planks, and after another twenty feet or so these, too, disappear, and they're picking their way across crudely hewn stone. Something changes in the air too. The air at the front of the tunnel was still and slightly dank. But the air here feels charged, as though there's a magnetic energy running through it. The odor has changed too: at the front of the tunnel the dominant smell was the faint sweetness of rock dust, but here there's a concentrated ozonic reek, as though they were inhaling the scent of an approaching thunderstorm out of an apothecary bottle rather than just in the atmosphere.

"Oof," says Artie. "We must be close."

The moment the words leave her mouth, the air in the tunnel is hewn by noise. A squeal, high-pitched, violent. And then this sound gives way to a scream. This must be it. This is the sound she knows she can't hear, the sound that she knows will destroy her body and drive her to madness, but even in the grip of her terror she feels a sense of completion, of grim satisfaction, because she's hearing it at last, the sound she's been tracking for three months now: the cry of an amputated god, the sustained, wordless scream of the Shrieker.

25

This is not merely a scream. It is the sound of the world being torn, howling like a rupturing sheet of metal. The sound of time itself shredding as something blindly claws through it.

"Oh, no," Artie says. "Oh, no."

Theodore is right next to her, but she doubts he can hear her. She can't hear herself. She has her hands clamped over her ears. She's dropped her lamp. Her fingers dig into the back of her head. Maybe if she can block out the sound, it'll buy her some time. She can't really block much out, though; the scream is everywhere. It feels like it's already penetrated her all the way down to the bone.

How much time does she have, anyway, before her teeth loosen in her jaw and her mind loosens in her skull? Probably not long. Probably only seconds. How long has it been? Has it been seconds yet?

Everything is reeling, the tunnel is reeling, she has vertigo from whatever the scream is doing to her ears, to her brain. The tunnel seems upside down; it struggles to right itself. This is the part where she'd retreat, if she were a man with a gun, sent down here by the city. But instead she takes a step forward, what she thinks is forward. She wants to see this thing. She didn't come this far not to see this thing.

She misjudges her step, loses her balance in the spin, over-corrects, stumbles. A rock bashes a hole in the knee of her suit and bloodies the flesh beneath. Her hands splay against the stony floor of the tunnel, and the sound of the Shrieker pours into her unprotected head.

She clenches her eyes shut. In the darkness, though, she thinks she can feel the process, the aging. The Shrieker's horrible consumption: she can feel it happening to her. Her hands throb. Her joints begin, suddenly, to ache, as though they've had some vital quality sapped out of them.

She forces herself to open her eyes rather than lose herself to tracking these sensations. She stares down at her hands. For a moment, in the wild lamplight, it looks as though her skin is melting away, revealing blackening bone below. She moans. But it isn't real: it's just leaping shadows. At least for right now. They still have time; she doesn't know how much.

She moans again. No one can hear her. She gathers her lantern as she clambers back to her feet, tries to see if there's a way that she can hold its wire handle while simultaneously blocking her ear with the back of her hand. This arrangement puts the flame right next to her eye; she has to squint; it makes it difficult to truly make out anything that lies ahead. But she advances. This time she's steadier on her feet. She looks back to ensure that Theodore is with her: he is. Together they round the tunnel's final bend.

And then she's there, on the threshold of the Shrieker's lead prison. It's as Gannett described it: a cube of metal, inscribed with strange symbols, standing in the center of a crypt crudely hewn from the city bedrock. The cube, as she expected, has opened: on the side that faces her, innumerable planes of thin metal have folded back from a central point, crumpling finely as they peeled away. The end result resembles nothing so much as the delicate layers of a rotting flower. She stares into the center of it. And at the center is darkness. And in the darkness is the Shrieker, emerging now to meet her.

Eight feet tall. Maybe more. It towers over her, this screaming thing, yet its presence seems somehow insubstantial, like it's not all entirely there. It seems like only a portion of it is here in this world, parts of it appearing only as tatters and shreds, like rags caught on a wire, whipping in an unfelt wind, the wire whining, then disappearing again, replaced by new parts writhing into existence. She can't quite make her eyes make sense of what she's seeing; she tries to take these perceptions and shape them into a body, something she can fight or defend herself against. She trains her eyes upward to the top of the looming form, locks in on a nucleus of activity there, a foul accretion. She decides that she must be looking at the head.

It doesn't have a face. There's just a mass of raw, bluish matter whirling about a central point, but that central point is nothing, just a hole punched in the air, a pit around which everything seems to twist, the exact point where time is being torn, the point from which the scream emerges.

She stares into that point: in her mind it begins to open into a yawning void. She is overtaken, for a moment, by memories of vast spaces. Standing at the edge of the harbor, last year, looking out at the horizon. Losing herself, as a child, in the dizzying depth of a clear fall sky, imagining it beneath her rather than above her, imagining it as an abyssal thing she could drop into and fall forever.

She emerges from this into another memory, some morning, in a classroom, learning mathematics, frowning as she tried, pencil point broken, to solve a complicated sum in her mind. That feeling—of an abstraction hanging in your consciousness as you struggle to make it cohere—that's what she feels when she looks at the Shrieker, on some level, somewhere behind her horror.

But it's the horror that grounds her, that brings her back to her body. There is blood in her mouth. Her gums, dry, are receding. It hurts. She spits. Not my teeth, she thinks. Please.

In terror, she turns her head away from the deteriorated being before her. She looks at Theodore. Has he started doing the spell yet?

She is dismayed to see him fumbling. His lamp is sitting on the floor of the tunnel; he juggles the notebook and the watch from one hand to another, finally dropping them both. My god, Artie thinks. What is he doing? There's no time—

He lifts both his hands. His arms are trembling; his whole body is trembling. But he makes his hands assume a specific configuration; it feels familiar to her, somehow; she's seen it before—

It's the Cat's Approach.

It creates a sphere of silence, she remembers. If you were a thief, you could project it on your feet, and you could creep about silently. But you could—really you could, she suddenly realizes—you could project it anywhere.

And Theodore is aiming it at the Shrieker's head, at the dead, still center of that swarming nucleus—

And just like that, the Shrieker's howl winks out. Artie turns to look—the being is still there, still thrashing in its wretched throes at the entrance to the cube—but now the only sound in the tunnel is Artie and Theodore's ragged breathing. She looks again to Theodore. He keeps his eyes on the Shrieker, keeps his hands in the air, his face tensed with the effort of the concentration it takes to keep the Shrieker's head surrounded by the sphere of silence. He won't be able to keep doing that forever. And so Artie has to move.

She sets her own lamp down; she scrambles back over the uneven jumble of rock to reach the watch, glinting in the light, finds the notebook next to it. She falls to a kneeling position, gathers these items closer to her, flips through the pages of the notebook. She doesn't know how to do magic. She's never done a spell before. But Dorothy has prepared the incantation. Dorothy said she's standing by to help.

There is no sound but the sound of their breathing. She whispers "Please, please, please," partly in the hope that Dorothy will hear her somehow, partly just to pour something out, to disrupt the troubling silence. Speaking words into the air, any words, covers up the sound of her breath—and this helps distract her from the fact that she is a living being, a creature, exposed and gasping and stumbling and vulnerable in front of this hostile, alien thing.

She does not look up. She does not want to see the thing. She looks at the notebook. She holds it in one hand and the pocket watch in the other. She tries to read the crabbed handwriting in the wild light.

She stops herself from saying please. There's no time left to ask anything anymore; there is only time to act. She finds some last gram of inner calm and comports herself. She opens her mouth and reads the first words of the incantation.

Is this working, she has time to think.

And then it is as if Dorothy jumps into her skull. It feels as though her head is suddenly wreathed in green fire. And with Dorothy comes the body of Dorothy's knowledge. She knows, suddenly, how to do what needs to be done.

The words of the incantation are coming easily now, a complex stream of syllables pouring out of her, like water clattering over stones. She doesn't even really need to look at the notebook anymore: she knows what to say.

She looks up at the Shrieker. She understands it now: if the Shrieker is a set of unresolved mathematics, a problem for the solving, then now, armed with her new knowledge, she has solved it, simply and completely. The cerebral itch of it gives way to satisfaction. And the horror she feels shrinks away in the light of this satisfaction.

The Shrieker seems to understand her, too, now. It understands her as an enemy. It understands that it must put a stop to the torrent of words rushing at it; that those words threaten to dislodge it from the stronghold that it inhabits here, in Artie's time.

Artie takes another step, words pouring off of her tongue.

The Shrieker sends one of its tatters out at her face, a tendril coming at her, fast as a whip, as though it intends to strike her tongue, to cleave it in two. Artie yanks her head to one side, and the tendril strikes her cheek, passing through flesh: she can hear the small, soft *vip* of a wound opening, she can feel blood cascade warmly down her face. She stops saying the words of the incantation. And with her head turned she can see Theodore: she watches with dismay as he coughs and splutters. He doubles over, drops his hands—he can't hold the Cat's Approach any longer. And the Shrieker's scream starts up again like a rising siren.

She stumbles backward; she has to get away, get out of reach.

And then—something seems to pop in Artie's head: an awful feeling, a darkening blossom seeming to spread open in her mind. She wonders if she's about to have a seizure, or whether something has gone wrong with her brain.

It's Dorothy, she realizes suddenly. Dorothy is dying.

"No," Artie says. "No, you can't. It isn't fair." Tears spring into her eyes. The crown of green flame wobbles unstably.

But she can't stop. The knowledge that she has won't allow her to stop. The Shrieker is beginning to unfurl again, a horrible, etiolated, batlike thing regaining its wretched majesty, and she knows that she needs to complete this, and complete it now, or she'll never get another chance.

Artie scrambles back a few more steps. Safely out of the Shrieker's grasp, she returns her gaze to it. She begins, once again, to speak Dorothy's words. She extends her arm to its full length, locks her elbow, stiffens it like a plank. In her right hand is her watch, throbbing with eldritch power; she points it at the Shrieker as though she were training a lens on it.

Nothing is happening. It isn't working. The Shrieker keeps on growing, as though blossoming. Her arm unlocks; her hand drops back to her side; the watch goes cold and still.

You're too far away from it, Artie thinks. Whether this is Dorothy advising her, or just her own observation, she can't be sure, but she knows the observation is true. The range of the spell isn't infinite. You need to get closer. You need to really see it, up close, or this won't work.

I can't, she thinks. There's blood all over her face. If that thing had hit her throat in the right place, she'd be dead. I can't.

Yes, you can, she tells herself. You're not a person who isn't brave.

She regains her footing. She takes a step forward, across the uneven floor of the broken tunnel. That's all you can do, sometimes, advance. You just have to be brave enough to take another step.

She holds up the watch.

Something seems to travel down her arm and out, through the watch face, some vital force; it strikes the Shrieker like a beam and the Shrieker staggers, sags, crumples backward, its scream stuttering.

Artie says the final words of the incantation; the crown of flame begins to flicker out. The notebook drops from her hand. But it isn't over. She takes another step forward. She's within the orbit of the Shrieker's whirling tatters, but they can't seem to harm her any longer; they don't even touch her. She lowers the watch for a moment, passes it to her left hand, and then she raises her right hand once again. She extends it, reaching out. She's an inch away from touching the core of the Shrieker—not its head, but some secondary mass she couldn't perceive before, something you could call its heart. It's shriveled, she notes, withered. An injured organ. Weak. Old. She could touch it, or—no—

Her hand clenches—she pulls it back—and then she puts her righteous fist straight through its heart.

It poses no resistance, and she understands, for just a moment, that this god is actually nothing, just a phantom.

The Shrieker recoils, the blow flings it backward, back into its box, and the peeled-back layers of the lead prison suddenly heave into motion, sealing the Shrieker back in.

The incantation has ended. The cube is sealed, the Shrieker silent within it. Artie takes another step forward, two, three, a little more uncertain now that the architecture of Dorothy's chronomancy, so vividly drawn in lines of light just moments ago, has begun to disintegrate in her mind, to go to ash. She doesn't know where the notebook is. But she knows how to complete the spell. The knowledge is fading fast, like a dream upon waking, but Artie only needs to hold on to one final action.

She touches the face of the watch to the central symbol engraved on the front face of the prison: the lock that holds the Shrieker in place.

At the moment the two surfaces touch, the glass of the watch cracks. The tiniest sound.

And then the cube disappears. There's no thunderclap, no flash of light. It's just no longer there, no longer in 1910. It's somewhere else. The electrical odor in the tunnel—the smell of a corroding light switch—is gone, replaced with the faint but distinct smell of seawater.

"Is that—is it over?" Theodore asks. He coughs. "Is it really gone?"

Artie turns to look at him. He looks weary; his handsome face has, perhaps, a line or two in it that it didn't have before. He stops speaking so that he can tug on his teeth with his hand: she can see that his gums are bleeding, just as hers were. But his teeth stay put. She checks hers with her tongue. They seem OK.

He stops touching his teeth. "You're bleeding," he says.

For the moment, Artie ignores this. "Dorothy is dead," she says. She sits down on a flat hunk of rock.

"Oh," Theodore says. "Are you sure?"

Artie considers the question; she reflects back on how it felt, all that power in her mind, going dark. "Yes," she finally says.

"I'm sorry," Theodore says. He makes his way over to where she's sitting, and sits down next to her. They slump against one another, let their shoulders touch. He offers her a handkerchief from his pocket, which she holds against her face to staunch the bleeding. And then it's a long time before either of them move again, or say anything.

*

It's Theodore who eventually stirs, who reminds them that they need to get up, eventually, and leave.

"I hate to point this out," he begins gently, "but I don't think it would be very wise for us to be found down here."

Artie blinks. "The watchman," she says.

"He won't chase Zeb forever."

"He might," Artie tries, a wan joke. "Zeb can be a nuisance when he wants to be."

Theodore musters a charitable smile, begins to stand. "Yes, he can. All the same, whatever time he's buying us—"

"Yes," Artie says, "you're right." She collects her notebook from where it's fallen, struggles up to her feet. Her knees pop. Her back is sore. She works her jaw experimentally. It's stiff, and the muscles around it ache. She hopes that this will fade, given time. But everything else seems to be OK. She can stand. She can walk. She can think. She takes the handkerchief away from her face: probes the edge of the wound with her finger. It's hard to tell how bad it is, here in the dark.

Together they make their way back to the mouth of the tunnel. Neither of them speak. Zeb's distraction worked well: the guard hasn't returned to his station. The fire from Zeb's bomb, or whatever it was, has gone out. They cross the planks that lead to the ramp and wearily climb their way out of the pit. They both know they need to put some distance between them and the work site, but before they make their escape Artie gives one last look back over her shoulder, down into the trench. It is quiet and still down there. It looks as though nothing ever happened.

*

"So," Theodore says, tentatively, after they've walked for a few minutes, rejoined the thin stream of people still traversing the main avenues at this hour. "It's gone. It's really gone. We sent it away."

Artie's head is down, against the wind, still keeping the handkerchief pressed to her face. She doesn't look at Theodore but she allows herself one curt nod. "We're not done yet," she says. "Briggs is still out there. He was in on what happened to those girls from the beginning—we can't just let him get away with it. I want to be sure—I want to be sure that those girls are going to get justice. Just sending the Shrieker away doesn't do that."

"No," Theodore says, "it doesn't. I was thinking about that too. By tomorrow Roop at the *Globe* should have our package—and, ah, perhaps against my expectations, I find myself in a position to follow up. Perhaps in person. I'll see what he thinks, in terms of putting together an exposé. Maybe we can go meet with him together."

Artie nods again. "I'd like that," she says.

They walk on in silence for a bit longer.

"All the same," Theodore says, stopping in his tracks for a minute. "We accomplished something tonight. Not without a cost, and the cost was high. But I think it's important to look for a moment at the accomplishment. To at least acknowledge it. Otherwise the cost was for nothing."

Artie stops as well. "Yeah," she says. "We did something."

"We did it well," Theodore says.

"As well as we could," Artie says.

"And not without help."

"No, not without help."

They look at one another, and they each smile wearily, but sincerely. She lets the handkerchief drop away from her face for a second and he manages to get a look at the wound.

"We should get you to a hospital," he says.

"It's OK," Artie says.

"A doctor," Theodore says. "He could—"

"No," Artie says. "I have gauze at home. I can clean it. It'll be OK."

"You're going home?" Theodore says. "You could—just so you know—you could come back to the townhouse with me. Take up your spot on the settee again? I have gauze there, too, I think, and I'd feel better if—"

Artie shakes her head. "I'd better get home tonight," she says. "I haven't been there in forty-eight hours, and—my parents—well, I'm not sure I'd say they're likely to be worrying, but they've probably noticed my absence at this point. I'd like them to at least see that I'm, you know, alive."

Theodore grins. If he feels disappointed, he shows no sign. "Yes," he says. "I'm glad you're alive, Artie Quick."

◆

She catches a streetcar back to her neighborhood, rolls her head on her neck as she rides, slowly, imperfectly working out the kinks that have settled there, keeping the handkerchief pressed to her face the entire time, ignoring the looks from the few other riders out at this hour.

When she disembarks, the night is cold, but the air is still: the wind has died down at last. A small mercy. She stuffs the bloody handkerchief into her pocket as she closes in on home, hoping that she can wash her face before encountering either parent. She blinks to clear her eyes.

There's someone sitting on the stoop of her building, huddled there in a bulky coat with a high collar.

Artie slows her gait, suddenly suspicious. She's not convinced, not at all convinced, that Briggs hasn't figured out that she and Theodore are onto him. This could be some new goon, Horace Spivey's replacement, sent here to kill her.

But that's ridiculous, she thinks. How could he possibly know?

Hypothesizing for a moment: maybe when Dorothy broke that window earlier, maybe the nurse heard it, investigated. She could have called in Briggs; Briggs could have realized that Dorothy was lucid; he could have started putting puzzle pieces together somehow—

But that doesn't make sense, Artie thinks. Dorothy was available to help them when she was down in the tunnel; she could hardly have spent her last energies on that if she was under the hot light of Briggs's attention.

Or maybe—another hypothesis—maybe it was Zeb? Maybe the watchman caught Zeb, brought him before Briggs; she can imagine the interrogation; maybe they extracted information from him—

Her gait slows further, and finally she stops, maybe ten feet from the stranger. She peers openly, too weary to attempt any subterfuge. If someone has come to kill her, they'll just have to fight it out here on the street.

The stranger lifts their head and looks back at her.

Artie blinks again. She suddenly remembers that she should be committing identifying characteristics to memory, just like *Criminal Investigation* suggested, just like Winchell taught her. But it isn't easy. The nearest streetlamp is some distance away, and the person's face is hard to read. She can't quite discern the stranger's age: she notes a strong bolt of gray in their cropped hair, and their face is weathered, lined with fine wrinkles, but even in this bad light Artie can detect a certain youthfulness in the stranger's presence, a twinkle around their eyes—not quite mirth, but an alertness that feels precocious, even on this aged-looking face. And it carries with it a note of familiarity; there's the feeling that this person isn't quite a stranger after all.

Artie also can't quite make out the person's gender. This should be easy: the crop of their hair is close, and they're wearing pants, not a dress—these things suggest that the person is a man. But Artie knows full well that these things don't prove that a person is a man. After all, Artie's hair is cut short, and Artie wears pants—

And that's when they realize.

They're looking at themself.

26

"I see you get it," says Older Artie. Their tone is terse, their voice brusque—not exactly what Artie expected. "I'm you, from the future. You figured it out quick. That's good, because I'm not here for that long; I didn't want to waste a lot of time doing a whole thing where I have to convince you that I am who I say I am."

Artie blinks. They don't say anything. They're still trying to take it in.

"Just—come here," Older Artie says. "Come sit. I know it's been a long night. I remember that much. You're gonna feel better if you get off your feet."

"OK," Artie says. They feel a bit like they're in a dream; like they've become untethered from reality. But honestly, after battling an untethered god in a tunnel, they can't say that it's the strangest thing they've seen today. And again, like a dream, somehow the strangeness of it seems almost normal, as though it were expected all along. So they take a step. They close the gap between themself and the stoop, and they sit next to Older Artie.

They look themself in the face. Identifying characteristics, Artie thinks, almost reflexively. Even at a distance they'd noted an alertness in Older Artie's eyes, and that's the first thing they note now too: Older Artie's inquisitive, interrogating eyes. They realize that they're studying Artie just as certainly as Artie is studying them. And Older Artie watches carefully as Artie notices the next thing: a scar that runs along the length of their eyebrow.

Artie's hand goes up, touches their own wound, in the matching position. Their fingers come away stained with blood.

"Yeah," Older Artie says, reflexively mirroring the gesture: tracing their own scar with their own fingers. "That never really heals right."

"Theodore said I should go to the hospital," Artie says quietly.

"He was right!" says Older Artie. "I mean, sort of. At the end of the day, it's just a scar. You get used to it. And if you'd gone to the hospital, you wouldn't be here, talking to me. Right?"

Artie doesn't answer. They feel disoriented thinking about it, a little nauseated, sorrowful, too, as though the appearance of this person has revealed something that's been lost. A long silence ensues.

"Do you want a cigarette?" Older Artie says, mostly, it seems, to break the pause, fishing a box out them from a pocket of their coat.

"No, thank you," Artie says. "I don't smoke."

Older Artie fixes Artie with a flat expression. "Yes, you do," they say. "I mean, we do. That's one of my favorite things about being back here—you have good cigarettes in 1910! No filters yet, no additives."

Additives? Artie feels confused on top of their deepening misery. "I'm—not sure what to tell you," Artie says. Why is the conversation going this way? They don't know what exactly they would have hoped for, if they'd ever imagined having a conversation with their future self, but sitting here, bleeding from the head, getting into an argument about the composition of cigarettes that they may or may not have a habit of smoking wasn't it. The hint in the statement—that maybe this isn't the first time Older Artie has been back, back here, in 1910—hasn't gone unnoticed by Artie, but they are feeling a little too misunderstood, too sullen and sad right now, for the hint to hold the interest that it should: it goes a bit colorless and inert.

"It doesn't matter," says Older Artie. "Really. Forget it." They get their cigarette lit—the lighter is a shade of bright green that catches Artie's eye—and take a drag on it; they stare out into the street, having seemingly caught a touch of Artie's melancholy. They exhale sharply, blowing smoke out, careful to aim it away from Artie's face.

"This is weird," they say, setting the box of cigarettes and the lighter down on the stoop. "I'm sorry. I knew it was going to be weird. I mean, strictly speaking, I'm not even supposed to be here, with you, I mean. This type of thing is—it's just—it's totally forbidden. But—I told Continuity Control that this is the way it happened; they don't really understand how it happened, but they know it did, so they were sort of in a corner, so they told me, OK, just this once I could go—"

"I don't understand," Artie interrupts, nearly in despair.

Older Artie nods vigorously, and drags again on their cigarette; exhales. "Sorry," they say. "It's just—it's a long story. The main thing that you have to know, the thing I'm really back here to tell you, is that the Shrieker—it isn't gone. I mean, it's gone for you, gone for now, but it isn't dead."

"We just sent it into the future," Artie says. This isn't news.

"That's right," says Older Artie. "And you sent it to a time when it's underwater. That was—that was really smart, actually. That buys some time for people who need it. It saves lives."

"That part was Dorothy's idea," Artie says.

"Yeah," Older Artie says. "Dorothy's plan. I remember that. But you implemented it. You made it work. We did."

Artie smiles at this, their spirits lifting somewhat. But then they hold these feelings in check. "It doesn't stop the Shrieker, though, does it?"

"No," Older Artie says. "It doesn't. Not forever."

"We just sent it into a different time," Artie says. "Where it is someone else's problem. I worried about that—it felt wrong."

"It's not wrong," Older Artie says firmly, looking Artie in the face. "That's the best solution that's available to anyone, for a while. To sort of bounce it around from point to point. That's how the Shrieker gets stuck in 1909 in the first place—people from the future imprison it, and send it here. Yes, it's kind of a mess, people in one time period foisting the problem off on people in another time period. But it's not wrong. The good news is that there are good people in every time. There's always someone who will fight it."

Artie takes this in. "You said it's the only solution available for a while," they say eventually. "Do we eventually come up with a different solution? Do we eventually stop it?"

"That's what they say," Older Artie says. "I haven't lived long enough to get to the point where that happens, but I've met people who know how it all goes down. It's complicated.

It requires a lot of coordination, and convincing people, and it takes a long time, and—people die, making everything happen the way it should. But, yeah. We win in the end. Or so I'm told. What I need to tell you is just—be ready. You have a role to play in all this. Somebody's going to come—it won't be that long from now—and they're going to tell you that you need to work with them, and you won't be sure whether you can trust them, or what's happening, not really, and I'm just here to tell you that when they show up and tell you that it's time to go, you have to be ready. You have to just remember this conversation, and go."

Artie considers this. "OK," they say finally.

Older Artie nods at this. They take another drag on their cigarette, check a device strapped to their wrist that Artie recognizes as a kind of watch.

"OK," Older Artie says in return. "That's out of the way; we've got a few minutes to spare. You want to know anything, about the future?"

"Uh!" Artie blurts, caught off guard by the question.

"Ask quick," Older Artie says.

Artie thinks for a second. "Briggs," they say finally. "Police Commissioner Jameson Briggs."

"Ohhh, yeah," says Older Artie. "That guy. He goes to jail!"

Artie brightens at this. "He does?"

"Yeah—Theodore's man, at the *Globe*? Roop, or whatever his name is? Stand-up journalist. Good writer! He does the job. The whole story never quite comes out, but—enough does. The mayor gets implicated too—"

"Oh?" Artie says.

"Yeah, don't get too excited—he doesn't go to jail. But he does lose his bid for reelection, and it's   it's the girls, the girls in the nursing home. He can't disavow knowledge of that, and that brings him down. Fitzgerald takes over as the new mayor."

"John Fitzgerald?" Artie asks. "Wasn't he just the mayor, though? The last one?"

"Yeah, he comes back, I think?" Older Artie says.

That seems a little weird, but Artie doesn't want to talk about the next mayor, or the next president, or who wins the next World Series. They consider the question. What else do they want to know?

A question rises; they reject it, then it rises again. Finally, to get it out of the way, they ask.

"Do Theodore and I get married?"

Older Artie raises their eyebrows, doesn't answer immediately. "No," they finally say.

"OK," says Artie, but a frown passes across their face. "I have a question," they say, after a moment.

"That's what you've been doing," says Older Artie. "Asking questions."

"These answers you've been giving me," Artie says. "Are they—I'm not quite sure how to put this. Are they fixed? Are they permanent?"

Older Artie regards them wryly. "You want to know if you can change the future."

"I—guess so?" Artie says. "Yes?"

"And that's what you'd change the future for? Out of all

the possible things? You'd want to make sure you ended up with Theodore?"

"I don't know," Artie says.

"Do you want to end up married to Theodore?" they respond eventually.

Artie thinks about it for a moment. The moment stretches on, lasts almost a minute.

"No," they say.

"OK, good," Older Artie says. "'Cause you don't."

The frown returns.

"What," says Older Artie.

"Nothing, really," Artie says. "It's just that—Theodore is a good man."

For the first time in this conversation, Older Artie smiles, and for the first time the full winsomeness in their face emerges. It is like a door is being opened. "He is," Older Artie says.

"He just—he deserves to be happy."

"And what," Older Artie says, the smile expanding, "you think you're the only person who can make Theodore happy? Theodore is a happy person by nature; you really don't need to worry about him. But if you're wondering if he ends up with someone, he does. It's—again, it's a long story—but, yeah. You're going to like her. Let's leave it at that."

"And what about us?"

"Us like you and me?"

"Yes," Artie says.

"What about us?"

"Do we—how did you put it—do we end up with someone?"

"Oh." Older Artie smirks, drags on their cigarette, exhales out the side of their mouth. "That's a little complicated right now. Ask me again in six months."

"Will I—see you again in six months?"

"No," Older Artie says. They stub their cigarette out on the step. "Don't worry. You'll figure it out. You'll have fun. There's some hard stuff ahead, too, but—I don't know. It's not all bad. You'll see."

"OK," Artie says, not entirely satisfied. Older Artie looks them over.

"OK," Older Artie says with a sigh. "You want to know the truth?"

"Of course," Artie says. "Always."

"Yeah," Older Artie says. "I figured. You and I—we're like that. We always have to know. So the truth is—the truth is there's a reason I came back. And it isn't just to give you a heads-up that you're gonna be contacted by people from the future; it isn't just to tell you that you should go with them when the time comes. That's all—I don't know. That all seems secondary. Like—there isn't really any chance that we wouldn't have gone."

Artie contemplates this. "No," they say finally. "There isn't."

"So, the real reason," Older Artie says, "is that I wanted to tell you something. I wanted to tell you—I wanted to tell you that, in a way, Zeb is right."

"What?" Artie says.

"Hear me out," Older Artie says. "I don't mean he was right to become a criminal."

"He killed some kid—"

"Yeah, yeah," Older Artie says. "I don't mean any of that. I don't mean that he's a good person. He's not. I just mean that he was right about one particular thing. And the thing—it's the reason he leaves. The reason he runs away. Like—I remember—you always think he runs away to do crime. He runs away because crime gets its claws into him, something like that."

"Something like that," Artie says.

"But it's not that," Older Artie says. "He leaves because of your parents. He leaves because your parents can't take care of you. Of either of you. He's the one who figures that out first, and he's right."

"They take care of me," Artie protests.

Older Artie continues, as though they haven't heard. "Zeb doesn't know what to do about that, and eventually he just leaves. That's how the world of crime gets to him. That's the answer you were looking for, with Winchell. You want to know why Zeb becomes a criminal, and it's that: he figures out that the world of crime will take care of him better. And he's right, it does. He's wrong, in a way, to leave you—he shouldn't leave you alone. But he's not wrong to realize that he's not being cared for."

"They keep a roof over my head," Artie says. "They get me three square meals a day—"

"Do they?" Older Artie says. "You eat half your meals with Theodore nowadays. You buy your own lunch on the days when you're working—"

"They protect me," Artie says.

"Do they?" Older Artie says, again. "They check in on you? They ask where you've been on the nights you don't come home? Did you ever feel like you could turn to them as you were running around doing all this dangerous stuff? What do you think they're going to do when they see that nasty gash on your face? They're going to make sure you get the treatment you deserve?"

Artie doesn't say anything.

"Listen," Older Artie says. "I'm not here to make things harder for you. I'm just here to tell you one thing: you deserve better. Zeb sees that before we do; he acts on it. You and I? We're very astute, very good at noticing all sorts of things. But that one? That we deserve better? That one we need somebody to tell us. So here I am: telling you."

Artie sits with this for a moment. They have a feeling they'll be sitting with it for quite some time. And then they shunt it aside.

"OK," they say.

"OK," Older Artie says. They check their watch again, climb to their feet. "Time's up."

Time's up. But nothing happens. Artie takes this opportunity to look them over, head to toe. They dress in a way that makes them look masculine, and Artie tries to commit the entire presentation to memory: their work shirt, the dull, heavy canvas of their pants, their beat-up boots. Artie wants these clothes: they want to look like this. They wonder how Older Artie makes their chest look flat; they try to discern whether they've bound their breasts with fabric, or what.

Older Artie, noticing this, remarks: "Don't worry about your chest," they say, "Those won't be there forever."

Artie gives a start at that. "What?"

"It's a fact."

"Wait," Artie says. "Where do they go?"

But Older Artie can't answer; they've disappeared. It's exactly like when the Shrieker was sent away: there's no flash of light, no puff of smoke, no thunderclap. They just don't exist anymore. It isn't even like they disappeared. It's like they were never there.

But they *were* here, Artie thinks. Here with news.

It's cold outside, but Artie doesn't want to go in, not just yet. In a minute they'll go. In a minute they'll face their deteriorating mother and their drunken father; they'll make up some story to explain where they've been, the gash on their face. And in the morning they'll go in to Filene's and see if they still have a job, or if they have to start all over, somewhere else, for the time being.

But they don't want to do any of that just yet. First they want to take a minute. They just met their future self, received some very interesting information about the next decade or two of their life; they feel like maybe they deserve to just sit on the stoop for a minute and look out at the street while they think it over.

They touch their chest through their suit, uncertainly. An alley cat, black with white feet, pauses in its route to give Artie a look, and then continues on its way.

Maybe they should write it all down. They still have their notebook—they clutched it the whole way home, and it sits in their lap now—though somewhere in their adventures they've lost their pencil. Their father, the carpenter, always has pencils. Maybe they'll go inside, and creep upstairs, and let themself in. Maybe no one else will be awake, and they'll get a pencil, and go into the privacy of their room, and write it all down, the things that they know, now, will happen to them.

They'll write down "You deserve better," and see how it feels.

In a minute. They'll do it in a minute. For now, they just want to think it over. They don't even want to think it over, actually. They just want to sit on the stoop and breathe, and be alive, to take in the details of the world one at a time.

They look down, marveling at the sheer physical presence of the stoop, and they see Older Artie's box of cigarettes, the emerald green lighter.

They pick up the lighter: they're surprised to find that it weighs almost nothing; it's almost flimsy. They thought it might be made out of stone or some kind of precious metal alloy, but it's actually made out of some kind of resin or cellulose. They feel like they've seen something like it before, and they puzzle for a long moment before they can place it: the clerk who works in the accounts room at Filene's wears a visor made from a transparent green material much like this. They examine the tiny, ingenious sparking mechanism, and after a minute or two of fumbling they get it to produce a flame.

The cigarettes are good, here in 1910. That's what they've been told. They open up the box and pull one out, place it between their lips. They follow the steps. Light the lighter. Bring the flame to the cigarette's tip. And draw a breath.